AISERTOWN

A Novel

Greg Swiatek

NFB Publishing
Buffalo, New York

Cover Photos by David Luchowski
Poem and translation assistance by Michael Gomlak

NFB Publishing/Amelia Press
119 Dorchester Road
Buffalo, New York 14213

For more information visit NFBpublishing.com

To Edward "Big Daddy" Swiatek; an extraordinary father and man

To Al Zizzi; that's twice now

Most of all to Susie, my wife of fifty years. How did she do it?

My Toronto

Oh hodge podge of ethnic groups
melting pot of world's unwanted
Your midnight sparkle
Your sidewalk cafes
safe havens in restless
world of conflict. Remind me not
of liberty rescinded – affection regained
skyline of stubble, towering art
motivating our dreams,
discontinuing negative discourses
Eaton and Sheraton Centre houses
of our afflictions and affections.
Holding hands down Yonge Street
sipping brew at the library,
savoring the bluffs at Scarborough,
scrutinizing wares at Kensington
With both our hearts beating life
Into each other.

By Michael Gomlak

Glossary of Polish Words and Phrases

(In the order of their appearance in the text)

Matka boska, tokye hot – Mother of god, it's hot.

Psia krew – Dog's blood

Pieniadze jak nevyem – Money like crazy. Lots of money.

Obcy – Outsider

Niemnec – Foreigner, usually refers to a German

Ojcze nasz ktorys jest w niebiesiech swiec sie Imie Twoje – Our Father
    who art in Heaven

Boze – God

Idz do domu - Go home

Matka - Mother

Niech bedzie pochwalong Jesus Chrystus – Blessed be the name of `
    Jesus Christ

Na wieki wiekow, amen – For ages everlasting, amen

On sie powinien ciszyc – He should be proud

Nie – Yes

Co oczynie widga to serce nie boli – What the eyes don't see, the heart
    won't hurt

Idz z bogiem. Bog z wami – Go with God. Stay with God.

Jaksie masz, ma? – How are you, ma?

Dzia-dzia – Grandpa

Jesu kochany – Dear Jesus

Rany Boskie – God's wounds

Witaj krolowo nieba I Matko litosci – Polish prayer - Hail heavenly
    queen and merciful Mother

K'toi wzdychamy placzac z padolu wiezniowie – Prayer continued - To
    you we send our mournful sighs from this valley of tears

Glupi – Crazy

Pan, Pani – Mr. Mrs.

Kaczka – Duck

Psipsia – Female sex organ, pussy

Czy nie – Is it not

Taki – Such

A co to? – What is this?

Dziekuje – Thank you

Pies, moya pies – Dog, my dog

Dobrze – Thanks

Tutaj, pani – Here, Mrs.

Czanina – Duck's blood soup

Nasze ptaki – Our birds

Zeby nie ten dech, to by czlowiek zdech – If not for the smell, a person would die.

Sie modli przed figuram a ma diabla za skoram – He prays before the holy statue but has the devil within him

Cieszmy sie pod niebiosy wznosmyz... A Jezussa przywitajcie No wonaradzonego – Polish Christmas song – Happy under heaven, we sing with lifted voices and celebrate the birth of Jesus, infant son of the purest mother. Beat the drums and sound the trumpets. Jesus, savior of the world.

Piesni - Songs

Lulajze, Jezunie, moya perelko ... Matulu w placzu utulaj – Polish Christmas song – Lullaby, sweet Jesus, my pearl and precious treasure. Sleep in the love of your mother's arms.

Dzisiaj w Betlejem – Today in Bethlehem

Wigilia – Christmas vigil and celebration including meatless meal and breaking of the

Oplatek – Wafer, used to wish on at Christmas

Nie smuc sie dzis tatusiu….. Usmiechij sie do mnie - Polish wedding
song, Don't be sad today, Daddy. Don't be sad over me. For
today is my wedding. Try to smile at me.

Nie za pomne tatusia … co mam – Another stanza of the wedding song.
I'll never forget you, daddy, because you always loved me. You
always worked for me. You gave me everything I have.

Czepina – Polish wedding ceremony and song

*Krakowianka*s – Polish peasant dancers

Pije Kuba do Jakuba – Polish drinking song: James toasts to Jacob,
Jacob to Michael I drink, you drink, we all drink together

Ale zimno, nie? – Cold, isn't it?

Ten co rychlo staja temi pan Bog daje. – He who rises early, him the
Lord blesses.

*Czekaj, czeka*j – Wait, wait

Zeby babka miala jajka to by byla dziadkiem – If grandma had a beard
(balls) she'd be grandpa

Chodz tutaj – Come here

Pamietasz – Do you remember?

Tak, tak – yes, yes

Taki duzy – So big

Ciotka Rose – Aunt Rose

Play cards, cy co? – Play cards or what?

O Jezu niech po smierci … O Maryo, upros nam… – Polish prayer
seen earlier. Oh Jesus, let us, after death, be admitted to thy
presence. Oh Mary, plead for this our great desire.

O Jezu, Jezu … nit przebrany. – Polish prayer continued. Oh Jesus,
dear Jesus, my beloved. Jesus of great mercy never lacking.

Izba – cottage

Dziennik dla Wszystkich – Everybody's Polish Daily

Pioran – Thunderbolt

Zaplomnial wol jak cielenciem byk – The bull forgot when he was a calf

Swieconka – Easter basket and ceremonial blessing of Easter baskets in
church

Jenna – Oh dear

Zebys struchla – Drop dead

Sczesliwa bestija – Lucky bastard

Taki szkaradny – So ugly

Mala Wladek, synulek – Little Walter, my young son

Piana – A drunk

Zeby cie diabi wzili – May the demons take you

Spac – Sleep

Ja niewiem – I don't know

Kaisertown: 1951

Within everyone's memory it had been called Kaisertown, the fourteen block area surrounding Clinton Street on Buffalo's East side. It was bounded on the north by the huge Clinton-Bailey Market and the Niagara Frontier Food Terminal and on the south by South Ogden Street which stood at the edge of the city line adjacent to the sleepy suburb of West Seneca.

There was controversy attached to the origin of the name itself. Some people claimed that the reference to "Kaisertown" was a carry-over from the former predominantly German character of the area, hence street names such as Weiss and Weimer. Later, when the Polish immigrants from Galicia moved in and displaced the Germans, the old name was simply retained for convenience and familiarity. Others said that "Kaisertown" was really an uneducated bastardization of "Casimir Town" after the beloved Polish ruler and saint. Nevertheless, the area in question was not large. You could walk from one end of Kaisertown to the other in an hour unless, of course, you stopped in for a drink at each of the bars that lined its streets. In that case the trip could last a lifetime and in many instances it did just that.

Indeed, bars, bakeries, and churches were the hallmarks of Kaisertown throughout its Polish history. One short block between Roberts Street and Kelburn alone sported three saloons, all catering to the Worthington Pump work force, the area's largest employer. Smoke belching from the foundry and machine shops and hissing from the blue-green glassed Navy Building kept the Polish immigrant breadwinners happily employed and spending liberally at Tubby's, the Pump Inn, and Lefty's Bar. In fact, all the Kaisertown gin mills did a brisk business. Men crowded around after work on a daily basis, drinking their shots and beers, gossiping, playing pinochle and poker, or watching the Friday night fights with their paychecks cashed and pockets full of money. 'Psia krew, dat wop Basilio, he ken take a punch, nie? You gotta hand id to him.' Zip's Lounge, Gay's Club (no reflection on sexual orientation back then), the Orange Front, Weichek's, Bill's and El's, Benny's, Stan's, Ray's Supper Club, the trio at Worthington, as well as a dozen more midblock establishments opened their doors to the Polish drinking public. Most of the saloons did an especially brisk business on Friday nights serving their patented fish fries, a happy juxtaposition of business opportunity, worker cash, and the dictates of Holy Mother the Church.

You could beat your wife and kids half to death, steal and rob the Jewish grocers and hucksters, drink and gamble yourself sick any day of the week, but, heaven forbid, a morsel of meat ever touch your lips on a Friday. The violation was no venial infraction, but a one way ticket to the fiery pit.

So the people filed into the back rooms of the bars for their weekly fish fries and a social night out, and many a wife made it a habit to meet her husband at the door to intercept the weekly paycheck before it was not so miraculously converted into shots of whiskey and glasses of beer.

Kitchen staffs were augmented on Friday nights to handle the crowds. Flushed and disheveled Polish matrons labored over the stoves in the back kitchens. They washed the dishes, waited on tables, and wrapped the hot take-out orders between paper plates and yesterday's newspapers. They complained about the heat and the work.

'Matka boska, tokye hot!'

But they enjoyed the camaraderie and the bustle of the evening and the chance to have an activity that was not centered around the hearth and home. Crispy breaded haddock, a mound of potato salad, coleslaw, slices of pickled beets, a couple of pieces of fresh rye bread and a pad of butter made up the standard fare. This was topped off with a cold Simon Pure, Genesee, or Iroquois beer.

Any street corner that did not have a gin mill on it was sure to have a bakery or two. Hyzy's, Goinski's, the Gold Ray, Maszlanka's, Blaszyewski's, Szeglowski's, Blandowski's, and Brzesinski's lined the prestigious Clinton Street and tempted each passerby with window displays of sweets while purposely opened windows permitted the sugary and doughy drafts to perfume the air around each establishment.

The staple rye bread lined the slanted shelves in warm rows. Their soft caraway spotted interiors were protected by a crackly crust shined to a hard gloss by egg whites brushed on just before the loaves entered the ovens.

'Pani wan id slice or whole?'

And the machine whirred as the loaves vibrated through the small vertical blades of the slicer.

There were also rogaliki, the crescent shaped rolls sprinkled with poppy seeds, schnekas large, sticky cinnamon buns with raisins and white icing, crumb and poppy seed kuchas, rum babas, and a dozen different panski, cream and custard filled, glazed, sugared, plain, or jelly filled. Some were rolled in chopped nuts, others covered with white or chocolate frosting.

The bakery clerks with their white smocks and little baking caps worked steadily from opening till closing time bagging the goodies or tying them in boxes with the strong string that spun off the rotating spools at the corner of the counter. They broke the string with a quick tug of their strong Polish hands.

'Pani is next.'

The Kaisertown bakeries were all small family affairs with the shop located in front, the ovens in the middle and the family's living quarters in the back or on the second story. The bakers' children were the envy of the neighborhood since they lived amidst the warm sweet fragrances of the shops and had the sugary baked goods at their fingertips.

As with the bar rooms, everyone in Kaisertown had his or her favorite bakery and generally defended its products against all rivals. Of course, this did not prevent certain tactical switches in loyalty when it came to savoring a particular item that was deemed superior at one bakery over another. Many people felt, for instance, that Goinski's had the best rye bread in Kaisertown, though Gold Ray and Blendowski's had their spokespersons too, but that did not stop these same customers from getting their crumb kuhas at Hyzy's or their Christmas pierniki and krushchiki at Maszlanka's. All was fair when it came to the Polish sweet tooth and since there was plenty of business to go around no merchant suffered.

While the taverns and bakeries of Kaisertown nourished the bodies of the Polish immigrant, the churches of the neighborhood made sure that their souls were not compromised in any way. More importantly, Holy Mother, the Church, was not to be denied her fair share of the workers' pay check.

Saint Casimir's was the largest Catholic church in Kaisertown. Tucked away on the back corner of Casimir and Weiss Street, it was an architectural marvel built on the vast and vaulted basilica style. Many historians and scholars from all over the country came to admire and study the holy edifice. This fact, however, was generally unknown and unappreciated by the local Polish parishioners. For them the external appearances did not matter all that much. To them the church was the "House of the Lord" and the focal point of their spiritual lives. It was where they came for consolation from life's miseries, where they took their children to celebrate the sacraments of baptism, communion, and confirmation, where they saw those same children march in processions and get married, and where finally they themselves would lay before the altar at the funeral mass.

For convenience sake Sittniewski's Funeral Home was located right across the street.

St. Bernard's and Our Lady of Czestochowa were simple, almost bleak structures in comparison to St. Casimir's. They had no architectural character about them, being purely utilitarian structures. Both were small churches. St. Bernard's was built of wood; Our Lady of Czestochowa, brick. They were situated alongside the Polish Catholic elementary schools they served and together with those schools formed a tight knot of both spiritual and moral instruction inseparable and interdependent. Every school morning was begun in church at mass. Polish, not English, was the language of instruction throughout the first three years of education. And every Sister Superior, in lieu of the priest, the bishop, the Pope, and God Himself, ruled her sacred domain with an iron will and a stout wooden pointer. Heaven protect the poor pupil who got in the way of either one.

Kaisertown was the heart of Buffalo's Polish community and woe to any other ethnicity, religion, or race that dared enter its borders. There were only two types of people in the Polish world orbit so aptly miniaturized in the Kaisertown neighborhood; the Polish, and the niemnec, the others.

The following stories are taken from the settings, situations and the lives of people living in Kaisertown through the transitional era of the fifties and sixties. Some events and characters have been fictionalized for dramatic purposes.

Dorothy Klein: South Ogden Street. "Obcy, the Outsider"

The girl moved the carpet sweeper back and forth across the threadbare parlor rug. 'Dorothy Klein, Dorothy Klein.' It shouted her name. 'Dorothy Klein, Dorothy Klein, Dorothy Klein.' It would not stop. She slowed her pace. 'Dor-o-thy Klein, Dor-o-thy Klein.'

"Shut up! Shut up!"

Faster she went. 'Dorothy Klein, Dorthy Klein, Dory Klein, Ory Klein, Klein, Klein.' It blared in her ears proclaiming her German ancestry and reinforcing her separation from friends and the Kaisertown community. It drowned out the music from the small plastic radio in the kitchen, her only source of joy this chore filled Saturday.

"God damn it, shut up!"

Then something else caught her attention, incidentally interfering with the music. She froze in place. Footsteps moved haltingly up the hallway stairs. The kitchen door opened, then slammed shut. Dorothy jumped and wet herself slightly. Something, a bag, dropped onto the floor with a heavy thud.

Dorothy stepped through the thick, squared columned archway into the dining room where an ironing board had been set up awaiting its turn at activity. On top of the ironing board sat a rust stained iron and an old ketchup bottle filled with water and fitted with a sprinkler top. A pile of laundry lay heaped in a splintered wicker basket on the floor.

Maybe, hopefully, her mother had forgotten something and returned unexpectedly. It couldn't be Timmy. He was still asleep. Just like him to sleep in on the weekend when help was needed the most. Nevertheless, Dorothy preferred the extra work to her brother's irritating presence and it was also one of the few times she had the radio to herself. The music soothed and distracted her.

Then he was there in the doorway; tall and burly, his hooded, blood-shot eyes barely visible below the brim of a tight leather cap. He was dressed in carpenter's coveralls over a dark blue shirt. High, black work shoes showed beneath his pant cuffs. The man shuffled his feet awkward-ly, then leaned heavily against the door frame. The girl took a frightened, instinctive step backwards. She felt the wetness in her panties.

"Yer, yer home early, dad. Did, did you get the job?"

"Shut yer mouth," replied the man. "I doan answer no questions from the likes a you. An shut dat nigger music off. I told you once before about listenin to dat shit."

The girl stepped into the kitchen and turned the radio off.

"Where's yer old lady?" the man continued.

Dorothy felt her knees shake. "She's at Bill's and El's. They've got a, a wedding banquet. Timmy's sleepin. I should get him up."

Dorothy made an attempt to walk past the man, but he made a sur-prisingly quick grab and caught the girl by her elbow. She could smell the beer and body odor on him.

"What you got on yer face?"

Oh god, the make-up. Dorothy had been practicing with her mother's lipstick and rouge this morning and forgot to take it off just a little that was all.

"Bad enough yer old lady works in a gin mill. You got to paint yer-self like a Polack whore."

Dorothy winced and tried to pull free. "I was only playing. I'll wash it off."

"I save you dah trouble," said the man and he dragged the girl backwards into the kitchen, knocking over a chair in the process before he leaned himself up against an old porcelain sink. Although unsteady on his feet, his grip was unbreakable. The girl's bare feet squeaked against the linoleum as she stiff legged tried to resist.

"No, no, I can do it. I can do it myself, please."

"Show you playin. Show you playin at bein a whore, a Polack whore," said the man. He turned on the water at the sink, waited a minute, and then shoved the girl's head beneath the cold stream.

Dorothy fought to break the hold behind her neck, but the shock of the water and her own fright and embarrassment cut off her breath. She sputtered and gasped, then began to cry. With his free hand the man clumsily grabbed a cracked bar of brown soap from the rusted wire holder on the wall. He rubbed it into the girl's face as her head bucked up and down and twisted from side to side. The soap was knocked from his hand, but he continued to rub, smearing the strong smelling, gritty soap residue across the girls' pursed lips and forcibly into her tight nostrils.

Dorothy lifted her feet up and down in a dance of torment before she felt the wet warmth of urine spread through her underpants and onto her slip. That last straw of humiliation buckled Dorothy's knees and under the added pressure of her father's hand, the girl fell to the floor. On the way down her chin hit the sink top and her teeth, like the edges of a cookie cutter pressing into soft dough, cleaved a crenulated pattern along the border of her tongue. Dorothy's mouth opened in a silent scream; a dark, blood filled hollow of pain.

"What's the matter, dad?" a shrill voice suddenly cried from the dining room entrance.

"What's happening to Dorothy?" It was Timmy, half asleep, half terrified.

The man, panting heavily, looked up at his son, then fell backward jarring the kitchen table as he attempted to avoid the writhing body of his daughter.

"Little Polack whore who insults her father. Paintin' her face wit make-up." He looked down pitilessly at his stricken daughter.

"Do it again, see what happens. I'll take you back down in the cellar. And you don't never ask no questions. I come and go as I please. Dis is my house."

The boy looked down at his sister. "I seen her with make-up lots of times," Timmy stated, looking like a loveable Dennis the Menace with his pajamas and blond cowlick. "She even puts on ma's perfume sometimes when she goes out."

The man's face tightened into a snarl and he lashed out an off balance kick at his daughter. The girl avoided the blow and with a squeal of fright struggled to her feet exposing the wet crotch of her underwear. She stumbled wildly out of the kitchen.

"Serves you right," said Timmy. "Hey dad, you want some whiskey? I know where ma hid the bottle."

Dorothy cowered in her bedroom, biting down on a bloody blanket stuffed in her mouth and pounding the mattress with her fists.

"That, that bastard," she cried. "I hate him. I hope it don't stop bleeding and I die. Then they'll throw him in jail. Let him die there of the DTs, howling like Stachu Klemp. He don't work. Nobody'd give that drunken Kraut bastard a job. When I get older, I'm going to change my name and have nothing to do with this god damn family."

The girl's nostrils flared as she panted heavily. She could still feel her father's thick, sausage like fingers stretching her nostrils wide as he wiped her face with soap. Dorothy pinched her nose against the memory. She stayed in the bedroom for the rest of the morning. Timmy, who shared the room, came and went a few times.

"You better get dressed and clean up and get the chores done. Ma's gonna be home soon."

"Little bastard snitcher," she yelled at him!

"I'm tellin dad on you."

Dorothy's mother took no action against her husband. She knew the futility and even the danger of intervention. "I toll yous boat to stay otta his way when he's drunk like dat, and doan say nuttin to him."

Lorraine Klein was a woman of thirty years, but she looked ten years older. Skinny, plain, and timid, she took out the misery and frustration of her life by chain smoking and immersing herself in the make believe world of afternoon soap operas. Her voice was raspy and low and she was given to long and sustained bouts of coughing. Despite her frail appearance she was a hard and dedicated worker holding down two jobs at Oleski's Dry Cleaners, and Bill's and El's Tavern. Ask any of her neighbors in Kaisertown about Lorraine Klein, nee Machiewski, and they'd all say the same thing. 'Hard working woman. Too bad she ain't got a pot to piss in with that niemiec, piok husband of hers. You marry outside your own dat's what you get.' And when she'd walk down the street with a black eye or bruised face the Polish ladies would just shake their heads and look the other way.

Dorothy's tongue and jaw were badly swollen so she stayed inside for the weekend. Her father was gone to the gin mills all day anyway so she was comparatively safe being locked in her bedroom long before he stumbled home late at night. She found escape in books and music. The family had no record player so she contented herself with radio tunes and often snuck the radio into her room when no one was watching. There, under the covers of her bed, she'd lay transported by the sounds to a far off place that had no definition, no boundary, but just existed in melody and fanciful musing. Nancy Drew, and Ginny Gordon were her favorite fictional characters, but she read almost any book she could get her hands on and understand. Of course, she did not have any books of her own. They were all borrowed from the Clinton Street Library.

Throughout the weekend Timmy made a big deal out of going outside by himself and playing with their friend next door, Jason Novak, or partaking of the neighborhood baseball games at Okie Diamond, the large open field and the City of Buffalo's unofficial boundary.

"Got a homer and a double today," he boasted to his sister.

"Liar," she replied.

"Yeah, just ask Jason. He'll tell yah."

"What did they do? Give you six strikes again?"

"So what. It was my ball. The one I found at Houghton Park. And Jason asked what happened to you too."

"You didn't say nothing did you?"

"Why not and I told him you pissed yer pants too."

"I hate you! Anyway, I don't wanna go outside and play. I rather read my books."

"You and yer stupid books. Yer gonna go blind. Ma said so herself."

"How would she know? She never read a book in her life."

Dorothy was twelve years old in that summer of 1956. Her brother was ten. The Klein family had lived on South Ogden Street in Kaiser-town for most of Dorothy's life. They rented a lower flat with use of the cellar in exchange for maintaining the yard in the summer and shovelling the driveway in the winter. Old man Pankow and his wife lived upstairs. They owned the house, the lot next door, and the old garage at the back of the lot. Old man Pankow was loaded with money.

"When he dies," the neighbors all said, "Psia krew, his kids, dey're gonna have it good. Pieniedze jak nevyem"

Long ago, when Dorothy's father had worked for Master Craft Studios, life on South Ogden had been bearable, almost pleasant. There was a steady income and her mother and father seemed happy. Her dad's small workshop in the basement was devoted to doing carpentry jobs for extra money. He built cupboards for Pani Pankow and tables, benches, and bookcases for neighbors. He used to drink back then too, but only on weekends. But when he lost his Master Craft job, and several others in quick succession, and Dorothy's mother had to go to work, things got very bad for the family. Although her brother and mother got their share of abuse, the burden of punishment for some reason fell on the girl's shoulders.

At first it would appear as though the father was playing with his daughter and the young girl would smile and try to laugh at the funny things he made her do. But then the playing would turn into cruel teasing and finally pain and abuse. When Dorothy was ten years old her father delighted in pulling down the girl's pants and pinching her bare bottom, or spanking her with a belt. Later, down in his workshop he made a special strap with a wooden handle and long leather thongs. The "pida" her mother called it. The slightest accident or mistake, like spilling milk at the table, or knocking over an ashtray, would set off his anger and bring out the strap.

One time, in the parlor with the whole family present, her father unexpectedly yanked down Dorothy's pants and underwear and bunched them tightly around her ankles. Whenever, the girl stooped to pick up her clothes, her father whacked her with the strap. Harder and harder with every attempt she made. Finally, in pain and humiliation, she had to waddle off to her bedroom with her pants still down and her ass bright red and welted. Everyone laughed, and even her mother joked about "the little penguin". Timmy added to the insult by laughing at his helpless sister and rubbing his index fingers over each other in the "shame sign".

Supper time at the Klein residence became an ominously silent and intimidating affair. No one spoke. Only the lonely clink of cutlery on the plates, and the sounds of muted chewing and swallowing were audible. If the children wanted something they had to stare hard and long at their mother until they got her attention. Only when she directed a question at them could they hazard a request.

'More bread, please.'

Dorothy's father, when he was home, habitually sat in a chair by the window hidden behind a copy of the Courier Express. Once in a while between chews he'd breathe in deeply, his whole body vibrating with the intake of air. The girl shivered in response. Goosebumps rose on her arms like a sudden plague. She'd stare at her father's hair tufted fingers clutching the edges of the paper. The fingers were thick and yellow nailed, the two middle ones on his right hand deeply nicotine stained.

One day the paper suddenly crumpled and collapsed and Dorothy's father's big round face with its cold snake eyes was suddenly staring straight at her.

"What you lookin at?" he hissed, his high forehead furrowing and reddening at the same time.

Dorothy gasped. Everyone else held their breath.

"I... I was just looking at the paper," she lied. Her dark eyes blinked uncontrollably and her face pulled away as if to avoid a blow.

"Den look at somethin else or I'll give you a slap across dat smart Polack mouth a yers."

The girl riveted her eyes onto her plate and did not look up again until she heard her father's chair pull away, and the paper flap and fall like a dead bird upon the table.

The children dared not leave any leftovers on their plates.

"Over feed yous," their father would say. "Good, den tomorrow yous can go without supper. Maybe dat improve yer appetite."

One of the few times Timmy got punished was for refusing to finish the cabbage on his plate. He had been arguing with his mother about it.

"I don't wanna eat it. I hate it. It smells like farts."

The father exploded from behind his paper. Dorothy could remember wetting herself from the sheer suddenness of the outburst. The man grabbed Timmy by the hair and yanked his head back and stuffed the cabbage into the boy's mouth. When Timmy choked and spat some cabbage on the floor, his father made him get down on his knees and eat it off the linoleum.

It was shortly after her beating over the makeup that good fortune finally smiled down on Dorothy. Her father got a night job working at the Statler Hilton Hotel as an elevator operator. He worked from 4 PM until midnight, and since he had to take a bus to work that meant he'd be gone from three o'clock in the afternoon until one in the morning.

"Remember," her mother warned, however. "Doan say nuttin about his uniform, nie? He hates id. Calls id dah monkey suit. So yous be quiet, or else."

That was fine with Dorothy and although the thought of planting a bag of peanuts and a banana in her father's lunch box occurred to her, the concept of self-preservation overpowered that momentary mischievous urge. She was content to revel in her new found happiness and freedom.

Dorothy Klein was an outsider in her neighborhood, a neimnec. At best she was ignored, shunned; at worst she was ridiculed. 'Yer mother is a DP and yer father's a Nazi. He's Hitler's cousin. The cops are gonna come one day and kick them outa the country and you and yer brother are gonna go to Father Baker's where the nuns will beat you and you will stay there forever because nobody wants to adopt a dirty neimnec like yous two.'

The only person, the only boy, Dorothy associated with during her youthful days in the predominantly Polish East side of Buffalo was her next door neighbor, Jason Novak. Jason was oblivious to her hateful German heritage. He never teased or called her names. He was different.

Years ago Dorothy had a crush on Jason even though he was a couple of years younger than she. In their childhood innocence they had promised that when they got older they would get married and move away from Kaisertown to some far off place, maybe even another country where they would live happily ever after, and, of course, Dorothy would get to change her name and she wouldn't be a niemnec anymore.

"Happily ever after." Dorothy loved that phrase although she never really believed such a state could be achieved. Maybe in books, but not in real life.

On those occasions that Timmy was being punished and not able to come out and play, Dorothy and Jason had their best times. Then they would play house up at old man Pankow's garage which was at the far end of the lot that separated Dorothy's house from Jason's. No one ever entered the large, barn-like structure except the children. The big sliding doors were locked, but a steady push in the lower corner allowed access. The downstairs of the building was open and barren and smelled of oil, grease and dust. Crickets chirped and silverfish scurried along the cool dark walls to find security in the cracked concrete corners of the room. In the heat of summer flies and wasps banged futilely against the small dusty panes of the high windows until they died of exhaustion or were killed by Jason and Timmy.

A narrow wooden ladder allowed entry through a broken trap door to a second story. Upstairs the air was hot and dusty. An old pool table with deep mesh pockets and a torn green felt top stood in the middle of the single room. There were no balls or cue sticks. Two broken backed wooden chairs flanked the table. Jason's asthma bothered him whenever he spent too much time upstairs, but when he was with Dorothy he never complained.

Dorothy got goosebumps on her arms and thighs whenever she and Jason entered the garage alone. It was their secret world. The two children spoke in whispers when inside. And Jason, whom Dorothy believed was very handsome, and had the most beautiful eyes in the whole world, was different when Timmy wasn't around. He wasn't wild and uncaring. Instead he enjoyed sitting and talking with her as they discussed all sorts of things: teachers, parents, friends, and books. Jason had read even more books than Dorothy. His father actually had a library right in their house with hundreds of books. Dorothy never saw a book in her house unless she had bought it in herself from the Clinton Library. Jason's house was just one lot away from hers, but it was an unreachable distance across a wide gulf of differences, or so it seemed at the time.

Jason: South Ogden Street: "A co to? What do we have here?"

When the boy was very ill, his mother would come into his bedroom at night. She would light the candle in front of the bambinko on his dresser and kneel down to pray. The boy watched through slivered eyelids. Maybe it was an angel at the foot of the bed, the strands of her hair glimmering red and gold as the candle flame played peek-a-boo above the red lip of the glass. No, angels had wings. They had to have wings. That was for sure. The boy shuddered under the blankets as the white clouds poured out of the round black box on the night table. He breathed them in. Clouds were near heaven, near boze. They were good for him. His mother spoke the other words into her hands telling stories to boze. "Ojcze nasz, ktorys jest w niebiesiech, swiec, sie Imie Twoje…"

Jason did not understand the words, but boze did. Boze knew everything. He would listen to the words and the boy would get better. The pain in his chest would ease and the breath return to his lungs. When his mother placed her hand against his forehead, a wave of unease suddenly swept over the boy. His toes curled. He twisted them into his blanket and shut his eyes tightly.

When the boy's father came home with his briefcase in hand, he first spoke the other words to Jason's mother. Then he went directly into his son's room. He left the other words behind.

"Get your rest and you will be up and around in no time. It could have been a lot worse, TB or polio. The vaporizer will help. I'll read you a story tonight."

Jason did not like the night time. The flickering candles made strange, scary images on the bedroom walls and ceiling. The bambinko's shadow was the biggest. Brooding and breathing, it dominated the room like a black ghost. And night was the time that the bogey man, who was the devil's cousin, came out and looked for the souls of bad boys and girls. That was why Jason prayed to his guardian angel before he went to bed. Every child had a guardian angel who protected them from the bogey man as long as they were good boys and girls. If the children turned bad, however, the guardian angel would cry and if the badness continued then the angel would give up and go back to heaven. Then the boy or girl would be all alone and the bogey man would come for sure and carry them off to hell where they would burn in red hot fire. No one could help you, not your mother, or father, not babcia either. In hell you were all alone to burn in the flames forever and ever. There was no escape from hell.

Only when Jason was fully recovered from his asthma attack was he allowed to venture outside and play with Dorothy and Timmy next door. And then, 'No running' his mother scolded, and she would watch him from the kitchen window as he crossed the empty lot that separated the two houses.

Jason's mother did not want him playing with the Klein children next door. Pani Klein was Polish and a Catholic, but her husband was a piok German, a niemnec and so then were the children. That's just the way it was. Jason should stick to his own; his cousins and Polish friends. Nevertheless, Jason's mother deferred to her husband who reasoned that the children, Timmy and Dorothy, were too young to know better. Furthermore, they were always nice and polite calling her, "Pani Novak" whenever they met her on the street or in the yard. She liked that.

"Oh Timmy, Oh Dorothy," Jason called at the side door. The narrow driveway was cloaked in a chilling shadow since the sunlight rarely penetrated between the tall houses. Jason shuffled his feet and waited, studying the bright green moss that grew tenaciously between the cracked slabs of gray concrete in the driveway.

The Klein house was different from Jason's although the architectural lay out of nearly all the houses on South Ogden Street was the same. Jason sensed the unfamiliarity from the first moment he entered and he found it strangely exciting. First of all, Dorothy and Timmy's house didn't have any pictures of Jesus or Mary on the walls, no Last Supper. There were no palm leaves or even a bambinko. At Christmas there was no angel on top of the tree and no manger below.

Jason's house was clean and tidy, nothing out of place. Dorothy and Timmy's was a pig sty. Clothes were lying on the floor or thrown over chairs. Dishes filled the sink, and overflowing ashtrays and empty beer bottles were scattered everywhere. Odd odors of strange foods hung in the air. And Pani Lorraine often walked around the house with only her slip on and she didn't even care that Jason was there. The boy could see things he knew he shouldn't be looking at, but he never told his parents. Pani Lorraine also smoked which was probably a sin for a woman, but Jason wasn't sure.

Jason had a dime saved up from his babcia's last visit and today he was treating his friends to candy at Charlotte's store. When the children emerged from the driveway the first thing they did was turn and run for the corner. Dorothy's shorts hung loosely from her thin legs and flapped like a flag on a pole as she ran with wild abandon. Timmy's shoes were too big for him and gave him a decidedly clown like appearance. Jason could not keep pace with his companions. He soon felt the dangerous shortness of breath come on. He stopped immediately and walked the rest of the way. Timmy was already mounting the store steps, but Dorothy turned back when she saw Jason stop.

"You alright, Jason?"

"Yes, thanks. Just short of breath. I'll be OK." Jason did not let go of Dorothy's hand until they got to the front of the store.

Charlotte's store was built several steps up from the street. The enclosed area beneath the steps had become, over the years, the accidental repository of innumerable coins that had fallen between the cracks in the stairs. At least once a week the neighborhood children huddled on the steps and, cupping their hands to their eyes, tried to espy some of the lost treasure. Pennies, nickels, dimes, rumor had it that even an almighty quarter, lay hidden in the dirt and darkness below. Bobby Mynka claimed to have seen the actual quarter roll out of Pan Radomski's pocket when, in something less than a sober state, that gentleman ascended the store stairs one Saturday afternoon.

Whenever the door to Charlotte's store opened, a bell rang overhead summoning hither Mrs. Charlotte or her husband, Mr. Charlotte, from their living quarters in the back. By the time the woman with the tight bun in her hair, the white apron, and glasses held in place by a band of little pearls, stepped into the room, the three children were already kneeling in front of the candy counter poking at the glass and discussing their prospective purchases. Mrs. Charlotte grimaced when she caught sight of her diminutive customers. "Jesus Kohany," she sighed.

The store was not large, but it sold an amazing variety of groceries and household products. It had a meat counter with a slicing machine and a good selection of cold cuts: baloney, krakaska, tongue, liberka, pepperoni, hard sausage, and ham. The sacked loaves of Bond and Wonder Bread, new to the market, came in their own packages. There was an ice cream freezer stocked with popsicles, fudgesicles, Skippy cups and Mr.

Bigs. Shelves overhead held bags and metal cans full of pretzels and potato chips. Next to the freezer was a rack of comic books and magazines and a big red pop cooler with an opener built into the side that collected all the caps.

With space at a premium, high shelves laden with cans, boxes, and jars ran to the ceiling. In order to reach the items on the top most shelves Mrs. Charlotte had to use a funny pair of pinchers on a long handle. Mr. Charlotte was much better at using the tool because he could catch all the stuff when the pinchers let go. Mrs. Charlotte couldn't and she was always dropping the pinchers and running away holding her head in her hands as the packages came tumbling off the high shelves. When the children were in the store and heard someone ask for a top shelf item they all stopped what they were doing and gathered around to watch Mrs. Charlotte and the pinchers. The ceiling of the store was made of pressed tin and had a big slow moving fan in the middle. Also hanging there were several strips of sticky curled paper raisined with flies and other insects.

"Do yous know what yous wan it?" asked Mrs. Charlotte looking old beyond her forty years. It never ceased to frustrate her that no matter how often the neighborhood kids came into the store, they could never remember the prices of the candy.

"How much is those red dollar ones?" asked Timmy.

"One cent.'

"What about them candy pies?" asked Dorothy pointing to boxes of tiny chocolate, vanilla, and strawberry pies complete with little metal spoons.

"Two for a penny."

The children conferred out loud. "We could get two pies each and one of them dollars. How much is the ribbon candy?" asked Jason.

"Penny a strip."

"Do you like ribbon candy?" he asked his friends.

"Timmy does," replied Dorothy. "He eats the whole thing, paper and all."

"So what," said Timmy.

"Sew buttons," replied Dorothy.

Just then the bell over the door sounded and Mrs. Charlotte gratefully got to her feet and went off to serve another customer.

"Let me know when yous are done," she said.

The three friends hesitated for a moment eavesdropping on the new customer's order. No top shelf items so they went back to the candy. When finished each left with a small paper bag full of assorted goodies. In front of Pani Dombrowski's house, next door to Timmy and Dorothy's, the children suddenly stopped.

"Look it alla the ants," said Timmy.

Beneath them on the sidewalk an immense mass of black ants was issuing forth from a crack in the concrete and flooding the surrounding grass. The friends promptly sat down to examine the situation more closely.

"How do they know where to go?" asked Timmy as he squashed a few with his thumb.

"They remember their neighborhood," answered Jason. "And they never go so far that they get lost."

"How can they tell which is which?" asked Dorothy. "They all look alike."

Jason was pondering a reply when Pani Dombrowski came waddling down the narrow sidewalk beside her house. The old woman's heavy, blue veined legs were exposed just below the house dress she wore. The fat of her ankles crushed down and spilt over the sides and heels of her worn slippers. She carried a steaming kettle in her hand.

"Ged oud it yous," she said. "Idz do domu."

The three children stood up, clutching their bags of candy, but did not leave. Pani Dombrowski waved her hands at them as though shooing flies. She then measured her aim above the ants and tipped the kettle. The cloudy water spilled out and bathed the sidewalk in steam.

"Idz do domu. I tell yer matkas."

The children reluctantly moved off. They passed Dorothy's house and turned down the worn pathway that led alongside the hedges where the tall Rose of Sharon and the Bleeding Hearts grew. Timmy reached out and squeezed one of the small heart shaped flowers. It gave a little "pop".

"You kill them by doing that," Dorothy exclaimed.

"So what," replied Timmy.

Inside the old garage they settled down on the floor in front of the low multi-paned window on the second floor overlooking the lot and neighboring yards. It was getting hot. Later the heat would increase and the wasps which had stucco nests across the ceiling would become loud and menacing. Jason could not remain here for long so they ate fast. Out the window they watched Jason's mother go to the garbage shed and saw the cats who foraged there slink out the back way when they heard the latch move. They observed Pani Lorraine, Dorothy and Timmy's mother, glide past the dining room window still in her slip with a cigarette in hand. And they watched as Stachu Klemp sniffed at the elm tree near the street before lifting his leg.

Jason remembered being here when his father's secret friend, "the Professor" came to the house. His mother was away at Aunt Catherine's. The friend left before she got back, but Jason told her about the visit. That night there was a loud argument between his parents.

"I hate it when they're hard and the stupid spoons get all bent up," said Dorothy whose knees were black from kneeling on the sidewalk and garage floor. Her curly reddish brown hair was in two long braids and she looked rather homely with her freckled nose and sweaty red face. Still Jason liked her, liked her a lot, and would even have admitted as much except for his fear of being called a "girl smeller" by Timmy.

"Tomorrow's Sunday," said Jason. "I hate Sundays when it's nice outside and you gotta get dressed up and go to church."

"We don't go to church no more," volunteered Timmy.

Jason was startled. Missing mass was a mortal sin and a one way ticket to hell if you didn't confess and do penance.

"And we can eat meat on Fridays too, not like yous Catholics," added Timmy.

"What religion are you?" asked Jason.

"Lutheran," said Dorothy.

Jason had known all along that the Kleins were different, but this was more than he bargained for. He was afraid his two friends were easy pickings for the devil. High above them in an elm tree they heard a prolonged buzzing sound.

"Spider sucking the blood outa a fly," said Dorothy.

They listened in silence as the buzzing got louder and louder, then dropped off.

"It's dead," added Dorothy with a wan smile at Jason as though she was in sympathy with the fly.

Jason swallowed his candy and smiled back. Poor Dorothy, he thought. From the yard they heard Pani Lorraine's voice calling, "Dorty, Timmy."

The children threw their remaining candy in their bags and bolted for the stairs. Together they waited at the garage doors for the calling to stop before going their separate ways.

After his two friends disappeared, Jason remembered the ants in front of Pani Dombrowski's house. The water was gone and the ants lay dead in a long narrow sidewalk crack filling it like the poppy seeds in the kuchas his mother bought at the bakery. The remainder were formed up in an irregular circle like the remains of an old stain. Suddenly a lone ant made its way from the edge of the grass and ran to the faded circle of its dead brothers. When it made contact, however, it immediately veered off toward the sidewalk crack. There it paused, waved its feelers in the air and then looped around in the opposite direction at a frantic pace only to return to its original spot. The ant was alone and knew it, Jason reasoned. All its relatives and friends were gone.

'Without yer family you ain't got nothin,' his mother often warned him. Another ant hill wouldn't take the lone survivor either. Jason remembered when he and Timmy mixed ants up from two different places and they fought until one bunch was all dead. Jason's fist descended on the ant with a thud. The ant curled into a tight ball, but managed to unwind itself and wobble drunkenly off. Bang, the fist came down again. The small body constricted, creaked open slowly and lay still.

Jason got up and ran for home. It was a brief stint, but it was enough. Jason stood panting in his own backyard. His breath got shallow. He opened his mouth widely and tried to gulp in air, but there was a void where his lungs used to be. The boy looked around frantically, his body held in suspended animation. Flies spotted the sun soaked boards of the house. They buzzed loudly, their blue and green bodies shining like precious jewels. Flies died easily, Jason thought, not like ants or wasps.

People were flies.

Jason looked up at the white puffs of cloud and the blue sky. No airplane could fly to heaven. Only your soul could get that high. The boy fell to his knees and his head dropped. He had sucked in the world and it was now trapped inside his body. Then his mother appeared, or was it an angel.

Timmy Klein: "Jak Swiat Swiatem Polak z Niemcyn nie be Dzie Braten. As Long as They Live, Poles and Germans will Never be Brothers."

Timmy carried a pair of steel and pearl framed opera glasses that he stole from Pani Pankow's apartment. His friend, Jason Novak, had with him a small retracting telescope that belonged to his father. They headed across Griswald Street to Okie Diamond. Dorothy was not with them. She had long ago given up the pleasure of their company.

Okie Diamond was the name given to one large section of open fields that marked the western edge of Kaisertown and led from the City of Buffalo proper to the scattered houses of Cheektowaga and West Seneca. It was a large natural playground for different groups of Kaisertown youth who played and fought amidst its grassy fields, cattail swamps, and scattered copses of crabapple trees and sumac bushes.

"Let's go into the trees and look around from there," suggested Timmy. "Nobody can see us if we stay low. We'll be the James brothers. You can even be Jessie and I'll be Frank. I wish we were real brothers and I didn't have that bitch Dorothy for a sister. Wouldn't that be cool? Wouldn't it?"

Jason did not respond. The two boys continued on, crouching low and occasionally scanning the horizon with their binoculars like two African hunters on the prowl for big game. When they slipped into a cluster of sumac bushes each boy furtively reached up and cracked off a clump of the purplish red fuzzy berries that grew on the low trees. They sucked on the sour buds spitting out the downy pulp. Again they examined the surrounding territory.

Directly in front of them about two hundred feet away they spotted the forms of two people lying in the tent like opening of a spiky, low branched crab apple tree. From any other vantage point the couple would have been completely hidden, but Timmy and Jason could see them clearly.

"Son of a bitch, it's my sister and that prick, Danny Sokolowski," said Timmy in a whisper. "Stupid Kaisertown jerk-off. Thinks he's so tough. I thought she broke up with him and was going out with Chevy. Dumb Polacks both of them anyways." Timmy glanced quickly at his friend, but Jason did not say anything.

The boys raised their viewing devices to their eyes and watched the couple. Something interesting was happening.

"Look at that," said Timmy excitedly. "He's got her tits out."

Jason screwed the telescope tightly into his eye socket.

"Wait till the old man finds out," continued Timmy. "He's gonna beat the shit outa her. You should see how she cries too. Face gets all red and her lips twitch like a dying cat. She tries not to cry, but he beats her till she does. Whacks her on her bare ass. It's great."

"Not so loud," cautioned Jason. "They might hear us. They aren't that far away."

Back in the bushes the boy rubbed and squeezed Dorothy's exposed breasts. He then unzipped her pants and put his hand down between her legs. The girl didn't protest. She let him do it.

"Damn," said Jason, "all them times we were alone in Pankow's garage we never did nothing like this."

"My sister's a whore," said Timmy.

Both Timmy and Jason had taken to swearing lately and they were both intensely interested in sex although they weren't exactly sure about the specifics. For a while Jason had been smuggling out his father's art books for him and Timmy to peruse up in old Pankow's garage. And one time Timmy got his hands on a dirty comic book that his father owned. It showed Popeye and Olive Oil screwing. Even Brutus got into the act one time when he kidnapped Olive Oil. He had a huge dick and Olive Oil was screaming the whole time they did it even though she had a smile on her face. At the end Brutus sold Olive Oil to Whimpy for a hamburger. None of that could compare, of course, to the real live adventure that was unfolding right before their eyes.

"God damn it," said Timmy. "He's given it to her now."

In front of them they could see the boy's bare ass between Dorothy's legs. Her panties and jeans were bunched around one of her sneakered feet. The other leg, bare and bent at the knee was positioned against the boy's pounding body.

"Jesus," marveled Jason.

"It's over," said Timmy. "Look, he getting off of her."

The two friends watched as the boy removed something from his penis and tossed it away. He stood over Dorothy who was still laying half naked on the ground. She got up and tried to hug him, but the boy turned away scanning the horizon apprehensively. He never noticed Timmy or Jason who were directly in front of him. At Griswald Street Dorothy went one way and the boy the other. She turned to stare at him a couple of times, but he never looked back. When the coast was clear, the boys ran over to the site of the seduction.

"Yer sister's body looked great," Jason said enthusiastically. "Man, with this little telescope I could see every detail."

"Yeah, I seen her naked in the bathtub plenty of times," replied

Timmy. "What's this here?" The boy stared down at Danny's used condom unsure at first just what it was. Jason prodded it with his foot, then remembered the boy pulling it off.

"It's a safety," said Jason. "You gotta wear one of these when you're doing it, or else the girl gets a baby for sure. My cousin Larry, was telling me about them. He can get one for me if I need it. You know, I would love to get a closer look at everything. I never seen a real live naked girl before, just pictures and they weren't all that great either. They never show the good parts. You know between the girl's legs."

"Yeah," nodded Timmy and he stooped down and gingerly picked up the used condom and tied the top off in a knot. Then he wrapped it in a handkerchief and put it in his pocket.

"What are you doing?" asked Jason with a grimace on his face.

"Listen," said Timmy and he told his friend about his plan.

The next day Timmy told Dorothy that he and Jason wanted to talk to her in secret down in the cellar. They met in a room beside the coal bin, a storage room filled with newspapers, rags, and old tin cans that were stripped of their labels and crushed flat.

"What do you two want?" asked Dorothy irritably. "Make it fast."

"We seen you yesterday," said Timmy without hesitation. "Seen you and yer boyfriend, Danny Sokolowski, an everything."

"I don't know what you're talking about," she said.

"We seen you screwin," Timmy continued. "And I'm tellin dad. Jason seen it too and he'll back me up."

Dorothy gave Jason a bewildered look, but the boy avoided her gaze and stood his ground beside Timmy.

"You're making it up just because you saw us coming from Okie Diamond, but that doesn't mean we did anything."

It was then that Timmy brought out the safety and dangled it in front of his sister. The girl flushed red on the spot, then made a grab for the used condom, but Timmy quickly snatched it back again.

"Why didn't you tell already then?" asked Dorothy apprehensively.

"Because Timmy began…"

"Because what?"

"Because we're willin to forget what we seen on one condition." He winked at Jason.

"What's that?"

"We won't say nothing and save you the beating of your life if you take all yer clothes off for us right now and give us a good look."

"Fuck you, you little bastards. I ain't doing it." Dorothy looked instinctively around as if there might be other people hiding in the corners of the room.

The swearing startled Jason, but had no effect on Timmy. Nothing made him happier than to see his sister suffer and he never missed a chance to bring that suffering on if he could help it.

"OK, then. I'm tellin dad. You'll scream pretty loud when he gets his hands on you, you little slut. Maybe I'll sneak Jason over to get a peek at it too. Watch you get stripped naked anyway and your ass whipped."

"We just want one look," Jason added.

"Et tu Brute. I should have known," Dorothy responded. "If you tell anybody about this, I'll get Danny or Chevy to beat the shit out of you, both of you. And what about that safety?"

"I'll throw it out. What do I want that thing for?"

Dorothy stepped further into the room and closed the door behind her. "Get back," she said. "You're too close."

Dorothy turned her back to the boys as she slipped off her blouse and squirmed out of her jeans. She then hesitated for a moment hoping for a reprieve. None was forthcoming. She took off the rest of her clothes.

Jason's face was red and there was a noticeable bulge in his pants. Timmy was unmoved.

"Yer socks too," he instructed. "And turn around. We wanna see yer cunt."

Dorothy meekly obeyed. She was less assertive with her clothes off. She pulled at her socks like a child, toe first. Then she quickly turned around.

"I ain't doing no more," she suddenly cried out looking straight at Jason. Leave me alone. Just leave me alone."

She put her face in her hands. Jason and Timmy hesitated giving themselves a final and prolonged look at the naked girl, then they hurried out the door and made a beeline for old Pankow's garage.

"Holy shit," said Jason. "That was great, but I felt sorry for your sister too. She looked so sad. We used to be friends."

"Fuck her, Timmy replied. "She ain't no good for nothing. Anyway you can't be no friends with girls. They're only good for one thing and we both know what that is. I hardly see her anyways. She's always out now that the old man is working nights. Besides I'm not through with her yet."

"What do you mean?"

"I'll tell you later. Hey, you wanna go spear some frogs over at Okie Diamond? I got the spears downstairs."

"No, I don't like doing that. It's cruel."

"Big fuckin' deal. Who cares about a bunch of stupid frogs?"

"No thanks. You go with somebody else."

"Just who would that be around here? Yer the only friend I got and sometimes I ain't too sure about you. Just remember you wouldna seen my sister without me."

"Yeah, thanks. I'll see you later," Jason replied. "I gotta go home for supper."

"Yeah, right." Timmy muttered to himself as Jason made his way out of the garage.

Timmy didn't run into Jason until he finally caught up with him at Charlotte's store a few days afterward.

"Hey, I been calling you, but yer mother told me you couldn't come out and play," said Timmy in an interrogating tone. "What's goin on? And was that that skinny bitch Tina Kaszpczyk I seen you talking to? You ain't been hanging around wit her, have you?"

"I just said hello. She was coming out of the store when I was going in."

"She's a stuck up little bitch. I hate her and she's flat as a board too."

"She's not that bad," replied Jason. "Nothing like your sister though. Man, I gotta say Dorothy's got a great body."

"Hey, yeah, and guess what?"

"What?"

"My stupid sister ran away from home. She took off to our babcia over by Glenn Street."

"Why? What happened?"

Timmy responded with a quick smile. "I told on her."

"You what?"

"I told on the bitch, about her and that prick, Danny Sokolowski. She had it comin. You shoulda seen it. We were at the table for supper and I took out that safety, you know, and I showed it to the old man. 'What's this thing, dad?' He almost choked. Dorothy got beet red. We had chicken soup, you know, and there was this noodle hangin outa her mouth. 'I seen Dorothy and a boy in the fields. He was on top of her and when he got up he threw this thing away. What is it, dad?'"

"Timmy you were supposed to get rid of it. We promised."

"So what. Who cares. Listen. Boy, did the old man go crazy. He grabbed her and dragged her down into the cellar. Good for her. I just wished I could a seen it all. The old lady went down, but she got a punch in the nose for her trouble."

Jason dropped his face in his hands. "We promised," he said over and over.

"He beat her for half an hour and who knows what else he done. When they came upstairs she was naked. All snotty nosed, red eyes and she had big red marks all over her ass and the back of her legs from the strap. But she wasn't cryin no more. Looked like a fuckin' zombie.

"Then he took all her clothes and locked em away. She had to walk around the house naked. You woulda liked that. She finally ran off. That friend a hers, that Janie, she helped her."

Jason looked straight at Timmy. "I don't think I want to be your friend anymore," he said.

"Who cares," Timmy replied quickly. "Who needs a girl smelling Polack asshole like you anyways? I can have more fun without you."

Dorothy: *"My Man Don't Love Me. He Treats Me, Oh, So Mean."*

Dorothy had outgrown the company of both her brother and Jason. Timmy was simply too unbearable to be with, and Jason, at two grades beneath her, was now too young. There was no way that a freshman high schooler could be seen with a boy from the seventh grade. Still some sentiment lingered although the girl would never openly admit to it. Other boys, her age and older, were paying attention to her now and with both her parents working she had time and freedom on her hands. The first of her boyfriends was a boy named Danny Sokolowski.

Dorothy had a crush on Danny and since he was popular with the other girls at South Park High she took a special delight in capturing his attention. Teach those Polack bitches. Niemnec or not, the best looking boy in class likes me, not you, Dorothy enjoyed the thought. She willingly let him kiss her and feel her up. At first from outside her blouse, but later she let him undo the buttons and put his hand inside over her bra. Dorothy didn't get much pleasure out of it, but Danny liked it and she wanted him to be happy with her.

Whenever Danny got Dorothy alone he was obsessed with her, kissing and squeezing her constantly, but at other times, especially at school, he hardly seemed to notice her. He never ate lunch with Dorothy even though they were in the cafeteria at the same time. He sat with his buddy, Bobby Grabowski, and a couple of other boys.

After school one day, Danny invited Dorothy to his house on Fenton Street. No one was home. The two of them sat in the parlor, a small room, but filled with expensive furniture. The rug was an orange and brown color and real thick. Dorothy could feel it give way softly beneath her feet.

"Take yer shoes off," Danny cautioned her when they entered the room. "We're not allowed in here unless my parents got company."

"It hardly looks used at all," the girl said feeling uncomfortable and somehow threatened by the rich surroundings. God forbid if Danny ever caught a glimpse of her flat on South Ogden Street.

Two shiny glass topped tables flanked the sofa. Protected by doilies, these tables held a couple of large lamps in the shape of white robed women with golden colored hair supporting tall green lamp shades in their outstretched arms. The shades still had their plastic covers on. Drapes of a similar hue framed the parlor window whose leaded upper portion was veiled by a scalloped lace valance. A golden rope tied in an elaborate knot held back the curtains themselves. A chair and a hassock completed the room except for a plaster cast fireplace centered on one wall. A fake log fire sat in its hollowed center.

"When you switch it on, the bulbs get hot and turn these little fans that give you a red glowing light just like a real fire," Danny explained. "Best when it's dark out though."

Danny nervously put his arm around Dorothy and kissed her. Their teeth clinked for a second, then he put his tongue in her mouth. Dorothy closed her eyes and winced. She didn't like kissing. With lots of fumbling and cursing Danny took her blouse and bra off for the first time. Dorothy was embarrassed and kept her head down. From her perspective, however, she could see a large bulge in Danny's pants. Danny pushed her upright and rubbed her naked breasts hard. His kisses got hot and sloppy and ran all over her face. She felt sick. Finally Danny paused and asked her if she loved him.

"Yes," Dorothy responded looking at him directly for the first time. Her cheeks were flushed, coloring red the spaces between the tiny freckles across her nose. Her eyes were wide.

"No, you don't really love me," Danny said as he continued to play with her breasts, squeezing them painfully.

"I do," insisted Dorothy. "I wouldn't be lettin you do all this if I didn't."

"I don't got no safety with me," Danny said. "Bob was supposed to get me one, but he couldn't or somethin."

Dorothy had no idea what he was talking about. At the same time Danny had managed to get his penis out of his pants and he was now rubbing it with his free hand. Dorothy had never seen a full- fledged erection before and she was surprised by the size of Danny's cock, or prick, or whatever she was supposed to call it. She had seen Timmy's plenty of times. He had even taken it out and waved it at her on several occasions. But it was small and ugly, and had those wrinkly balls, ughh. But Danny's was big, and shiny, and smooth, and hard. The girl was fascinated by it, but she was too embarrassed to stare.

Dorothy knew you could get pregnant if she had contact with boys, but she wasn't exactly sure about the procedure except that the boy had to put his cock inside of her pussy. That much was certain. What happened next she didn't know. Janie had told her that if a boy took his thing out right away then you couldn't have a baby. Also Janie said that if you peed immediately afterward then that would stop you from getting pregnant. Of course, Janie was such a simpleton there was no way Dorothy was taking her word for it.

"Maybe then, if you love me, and we can't do it right now, then maybe you could just give me a blow job?" Danny continued. "If you really love me, you'll give me a blow job."

Now Dorothy had heard the term, "blow job" more than once in her life that was for certain, but she didn't know exactly what it meant. Judging from the term itself she figured at worst she'd have to just purse her lips and blow on Danny's cock. Maybe somehow that made boys feel good. Who knew. Wasn't much to it evidently, but she thought she'd ask anyway.

"How do you do that? Give a blow job, I mean?"

"Don't you know nothing?" replied Danny. "I thought you were with boys before. Bobby Grabowski said you were a little niemnec whore."

Dorothy winced at the words, but said nothing.

"You put it in yer mouth, stupid, and then move yer head up and down. A blow job, you know. Come on. If you really love me, you'll do it."

"Put what in my mouth?" Dorothy asked.

"My dick for Christ's sake. What did you think?"

"What?" gasped the girl looking down at Danny's large, throbbing cock as it bobbed up and down like a diving board. "I, I don't know. I..."

"And I was goin to ask you to go steady too," replied Danny.

Now going steady was the biggest deal for the girls of South Park High School. Only a few girls had that honor bestowed upon them, Judy Burkowski being one of them. Judy Burkowski, the most beautiful girl in the freshman class. She was so gorgeous and sought after by the boys that any other girl would have traded their virginity and their right breast to change places with her. She had a boyfriend who was a senior and had his own car.

Danny suddenly sat up and swung Dorothy down, her face across his lap. His hard erection almost took her eye out.

"Come on," he insisted. "Yer spoilin it. We could go steady and everything."

"You won't tell anybody, will you?" Dorothy asked. "And what about your parents and your little sister?"

"They won't be back till five o'clock. My father's picking em up."

The boy peered into the dining room where a large clock on the wall read 4:30 PM. "Come on, Dorothy. You said you loved me. Yer friend Janie gives blow jobs all the time."

"What? Janie Toporciak?" Dorothy shouted out in disbelief.

"Yeah, we buy her Hostess cupcakes and she gives us all blow jobs."

"Janie! She never said anything to me."

"And she wasn't goin steady or nothing," added Danny. "Come on. It's gettin late." And he pushed his penis against her closed lips.

"It's, it's all sticky or something," Dorothy protested weakly.

Danny wiped himself with the edge of his shirt. "That's nothing. Happens all the time. But be careful. Don't get any on the couch or my mother will kill me."

Dorothy closed her eyes and opened her mouth.

"Yeah, that's good," Danny moaned. "Now move yer head up an down. Up an down. But watch yer teet."

After the initial repulsion, Dorothy found the practice pleasurable. The head and shaft of Danny's cock in her mouth, all wet, hard, and smooth, felt good, and the boy's helpless excitement gave her a feeling of power and control. The mood was momentary as Danny began to quiver and gyrate more forcefully, pushing his penis farther and farther into Dorothy's mouth. The girl began to fight for air. Her cheeks puffed out and her nostrils flared with each difficult breath. She struggled not to gag. Danny moaned and thrust more wildly. Dorothy's lungs felt like as though they were going to explode. Finally, unable to breathe at all, she lifted her head and sat upright.

She gasped and smiled weakly. "I, I couldn't breathe anymore," she apologized. "Was I doing it right?"

Danny said nothing. He was staring instead in rapturous dismay at his erupting penis as it, like a mini volcano, shot forth thick gobs of sperm all over his pants and onto the sofa.

"Jesus Christ, what did you stop for, you dumb Kraut bitch?" he yelled while still twitching to his climax. "Lookit what you made me do. I got it all over the couch. My mother's gonna kill me."

"I'm sorry. I, I didn't know. I couldn't breathe," Dorothy stammered. She had never seen an ejaculation before and thought that Danny was hurt. "Are you OK? Can I get you something?"

"A washrag! Get me a wet wash rag, you idiot!"

As the boy stood up several drops of semen puddled onto the rug. "Oh god damn it. They're gonna be here in a few minutes."

Dorothy returned after finding the bathroom and the washcloth.

"It's all yer fault, you stupid jerk," he shouted again as he grabbed the wet rag from her hand. "And you better get outa here. My mother catches a girl in here, especially one like you and she'll kill me."

Dorothy was still naked from the waist up. Her breasts heaved from the exertion and panic. She grabbed her blouse off the couch and held it in front of her. She walked towards the doorway, then looked back at Danny hoping he'd say something. He ignored her. In the hall Dorothy put on her bra, buttoned her blouse and put her shoes on. Her breathing came regularly now. She could still hear Danny cursing from the parlor. She hesitated, then decided to wait. Finally, she heard a car pull into the driveway. Only then did she exit the house.

"Good afternoon, Mr. and Mrs. Sokolowski," she said. "Nice day, isn't it."

Dorothy and Janie Toporciak strolled down Clinton Street. Dorothy never mentioned the cupcake reference that Danny gave her at the end of the school year. This was summer vacation, Danny was gone and Dorothy was free. As usual the two girls were dressed the same in tight blue jeans and white men's shirts with the tails hanging out. They had white socks and sneakers on their feet and black kerchiefs tied high on their chins. At the corner of Weimer they stopped to put their makeup on using the Gold Ray Bakery window as a mirror: some eyeliner, rouge, and a heavy coating of pearl colored lipstick.

Janie's chubby face and her puckered lips gave her a decidedly fish-like appearance. Nevertheless, when she asked Dorothy how she looked, Dorothy answered with a cheerful and sincere. "Beautiful! You look beautiful."

The two friends lit their cigarettes and continued the walk down Clinton Street towards Houghton Park.

"I got mine last year," said Dorothy. "Nobody ever told me anything. I didn't know what was going on. I thought I was dying, that I had cancer or something. I told my mother and she said. 'Yer a woman now.' And threw me a box of Kotex. That was it."

"My mudder toll me before it happened, but I was still scared as hell," said Janie. "I never like to see blood, especially when it's mine. Hey, you got a garden at home?" she added.

"No," replied Dorothy. "We used to have some flowers in front of the house. Why?"

"You ain't suppose to go inna garden you got yer periods," explained Janie. "My mudder toll me. It makes all a dah vegetables dry up and die. I doan know about dah flowers dough."

Dorothy didn't reply. Some things with Janie were best left unchallenged. Wonder what farm women did, she thought, nevertheless.

"Oh, Oh," said Dorothy nodding to Janie. "There's Danny and Bob on the next corner."

"Dat dumb Dave Murowski's wit em too," Jamie added. "I hate him. Let's cross over to dah udder side a dah street."

"Too late. They seen us."

The girls quickened their pace and stared straight ahead as they walked past the boys.

"Hey dere Janie, you wanna cupcake," a voice called out.

"Oh shit," said Janie.

"Just don't say anything," added Dorothy. "Keep walking."

"Hey Dorothy!" It was Danny's voice. The girl winced. "Wait a minute. I gotta stop at the bubble gum machine at Ben Franklin's and get you a ring so we can go steady. Ha, ha, ha."

"Janie, I got a cousin works inna bakery. If I get you a job dere, will you give all of us a blow job?"

The boys' voices were followed by peals of laughter. The girls hurried their steps.

"Hey Dorty," said Janie after only another block. "I'm sorry, but I gotta stop up dere at dah butcher shop. Godda stick in my side."

"Sure. We ain't going to get rid of these morons anyway."

Up ahead at the entrance to Tedlinski's Butcher Shop stood two figures in a darkening doorway. When they got closer Dorothy recognized them as two older Kaisertown toughs known as Chevy and Mack.

"Hiyah," said Janie as she stopped at the entrance to the store.

The large windows of the shop were plastered with homemade signs advertising various cuts of meat. A large banner spread across the storefront read: "We make are own Polish Sausage, Fresh and Smoke." It was after six o'clock and the store was closed. The two boys looked at the girls, sizing them up conspicuously. The boy named Chevy took a heavy drag on his cigarette. He was actually handsome Dorothy thought despite

the sneering expression on his face. He wore his slick backed hair in a
DA cut. There was a pack of Camels rolled up into the sleeve of his tee
shirt. His exposed arm was well muscled.

"Yous broads runnin from somethin?" inquired Chevy.

"Dem guys is bodderin us," said Janie, pointing to the three boys fast
approaching the store. "Dey woan leave us alone."

Chevy and his pal stepped out from Tedlinski's dim alcove into the
evening light of the street bringing the pursuing boys up short.

"Where yous punks goin?" asked Chevy as Danny and his buddies
screeched to a halt. Mack looked the three up and down, then snorted in
derision.

"Ah, hiyah there, Chevy," one of the boys said. "Hey, you know my
cousin Paulie Czajka? He lives over by Fredro Street?"

"Never heard a him," replied Chevy cutting the conversation short.

"We was just followin dem two whores dere," added Dave.

"Yeah, they give good blow jobs, especially that fat one there. You
got some Hostess cupcakes den yer in business wit her." The three boys
laughed nervously.

"Very funny," said Janie, her voice breaking slightly.

"I doan tink dat's no way to talk to no broads," said Chevy. "What
dah fuck's wrong wit yous guys? Yous ain't got no manners?"

The boys gave a collective and audible gulp. Despite their extra numbers they were no match for Mack and Chevy. Mack was a bull dog of a
boy, and Chevy bigger and tougher yet.

"Whadda yous broads tink we oughta do wit dese punks callin yous
whores and everyting?"

"Beat dah shit outa dem," Janie blurted out.

Danny and his friends took a step back, but not before Chevy
grabbed Danny's shirt. With one quick move he sent a crunching punch

into the boy's face. When he let go of the shirt Danny collapsed back into the arms of his friends. Blood streamed from the boy's broken nose and lacerated lips. Danny sobbed in pain and humiliation. Dorothy was horrified.

"No, no. They weren't bothering us that much."

Danny and his friends took that moment to turn and run. Mack yelled after them. "Chickens! I never liked dat Sokolowski anyways. Wise ass punk."

Chevy and Mack now accompanied the girls to the park although both Dorothy and Janie were uneasy and would have preferred to be alone.

"How come I ain't seen yous two broads aroun here before?" inquired Chevy as he and Dorothy dropped behind the other two.

"I don't know," answered Dorothy. "We come here from time to time. We graduated from 69 last year. Now we're going to be sophomores at South Park"

Chevy snickered. "I quit a couple a years ago. Don't need no school. I'm gonna be a mechanic. I work at Strow's Garage right now by Clinton and Bailey, yah know. Savin for my own car. I ain't got no use for no teachers. Dey tink dey're so smart. Bet you none a dem could replace a fan belt on dere car if it broke. What good is all dat book stuff? It don't teach you nuttin you need in real life. You wanna cigarette?"

"Yeah," Dorothy said smiling at Chevy's impassioned argument against higher education. She stopped for a light at Chevy's cupped hands. The street lights blinked white once, twice, then went on as the group entered the park. Nine o'clock, Dorothy thought.

"What's yer name anyways?" Chevy asked.

"Dorothy."

"Dorothy what?"

Dorothy hesitated. "Klein, Dorothy Klein."

"Dat doan sound Polish. What is it? It ain't German is it? My uncle was killed in the war over by dah Battle a dah Bulge. I hate dem fuckin Krauts."

"No, it's Austrian."

"Good, not dat I mind dat much. I'd go wit a Kraut broad if she was good to me. Know what I mean?"

"I guess," Dorothy acknowledged.

The call of the robins sounded loudly in the duskiness of the dying evening. Dimming images of strolling couples and scampering children moved indistinctly in the twilight. The distant lights of the baseball field were on. A night game in progress. Beyond the tennis courts and the looming edifice of the Shelter House, rolling lawns of grass and small copses of trees extended to the wild margins of Buffalo Creek.

"Mack, check if it's still dere," said Chevy. "I'll bust someone in dah mout dey took it."

Mack let go of Janie's hand and reached into the hollow of a tree, a dark, deep split in the lower fork. His arm disappeared to the elbow.

"Here she is," Mack said triumphantly as he withdrew a bottle of Thunderbird wine from the tree and held it high like a midwife displaying a baby.

"Yeah, alright. Now we ken have a liddle celebration."

At the back of Houghton Park only the occasional sound filtered down from the park proper. The wine was passed around. Janie giggled and slapped jokingly at Mack's exploring hands. Dorothy's insides glowed with warmth from the sticky sweet liquid. Chevy had her shirt unbuttoned and was squeezing her breasts and kissing her. His alcoholic breath sickened her slightly. Chevy was more practiced than Danny, confident and bold.

"Me and Dorty here is goin for a liddle walk," said Chevy after the last of the wine had been drunk. "Yous two behave yerselfs while we're gone."

Dorothy's white shirt flapped like a ghost in the night. Underneath it her bra had been lifted over her breasts. The two figures moved to the bottom of the hill and lay down in the grass. Dorothy could smell the freshly cut chlorophyll freshness all around her. The night sky was clear. Away from the lights of the Kaisertown streets, and the ball diamonds of the park, she was amazed at the number of stars that were out. Must be a million she thought as they whirled around her head like a slowly revolving record. Stars fell on Alabama.

Chevy was kneeling in front of her. Dorothy felt a tug at her belt, then her shoes were taken off and her jeans along with her panties removed. She gazed up at the night sky. It was such a beautiful night, why not. In a week it would be her fifteenth birthday, August, Eighteenth.

Suddenly a light blinked in the night sky; then another, and another. Falling stars or fireflies? Dorothy tried to sit forward and make a wish. She was about to say something to Chevy when she felt a tearing pain inside of her that took her breath away and forced her back against the ground.

"Yeah, yer my kinda broad," she heard Chevy's voice. "Doan worry. I godda safety on."

The boy moved up and down, pushing and pulling at the girl's clinging insides. Dorothy groaned and squirmed beneath the onslaught. She felt Chevy's hand cup and pinch her bottom.

"Dat's it. Dat's it," he kept saying. "Dat's good, huh. You like it, huh."

Dorothy flexed her legs back and forth alternately to relieve the pain. Her head moved from side to side as the boy's pace quickened and his thrusts grew more powerful and penetrating. Only the slope of the hill prevented the girl from being propelled along the grass. She grabbed the boy by the back of his shirt and hung on tightly, praying for him to stop. Stop. Stop.

Then with an equally sudden and tearing wrench, he withdrew from within her, and a dull throbbing ache replaced the sharp pain. Chevy stood up, pulled the condom off with a snap and threw it onto the grass. He then zippered up his pants and called to Dorothy.

"Led's get goin. See what Mack and yer girlfrin is up to."

Dorothy sat forward slowly. She hung her head down as a vinegary flow of moisture dripped from the roof of her mouth onto her tongue. She swallowed it back and wiped her mouth with the sleeve of her shirt. Then she pulled her bra down and started to button herself up. She struggled to stand up until finally Chevy took her arm and steadied her. In the darkness the white of the girl's bare ass cheeks stood out clearly and Chevy gave them a hard sharp slap. Dorothy almost toppled over.

"You had too much wine maybe," he said. "Pud yer pants on. I god yer sneakers. Hold onto me."

"Thanks," Dorothy replied as she hiked up her panties with one hand.

Janie and Mack were not at the picnic table. The lone wine bottle marked the spot. Chevy and Dorothy continued towards the side entrance to the park. Only the night lights were on now, spaced at far intervals along a cindered walkway. Hundreds of moths of all sizes fluttered around and dive bombed the pathway lights. Dorothy was fascinated by their erratic, suicidal flights. Several dying creatures littered the walk. Chevy crunched across them unceremoniously.

Each step that Dorothy took was accompanied by an inner pang of pain. She tried to walk normally, but fancied that she was hobbling bowlegged. Chevy was preoccupied lighting another cigarette. Near the darkened tennis courts they met Mack and another boy. Janie was not with them.

"I dunno what got into her," said Mack. "Wasn me. Ha, ha, ha. She got a cryin jag on an took off."

"She gets like that sometimes," said Dorothy. "She'll be OK, but I'd better go and see how she is. Probably went home."

"Remember, see yous tomorrow, same time, same place," added Chevy as he stuck his tongue out and blew a smoke ring into the air.

Dorothy could hear the boys talking and laughing as she continued towards the side exit. Babe's was closed now although the pleasant odor of sodas, sundaes, pop, and bubble gum hung in the air around it. Papers and bits of colored glass littered the sidewalk. The old bricks of Casimir Street could be seen beneath several crumbled sections of black asphalt recently spread between the high stone curbs.

Dorothy's own pain was drowned out now by her concern for Janie. Poor Janie, her self-image was even lower than Dorothy's. As the girl passed the vacant lot adjacent to Babe's she heard a voice call out. She stopped, then backed up warily into the street.

"Dorty! Dorty," the voice sounded high pitched and unnatural. "Id's me. Help me. Come back." It was Janie. Dorothy ran to the curb.

"Where are you? I can't see anything."

"You godda help me, Dorty. I can't come oud. It was dat Dave an dah rest a dem. Dey took all my clothes and they made me, made me... Help, I ain't got nuttin on."

Dorothy walked into the darkness and saw her friend standing there cross legged, arms covering her breasts. Dorothy held Janie's pudgy naked body close to her. Janie was trembling and sobbing.

"I, I, I di, didn't know whad to doooo. I was dizzy from dat wine.

61

They were waiting here. They had a bunch of cupcakes. Made me eat them and after each one I had to, to. You know. They made me. I was sick and barfing, but they kept making me. And they laughed and took my clothes. Them fucking bastards. I'm gonna tell Mack to beat dah shit outa all dem bastards. Lookit what dey did to me. All my clothes." Janie clutched Dorothy tightly by the shirt with her clenched fists.

"Look," said Dorothy. "I'll give you my shirt. It's long with the tails out. Should cover you enough. We can take Casimir all the way to yer street. It's dark and late. Nobody will see us."

"Oh boze, my mudder will kill me I come home wid no clothes." Janie started to cry.

The girls clung to the sidewalk; Dorothy in her bra, Janie naked except for the white shirt.

"Whad if dey're still around waitin for us?" whimpered Janie.

"Come on."

Thank god for the tall elms that fronted nearly every house, and luckily it was not one of those sweltering August nights in Buffalo. If so the whole neighborhood would have been outside sitting or rocking on their porch swings trying to keep cool as the bricks and boards of the Kaisertown houses gave back the stored up heat of the day. They got to Janie's house after midnight. Dorothy had to say a quick goodbye, reclaim her shirt and get home before her father returned from work.

"Tanks Dorty. Yer my best friend ever. God bless you."

Dorothy's house was the second from the corner not counting the double lot that Charlotte's Store occupied. As she turned into her yard she saw the Clinton St. bus, big and aglow with its cold white lights, pass the corner of South Ogden. It would stop midblock. If it was her father's bus, he would be home in five minutes. If he was already in the house, the downstairs door would be locked and Dorothy would be in big trouble.

She was in luck. Dorothy paused inside the hallway to catch her breath. She took a perverted delight in the delay as she pictured her father walking home, each step bringing him closer to the door behind which she now stood.

"Love to see him in his monkey suit," she whispered to the darkness.

The ache between her legs was still there, but it wasn't as bad as she had imagined. She had experienced worse cramps. Anyway, it was bound to happen. Too bad it wasn't Danny though. She would have preferred Danny.

Dorothy undressed, and stealthily slipped a kotex pad between her legs before sliding into bed just as the kitchen door opened. She gasped. He was home. At the same time the girl heard a whispered voice from across the room.

"I'm tellin dad you was out late."

"Leave me alone. I haven't done anything to you."

"I'm tellin unless you gimme a quarter," Timmy persisted.

"I don't have no quarter. I got fifteen cents is all I've got."

"You can give it to me in the morning, and then owe me the dime. An don't forget or I'm tellin."

Dorothy sighed. Welcome home she said to herself.

Jason: *"Rozumi Popolsku? Do you Speak Polish?"*

"Niech bedzie pochwalony Jesus Chrystus," Jason's babcia came for a visit.

"Na wieki wiekow, amen," Jason's mother replied.

Babcia wore long dark dresses and high shoes with lots of laces and her stockings were thick almost like socks. Jason loved his babcia. She gave him pennies, and nickels and sometimes even a dime for his piggy bank, and she brought him a Heath Bar each time she visited. His mother claimed that babcia loved Jason more than any of his cousins.

"Rozumi popolsku?" was always the first thing babcia said to Jason, and his mother would laugh at her son's awkward attempts to repeat the words.

"Edda don't wann him to learn Polish. He's afraid when he grows up he won't talk English good."

"On sie powinien ciszyc," replied babcia with a toss of her head. Her big breasts stuck out like pillows and cushioned Jason's head whenever she cradled him in her arms. Up close Jason could see babcia's face with its sunken, rouged cheeks, and lips that were creased like the edges of an apple pie crust.

"Is Florian still by dah ships?" asked Jason's mother as she took up some ironing.

"No, he quit it dere, Berta was sayin."

"Bertha, my poor sister, what she's got wit him, nie? Can't keep a job, but dat's one ting wid her. You doan say nuttin or she tell you right out, 'It's my life an my husband. Keep yer nose outa it.' I feel sorry for dah girls, Frances and Nelly. The whole bunch ain't got a pot to piss in."

"Co oczy nie widga to serce nie boli," replied babcia.

When babcia was ready to leave she bent down for a goodbye hug and kiss from Jason. She almost smothered him. She smelled like flowers.

"Idz z bogiem."

"Bog z wami."

Every Sunday Jason and his mother met babcia on the corner and went to church together at St. Bernard's. Jason's father stayed at home and read his books or listened to his music with no singing in it. That's why there were mice in the cellar Jason's mother said.

Jason worried about his father not going to church. Every time you missed mass that was a mortal sin. Only one mortal sin was enough to send you directly to hell. Maybe when he got older his father would go to church every day like Pani Dombrowski to make up for what he missed.

Jason was supposed to go to Catholic school like his cousins, but his parents had a big argument about it and he wound up attending School 69 instead. He was glad. In Catholic school you didn't even learn English until Fourth Grade and you were taught by nuns, sisters, or crows as the children called them. And the nuns were mean. If you were caught chewing gum you had to stick it on the end of your nose and keep it there all day. And the nuns would hit your hands with rulers and make you kneel in front of the whole class if you disobeyed even if it was an accident and you didn't mean it. And if you ever got sent to Sister Superior you may as well head down the railroad tracks to Black Bridge and jump off. Most of the kids peed their pants before they even opened the door to her office.

In exchange for sending his son to public school, Jason's father had to promise to allow Jason to receive all the sacraments of the church. For Jason that meant a year of religious instructions at St. Bernard's leading up to his First Holy Communion. "Religious Instructions" was a cooperative proposal that created a cease fire in the Catholic-Public school rivalry over pupil enrollment. At the same time it was an acknowledgement of the power the church still exercised in the Polish community. It allowed public school students who were Catholic to get religious training and preparation for the sacraments of the church, all on public school time. Jason's father claimed it was illegal, but did not pursue the issue in order to maintain peace in the family.

The Instructions were held every Monday afternoon from 1:30 PM till 3:00 PM. This gave the Catholic school kids a half day off and one-upmanship over their public school rivals.

Jason could sense the change in atmosphere the minute he walked into St. Bernard's School. It felt and smelled like a church and it was just as quiet and scary. He opened a door which had the sign, "First Holy Communion Class" taped on its frosted window. Inside, a large crucifix hung above the front blackboard. Underneath it were two pictures: one of Jesus and one of the Virgin Mary. Both were showing their open hearts wrapped in thorns with blood dripping from them. Jesus and Mary had sad, painful looks on their faces. Jesus and Mary were never happy, Jason had long ago figured out. The blackboard itself had the name, "Sister Salomea", written across it in a very fancy style. And sitting at the desk in front of all this was the good sister herself; small, wrinkled, and meaner looking than Stachu Klemp guarding an old bone. Jason took a deep breath and stepped forward. The eyes of the huddled and silent pupils who had preceded him were instantly riveted upon the boy. Jason was puzzled and afraid. He didn't know where to sit.

"Fine a empty desk an sid id down," came a piercing voice from the front of the classroom. Jason did not bother to confirm its source, but moved quickly to the first empty desk and sat down. The boy got lots of sympathetic glances from his fellow sufferers. Then he slumped down in his seat and got ready for an hour and a half of terror.

The desks were unfamiliar and uncomfortable. They were made of black wrought iron and wood worn gray from use, and they were connected in long rows so that none could be moved independently. Sister Salomea, who looked like a mummified bird of prey, wore the traditional black, hooded nun's habit with a large, beaded rosary tied around her waist. The crucifix at its end trailed nearly to the floor. Her stiff white cap rim left a furrow on her heavily wrinkled forehead. Jason's cousins told him that underneath the cap, the nuns' heads were shaven.

"Bartkowski, Paul; Chipua, David," Sister Salomea read the roll call, last name first, not like in School 69 where they always called you by your first name. After each response of "Here" or "Present" the sister made a quick check mark in her attendance book. When she finished and shut the book with a bang, all the pupils bolted upright in their seats.

"Who is our 'evenly Fadder?" Sister Salomea began abruptly.

The pupils squirmed in their seats and suddenly took a particular interest in their pencils and desk tops. Not one of them said a word in response since most were not even sure what the good Sister had asked them.

Sister Salomea scowled down at her charges. Hers was a heavy burden. She next grabbed the attendance book and ran her skinny skeletal finger down the list of names.

"Gardon," she finally thundered. "Who is our "evenly Fadder? Answer!"

A cute girl with pigtails who sat in the front seat of the second row stared blankly ahead as a sigh of relief spread throughout the rest of the class. Her lower lip soon began to tremble and tears welled up in her eyes. One rolled mournfully down her cheek.

"Doan be a baby," snapped Sister Salomea. "Bose is watching you. Now all a yous. Dah proper response is, God. God is our 'evenly Fadder who made it everyting. He made us too, an He loves us because we are his children. Now who knows aboud dah tree in one concept a God? Whad do we mean when we say tree in one?" Now Jason's father had recently tried his hand at golf and Jason had heard the expression "Hole in One" but he wisely decided to keep that information to himself. Instead he watched the clock on the wall whose hands did not seem to be moving despite the loud ticking sound that echoed in the room. No one raised a hand prompting Sister Salomea to throw hers up in despair.

"Dat's dah trouble when yous go to dah pubic school," she bellowed. "Dey teach yous everyting but nuttin about God. Yous can not fool God. Yous ken take dah communion wafer in yer mouts, but it doan mean nuttin if yous doan accept God in yer hearts. If yer parents had any sense dey would put yous in dah Catlick school before it's too late."

Sister Salomea stared at her charges in order to let the message sink in. Then she returned to her question and when no response was forthcoming she continued her monologue.

"God is tree beings in one: God, dah Fadder; God, dah son; and God, dah Holy Spirit."

Jason remembered the sign of the cross.

"Dis is dah tree in one. God is tree, an God is one. We ken not explain it no bedder den dis. It is one a dah mysteries a God, dah tree in one. So now yous say it after me."

The children dutifully repeated the lesson but by and large had no idea what the phrase meant.

At Religious Instructions Jason learned how close he had actual-ly come to being damned. He was not a good Catholic after all. Sister Salomea may be mean, but she was saving his soul. Before long Jason could rattle off the Ten Commandments although he wasn't sure about some of them like, "Coveting your neighbor's wife." And there were other important Church laws that the Sister drilled into the pupils' heads: fast on the appointed days, give money to the support of the Church, and confess your sins at least once a year and take communion. That was for grownups, with kids it was more often.

As usual, Jason's father had a different opinion. He claimed none of that stuff was even in the Bible; that the Catholics had made it all up themselves.

When the time of his Communion approached, Jason's mother took him on the bus to Broadway and bought him a new white suit at Sattler's. She also got him a pair of white shoes and a white bow tie.

"Jus like a liddle angel, you look," she said proudly.

The salesman smiled. Holy Communion time was good for business.

With the day drawing closer, Sister Salomea rehearsed her instruc-tions: "Yous muss say, 'Bless me Fadder, for I have sinned', when yous see dah priest. Den yous tell all yer sins, mortal and venial sins. Doan leave nuttin out."

Just one mortal sin on your soul and the devil would laugh and torment you for all eternity, Jason knew. And there was nothing anyone could do about it, not Sister Salomea, not Father Kolinski, not Jason's mother, nobody.

At least with a venial sin you had a chance because then you went to Purgatory where your sins were slowly burned away. That was pretty bad too, not to mention painful, but at least you got out of there. Maybe it would take a thousand years, but that was better than hell which lasted forever.

"Den dah priest give yous yer penance," Sister Salomea went on. "So menny Our Fadders, or Hail Marys. Den yous come outa dah confessional and circle around to yer places wit her heads down. Dere yous say dah penance."

Sister spoke loudly in church. Maybe God didn't mind if a sister did it. Must be nice to feel so comfortable. Jason was always timid and afraid in church. After all you had God there and all the angels and saints just waiting for you to make a mistake so they could punish you.

"An yous ken not eat nuttin on dah day of yer First Holy Communion. Nuttin," continued Sister Salomea. "A drink a wadder, dat's all. No juice or pop, or the holy wafer turn black in yer mouts."

Jason was shaking and sick to his stomach as he waited in line at the confessional. He could hear the others in his group reciting their sins. He wished there was a door on the confessional as there was in St. Casimir's instead of just a curtain. What good was a curtain?

Teddy Lewandowski emerged red faced and eyes lowered. Jason was next. He stepped inside and knelt down. In front of him a small door on a screened window slid open. He could see a silhouette behind it. There was a soft tapping sound on the wall. Jason frantically tried to remember his carefully rehearsed confession. He just had the whole thing down by heart but now his mind drew a blank. The tapping sound was repeated, louder this time and followed by a deep voice.

"You in dere, confess!"

Jason's head whipped backward.

"Bless me, Father," he began in a trembling, barely audible voice.

The priest mumbled something that sounded like a Polish swear word Jason's father occasionally used, but the boy wasn't sure. Priests probably had special permission anyways.

"Talk it louder," the priest urged.

Jason rattled off a list of sins, real and imagined in a booming voice that could have startled the pigeons off the church roof top. When he was done, he was sweating and could not remember a single thing he had said.

"Ten Our Fadders, an ten Hail Marys," the priest said, and the little door on the screened window slammed shut.

When he emerged from the confessional all eyes were on him. Jason turned red, lowered his head and almost ran around the aisles back to his seat. He nearly had an asthma attack in the process.

On the appointed Sunday, the Holy communicants marched slowly down the main aisle of St. Bernard's Church. The church was festive with flowers. The young charges beamed with pride while hiding an interior filled with trepidation. The parents in turn craned their necks and pointed their children out to one another, a needless exercise since the congregation was like one big intimate family anyway.

"Dere she is, my Sophia. Ale ladna!"

"Johnny, my God, he looks like such a little angel."

Jason looked around for his mother, but could not spot her. She was there somewhere with babcia, and Aunt Catherine, Jason's godmother.

All the children were dressed in white; the boys in suits, the girls in veils and dresses that shot out from below their knees in wide hoops and flares. Even though the number of girls was roughly the same as the boys, their line was twice as long. Sitting was even more of a problem for the girls as they kept bobbing up and down trying to arrange their rocketing, swiveling skirts.

Father Kolinski stressed the importance of the day and reminded the youngsters and their parents that this was the beginning of their active Catholic lives. From now on the children must work hard and obey

Holy Mother, the Church, for it was their guiding light and salvation. In the meantime, Jason was wondering how much money he'd get at his communion party, and if he'd break the current family record held by his cousin Nelly with a total of $285.

After the lengthy sermon, Father Kolinski returned to the altar. Communion was about to begin. The children had their eyes riveted on Sister Salomea who would give the signal to file out. The good Sister had her most dependable students strategically stationed at the head of each aisle. Jason was second in line. The procession had to go down the center aisle of the church in two lines, then split left and right to fill in the spots in front of the altar. After each child received the communion host, he or she got up, and circled around the side aisles. Then they'd come back up the main aisle from the rear to their original seats never interfering with those still moving forward to the altar.

Luckily the foul up occurred near the end of the procession when there were fewer pupils in motion. That was when Tommy Toporchuk, deep in religious meditation no doubt, cut up the main aisle when he was finished with his communion. Several others, with eyes downcast, religiously followed Tommy's wayward heels. This brought them in line for a head on collision with those who had taken the proper route and were at that time heading down the main aisle from the rear. But the omniscient eye and swift movement of Sister Salomea, who displayed the agility of a half back on the Bishop Ryan High School football team, intercepted the transgressor and quickly got everyone back in order.

The congregation smiled the whole thing off. Nevertheless, it was a good thing Tommy Toporchuk was a public school student, Jason figured. Life wouldn't be too pleasant if Tommy had to see Sister Salomea ever again after this day. A stint in purgatory might look like at walk in Houghton Park by comparison.

Jason now had the body of Christ on his tongue, and his stomach lurched in sympathy with the awful burden. Don't bite it. Don't bite it. It will bleed, he kept telling himself as the host formed a gluey pad in his mouth. He swallowed. The pasty wafer grabbed the roof of his mouth and hung on for dear life. Now what, as panic gripped him? He couldn't scrape it off. Only the priest was allowed to touch the host with his fingers. Could Jason prod it off with his tongue? Jason thought of Stachu Klemp when the dog got a piece of bone caught in his mouth and was rolling in the dirt pawing at its muzzle. Jason's father risked his life, not to mention several fingers, in removing the fragment. But Stachu let him pull it out and never tried to bite him. Jason calmed down and waited until the wafer disintegrated to a skeletal film and then disappeared.

Jason's communion party was a typical Eastside Polish celebration. All the family was there: aunts, uncles, and cousins without exception. Babcia gave Jason a big hug and kissed him in front of everybody, and each family handed Jason an envelope stuffed with money. Aunt Catherine alone gave him twenty-five dollars. A person's godmother always gave the most. Jason also knew that if anything ever happened to his own parents he would go and live with Aunt Catherine, Uncle Dan, and his cousin, Paulie.

"Id's good to have a famly takes care of you. You doan gotta worry wit my sisters. Not like the old man's bunch," his mother reminded him.

When the party was over Jason and his mother counted out three hundred and sixty dollars. He had broken the record. He was rich. Unfortunately his mother took all the money leaving him a lonely quarter to spend at Charlotte's store. In the meantime, Jason's father wondered out loud if this was a celebration of the sacrament of Holy Communion or just an excuse to collect a lot of cash.

"Doan you say nuttin," his mother scolded. "My sisters' kids got dere's. My kid's getting his share too."

To be sure, Jason did not see much of his father's family, and had never met his other babcia although she too lived in Kaisertown. After the stories his mother told him, Jason didn't want to meet any of that family anyway. "Dah old lady kick us outta her flat over by Kelburn Street. Psia krew, an you wit dah asthma too." All the relatives Jason knew were on his mother's side.

Jason's mother's maiden name was Krupka, but because there were only girls in the family and they were all married now, the family name had disappeared. No Krupkas appeared in the Buffalo phone book. They were a lost family. The Krupka sisters were saddened and sensitive about this fact, but helpless to change it. It was their lot in life and this in turn fostered a virulent clannishness and protectionism. The sisters constantly argued, one upped each other, and interfered in one another's lives, often without invitation. And babcia, long widowed, was idolized as the family matriarch.

That was why despair and desperation gripped the family when two years after Jason's communion, his babcia fell seriously ill. Babcia had already been forced to sell her house on Weaver Street and move in with Aunt Catherine on Meadowbrook. She had her own room, but nevertheless, babcia missed her old house and her belongings.

"Yer mudder was born in my house," she told Jason. "All dah kids but Stella, dah oldess. I raise my whole family dere, me and dzia-dzia. Den lader I gotta move id out. Yer old and dey say, 'Out you go!' Jason, id's a curse to be old."

Babcia's hair was silver and her face thinner and more wrinkled than ever before. Jason could hardly recognize her lying in bed. A picture of the Virgin Mary hung on the wall in babcia's room. This year's palm leaves were dry and yellow behind it. Three candles in red church glasses burned on top of the dresser. The room was dark and smelled of medicine.

Jason's aunts hovered attentively around the bed of their stricken mother sensing the inevitability of her death but refusing to consciously come to terms with it.

"Jak sie masz, ma? You wann it anudder pillow? Wan more wadder? Time for dah medicine, ma. It make you bedder. Bedder."

Jason was outside with Michael, Nelly, and Paul. Both Mike and Jason were Chicago White Sox fans and had the baseball card of every player on the team and never traded them. Paul was a Yankee fan. Mike and Jason hated the Yankees so they feuded constantly with their cousin. Even though the Polish baseball star, Ted Klusziewski, played on the Chicago team, Mike's hero was Nelly Fox, while Jason liked Minnie Minoso. The four cousins were playing "three flies in" with a tennis ball, throwing it up instead of using a bat, when a big black car pulled into the driveway.

"Wow, look at that," said Mike. "It's a new Caddie."

Mike was an expert at identifying cars. He'd often sit on a street corner with his cousins and rattle off the make and model of every car that drove by. "There goes a Buick, Special; Olds 88; Chevy, Biscayne, and there's a Impala, beautiful."

The door of the Cadillac opened and a man shifted his massive bulk to get out from behind the wheel. Jason recognized him as Father Majewski from St Casimir's, babcia's old church. Jason and his cousins stood next to the car in open mouthed admiration. The priest, who was panting from his exertion, eyed them suspiciously.

"Yous kids," he said as he walked to the front of the car. "Doan play round by dah car. I doan wan it scratch. Rozumisz?"

Aunt Catherine met the priest at the door. She was all bows and signs of the cross.

"Thank you, Father. Thank you for comin. Inside please." Another sign of the cross as she held the door open.

Inside the house the aunts scattered before the priest like hens in front of a barnyard dog as Aunt Catherine led the way to babcia's room. The priest carried a long shiny wooden box. When he put it down, the top swiveled in his hand and he withdrew a thick white candle, a vial of holy water, and a prayer book. The aunts crossed themselves and immediately broke into loud sobs. Father Majewski silenced them with an irritable wave of his hand. He took a scarf out of his pocket, kissed it, and put it on, then with a groan he knelt beside the quiet form of Jason's babcia.

That evening despite the priest's prayers, babcia died. A day later her body was "laid out" right there in Aunt Catherine's house. From that moment on Jason told himself he'd never sleep overnight at Paulie's again. The open coffin sat under the large parlor window. The couch and chairs were pushed against the walls and several wooden, folding chairs were added to the room. The walls were all painted white and there was no wallpaper in Aunt Catherine's house and no knick-knacks. She was the youngest and most modern of the sisters.

Babcia had on a blue dress and wore her big brooch with all the bright stones on it. Jason at one time thought they were diamonds, rubies, and emeralds, but they were only glass. Babcia's face was a baking powder white with brightly rouged cheeks and red, red lips. Even when she went to church babcia never wore that much makeup. To Jason it didn't really look like his babcia. Her soul was gone, he knew. Maybe that was why. It changed the way a person looked.

The aunts stayed in the parlor with the coffin and talked quietly amongst themselves, telling stories about babcia and the old days, and greeting the many people who came to "pay their respects". When Father

Majewski returned to pray over babcia, the aunts were once again thrown into panic. They genuflected everywhere, bumped into things, and constantly crossed themselves as Aunt Catherine escorted the priest to the coffin.

Jason's father, who sat drinking at the kitchen table with several of the uncles, said that the priest reminded him of a fat walrus taking a shit. The uncles, with the exception of Uncle Dan, who made a hurried sign of the cross, all laughed.

"Catherine show you half dat much attention," said Uncle John to Uncle Dan, "you be laughin too."

The cousins who showed up with their parents regularly gathered at the top of the cellar stairs to converse and comment on the visitors while listening in on the conversations at the kitchen table. When the priest departed the discussion amongst the adults got heated. As usual Jason's father was in the thick of things.

"Jesus would turn over in his grave to see these fat cat priests walking around with their fancy clothes and jewelry and driving expensive cars. What happened to the vow of poverty, and the idea of giving your riches to the poor?"

Uncle Dan crossed himself again. "You shouldn't talk like dat Edda," he said. "Fadder Majewski is in line to be monsignor, maybe even bishop someday. And he came today, didn't he, and when she was sick too for dah Las Rights."

"Yes, because Catherine and the others give half your pay checks to the church each year. When Pa Pete died the sisters had to pay fifty bucks to get Majewski to say the funeral mass because the old man was behind in his pew rent. Who knows what Catherine paid this time around."

"Dey say Majewski's got dah rectory at Casimir's all decorated like a palace in Rome dere wit furniture imported right from Italy. And he drinks dah bess brandy and smokes dem Cuban cigars, nie. Taki expensive," added Uncle John.

Sitting below the level of the hallway, the assembled cousins could see everyone who entered the house. Nevertheless, their position did hold some handicaps. At night the cellar immediately below them was dark and shadowy, and more than a little scary given the present circumstances.

"I wouldn't sleep in no house that had a coffin in the parlor," said cousin, Larry who was older than the others.

"Dat's why Paulie sleeps by our house," said Nelly. "But my mother said babcia loved us an wouldn't hurt nobody so dere's nothin to be scared of."

"If babcia is in heaven with boze, why is everybody so sad?" added Jason.

"Because people rather be alive here on Earth, den dead in heaven," said Larry.

"Heaven's boring. What do you do all day?"

"I heard Aunt Stella talking upstairs," Mike began. "She said dat on the night babcia died Aunt Stella heard three loud knocks on the wall at her house. It was midnight. When she got up and looked outside where the knockin came from she seen babcia under the streetlight walkin away. Aunt Stella called out, but babcia never turned around."

The cousins huddled closer together. Before this Mike and Jason had been somewhat preoccupied with the view up Nelly's skirt as the girl sat with her legs nonchalantly apart just above them. Now that perspective was forsaken for a watchful eye on the bottom of the stairs.

"Auntie Mary said too dat around the same time dat babcia died some cats in her yard started screamin. They screamed all night long, and in the morning she found one of them dead."

"Lots a things happen when people die," added Mike. "My father said that when dzia-dzia died long time ago, they heard knocking too. My dad got up. In the kitchen he seen a man standin in the corner. He man was real big, tall, and my dad couldn't see his face, but the man had dzia-dzia's cap on. The next day dzia-dzia was dead, and they never found his cap again."

"I think…" Jason began to say as he pointed to the bottom of the stairs. "I think something.." Before he completed his sentence the boy bolted up the stairs, pushing his way past his startled cousins. They needed no explanation and in a second the entire troupe was scratching its way upward towards the light of the hallway.

"Something touched my leg," screamed Nelly as they became wedged three abreast in the doorway.

Luckily Paul fell down and the rest of the cousins scampered over his body to freedom. They then dragged Paul up by his arms, and slammed the cellar door shut. "Was it babcia?" asked Nelly.

That night Jason was haunted by dreams. He found himself kneeling beside babcia's coffin. There was a crucifix on the wall above him. The fragrance of flowers was strong. While Jason bowed his head in prayer, he became aware that something was happening in the room. He glanced up and noticed the figure of Christ on the cross had moved. Its neck now craned macabrely forward supporting an unusually large head with deep red eyes which were peering into the open coffin. Inside the satiny white lining babcia was sitting up and staring at her grandson.

"Jason, Jason, help me. Help yer babcia."

Jason screamed and woke up. In a minute his mother was in the room. "Babcia always loved you the best. She's in heaven now, lookin out for you. Doan worry. I miss babcia too," she went on. "Jenna, you doan know it. And are you gonna miss me like dat when I'm gone too, my synek? You gonna miss, yer mama?"

She started to cry and Jason, in turn, cringed holding his mother in his arms. Jason continued to dream throughout the night. He found himself floating above his street, South Ogden Street, looking down on the activity below. Everything appeared perfectly normal. Pani Dombrowski was sweeping her sidewalk with a big straw broom. Dorothy and Timmy ran past her heading for Charlotte's Store. Each grasped a few pennies in their dirty, sweaty hands. Stachu Klemp had just relieved himself on Pani Tokacz's lawn and was kicking up little clumps of dirt with his hind legs. Everything was just as Jason had witnessed it a hundred times before, but there was one big difference. Jason was not part of the scene. He was dead. It was his soul that was now looking down on the present where life went on without him as if he had been of no more importance than an ant. A burning sense of indignation and injustice seized him. It wasn't right he told himself. It just wasn't right! Again he woke up, but he kept quiet this time so as not to attract his mother's attention.

The funeral was held the next day. The aunts were visibly agitated as the coffin was closed and prepared for removal to St. Casimir's Church for the final mass, and then to St. Stanislaus Cemetery for burial. The aunts had all kissed babcia goodbye. Then an eerie hush fell over the scene as Jason's father and five other uncles entered wearing black suits and gray colored dress gloves. They positioned themselves three abreast on each side of the coffin. Unexpectedly, like a thunder clap in a cloudless sky a loud collective wailing broke out amongst the women.

"Jesu Kochany! Rany Boskie! Oh Jenna, No, ma. Matka, no!"

It was a gray and cold day at St. Stan's. Flocks of blackbirds rose and fell in unison across the dying lawns of the cemetery, their undulating flights mimicking the breathing of an unseen beast. Jason felt his own breath become shallow and painful. The aunts and children sat on folded chairs while the men stood behind them. Father Majewski sprinkled holy water on the casket. Then he took out a prayer book and led everyone in song. They all knew the lyrics by heart.

"Witaj Krolowo nieba i Matko litosci."

Suddenly the entire assemblage stood up in unison as their voices grew louder and soared higher trying to penetrate the dark clouds above them. Jason could recognize his own mother's voice amongst all the others. It was beautiful and clear.

"K'Tobi wzdychamy placzac z padolu wiezniowie."

Then two men stepped forward and began to turn a large crank. Jason saw the coffin shudder, then start to drop into the ground. He noticed all the gray gloves piled on the lid. No one was getting them. The aunts now flew into fits of hysteria with the uncles straining hard to hold then from the grave's edge. Slowly the coffin disappeared, mingling with the darkness at the bottom of the grave.

Jason's aunts were exhausted and limp as they were escorted away from the scene and into the waiting cars by their husbands. Each person, in passing, grabbed a handful of earth from the adjacent mound and sprinkled it into the open grave. Down below in the blackness Jason could hear the earth rattling on top of the coffin. Could babcia hear it? Jason's mother was sick in bed for a week after the funeral.

Timmy: "Pierwsze Sliwki Robaczywe. Early Plums are Wormy."

Timmy hunted frogs on his own that summer of his break-up with his friend Jason Novak. At Okie Diamond he prowled the shoreline of the large pond with his sharpened and fire hardened wood spear. His subconscious disappointment at lost friendship made his character grow meaner and more callous. He jabbed and hurled his spear at the swimming and sunning amphibians, then left them to die. The stricken frogs floated weakly kicking on the surface or sat on lily pads, intestines spilling out, bleeding their lives away. Their expressions never changed, no look of pain or doom on their faces. They just stared and blinked impassively until they died. Timmy also hunted birds with a slingshot, and blew up their nests and chicks with firecrackers. He occasionally teamed up with other boys in the neighborhood, but no friendships were ever formed.

"There he is on that second branch, the big one. See im? Against the trunk," Timmy pointed upward into the foliage of a lone oak tree which stood on the edge of Okie Diamond. "Can't you morons see him? Right there." And he emphasized his directions with the flight of a large stone which bounced off the trunk of the old tree. The frightened cat hiding there emitted a sharp yowl and dug its claws desperately into the bark.

"OK, yeah," the other two boys exclaimed as the animal's cries pin-pointed its location.

"Alright then, ready, aim, fire."

The boys each loosed a stone from their hands.

"Again, ready, aim, fire."

Two of the projectiles hit the calico cat square in the back. Stunned, it lost its grip and fell clumsily through the branches.

"I taught cats always landed on dere feet?" said one boy.

"Probly a Nazi cat," laughed the other with a nod towards Timmy.

Timmy gave the boys a scowl. Then he picked up the cat by its tail and, gripping it hard, whacked the animal's head sharply against the tree. Once, twice. Blood spurted from the cat's eyes, ears, and mouth. Timmy swung it around in a half arc spraying the two boys with its blood.

"What the fuck you doin, you German bastard?"

"Crazy Nazi."

Timmy jumped towards the boys, winging the bleeding animal around his head.

"Geronimo," he shouted. "Charge."

The boys turned tail and ran down Dingens Street. "Klein, dah Kraut. Niemnec."

"Fucker. Yer sister's a Nazi whore."

The boy slowed his pursuit. "Run, chicken Polacks, run."

Timmy was a tall, blond boy who retained the Dennis, the Menace cowlick of his youth. At a casual glance he was good-looking, but a closer inspection revealed a thin lipped scowl permanently worn into the countenance and a pair of cold shark eyes that, while watching you being torn in half, would not even blink in sympathy.

Timmy threw the cat's body onto the curb before turning onto the main pathway into Okie Diamond. The boy then followed a secondary trail that wound its way up the side of a small knoll. From this vantage point he could survey the fields below him. Two rings of blackened stones with charred wood and ash in their centers marked the old campfires of the Kaisertown youth who frequented the fields. Here they roasted the hot dogs and baked potatoes into lumps of charcoal which they eagerly devoured.

The boy knew Okie Diamond intimately although his days of participation in the neighborhood softball games and trysts of tag were long gone. Even before the other children outgrew the activities, Timmy had been excluded from their romps. Nobody called him out to play. His cruelty and selfishness made him a pariah.

"What I need up here is a broad," mused Timmy out loud. "Yeah man, that's what I need. Like that prick Jason thinks he's so smart with his little slut, Tina. 'Oh Jason, yer so romantic. I love you.' And he done whatever he wanted with her too."

Timmy lit a cigarette, one of three he had lifted from his mother's purse this morning. "I wish Dorothy was still at home. Man, I loved watching her skinny ass get whipped. Now there's only me and the old lady. Otto hardly comes home no more. Just often enough to beat up the old lady and grab a piece of ass. Fuckin away and slappin her at the same time. She must like it. She put up with his shit all these years. Dorothy's the same, a cheap whore."

A distant movement caught Timmy's eye. Down the street a dog was approaching the body of the dead cat. Timmy stiffened and sat up. Sure enough, it was Stachu Klemp.

"I shoulda killed dat nut lickin bastard when I had the chance," Timmy complained. "All that poison, and I had to buy them hot dogs myself. Just one more whack with dat shovel. If that stupid asshole Novak hadn't a come around."

Timmy saw the dog, a large black and white mongrel with matted, burr covered hair, drag the cat into the bushes. A short while later it emerged, bloody jawed, along the Okie Diamond trail. The boy hugged the contour of the hillside for cover. He didn't draw a breath, a cold sweat pearled his forehead. Stachu Klemp raised his nose high in the air and took several loping strides up the pathway before breaking into an open run. Timmy stood up.

"You cock sucker!" he shouted and bolted down the far side of the hill at full speed. His momentum knocked him off course and he tore through a stand of young willows whose buggy whip branches lashed the boy's face and body. He emerged on the other side latticed with welts.

"Son of a bitch," he hissed as he staggered for balance back along the path like a tightrope walker making a mad dash for the safety of the platform. Tall grass and cattails appeared before him. It was the margin of the pond. Timmy grabbed a substantial stick laying along the shore. Tiny frogs rain-dropped the water's surface as the boy splashed in. He felt the wetness embrace his legs; ankle deep, knee deep, mid-thigh.

"Dat fucker, I'm gonna kill him for sure one a these days. Pour gasoline on his ass and light him up."

In the middle of the shallow pond Timmy turned to face his pursuer. Stachu Klemp snarling and pacing like a caged lion kept to the high ground that encircled the pond. The dog's dark teeth were barred and the hair along his back and shoulders stood upright in anger. Timmy held the stick in a death grip lest the animal enter the water against him.

"Come on, you ugly bastard. Come on," shouted Timmy as he slapped the surface of the water with the stick only to have it break in half from the impact. "Ain't this just fuckin great," the boy gasped. "Maybe I can just stab him with the broken end."

The dog laid down in the tall grass where it waited in relative comfort for the boy to make the next move. Whenever Timmy ventured a step in any direction, Stachu Klemp picked up its head and cocked its one good ear in the boy's direction. Two steps and the dog stood up salivating and snarling.

Over the next half hour the stalemate continued. Timmy's mood alternated between seething anger, "Bring it on, you bastard," to abject resignation, "Might as well fuckin drown myself. Won't give him the satisfaction of a bite."

Finally, with his legs white and puckered from the swamp water, Timmy noticed Stachu Klemp sit up and stare down the trail that led away from the pond towards Wheelock Street. The dog's ear perked up and its nose sniffed the air. Soon Timmy heard the footfalls of someone's approach. These were accompanied by strange guttural sounds that Timmy first thought came from the dog.

"Hey, hey, help me. I'm over here. Help!"

The dog looked nervously at the trail, then back at the pond. Timmy yelled even louder and threw his broken stick at the animal missing it by several feet. Nonetheless, the effort was enough to finally spook Stachu Klemp. Timmy saw its mangy tail disappear just as a chubby, pimply faced boy, who was apparently talking to himself, came into view. The boy carried a small knapsack on his back and a toy revolver in his hand. From his belt dangled a holster and a pair of toy handcuffs. A large sheriff's badge was pinned in the middle of his chest.

"For fuck's sake," laughed Timmy. "My hero, Glupi Wladek. Hey crazy boy, give me a hand over here, huh."

Glupi Wladek stuck his gun in its holster and smilingly offered his hand to Timmy and effortlessly pulled the boy from the muck bottomed pond. He then made some unintelligible sounds and patted Timmy strongly on the back.

"Jesus Christ, you smell like a dog's asshole. Get yer paws off of me," said Timmy with a grimace. He soon relented, however.

"I am glad you came by. Saved me from that fuckin dick licker. Too bad that wasn't a real gun." 'Course, a moron like you probly blow his fuckin nuts off foolin with it. You wanna cigarette? Lucky I had em in my shirt pocket." Glupi Wladek nodded and put two fingers to his lips. When Timmy had lighted the cigarette, Wladek held it with an awkward spread-eagle hand and puffed vigorously engulfing his face in smoke. He then coughed loudly flashing a brown toothed grin. Timmy lit his own cigarette and stared unbelievingly at the other boy.

"Yer fuckin old lady musta just shit when she first laid eyes on you. She still alive or she kill herself? You sure Stachu Klemp ain't yer father?"

The sun was setting behind the crabapple hill. Timmy blew a solitary puff of smoke into the evening's yellowing air. Glupi Wladek watched it rise, then he breathed out a similar wisp himself. Timmy repeated the action and watched as the other boy mimicked him.

"Yer a real fuckin ape, ain't you?"

Timmy took his hand and scratched the top of his head. "Ooo, Ooo, Ahh, Ahhh."Wladek did the same. Timmy nodded and unzipped his fly. He then pulled out his penis and pretended to masturbate, grunting and groaning and tilting his head back. Wladek followed suit. But he was jerking off for real much to Timmy's delight. Timmy quickened his hand and started shuffling his feet in a small circular motion still gazing heavenward. When he glanced down he could see the rigid shaft of Wladek's penis.

"Ooo, ooo, ahh," he repeated then stepped back to watch.

Wladek's sexual arousal and his spinning movement completely disoriented the boy. Like a whirling dervish Wladek spun into the grass ejaculating as he went. Timmy bent over in laughter and clapped his hands in glee.

"What's the matter, you asshole? You can't piss and fart at the same time. Ha, ha, what a idiot."

Wladek stood up and tucked his dripping penis back into his pants. He brushed the grass and leaves off his clothes and straightened out his packsack. He then nervously searched through his pockets until he finally held up a shiny pocket watch. He pressed the time piece to his ear and a big smile spread across his face. He gurgled and pointed to the watch before showing it to Timmy.

"Hey, I'll tell you what," Timmy remarked. "I'll give you a dollar for that watch. It's not worth that much, but since you helped me out and everything..."

Wladek shook his head and snatched back the watch.

"Alright puke face, I didn't want it anyways. Just doin you a favor."

Out in the distance the street lights blinked into awakening. Glupi Wladek stared up in surprise. A certain panic seized him and he started braying like an animal. Then he broke into a shuffling run, his toy holster and packsack slapping against his side and back. Timmy followed behind, way behind.

"Don't want anybody to think I'm actually friends with this asshole," he said. From a far off backyard Timmy could hear a woman's voice faintly calling. "Wladek, Wladek."

Ahead of him the boy stopped, turned around and thumped his chest. "Vaaaek, Vaaek," he shouted. Then he pointed to Timmy and nodded his head.

"Oh sure, I get it," said Timmy. "You think I'm gonna tell you my name. Then you can tell everybody we're good friends, like Dean Martin and Jerry Lewis."

Wladek continued his efforts.

"For fuck sake, alright, just shut up and hang onto yer nuts. My name is Jason, Jay–sin," and Timmy pounded his own chest. "Jay-sin."

"Jaasn, Jaasn," Wladek attempted the name and laughed contentedly before being thrown into a panic once again by the sound of the woman's voice.

Glupi Wladek shuffled down South Ogden Street towards a lone house separated from all the others by several weed covered vacant lots and disappeared into the yard.

Timmy himself went home, changed his clothes and stole some money from his mother's dresser drawer. At Charlotte's Store he bought a pack of Lucky Strikes and while Mrs. Charlotte rang up the sale Timmy stole two packs of chewing gum off the counter. Serves her right for leavin dat stuff out in the open, he thought.

On the corner Timmy stood and smoked his cigarette. Tasted great. He shook his head in remembrance of his encounter with Glupi Wladek.

"Surprised his old lady lets that idiot roam around like that," Timmy muttered. "What if the horny bastard takes a liking to some little neighborhood girl? Fucker is as strong as a bull." Just then a girl turned the corner. When she noticed Timmy she quickened her pace.

"Well, if it ain't tiny titty Tina," said Timmy. "What you doin out so late?"

"None a yer business," the girl replied.

"Whose business is it? Jason's?"

The girl gave no response.

"Hey Tina, Jason says yer a lousy lay, ha, ha, ha," Timmy shouted as the girl broke into a run. "An you ain't no good at blow jobs either."

Boy, I'd like to get her upstairs in the old garage, Timmy mused. I'd have her screamin fast enough, that stuck up little Polack bitch. Timmy finished his cigarette. He had no friends since Jason parted company with him. Timmy's snitching on Dorothy and his torturing of animals was too much for his neighbor. It was Jason too who stopped Timmy from trying to finish off Stachu Klemp with a shovel.

"Why Timmy, why?" Jason had asked.

"What do you care? It's none of yer business anyways. Go hang around with yer new Polack buddies there in Kaisertown. I don't need you. I don't want you. Yer too boring anyway."

Indeed, the word boring pretty well summed up Timmy life of late. What he needed was something to burst the bonds of boredom and set him free. He needed some action.

Tedlinski's Butcher Shop: "Pork Chops, Today, Pani? Nice and Lean, Nie?"

Tedlinski's Butcher Shop was an institution on the corner of Clinton and Willet Streets. It was run by Theodore, "Ted" Tedlinski, his wife, and two daughters. Pan Tedlinski was instantly recognizable around Kaisertown by the huge, blue veined proboscis that dominated his face. It was his distinguishing feature. Pani Tedlinski was a small woman with no remarkable physical characteristics, neither attractive nor repulsive. The Tedlinski daughters unfortunately got their "good looks" from the paternal side of the family prompting the Kaisertown ladies to predict the two would inevitably wind up as "old maids" a term of both derision and great sympathy.

The butcher shop was a large, light brick, two story building with the business occupying the front section of the ground floor, the family quarters in the back, and a large rental flat on the second floor. The front entrance was set in a small elevated alcove constructed of large translucent glass blocks.

The interior of the store was vast and open and all white in color except for the honey hued hardwood floors which were liberally and daily sprinkled with fresh sawdust. Glass display counters, full of meats, poultry, and fish ran nearly the full length of the room bisecting it into two unequal sections. The meat preparation and work area was the smaller of the two sections. The grocery and dry goods sections with its numerous shelves, barrels, crocks, weight scales, and bushel baskets was the larger.

Like any fine artist, Pan Tedlinski, made sure his tools were up to the task at hand. Therefore, the work area was well equipped with various cutting and slicing machines, a large sausage stuffer, thick wooden butcher tables, and wrapping tables with rolls of stiff brown paper and spools of strong white string. Several knives, saws, cleavers, and sharpening stones lined the wall above the tables. A large walk-in cooler occupied the entire back corner.

"An for you today, pani?" was Ted's invariable greeting to his customers. After which he'd list the various specials of the day, enticing the women towards his most profitable products. "Pork chops today. Nice and lean, nie?"

Ted was quick to spot a new customer to whom he'd display a special obsequiousness offering small free samples, or an extra portion or as a grand gesture a rounding off of the bill in the customer's favor. He'd interject, "Tank yous", throughout the purchases ending with a final, "Calm again", to show his appreciation as well as the expectation of a return visit. At the same time, Ted was careful never to slight his regular customers whose business had been won and nurtured over the years. He understood that return business was the cornerstone of success and the mark of a good entrepreneur.

Ted took special pride in his meat offerings. A bigger nor better stocked counter was nowhere to be found in Kaisertown. He'd even venture that it rivaled many a stall at the Broadway Market itself, if anyone stopped to judge objectively.

Whenever Pan Tedlinski brought forth a particular cut of meat for his customer's inspection he did so with a special flourish, presenting the piece on a sheet of brown paper as though it was a fine bit of jewelry cushioned on a rich pillow.

"See id, pani, nice and lean, nie?"

"You could trim it more. Too much fat."

Ted would stagger back from such a comment as if hit with a meat mallet.

"Pani, you need it some fat for dah flavor, nie? Dat's a good piece of meat, but for you, if you wan it, I take some off."

Inside the glass counters, lying on trays atop beds of crushed ice were countless varieties and cuts of meat: pork, beef, even lamb, along with poultry, fish and innumerable Polish delicacies. There was mock chicken; corn breaded veal stuck onto round sticks; coils of Polish sausage made by Pan Tedlinski himself from fresh pork butts. Both fresh sausage with its pale grayness and strong garlic flavor and aroma, and the rich, red, smoked were amply represented. Shoppers had to special order at Easter because of the demand. The homely, plucked bodies of chickens and ducks filled one case, the heads and feet still intact. Ted would trim them to order. And next to each duck set in the crushed ice like a small trophy, lay a half pint bottle of black blood.

"Kaczka wit dah blood. OK, pani? Good fresh duck. You like id?"

Other delicacies graced the counters as well: oxtails, tripe, tongue, pigs' tails and pigs' feet in the vinegary gelatin known as galiritta, along with coils of thick skinned kishka. The latter was a favorite breakfast food of Ted himself who enjoyed it fried and served with eggs and fresh rye bread and butter.

A wide selection of cold cuts, far superior in both number and quality to those found at Charlotte's Store, were also on display. Hams, slab and sliced bacon, fat weiners linked together in an almost endless coil, and red ground beef completed the array of meats. The final counter was devoted to fish: smoked white fish with their tanned and crispy skins, salty blind robins, perch and haddock fillets, and jars of pickled herring, half of them in plain brine and half in cream.

Several Polish ladies clutching fabric shopping bags argued, gossiped and shouted across the counters with Pan and Pani Tedlinski. Other women strolled amid the aisles and shelves inspecting the produce and packages. All were under the fretful gaze of Ted himself who didn't trust his delicate goods in the coarse handed grip of his country women.

The action in the store was loud and prolonged. Whenever there was a slight lull the Tedlinski clan ate their lunch in shifts. Often they had to be content with merely munching on a slivered slice of ham or hard sausage as they labored. Ted especially enjoyed these moments of shopping mayhem as they foretold good receipts at the end of the day. And the day's end usually came at five o'clock although Ted would linger if customers were still present. Meanwhile, the Tedlinski girls would grab their push brooms and sweep the dirtied sawdust into garbage pails and then spread a fresh golden replacement evenly around the floors.

The senior Tedlinskis cleaned up behind the counters, wiping down the cutting boards, slicing machine, and other tools of the trade. Left over meats were appraised for freshness with sale items identified for the next day and Pani Tedlinski selected the most vulnerable cuts for that evening's meal. Then everything was stuffed into trays and secreted in the large walk-in cooler. The glass counters were washed, top and bottom and left out to dry overnight. Finally the lights and overhead fans were turned off and another business day came to an end.

Ted was always the last to leave the store. He locked the front doors, made final modifications to the sale signs, and collected the receipts into his leather money bag for deposit in the large safe in the bedroom prior to Friday's trip to the bank. If it had been a good business day, Pan Tedlinski would be jovial and talkative at the supper table extolling the virtues of the free enterprise system and explaining the various intricacies of the business to his daughters. The two large nosed Tedlinski girls, however, were far more intent on feeding than listening, although out of habit and filial respect, they nodded politely and mumbled at all the right times.

If the day had gone poorly, however, gloom would descend upon the table as Pan Tedlinski bemoaned the passage of the good old days, railed against the A&P stores for taking away his business and contemplated retirement from the strains of running a family enterprise in such a hostile economic climate. And the large nosed Tedlinski girls, future old maids of Kaisertown, ate on.

Jason: Santa, Salvation, and Safeties

Jason sat in St. Bernard's Church listening to the priest drone on. Everything was in Latin which, Jason was convinced, no one in the entire building understood. I wonder if he evens knows himself or is he just reciting words from memory, Jason wondered. Anyway, could any of this bull shit really be true; the virgin birth, creation in six days, not to mention Sister Salomea's infamous, "tree in one." But should he take the chance? His mother always cautioned him, "You wanna be a ateeist like yer father an go to hell? Hell is forever and ever."

It reminded Jason of a discussion at a Christmas time long ago.

'Mom, how can Santa's sleigh with them reindeer fly? Reindeer can't fly.'

'Santa ken do anyting. He's magic.'

'And then he's got to visit every single kid in the whole world. All in one night.'

'Santa's magic. Dat's how he does it.'

'And how does he really know if you're naughty or nice? I mean, he's got to check up on every single kid everywhere in the world on every day of the year?'

'Like I toll you. Santa is magic. He knows everyting.'

'And how does he carry all them presents around and know which ones to bring to each kid, what they want for Christmas?'

'Santa knows yer taughts, but you shouldn even worry about dem tings. Santa is magic. Dat explains it all.'

'Santa sounds a lot like boze, like god.'

When Jason expressed the same concerns to his father the reply was simply. 'Well, Jason what do you think?'

"Bless me Father for I have sinned," Jason began. He had decided to bypass confession at St. Bernard's and go instead to St. Casimir's where no one knew him and the young priest there was said to give very lenient penances. When Jason came to the part in his confession of "impure deeds", however, the priest interrupted him.

"Whad impure deed you talkin aboud my son?"

Oh shit, thought Jason. A priest never interrupted his confession before. How was he going to get out of this one? His father always told him that honesty was the true mark of a man so he decided to try it.

"I, ahh, me and my friend, sort of a friend, we made this girl we knew take all her clothes off so we could look at her."

Jason could see the form on the other side of the screen move closer to him.

"How old of a girl was she?" the priest asked. "Did she have dah poobic 'air on dah psipsia?"

What the hell is he talking about? Jason wondered. The priest's thick Polish accent was throwing him off. "No," he replied figuring it might be wise not to blindly admit to anything.

"Oooh," the priest moaned. "Taki young girl. Tell me. Did yous make her perform for yous in eny way? Tell me everyting. Omission is a sin."

Jason wound up backtracking all the way to the scene at Okie Diamond while the priest grew more and more restless on the other side of the wall.

"Taki young girl, undeveloped like dat, in dah act a fornication. Id's a sin. Czy nie? Yes, a sin, a sin, a sinnn."

OK, I get the point Jason felt like saying, but he dared not prolong the indelicacy of his situation. The priest's voice grew distant. The confessional shuddered slightly, and then the screen door shut with a quick bang only to open again just as suddenly.

"Fifty Our Fadders, an fifty Hail Marys, an return here again next week for yer confession. Doan forget!"

"Fifty of each! Son of a bitch, that's the worst I ever got," moaned Jason under his breath.

"Hail Mary, full of grace. The Lord is with Thee," he began in mindless repetition. His thoughts wandered as he prayed. Where is heaven anyway? How does it fit in outer space among all the planets, stars, the galaxies? Why do you even need them if everything important happens just here on Earth? It's kind of a waste to create all that stuff for nothing.

"Blessed are Thou amongst women." And why the long wait with evolution? What was the point of a world filled with dinosaurs and little mammals and creatures that existed long before man appeared? What were they doing walking all over the Earth taking up space and time? They couldn't worship or praise God.

"And blessed is the fruit of Thy womb, Jesus." When old man Klemp fell down in the street drunk as a skunk with his false teeth falling out of his mouth, nobody stopped. Nobody but Jason's father. The nuns on the corner crossed themselves and looked away. Jason's mother cursed under her breath. 'Doan you touch dat piok and embarrass me.' Kids pointed and laughed and ran to pick up the spilled change. Jason's dad stopped the traffic, got old man Klemp to his feet and helped him home.

But Jason's father never went to church. He was heading, therefore, non stop to the fiery furnace of hell while Pani Dombrowski who attended mass every day, and was the most miserable and mean old bitch on the block, would bask in heavenly bliss for all eternity, drowning puppies and kittens, and killing ants at the right hand of God, the Father.

"Holy Mary, Mother of God." The candle flames flickered above the red glasses on the large metal frames in front of the altars. Pray for a soul in purgatory. Where the hell was purgatory? That first one on the left, bottom row, thought Jason. That one. Such a little thing. It could almost happen by chance. Just this once. Show me! The candle continued to burn unchangeably almost lost in the uniformity of its fellows.

"Amen," said Jason and left the church.

It was a summer evening and Jason sat on the steps of his porch. The canvas awning cloaked the porch in darkness. No one was home. His mother had gone to Aunt Catherine's. His father had a meeting with the Professor. Another argument coming up, thought Jason. Mr. Durlak across the street was watering his lawn. A robin chirruped from the wet grass looking for worms. In the distance, a dog barked.

"Hi-yah, Jason."

The voice woke the boy from his reverie. He looked up. Two girls were passing by giggling and poking each other; Tina Kaszpczyk from Wheelock Street and a girlfriend. Tina had just graduated from the Eighth Grade at St. Bernard's. A few steps away from his porch Tina's friend turned and shouted back.

"Tina loves you, Jason."

"Shut up, you bitch," said Tina laughing and slapping at her friend. The girls ran to the corner one in pursuit of the other.

For the last year Tina had been a perfect pain in the ass for Jason. She sent him love notes and called him, "Lover Boy", a name his friends were quick to pick up on and add to that other horrible moniker, "Girl Smeller".

Now Tina didn't look quite so bad, Jason thought. Of course, she was no Dorothy, or Audrey Czajka, the sex queen of South Ogden, but all in all still not bad. Had it not been for his past awkward association with her, he might now have summoned the courage for a conversation or maybe even a future date at the Strand Show although Jason usually stayed away from the heart of Kaisertown with its gangs of boys on every corner.

Jason was about to walk around to the back of the house. The front door was locked. Polacks never use the front door his father observed long ago. It was then that Jason noticed Tina's friend returning alone.

"Hiyah Jason," the girl said.

"Hi, where's Tina?"

"Tina's mad at me for what I said about her havin a crush on you. It's true anyways. She's walkin around the block right now hoping you'll meet her."

"And if I don't?"

The girl shrugged her shoulders.

"What's your name?" Jason asked.

"Cathy."

"Where you from?"

"Inside my mother."

OK, thought Jason. That's encouraging.

"Guess I'll go home," she continued. "Ain't nothing doin around here. You wanna walk me home, you can."

The two of them walked down Clinton St. past St. Bernard's. Cathy lived on the dead end side of Weaver St. just one block up.

"You got a cigarette?" she asked Jason as they turned the corner.

"No."

The girl made a face of bored resignation.

"Tina's alright, but she's a baby, yah know. She never had no boyfriend. Maybe did a little neckin at a party. That's it."

"And you?"

"I used to go steady with Gleaner. You know him, Johnny Gleankowski lives on Cable. Pretty tough. Take you no problem."

Jason ignored the comment. Just then a car drove down Weaver Street headed for Clinton. Its horn blew and a boy waved out the window. Cathy immediately became animated.

"Hey! Yeow! Earl, Man."

Oh great, said Jason to himself, a real intellectual. The car stopped with a screech of tires and backed up.

"Who's yer boyfriend dere, Caddy?" asked the driver snorting contemptuously at Jason. The car's interior was dimly illuminated by the red glow of an unseen light. Little, white, fuzzy balls encircled the underside of the ceiling while a pair of dice along with a garter hung from the rearview mirror.

"He ain't no boyfriend a mine," replied Cathy. "I hardly know im."

Jason stepped back. Thanks for the ringing endorsement he thought.

"Wanna go for a ride?" the boy offered Cathy as he toned down the radio.

"Hey man, dey're playin "Peggy Sue". Leave it on," a voice called from the back seat. In the meantime Cathy made a bound for the car as the door opened.

"See you around, sucker," said the driver to Jason, and then they were gone.

Jason turned around and headed back home. Ironically at the corner of his street he ran right into Tina.

"Hi-yah, Jason. Was you lookin for me?"

"Yes, as a matter of fact I was," Jason lied.

Above them and partially screened by the branches of the tall elm trees Jason could see the street lights blink into life. The fragrance of the girl's perfume drifted around him. Tina was wearing makeup too; rouge and lipstick. She was prettier than he remembered. This is your chance, Lover Boy. Don't mess it up, he told himself.

Jason recalled the time last year that he and David Luchowski took two girls from their class to the Strand Show. Jason spent the entire first feature working up the courage to put his arm around his date. When he finally made the attempt he wound up drilling the girl in the ear with his elbow.

"You want to go for another walk?" Jason asked Tina.

"Sure," replied Tina with a smile and brightly sparkling eyes.

Halfway around the block Jason made his first bold move. He grabbed Tina's hand. Neither said a word, just walked silently, fingers intertwined. At the corner, Jason stopped and kissed Tina. All that time studying pictures and movies, getting his head tilted just right and his lips properly positioned, paid off. Jason performed perfectly.

"Yer so romantic," Tina whispered as she snuggled against him.

Not too close, Jason worried because the hard-on in his pants was beginning to resemble the diving board at the twelve foot section of the Shelter House pool. He distracted himself by thinking about Pani Dom-browski's flat feet and blue veined ankles. As they continued their walk, they kissed more frequently, French kissed too. It wasn't that difficult Jason discovered. Soon they found themselves at Tina's house on Whee-lock St. where they sat down on the steps of the porch.

"You got such beautiful eyes," Tina commented. "The other girls in my class say you got 'bedroom eyes'."

Suddenly a voice called from the walkway. "Tina, it's gettin late."

Then a thin woman with her head wrapped in a babushka appeared alongside the house.

"Tina, who's dat wit you? What yous doin out here?"

"It's Jason, ma. Jason Novak. We're just sittin here talking."

"Pani Novak's boy from Sout Ogden?"

"Hello, Pani Kaszpczyk," said Jason in the most pleasant tone he could muster.

"Oh, hallow, Jassin. An how is yer mudder doin?"

"She's fine, thank you."

"I didn see yous in church dis week. Was wonderin."

"We went to St.Casimir's instead," Jason explained. "They had a mass for my grandmother."

"Oh yeah, I see it in dah "Wszystkich"."

"Well, it's late, and I should be going," Jason said. "It was nice meeting you Pani Kaszpczyk. Tina, maybe I'll call you sometime?"

"I'd like dat Jason, very much."

As Jason walked away he heard Pani Kaszpczyk speaking to her daughter.

"Sudge a nice boy. Good family. His fadder is a big shot by Wordington in dah office."

When Jason returned home he noticed a light on over the kitchen sink so he knew his mother was back. It was eleven o'clock. In the summer time his parents weren't particular about how long he stayed out. Anyway, they had been arguing a lot lately and that prevented them from forming any comprehensive set of rules governing his behavior.

"Is dat you, Jason?" his mother's voice called from the bedroom. It was her sick voice.

"Yes," he answered. "Is dad home?"

"Doan mention dat one to me. Wid his Perfesser. He's god it time for everybody but his own famly. Matka boska, I god it such a headache."

The yellowish hue of the kitchen light cast a sad sunset glow throughout the room. As usual the kitchen was spotless; everything put in its place. Only two opened but capped bottles of Queen-O, orange and root beer flavors, Jason's favorites, marred the surface of the kitchen counter top.

The new fridge paralleled the stove. Jason remembered the old ice box that used to stand there, and he thought of the ice man with the old truck that poured water as the large crystal blocks were pulled forward with tongs from the canvass draped interior of the vehicle. The ice man, where was he now? Technology throws workers on the scrap heap of unemployment, his father used to say. Automation only helps the capitalist owners of industry. When machines do all the work, who will own the machines?

Jason saw the pillow and blankets thrown across the couch as he walked to the doorway of his parents' bedroom.

"Want me to get you something?" he asked. "A cold washrag maybe for your head?"

"OK, synek, dat would be good." His mother's room was like a side altar in church, dimly lit, immaculately tidy and fragrant with perfume. A large picture of the Virgin Mary clutching her exposed heart hung over the bed. Jason knew it was there even though he couldn't see it now. The bambinko that used to be in his room was on his mother's dresser surrounded by bottles of colored liquids and jars of creams and powders.

"Tank you. Yer a good son for me," she said in a feeble voice while grabbing his hand and the wet wash cloth at the same time.

With that, an intense feeling of irritation, almost revulsion swelled up in Jason. He didn't want his mother holding his hand, or touching him. Even her voice grated on his nerves. His skin crawled and a chill ran down his spine. That night Jason covered his head with blankets to drown out the arguing of his parents in the next room. He should have been used to it by now.

A couple of weeks later and Jason led Tina by the hand to the old Pankow garage. It was ten o'clock at night. A bright moon made visibility easy except within the long shadows that silhouetted the buildings and trees.

"I doan know about this," Tina balked as they entered the moonbeam streaked interior.

Jason turned and kissed her; the second kiss a soft and gentle afterthought.

"It's not fair," the girl whimpered. "You know I'll do anyting for you. My mother says I shouldn't let you take advantage of me."

"Do me a favor," Jason said. "Don't tell your mother everything we do."

Upstairs the moonlight shined in the little front window like a silver slide spilling itself on the floor where Jason already had a blanket spread out. He patted his back pocket. Inside were two safeties given to him several days ago by his cousin Larry Bingkowski.

"Did you ever do dis wit other girls?" asked Tina as they lay down on the blanket.

"Ahh, one or two," Jason lied not wanting to admit that he really had no idea what the hell he was doing.

"Who?"

"Tina, please. I'm with you now. You're the only one who matters."

"Do you love me?"

"Yes, I told you so lots of times. Come on, don't be so worried."

Of course, Jason was worried too. This was the first time. He leaned over Tina and pulled her tee shirt up over her bra. Next he unhooked the restraining device. No problem. No problem because he had practiced for two days with one of his mother's brassieres tied around a chair. Son of a bitch of an ordeal it was at first too, Jason had to admit. Tina's bra was hardly an essential piece of clothing. Her breasts were small and once the girl was on her back they all but disappeared.

"I know I don't got big boobies," Tina confessed. "You probly like girls wit big boobies."

"No, that doesn't matter," Jason lied again. "Yours are nice, beautiful."

He knelt beside her and quickly undid the girl's shorts.

"Jason, you woan tell nobody, will you? Doan say nuttin to dat Timmy, OK?"

"Don't worry," said Jason who could not stop staring at Tina's naked body. He nudged her into the moonlight a bit more, and moved her hands aside and rubbed the dark, curly hair between her legs.

"Spread your legs," he said. His cock bulged and throbbed with excitement. Good thing he had masturbated beforehand. Otherwise he'd be shooting off like a can of pressurized Reddi-Wip. Jason sat at Tina's knees, facing away from her. He took his wallet out of his back pocket and pulled down his pants. He then slipped the condom out of its gold foil wrapper. It was thin and covered in a light powder. Careful, he told himself. These things are valuable. It was all rolled up so Jason unrolled it quickly. No time to lose. Strike while the iron was hot, he encouraged himself.

Jason marveled at how big and long the safety looked. He placed the open end onto the head of his penis and pulled as though putting a sock on his foot. The condom advanced all of an inch before coming to an abrupt stop. He then tried yanking first on one side of the safety and then the other, hiking it up slowly. His erection began to fade; then several crotch hairs got caught in the rubber.

"Ouch, Owah," he whimpered.

"What's the madder, Jason?" Tina asked as she sat upright.

"Nothing. It's OK. Just putting on this safety."

"I'm not sure about dis," the girl said bringing her knees together and hiding her tiny breasts. "I'm afraid. What if somebody comes?"

That somebody probably won't be me, thought Jason as he glanced at his deflated erection beside the giant condom. Looked like a cocktail weenie next to a sperm whale's bladder. Exactly, how the hell was he supposed to get this thing on? Stick his wilted cock inside and grow into it? God damn. Then he remembered watching his mother put on her stockings. And the safety originally came all rolled up, didn't it.

Jason discarded the first condom and moved next to Tina. He began fondling her again. Properly aroused, he succeeded with the second safety and promptly threw himself on top of Tina. The girl groaned under his weight.

"Yer so heavy," she complained.

"Sorry, just getting ready," Jason apologized. "Now spread your legs, OK?"

Jason tried to insert his penis into the girl. The trouble was he didn't know exactly where to put it.

"Is, is it in?" he asked Tina. "Can you feel it?"

"I, I doan tink so," she replied.

He felt down with his hand. It was difficult to get even his finger inside of her. Boy, and everyone talked about how great sex was, Jason mused as he moved his less than poker stiff cock in line with his finger. OK, that seemed like the right place. Think of what you're doing, he encouraged himself. You're going to fuck Tina. She's laying here naked, with her legs spread. You're going to give it to her. You're going to fuck her brains out.

Thankfully Jason's penis responded. The trouble now was that he couldn't get much penetration and if his cock was to slip out now he doubted he'd ever get it back in again.

"Maybe if you lift your legs, or bend your knees," Jason suggested.

Tina pulled her knees up, and Jason felt himself penetrate deeper.

"Ow-wah, yer hurtin me," cried Tina. "Oww, please stop, Jason. Stop it."

But Jason didn't stop. He moved faster. The girl's cries excited him. This was it. He could feel the rough friction of his penis inside of Tina. Yes, a little more, more. He pushed harder and deeper as the girl squirmed beneath him. More and more. Yes, yes, yesss! The boy came in a sudden mind fogging explosion. Then he rolled of the girl with a thud.

I did it, he thought triumphantly. I did it with a girl, a real, live girl. Jason checked his safety. It was hanging halfway off his cock. Jesus Christ, I almost lost it. He removed it and held it up to the moonlight, a large pearl colored teardrop. It seemed intact.

"Is, is everyting OK?" Tina asked with a sob in her voice. "I guess I ain't no virgin no more, am I, Jason?"

She reached out for the boy who was still preoccupied with his accomplishment. "Jason?"

"Oh, sorry Tina. I was just thinking about how good you were."

"I was?"

"Oh yes, you were terrific." He bent down and gave her a kiss.

"It really hurt me though," she said holding on to him, unconcerned now, of her nakedness. "Does this mean we're goin steady 'cause I'm really gonna need you now, you know, Jason? No udder guy is gonna marry me. Yer the only one."

Pani Khula and Glupi Wladek: *"A Co To? What Do We Have Here?"*

"Wladek, time to ged up. Ged up now Wladek."
The woman pulled apart the curtains sending a thin beam of sunlight into the dark bedroom. A framed triptych of Jesus, Mary, and Joseph was partially visible on the wall above the bed. From one bedpost dangled a toy gun and holster, and a scapular and crystal rosary from another. On a small octagonal shaped table under the window lay a silver railroad watch on a chain.

"Wladek, whad are you doin dere? Wladek, No! I toll you, no. Stop dat. Stop dat right now. OK, I'm goin dah kitchen an get dah pyda."

The boy, a man almost in size at least, twisted beneath the covers and turned his face to the wall.

"You ged up. I'm fixin dah breakfass. Got yer oatmeal dat you like so much. I'm putting yer clothes on dah dresser. If yer nod up in five minutes I'm comin back wit dah pyda. I mean id."

Pani Khula returned to the kitchen, a large room dominated by a gas-coal burning stove used for both cooking and warmth. The mica windows along its front threw a checkered pattern of light upon the floor. In the depths of the snowy Buffalo winters Wladek loved to lay in front of the stove and peer inside at the dancing blue and yellow flames. The sight comforted him.

A massive oak table with two chairs occupied the center of the room. Two matching chairs collected dust in opposite ends of the same room.

In the corner beside the entry door stood a tall metal cabinet that housed Pani Khula's linens. Several sepia toned photographs and a pin cushion in the shape of an old fashioned lady's boot and bristling with pins and needles sat atop the cabinet.

Outside the kitchen window barren trees and yellowing grassy fields were visible on all sides because the Khula house had no immediate neighbors being separated from the rest of the block by a string of vacant lots.

Pani Khula had a small pension from her husband which helped with the bills. Had he worked longer on the railroad the payments would have been higher and Pani Khula's life easier. She had her hands full caring for Wladek.

The boy came shuffling into the kitchen. His face was dirty and his eyes crusted in the corners. His shirt was noticeably misbuttoned, and his shoes untied. He grinned sheepishly at his mother. He was a short boy, but stoutly built with a slight pot belly for he loved to eat. His face was wide and fleshy with tiny eyes of clear blue. His teeth were bad, and his complexion sprinkled with pimples and blackheads. His blond hair was shorn short in a brush cut that only served to accentuate the large size of his head.

Pani Khula smiled back at the forlorn figure of her only child, still a baby after seventeen years. She walked up to him and buttoned his shirt and made him sit down so that she could tie up his shoes. The boy spoke hoarsely and indistinctly to his mother, but she understood every sound he made and calmed him with the reassurance that his porridge was forthcoming.

Wladek sat down and made an awkward sign of the cross starting with a pat on his chest and ending with a mere wave at his forehead. Nevertheless, his mother was proud of his little accomplishment.

Once outside the boy wore one of his mother's old coats, and a pair of mittens and earmuffs. It was chilly, but not cold as the darkening days still clung to the memory of fall. The two turned the corner and stood parallel to the length of Oki Diamond. Here the odd couple often strolled the cracked and weed grown sidewalks that bordered the swamps and fields in search of discarded pop and beer bottles. Further ahead South Ogden Street led to the city garbage incinerator and the railroad shunting yards. There were few houses. Most was vacant land, the playground of children, and the home of countless rabbits, pheasants and foxes.

At this time of year Pani Khula and her son also made occasional pilgrimages to the railroad tracks where they scoured the sidings for scattered pieces of coal dropped from the passing cars. This they carted home in shopping bags to add to the cellar's supply for the coming winter season.

Wladek was familiar with the pathways of Okie Diamond for he often played there usually by himself, but sometimes with the neighborhood children who employed him to "shag" baseballs for them. "Glupi or Crazy Wally" is what they called him. Pani Khula took offence, but to the boy it didn't matter. Their friendship was all he cared about, and aside from the occasional practical joke, such as the time the boys got him to "jerk off" in front of the Young Ladies Sodality procession, the children of the neighborhood generally accepted him.

Pani Khula took her son to St. Bernard's every Wednesday and Sunday and every holy day of obligation. They always did the Stations and Devotions together as well. Wladek was well behaved in church as long as he had numerous prayer books with pictures for him to look at. Naturally, they never attended High Mass. It was far too long.

Around the house Wladek was very helpful. He cut the grass and raked leaves. He was responsible for keeping the coal scuttle filled. He also shook out the ashes from the furnace and in winter sprinkled them along the sidewalk for traction after shoveling the snow. And shoveling snow was Wladek's favorite winter pastime. He loved the monotonous process of scooping, lifting, and then throwing shovel sized sections of snow from the sidewalk. He'd work in a surprisingly methodical manner, shoveling from left to right, never the other way around, in even shovels full, and he never stopped or even slowed down until the entire sidewalk was cleared.

When his mother went to Tedlinski's, Wladek would pull the coaster wagon or sled and help carry the groceries. On wash day he'd help his mother by twisting the water out of the clothes before Pani Khula ran them through the wringers.

Occasionally Wladek accompanied the mailman, Mr. Fitzgerald, on his rounds. Once in a while he was allowed to carry the big bag. Just like Santa Claus, Wladek bragged to the mailman, but Mr. Fitzgerald did not understand the boy's garbled speech.

Pani Khula's husband, John, had died ten years ago leaving her alone to care for Wladek. It was no extra burden, except financially, because in fact, John had had nothing to do with the child since the boy was born. The man refused to be seen with his son, attending church at different times. He also immediately ended all physical contact with his wife, first taking a separate bed, and finally setting up sleeping quarters in the summer kitchen staying there year round despite the winter cold.

Poor Wladek had never known the love of a father. Pani Khula tried, but couldn't make up for everything. She couldn't take him outside and play catch, or teach him how to bat the ball. Too much for a woman alone. She occasionally saw Wladek at Okie Diamond playing with the other children. Glupi Wladek chasing the ball far off into the fields, running and stumbling. Glupi Wladek, the son she loved.

When he got older Pani Khula gave Wladek his father's railroad watch as a memento. He had received precious little enough from the man when he was alive, she thought.

Wladek attended the Special Class at School 69, but after that Pani Khula kept him at home. She didn't want him attending another school far away from Kaisertown. Then one day the police and Father Kolinski from St. Bernard's brought Wladek home. As was the case with nearly everyone in Kaisertown, Pani Khula was terrified of the police under any circumstances, but to see them accompanying her son sent her into a panic of confusion and fright. Thank goodness Father Kolinski was there. He knew that Pani Khula and her son were good Catholics, that they respected the rules of the church. The priest would tell them. Wladek stood silently next to the good Father. He had done a bad thing. He knew he was in trouble.

"They were playin a game," began the priest in Polish. "One of the other children told us. They were showing their private parts, the boys amongst themselves. But Wladek was curious about the girls too, and he grabbed the little Bartkowski girl and tore her shorts. The kids panicked and ran away. When Pani Bartkowski showed up Wladek let go, but you know, the girl was scared. The mother too. Your son didn't harm her, but he's a big boy, and strong. The police want assurances. They want to make sure you will watch him carefully in the future so that nothing like this ever happens again."

Pani Khula broke down and cried. She was afraid for both herself and Wladek. What would she do without him, her precious son? And what would happen to him? No one to fix his beloved porridge in the morning, no one to tie his shoes, no one to sing him to sleep at night. No one to love him as only she, his mother, could love.

So she promised the police. Father Kolinski stood by her, said he'd help, talk to the other children and the parents. A sermon or two in church. Everything would be alright. Wladek was a good boy. The Lord loved him too.

Pani Khula hated herself that day when she took out the pyda and beat poor frightened Wladek. She told him never, never to touch another girl again. She beat him till he cried and hid under the table. Then she dragged him out and beat him some more. Beat him and beat him. Better now than later. Now let him hurt and cry so that he learns his lesson. Now or he'll be gone from me forever, and she beat him until her arm wearied and she collapsed beside him on the floor. And Wladek wept.

That night she sat on his bed and stroked his wet hair and feverish face."Lulajze, Jezuniu, moja perelko," she sang softly. "Lulaj ulubione me piescidelko… Lulajze, Jezuniu, lulajze, lulaj."

Nelly Ostraski: Jason's Cousin: "Boze, Bedroom Eyes, and St. Veronica's Veil"

Nelly sat quietly at her desk, one of exactly thirty six desks in the classroom arranged in six rows of six desks each. Each row was securely bolted to the floor forming a single, unalterable unit. Six unerring chains of wood and wrought iron. Six little trains with look alike, frightened passengers locked onto the path of salvation. And patrolling the aisles like a train conductor hunting for stowaways walked the dark form of Sister Fidencia, Engineer of the Faithful, Conductor of Lost Souls.

The girl was hunched over her work tightly clutching a pencil in her sweaty hand. She was conscious of the cold presence of the nun somewhere in the classroom, but it was suicide to turn around. Nelly had to confine her eye movements to her paper and the blackboard upon which were written the English spelling words of the day.

At St. Casimir's, Polish was the language of instruction up until the Fourth Grade. After that, and largely as a result of pressure from the New York State Department of Education, the curriculum became more English oriented. "Bishop, altar, priest, divine," the words were written in the clipped, unadorned penmanship of Sister Fidencia.

Nelly wrote slowly, almost painfully with her right hand. The pressure exerted on her paper had torn a couple of holes in it already. The pencil she used was chewed to disfigurement. Most of the yellow paint was gone and only a speckled wet tube remained. A tiny twisted hunk of ragged metal stood on the end where the eraser once lay. The girl fidgeted uncontrollably in her seat. She knew for certain she would never complete the assignment. Soon Sister Fidencia would shout: 'Stop! Pencils down!" So Nelly had no choice if she hoped to finish on time. She squeezed shut her eyes, said a quick prayer, and moved the pencil from her right hand to her left.

Out of the corner of her hooded eye Sister Fidencia spotted the movement. When the old nun turned and cocked her head along Nelly's row she immediately detected a breech in the wall. The unbroken line of moving hands had been disrupted. The girl felt a cold shiver run through her body just before the ruler landed with a crack across her knuckles.

"Ow-wah," Nelly cried out in fright and pain. The pencil fell from her hand, rolled off the desk and landed at the black shoes of the nun.

"A co to?" asked Sister Fidencia, her furrowed face like a dried mud puddle with two dead pollywogs for eyes. She crumpled up Nelly's paper.

"Dis is dah work of dah devil's hand. God's children use dah right hand. Are you a child of god or not?"

"I, I don't know, Sister."

"Doan know? Den you bedder find out, nie? First it's dah hand, den priddy soon dah devil got control of yer body and soul. You want dah devil to rule over yer immortal soul? Look at me when I'm talkin."

Nelly raised her head. She was a pretty girl with blond pigtails and blue eyes, features which in Sister Fidencia's mind guaranteed her a one way ticket to hell.

"Now go to dah sideboard and beg dah Baby Jesus forgive you. Fifty times."

Nelly sobbed as she wrote: 'Dear Jesus, I am heartily sorry for having offended Thee.'

Using her right hand it would take her well past her lunch hour to complete the punishment. She wished she was more like Bobby Gomulak who sat across from her in the fourth row. Nothing bothered Bobby. No matter how hard the nuns hit him, or how often he was sent to Sister Superior, he just kept smiling and getting right back into trouble. As a result, Bobby spent many an afternoon cleaning the wax from the church candelabra with small flat wooden Popsicle sticks.

Nelly's torment at the hands of Sister Fidencia continued throughout the school year until it began to affect her behavior at home. The usually bright and cooperative girl became sullen and withdrawn. She rarely finished her meals, couldn't sleep, and balked openly at going to school. It took Nelly's mother a long while to uncover the problem.

Pani Ostraski, a hard working woman, who was stern but fair in the upbringing of her two daughters, took a morning off work and went straight to Sister Superior's office.

"I doan mind you give dah discipline," she explained. "Dah young ones dey need it, but dis about dah left hand is no good. So what she uses her left hand? Her fadder is left hand too. He gives dah money for dah collection at church wit his left hand. For dah girls' school he writes dah check wit his left hand. It's not good enough, we move Nelly to School 69."

Nelly had no more trouble with Sister Fidencia although her marks were never as good as they once had been and they stayed like that over her years at St. Casimir's School.

It was something of a ritual for the Polish women of Kaisertown to abandon their local butchers and grocers at least once a month to venture into the vast Broadway Market in search of bargains and ethnic specialties. In this regard Nelly's mother was no different so on the last Saturday of every month with her two girls in tow she got on the bus and trundled off to the Broadway Market. This week Frances refused to go along. All the better thought Nelly. She rarely had time with her mother alone.

"What you wanna get, ma," inquired Nelly as the vastly crowded and noisy market spread out before them like a Roman arena?"

"I look for dat tongue. Yer fadder has a taste and I haven't fixed it in a long time. Let's go by Kornichiewiez dough. I doan like Malecki's. Good sausage, bud not dah tongue."

There were a dozen women standing at the long glass counter belonging to Peter Kornichiewicz. The signs overhead proclaimed: "Try Korny's Cold Cuts" and "Tripe and Tongue, the best in Town." The clerk nearest to them was engaged in conversation with an old woman whose stooped shoulders barely cleared the counter top.

"Tutaj, pani," the clerk said to the woman who wore a long black coat and a clean white babushka with frayed edges tied tightly under her chin.

"Dziekuje, dziekuje," the old lady bowed several times and put a white wrapped package into her shopping bag. "Pies, moya pies," she repeated.

Pani Ostraski glanced at Nelly and smiled. "Dere really for her," she said. "Probably make some soup."

"Pani's is nex," called a voice from the counter. The clerk was addressing Nelly's mother. "Jak tam, pani today?"

"Dobrze," replied Nelly's mother. "You god id dah tongue? I wanna it a nice tongue."

"Sure, tutaj pani. The bess, nice and fresh. Korny's god it dah bes tongue in dah market. I bring id out you one."

"Tak."

The clerk held out the tongue on a piece of wax paper for both Nelly and her mother to inspect. "Looks good, nie?"

Nelly was not at all impressed with the red-gray slab of nib surfaced, up rooted meat that stared her in the face. "I don't know how you and dad can eat that stuff," she commented.

The clerk, a middle aged woman, thin bespectacled with her hair wrapped in a net smiled. She resembled a sick seagull.

"Dah kids now days dey doan know id what's good, nie, pani?"

Nelly glanced down the counter where several plucked ducks lay on crushed ice. Dark, red-black bottles of blood rested beside them. The words, 'doan know what's good' echoed in her ears. She remembered when as little kids, she and her sister had gone to visit babcia when she lived with dziadek Andy and still had her own house.

"She's out in dah back," he said. "Gotta kaczka from dah market. Makin czanina for supper."

The two girls recognized the name, 'czanina" as their favorite Polish soup: sweet, dark, and smooth. Chocolate soup, they called it. The girls ran outside. In the backyard they espied their babcia sitting on a stool with a deep porcelain basin on the ground in front of her. A live duck was trapped between the old woman's legs. Its head had been plucked of feathers which lay strewn around babcia's slippered feet. The bird stared blankly ahead as their babcia took a knife and made two deep incisions in the form of an X on the top of its head. She then grabbed the duck firmly by the neck and still pinning its body with her legs tilted the stream of blood issuing from its head into the basin. The day was cold and the hot blood steamed in the air. Nelly remembered her head spinning as she stood there mouth agape in a noiseless scream. Neither Nelly nor Frances ever touched czarnina again nor did they visit their babcia for quite a while afterwards. They were terrified of the old lady.

While Nelly's mother worked steadily at the Drescher Box Company,

her father was chronically unemployed, working only odd jobs throughout the City of Buffalo. Florian Ostraski's troubles were a result of his
free drinking ways, his independent mind and his ego. He'd often do jobs
for friends and acquaintances for merely a compliment and a bottle of
booze.

"Psia krew, Florian, yer dah bess electrician in town. How about
anudder beer?"

However, compliments never paid the bills so money was in short
supply in the Ostraski household on Glenn Street. Despite all this, Nelly's mother never complained, nor brooked any criticism of her husband
which her sisters were only too willing to offer.

Instead she took a job.

In later years this left Nelly at home alone after school before her
sister Frances arrived by bus from Villa Maria Academy. Each day Nelly
changed clothes and headed for the large two story garage at the back
of the house where she scooped several cans of feed from the grain sack
into a small bright pail. Above, she could hear the soothing drone of the
pigeons.

How wonderful to be a bird, she thought, playing hide and seek in
the clouds. Birds were better than people. They were never mean. The
Holy Ghost was a bird. At one time Nelly and her sister had named all
the prettiest pigeons in the coop. There was Bashful, who always kept her
head hidden in her wing, and Speedy, the fastest flier, and Sister Agnes,
very pretty in purple and white, Bialets, Swiety Annki, and Myszka, for
her size.

But since the Ostraski family often relied upon these birds for more
than the occasional meal, the practice was abandoned. It was too trau-
matic to see little Snow Ball on the chopping block scrunching her head
to avoid the sweep of their father's knife, then watching it being plucked

and finally served on a dinner plate with several forlorn looking companions.

"Nasze ptaki are for dah food too," explained Nelly's mother. "We godda eat. To waste food is a sin."

So Nelly picked at her food and wondered about god's laws.

Jason and Aunt Vickie often visited Nelly's house. Jason was Nelly's favorite cousin and over the years she had harbored a persistent, though silent, crush on him. Maybe it was his easy manner which drew Nelly to him for the cousins talked about everything together. Jason had been the first to know about Sister Fidencia, for instance, and Nelly, in turn, knew that Jason's real first name was John, not Jason.

Or perhaps it was Jason's inquisitiveness that captured Nelly's attention. Everything amazed and delighted him. He'd spend hours at the creek just watching the dragonflies crawl out of the water and transform themselves from ugly, creepy bugs into beautiful, sparkling creatures with cathedral wings and jeweled eyes.

"Look at how big their eyes are," Jason said. "I wonder if they can see stuff that we can't?"

In turn Jason's eyes mesmerized Nelly. You didn't notice them from far away, the girl observed, but when you got closer they were beautiful and entrancing like a cracked cat's eye marble, or an image in a toy kaleidoscope.

"Let's go play in the fields," suggested Nelly as she lifted the latch on the back gate. The two children ran along the line of mismatched fences which bordered the backyards of Glenn Street. From there they veered off through the tall grass sprinkled with milkweed, goldenrod and wild chicory and headed for a line of willows that marked the crooked course of a small creek.

The air was pleasantly cool beneath the canopy of leaves. They sat together on a stout willow branch overhanging the water. A Red-winged blackbird warbled from a nearby cattail stalk. Jason looked at Nelly and smiled, then he leaned over and kissed her; an innocent kiss, awkward but soft and on the lips. Goosebumps ran over Nelly's body like an army of ants scurrying over a sugar cube. They sat holding hands, legs swinging freely in the air below the willow truck. This was their sanctuary. They stayed the afternoon.

"Where yous two been?" scolded Nelly's mother at the back gate. "I been callin and callin. Doan go too far dat you doan hear me when I call. We're havin dah eats now. Aunt Vickie and Jason are stayin for supper. Lookit yer faces, all red wit runnin. Ain't good for Jason wit his asthma. Now go wash up."

The three children sat in the summer kitchen apart from the adults.

"Would yous two stop makin so much noise when yous eat?" said Frances who was not pleased with being excluded from adult company although she was only a few years older than Nelly.

The two younger children ate quickly and headed back outside.

"Wait a minute," shouted Frances. "Yous godda help me clean up the dishes. I ain't getting stuck doin everything myself."

"Ma said I got to play wit Jason. He's the guest, and not supposed to do no work," replied Nelly as they dashed from the scene.

"Boy, I can't wait to get outa dis house and away from you, spoiled brat," shouted Frances.

In the yard the old garage was silent now. Nelly's father had liquidated the pigeons last year upon complaints from the neighbors, and the City of Buffalo which ordered him to get a license. The family ate squab for six months.

The two cousins settled into the stout Adirondack chairs that stood at the open entrance of the garage. Both children recalled the bitter disappointment they had suffered years ago upon first seeing the Indians who sold the chairs. The Indians had come around with trucks piled high with furniture: single chairs, love seats, and gliders sticking out every which way and tied down with ropes. But those Indians! They were ugly and pot-bellied and smoking cigarettes, and they wore clothes just like white men. Where were Cochise, and Geronimo, Crazy Horse, Sitting Bull and Pocahontas?

"Frances is mean," said Nelly. "And if she wasn't here I could have the whole bedroom to myself. Our room's so small dere's not enough space for two beds so I gotta sleep wit her."

"I'm glad I don't have any brothers or sisters," Jason said. "All the brothers and sisters I know, every one of them, fight all the time."

A while later Frances came into the yard with her bathing suit on. She scowled at the two cousins, then opened a cushioned lounge chair and made herself comfortable some distance away.

"Let's go by Auntie Stella's," Nelly suggested noticing Jason's preoccupation with Frances' attire. "She's always got pop and stuff, OK? OK, Jason?"

The last house on Glenn Street, a small brown insulbrick bungalow with pillared front and side porches was owned by the children's Aunt Stella. Aunt Stella was the oldest of the aunties and lived alone following the death of her second husband, John Olchowski.

"My father says that Aunt Stella reminds him of the Wife of Bath."

"Who's the Wife of Bath?"

"She's a character in a book, The Canterbury Tales. My father has it in his library. I haven't read it yet. The words are different, not like real English."

"We don't have no books in our house," Nelly confessed.

That was another thing about Jason and his family, his father mainly,

Nelly noted. They were different. Uncle Eddie didn't go to church, and he read all the time and listened to classical music which no one else in the family could even understand. Jason too wasn't very religious, and didn't seem to be afraid of nuns, or priests, or even god for that matter. It was strange and enticing being with him, like eating forbidden fruit.

Aunt Stella was outside trimming some hedges which substituted for a fence along her backyard separating it from the wild fields beyond. She was a large, big breasted woman with a hoarse voice and hearty laugh. She had a glass of beer in one hand and a large pair of clippers in the other.

"What, dah coppers chasin yous, cy co? Ha, ha, ha," the woman laughed as the two children came running up.

Aunt Stella was always in a good mood which was why Nelly liked her so much. Whenever Nelly had been punished by her parents or gotten into a fight with her sister, she came to Aunt Stella. They would sit in the kitchen and talk, Aunt Stella with her glass of beer, and Nelly with a bottle of Squirt.

"Jenna," said Aunt Stella surveying Jason whom she hadn't seen in a while. "Whad a piece a man you getting to be, nie? Ha, ha, ha. Yous wann it dah soft drink and some potato chip? In dah kitchen, you know it, Nelly. Go ahead. I'm gonna finish wit dah clippin."

Nelly and Jason dashed through a gap in the bushes and onto a narrow sidewalk that led to the back door of the house. Bright pansies with their smiling whiskered cat faces grew in profusion along the border of the walkway.

"You want orange or Squirt?" asked Nelly. Squirt was her favorite, but she deferred to Jason who selected the orange anyway.

"I like Aunt Stella's house. It's nice and small," continued Nelly. "When I grow up I'm gonna have a house just like this one with a husband and four kids. Do you think cousins can get married, Jason?"

"Maybe, but I don't think they can have kids. Something about their blood being too much the same. Anyways let's have our pop on the front porch," he suggested and stepped into the parlor which in turn opened onto the small roofed porch.

Midway across the room Nelly stopped in her tracks; her eyes focused on the open door of Aunt Stella's bedroom. The girl took an unconscious step backward.

"Hey, what's the matter?" asked Jason.

"I forgot about the picture," Nelly stammered, pointing at the bedroom.

"What picture?" asked Jason suddenly curious. "I don't see anything."

"It's on the wall by her dresser," Nelly replied.

"I'm going to look," said Jason.

"No," insisted Nelly.

"A picture can't hurt you," Jason said taking her hand.

As their eyes got accustomed to the dim light in the bedroom they could distinguish a large dresser and a high backed wooden chair with a woman's slip, white like a ghost, thrown across it. A bambinko with its wide shirt and jeweled crown sat atop a dresser. The faint tinge of moth balls mingled with the lingering scent of perfume drifted within the room.

"I don't see any picture," said Jason disappointedly.

"There," Nelly pointed at a dark spot on the wall.

The two cousins peered more closely. Gradually colors and details emerged from the obscured image above the dresser. Thorns framed a darkened face brown with sweat and blood and with reddish hollows for closed eyes.

"It's a picture of Jesus," Jason said. "Just his face. He looks dead. There's something written on the bottom."

"It's St. Veronica's Veil. Don't read it," Nelly pleaded.

Jason moved closer and read out loud. "Look at the eyes. Look at the eyes and they will open."

Nelly screamed and ran from the room. Jason instinctively panicked and fled immediately behind her. The porch door banged shut as they sped down the steps and onto the sidewalk in front.

"Nelly wait," called Jason as he ran after his cousin. Nelly slowed and finally stopped half way up the street.

"Gees," remarked Jason. "All this running and I'm not even breathing hard. Must be getting better for sure. What happened back there, anyway? It's like you seen a ghost or something."

"I'm afraid," said Nelly.

"Afraid? Afraid of what?"

"Of boze, of god."

In the Eighth Grade Sister Superior came to Nelly's class to lecture the girls on the occasion of their graduation from elementary school. After all they were headed for high school next and a world of temptations lay ahead of them. They needed guidance. Brother Gregory from Bishop Ryan was performing the same service for the boys in an adjacent classroom.

"God, our heavenly fadder, has entrusted yous wit a precious gift," began Sister Superior. "It is like a beautiful vase, a beautiful, but very, very delicate vase dat if yous drop it just once, it will break. Break to pieces an yous can never put it togedder again no madder how hard yous try. Dis is dah gift of virginity dat God, our fadder, entrusts to yous. He wants yous to take care of it because if yous don't, yous will never be pure in God's eyes again. God, our fadder, wants yous to save yer precious gift of virginity until dah time yous get married. It is dah gift yous give to yer husband. It was God's gift to yous, and den yer gift to yer husbands. To go into a marriage widout dah gift of virginity is like yous take a broken vase and try to put water in it. It will spill out like yer husband's love for yous will spill out and be gone."

Nelly fidgeted in her seat. It seemed as though Sister Superior was speaking directly to her. Nelly looked away.

"Dah devil tries to steal yer virginity by workin through yer vanity which is a sin," the good sister continued. "I seen some of yous on dah street wit dah lipstick and yer skirts up over yer knees. Dah devil laughs when he sees yous all painted up 'cause he knows yer soul is comin to him. Now kneel down and pray to God to protect yous from temptation and save yer precious gift."

After school Nelly walked home with Marsha Garlock and Kathy Nowaciezski. Once out of sight of the building the girls hiked up their skirts and partially unbuttoned their blouses. Nelly, being the most modest of the three, only slightly altered her uniform.

"You know," began Marsha, "I doan give a shit about bein no virgin. I'm afraid, dat's all. Afraid of getting pregnant. You godda have a boy who knows what he's doin. Dah stooges we got here at Casimir's, dey got trouble zipppin up dere flies."

Nelly blushed at her friend's language. Nevertheless, she liked Marsha and her gruff, honest talk.

"If it wasn for my parents, I would a gone to School 69," added Kathy.

"My cousin goes there," said Nelly. "He says the teachers are real nice and call you by yer first name."

"Who's yer cousin?" inquired Marsha.

"Jason, Jason Novak."

"Oh yeah, I know him. Once in a while he hangs out by Babe's. I wouldn't mind givin him "my precious little vase". He's good lookin and he's got dese eyes, "bedroom eyes."

"What's bedroom eyes?" asked Nelly.

"You know, bedroom eyes," explained Marsha.

"Hey, Nelly, why doan you come out some night and hang around wit us. Go to Babe's or dah park?" added Kathy.

"My father says I can't date till I'm eighteen," said Nelly.

"Shit, I was hopin I'd be married long before I was eighteen," laughed Marsha.

The girls parted company and Nelly was left thinking about Jason, Jason and his bedroom eyes. She hadn't seen him for quite a while. What was he doing?

At the end of the school year Nelly was given permission to attend her Eighth Grade graduation dance, but without a date, of course. In this she wasn't alone. Of her thirty-five classmates only two had actual dates, and these were naturally other pupils from the same class. It was only by special permission, impeccable references, and intensive interviews that the nuns allowed an outsider to attend a St. Casimir's School dance. Throughout the history of the school no one, as yet, had qualified.

The school's small auditorium was converted into a dance hall with a teenage polka band of dubious quality, but affordable price, set up on an elevated stage. Below, arranged along each wall, was a long row of benches occupied on one side by fourteen boys, and seventeen girls on the other. Two boys who had dates sat on the girls' side with their companions. Eight nuns and half a dozen parents rounded out the night's revelers.

The girls, in their wide flared dresses that tilted like tea cups when they sat down, waited, with hands properly folded on their laps, to be asked to dance. The boys, on the other side of the room, appeared in no hurry to act. However, if the young ladies tired of the wait, they had the option of standing in line to waltz with one of the nuns.

"I'd rather get laid by a toad than dance wit one a dem crows," said Marsha.

"Not so loud. Yer gonna get us in trouble," replied Kathy.

"Who cares? We're almost out of this hole anyways. I can hardly wait, and no more Catholic schools for me. I'm going to South Park next year. How about you Nelly?"

"I gotta go to Villa Maria like my sister."

"If one a dem little assholes doesn't come over and ask me to dance, den I'm going over dere and ask them," proclaimed Marsha.

"You can't do dat," said Kathy. "Dah boy's supposed to ask dah girl."

"You think I bought dis dress for the hell of it? And a corsage? Look-it dem jerks. What are dey waitin for?"

At that moment, Bobby Gomulak, who had been pacing for several minutes along the far line of benches, walked across the floor. The band struck up a sour noted rendition of "For Your Precious Love" featuring the off key intonations of the accordionist. Mercifully the rest of the three piece band thundered into the number and drowned out the squeeze box.

"You wanna dance?" Bobby asked Nelly.

The girls looked up. Not exactly a knight in shining armor.

"Better grab it," said Marsha to Nelly "Might be your only chance."

"Ahh, OK. Sure," replied Nelly.

Bobby held Nelly stiffly as they shuffled around in an ever narrowing circle until they were virtually spinning in place. The boy's every third step landed squarely on Nelly's toes. He apologized profusely.

"It's OK," Nelly assured him. "Don't worry."

Nelly was actually a good dancer although no one would have

guessed it from the present performance. She had learned and practiced throughout her youth at the numerous weddings that highlighted the family's social calendar. She had been taught by some of the best, having polkaed, waltzed, obereked, and mazurkaed with her father, uncles, and cousins of all ages. Her father, in particular, was a lively and graceful dancer despite his large size.

'Piorun, dat's how he get me," laughed Nelly's mother. "Such a dencer even to dis day.'

It wasn't long, however, before this present awkward two step twirl was interrupted by the stern figure of Sister Paulicarpa, one of the evening's chaperons.

"Not too close yous two," she said placing her arm between the dancers. "Make room for dah Holy Ghost."

The children dutifully separated their bodies, but continued to dance. Bobby then whispered to Nelly. "You remember in the Sixth Grade when Sister Paulicarpa's pet goldfish died, and she was all upset and cryin over dem?"

Nelly looked at Bobby and nodded.

"It was me dat killed em," Bobby confessed. "Everyday when I went to sharpen my pencil I put salt in the water. In a few days dey were swimming on dere sides, den upside down."

'Jenna, Jenna, moya maly fishies.'

"I was so happy. Remember how she used to make me kneel in dah corner or squat over dah wastepaper basket? I hated her. Yer dah only one who knows."

Before the night was over Sister Superior led everyone in a prayer and then delivered a lengthy harangue in which she urged all the graduates to continue their education at good Catholic institutions.

"Dah older yous become, dah more yous will need Holy Mudder dah

Church to guide yous. Dah best education is at dah Catlick schools. Before yous leave St. Casimir's I will talk to yous about which Catlick high school yous should go to. An we're gonna send dah notes to yer parents too."

After the dance the three girlfriends walked home together. It was nine o'clock. Nelly had managed two dances with Bobby. Marsha got up once with Henry Beebek who was at least a foot shorter than she. Kathy remained a wallflower the entire evening. At the intersection of Clinton and Weimer the girls parted ways. Shortly afterwards Nelly saw Bobby Gomulak standing on the next corner.

"I, I jus taught dat I'd walk you home, maybe. If you doan mind," the boy stammered.

"OK, but just to the corner of Rejtan. If my father sees you he'll shoot the both of us."

"I guess dat explains why I never seen you around Kaisertown."

As they walked along Bobby fumbled for Nelly's hand. She could feel the tremble in his when he finally grabbed a hold. Next he stopped and tried to kiss her. Their lips barely touched when their foreheads banged awkwardly together. That stifled any further attempt and they walked the rest of the way in silence.

Nelly shuffled down her sidewalk alone, a saddened Cinderella. The next day her dress was packed up and shipped to Poland where it would adorn the shoulders of her old country relatives and be handed down for generations to come. A five dollar bill was sewn into the hem.

Later that summer Nelly's father got a job at the Buffalo harbor rewiring ships at dock. The extra money allowed him to build a separate bedroom in the attic for Frances. Nelly would get the old room to herself by default. Both girls were ecstatic.

The old dresser and iron framed bed were brought down from

their storage upstairs because Frances got to keep the original matching set. But Nelly got to shop with her mother at Sattler's for a new set
of curtains, sheets, and pillow cases. Aunt Stella contributed a knitted
bedspread and two dollies for the dresser. Everything was blue, Nelly's
favorite color.

Frances' new room faced the street and occupied the front third of
the attic. Its inner wall had been built around the chimney giving the
chamber extra warmth in the winter, not that it was essential since the
hot air rose unimpeded through the uninsulated house and heated the
entire attic. In fact, Nelly's mother regularly hung her laundry there to
dry during the winter months. When Frances' new bedroom was finished,
Nelly was expressly forbidden to enter. With her own room now, Nelly
professed to have cared less, but, of course, she was dying of curiosity
the whole time.

She finally got her chance for a peek on All Saints' Day, a Holy Day
of Obligation and an holiday for Nelly, who was in her first year at Villa
Maria Academy. Frances, who was in her final year at the same school,
was out on a date with her boyfriend, Vince. They had gone riding in his
car.

An explosion of pink and white greeted Nelly when she opened the
door to Frances' bedroom. A bolt of envy shuddered through the girl.
White lace curtains hung on two low, long windows that overlooked
Glenn St. The tops of the window frames were just even with the girl's
shoulders. A pink bedspread covered the bed with a white ruffle surrounding the bottom. Beside the bed lay a long fluffy pink throw rug. The
wallpaper had a white background decorated with pink and red roses.
Two white dressers and a rocking chair covered in a crocheted white af-
ghan completed the furnishings while a portable record player lay on the
floor surrounded by several 45 records. A full face poster of Elvis Presley

stared down from above the headboard.

Nelly walked cautiously throughout the silent room peeking into every corner. She even opened the sliding mirrored doors half expecting her sister to be lurking there. But there was no one. Shivers of a strange excitement washed over the girl. She stared at her reflection in the mirror, then suddenly turned around in alarm. Just the sneering face of Elvis greeted her. She moved nervously to the windows and peered out. Nobody. The room, the whole house was empty, save for Nelly. She ran her fingers across the buttons of her blouse, and then inexplicably, undid them. Breathing heavily she turned again towards the mirrors.

"No, no, "she said out loud. "It's a sin." Soon her blouse and bra lay on the floor.

"Oh, my God," she breathed, her face and neck blushed red and blotchy. She kicked off her shoes, and wriggled out of her pants. She turned her back to the mirror, then looked over her shoulder as she slowly pulled down her panties. That was when she suddenly heard a car door slam, and like a rap on the knuckles with a ruler, it jolted the girl out of her reverie. Outside the window Frances and Vince were walking up the sidewalk laughing and shoving each other.

"Oh my god," cried Nelly as she did a little dance of fright in the middle of the room and almost peed herself. "And they're gonna come right up here."

Nelly gathered her clothes and looked around like a naked beggar for shelter. She couldn't possibly hide in the bedroom so she scurried into the attic proper and like a rat dug herself a hole in the junk and debris. Amid rolls of felt paper, clothes trunks, lamps, a baby buggy, bird cage, cobbler's bench and shoe lasts she huddled down panting heavily, dying of fright and covered in dust and dirt which clung to her sweaty body like grit on sandpaper. Back across her path of escape she could see a line of footprints barely discernible in the dust of the attic floor leading directly to her hiding spot.

"Oh Jesus, no," she whispered hugging her clothes for protection.

Luckily Vince and Frances were too absorbed in themselves to see the footprints. However, Frances did notice that the door was ajar.

"I bet you dat little bitch was snoopin around in here," the older girl said. She turned around and faced the stairway.

"Nelly! Nelly, you little bitch. I toll you to stay outa my room."

"Hey, Frances," said Vince. "Forget it. She ain't around. You was callin all downstairs when we got in. Anyways, get over here. I wanna show you something."

"What? Oh, you pig! Put dat away. Somebody could come."

"Hey, it's two o'clock. Quittin time is five. Just keep the door open. Dat way if yer sister does come in the house, we'll hear her."

"Vince, dere'll be nothing to look forward to when we're married. I'll be old hat to you," replied Frances who, nonetheless, sat down on the bed.

"No, you won't. Dere dat's better. Don't hide yer face."

"I'm shy. It's so light in here."

Reflected in the triptych of the mirrored closet doors, Nelly could see what was happening on the bed. Her sister's pants were gone and her legs were spread apart. A pair of pink panties hung loosely from her left ankle, and Vince's hand was between her legs moving slowly in a small arc.

"Dat better? Yer not complainin now, are you?" said Vince.

"Nooo."

Nelly shifted her position, never taking her eyes off the mirror. The images blurred, then refocused. Vince's bare behind was now between Frances' legs. The panties were gone and the heel of the girl's foot drummed against the small of Vince's back keeping time with the tightening and thrusting of his buttocks.

"Dat's good. Dat's my Frances."

Nelly could feel her face and body grow warm. She felt the wetness between her legs, but frantically clasped them together to stifle the sensation and also prevent herself from peeing all over the floor. Nelly's problem was that she had no knowledge of sex, none whatsoever. She never knew how to interpret her feelings or desires except to know that they were sinful. When she first got her period her mother gave her a rambling, confused explanation of womanhood and sex, but Nelly had no idea what she was talking about.

Frances was of no help either, and the girls at school, despite their bold talk, were as ignorant as Nelly. Even watching Vince and Frances now, Nelly wasn't sure what was going on, except that her sister was committing a grievous sin which could damn her forever.

Back in the bedroom Vince and Frances were getting dressed. "I gotta go to the bathroom," said Vince. "I wanna flush dis thing down too."

"Are you crazy?" replied Frances. "What if it clogs up the toilet? I can see my father getting out his plumber's snake and pullin a safety outa the toilet. He'd kill me, and you too."

"I'm not scared of yer old man," said Vince. "I'm startin at Chevy next month and I'll be makin seven-fifty a hour. With dat kind a money we can get married as soon as yer done yer senior year. We can get a little flat, den in a couple a years our own house."

"Oh Vince, I love you so much," cooed Frances.

When Nelly heard the downstairs door slam shut, she got up from her hiding spot and tiptoed to the window of Frances' room. She waited until Vince's car pulled away. The girl frantically searched around for some receptacle to relieve herself. Anything belonging to her sister was out of the question so Nelly rummaged through the debris of the attic. She came across a tall hollow plastic statuette of the Virgin Mary holding the Christ Child. Nelly made the sign of the cross, turned the statue upside down and positioned it between her legs. Tears of relief flowed as Nelly filled the vessel to the brim. Then, unable to put the filled vessel down, Nelly descended the stairs naked and headed for the bathroom. She flushed the toilet and turned to hurry back for her clothes when out of the corner of her eye she noticed something swirling in the bowl. It looked like a little balloon, clear colored and momentarily suspended by some air trapped within it. Before Nelly could investigate more closely it sank beneath the whirlpool of water and was gone.

Nelly's years at Villa Maria Academy were not a particularly happy ones. The routine was much the same as at St.Casimir's and, of course, the nuns had not improved in either personality or professionalism. Nelly simply endured.

The only joy in Nelly's high school years was her involvement in the choir. She loved to sing, and she loved Sister Mildred, the choir director, who did not care in which hand the girls held their musical scores. Furthermore, the choir, with its practices and performances, broke the monotony and repression of the Catholic school routine. The members were even allowed out of school to entertain at old folks' homes, churches, and schools. In addition, Nelly had to attend evening rehearsals and this got her away from the house unchaperoned for the first time in her life.

On the bus at night she saw boys and girls going on dates, to dances, and basketball games. The couples would snuggle together, and talk and laugh, and sometimes steal a kiss. It seemed innocent fun to Nelly and not at all sinful as she was taught to believe. And how am I supposed to get married and have babies and everything when I don't know nothin about sex, Nelly fretted? I never even seen a naked boy before.

The climax of the choir's activity came at Christmas Eve Midnight Mass at Corpus Christi Church. The Villa Maria Choir would sing traditional Christmas carols punctuated by numerous selections from the Polish kolenda. It was an annual and much anticipated event in the East end community. Nelly hoped against hope that this year her parents could attend the performance. She told them about it weeks in advance and reminded them almost daily.

"Jenna, Nelly, you know it how busy we are at dah box factory at dah Christmas time. I'm so tired from dah overtime. Yer fadder, you know he's busy all week goin for work. We try, honey, but doan count on id."

In desperation Nelly even turned to Frances. "Hey Sis, how about you? Maybe you an Vince could come? He's got a car. I think you'd like the singing."

"Doan be ridiculous," Frances snapped. "Vince and me got better things to do."

"Watch it yerself," Nelly's mother warned. "Wouldn be a bad idea. I doan see dat Vince a yers in dah church so much."

Frances gave Nelly a withering look that so much as told the girl she'd never see her sister at Corpus Christi even if Elvis himself was doing the singing.

Practices were increased as Christmas approached until they were virtually daily affairs. Although the girls enjoyed the experience and the hard work, there was one element of the affair they could not abide. That was the choir's organist, Pan Tszarog, a wizened, hook nosed, chain smoker with a question mark posture and a dirty mind. Pan Tszarog was usually drunk halfway through the rehearsals since he was constantly sipping whiskey from a flask he kept hidden inside his clothes. He had the further habit of loudly breaking wind while openly joking about it.

'Zeby nie ten dech, to by czlowiek zdech.'

He wasn't above rubbing up against the girls either every chance he had and making only slight modifications to his behavior when Sister Mildred was present.

"Sie modli przed figuram a ma diabla za skoram," the good Sister commented, but as obnoxious as the old organist was, there was no removing him from the scene. He was a good friend of Father Wojek, the pastor of Corpus Christi, and therefore beyond reproach. Nelly wondered how a religious man like the Father could associate himself with such a worthless pig like Tszarog. It didn't make sense.

The celebratory night arrived. It was cold and frosty outside, with little snow, unusual for a Buffalo winter. The church was packed since many a Polish family was in the habit of celebrating their wigilja first, going to midnight mass afterwards, and then returning home for desserts, drinks and the breaking of the oplatek, and the opening of presents.

Nelly was glad her family no longer observed the meatless wigilja meal since the death of her babcia. The girl, along with each of her cousins without exception, could not abide the watery pea soup, the doughy tough pierogies filled with stringy cabbage, lumpy potatoes, and hard, hot cheese. Uggh! Only the adults seemed to enjoy the meal driven by some primitive hunger and the need to preserve a vanishing tradition.

High in the choir loft at Corpus Christi, the Villa Maria singers watched as the throng of worshippers assembled below them. The girls were dressed in light blue robes over their normal clothes. Pan Tszarog was similarly attired. Nelly couldn't tell if he was drunk or sober tonight. It didn't matter. The entire choir was a tightly woven group this evening. Solidarnose! They would sink or swim together.

"Jeden, dwa, trzy," Sister Mildred whispered to the girls and Pan Tszarog holding her fingers aloft. After "three" she dropped her hand abruptly. Pan Tszarog pressed the keys and the first clear notes of the organ sounded into the high vaulted ceiling of Corpus Christi Church and reverberated down to the pews below. The choral voices flushed like startled doves immediately behind the music and triumphantly welcomed the Christ Child to Earth.

"Cieszmy sie pod niebiosy wznosmy razen mile glossy, Bo wesola dzis nowina: Czysta Panna rodzi Syna. Bijcie w kotly, w traby grajcie, A Jezussa przywitajcie,Nowonaradzonego."

Altogether they sang eight piesni, and when they came to the "Lullaby of Jesus", the "Lulajze Jezuniu" there wasn't a dry eye in the church including Sister Mildred's and the choirs'.

"Lulajze, Jezunie, moja perelko, Lulaj ulubione me piescidelko, Lulajze, Jesunie, lulajze, lilaji. A ty Go, Matulu w placzu utulaj."

When the mass concluded and the procession of priests and altar boys had filed out, none of the parishioners moved until the choir finished the last song of the night, "Dzisiaj w Betlejem". Then amid audible praises and the visible wiping of eyes a general cacophony erupted as the congregation exited in turn.

Up in the choir loft it was all congratulations and hugs and kisses. Sister Mildred was ecstatic. Pan Tszarog was offering praises all around and copping a feel wherever he could. Nobody cared such was the feeling of joyful accomplishment. The girls descended the stairs where down below the happiness and congratulations were renewed amongst waiting friends and relatives.

However, little of this affected Nelly since her parents had not shown up. She waited patiently in the vestibule for Cynthia Kulikowski and her mother to finish talking so that she could get a ride home. She never heard the voice calling to her.

"I told you, Larry, this whole thing would go to her head. She's probably waiting for a limo to take her home. Fat chance we have."

Nelly turned around and looked straight into the smiling, sparkling eyes of her cousin, Jason Novak. He was in the company of Larry Bing-kowski, another of her many cousins. Larry was several years older than Jason, but for some reason the two boys had formed a common bond and were fast friends.

"What are yous two doin here?" gasped Nelly.

"What are we doing here? What are we doing here? I'm wounded to the quick," replied Jason. "How about you, Lar?"

"Yeah, me too," said the other boy, a strong youth in a leather jacket that magnified the breath of his chest.

"Not only did we want to hear our talented cousin sing, but we also happen to be on our annual Christmas Eve tour of all the Catholic churches on the East Side of Buffalo. And since Larry here is a major contributor to the Corpus Christi Home for Wayward Girls, we thought maybe we'd drop in and see how things were going," Jason continued.

"We woulda been here earlier," added Larry, "except we had to give a ride to a couple a nuns dat was hitch-hikin home from bingo."

"Larry, they don't play bingo on Christmas Eve," said Nelly with a smile. She was thrilled to see her cousins.

"Oh shit," said Larry. "Dat musta been last week."

"Have yous two been drinkin?" asked Nelly.

"Other than some sacramental wine, which is totally in keeping with the spiritual nature of this occasion, certainly not," added Jason.

Just then another voice called out Nelly's name. It was Sister Mil-dred. The nun gave the two boys a hard once over before addressing Nelly.

"Remember to clean adn press dat gown and bring it back after dah vacation, nie?"

"Hello, sister," interjected Jason. "I just wanted to tell you that it was a magnificent performance tonight. Really enjoyable and uplifting."

"Tank you," replied Sister Mildred immediately warming to Jason's good manners. "Yous boys are relatives a Nelly's?"

"My cousins," volunteered the girl.

"Dat's nice," said the good sister who did not approve of boyfriends. "An whad school do yous go to?"

Larry looked down at the floor as though he was examining the tiles for defects. Jason cleared his throat.

"Ah, Larry and I both attend Saint Francis of Athol Springs, sister. Yes, we're home for Christmas vacation."

"Oh, how nice, a good Catlick school. Yer mudders must be proud."

"Yes, they are sister. Larry's mother especially. You see, he's going to St. John Kanti Seminary next year."

Sister Mildred's eyes widened with pleasure, but before she could say anything, Nelly interjected.

"It's gettin late. We better get goin. Excuse me sister, but my parents are gonna be worried."

Once safely in the car the three cousins broke into laughter. "You son of a bitch," said Larry taking a playful punch at Jason's arm.

"Hey, Father Bingkowski, is that any way for a priest to act?"

"Yer such a charmer, ain't you, Jason?" added Nelly. "Oh sister, we jus loved the performance."

"What the hell. It made her feel good. No harm done. And it was good. We caught the last two songs. I have no idea what you were singing about, but the music was great."

God, is he ever good-looking, Nelly said to herself. And those eyes, those bedroom eyes.

"Yeah, I bet he could charm the pants right off dat nun too," said Larry.

"Nuns don't wear pants," Nelly corrected him again. "But if dey did, I think yer right."

"Who knows? Might be interesting," smiled Jason.

"Jesus Christ, Nelly. You bedder watch out. Dah son of a bitch ain't got no morals. He's liable to go after you next."

Nelly turned and looked inquisitively at Jason. "You wouldn't do that, would you, Jason?"

Life at Villa Maria took on the monotony and misery of a Buffalo winter. Nelly battled frustration and boredom and the batter thick Polish accents of the nuns. Even the once invigorating bus ride to and from school took on an oppressive cast with its bundled and silent passengers staring blankly out the dirty windows at the bleak snow blanketed cityscape.

Nelly entered the downstairs hall of her house. The humid warmth felt inviting until it was shattered by sudden shouting and cursing from the kitchen. Nelly's father was at it. He was unemployed again and probably drunk too, thought Nelly.

"I'll tell you what dat bastard's gonna do. He's gonna marry her, dat's what. He's gonna do dah right ting by her."

Frances' voice screamed in response. "You don't have to worry about dat, daddy. He was getting me a ring for my birthday anyways. We love each other, so who cares?"

Nelly walked into the kitchen. Her school bag hung limply from her arm.

"Is Frances gettin married?" she asked.

Her father turned on her immediately. "An here's anudder one. Doan tink yer gonna be like yer sister. No goin out wit boys for you. No, not until yer eighteen, maybe twenty."

"I, I didn't do nothing," Nelly sobbed.

"Florian, take id easy," said Nelly's mother. "Dey're our daughters, you know. You gotta help dem, not yellin all dah time."

"Shoulda done more yellin before, maybe dis wouldn a happen. An jus how we gonna pay for dis weddin? You ever tink a dat?"

"Eighteen. It's not fair, not fair!" said Nelly.

After Florian departed for the local gin mill, Nelly's mother called her daughters together. "Id's all my fault," she began. "I, I never told yous nuttin about dah sex or babies. I didn't know how to."

"Lookit, ma," Frances began with an uncomfortable glance at Nelly. "It's not yer fault. Me an Vince, we figured we were gonna get married anyway, so, you know, what difference did it make?"

Frances stared again at Nelly who now understood the full scope of the problem.

"Don't you got homework or something?" she asked.

"Ma said I could be here."

"Mama," Frances continued. "I jus love him dat's all. He's the first boyfriend I ever had, and he treats me real good. We been goin steady for two years, an we plan to get married and be happy. Yous'll see. An Vince is makin good money by Chevy, more money den daddy ever made."

"Doan you say nuttin agains yer fadder. He work hard. Jus can't hold onto a job, dat's all. An no madder what he says, he loves dah both a yous. He's hurt right now, but he'll ged over id."

"I'm not sayin," answered Frances. "It's just dat wit Vince havin a good job we can get married right away. Look it Dolores Pajak and Bobby. He's just workin at the garage and car wash. Dey got a little kid an dere liven by her babcia and doin OK. We figure we can get married on my birthday. I won't even be showin by den."

"Can I be the Maid of Honor?" asked Nelly. "I never stood up at a weddin before."

Frances managed a smile and nodded her head.

"Where you gonna get yer gown?" Nelly continued.

"I was thinking at the Modern Bride by Broadway. Dey got some beautiful gowns in the window. Dere was this one: organdy wit scalloped neckline an this little appliqué all around, an puffy lace sleeves, a princess waist, an a long train, but not too long, you know, dat it gets in the way."

"What about the Bargain Bride on Bailey?" asked Nelly. "Or Wanda's here in Kaisertown?"

Frances frowned. "I jus can't see myself buyin a wedding gown at a place called, the Bargain Bride, and Wanda's, I dunno, she's too Polish."

"Wanda's good dressmaker, dough," added Nelly's mother warming to the topic herself. "An yous shoulda seen dah gown dat I had it. Remember dah wedding picture in dah parlor? Taki beaudiful. Yer fadder give me dah money. Such a big train, an long veil too. Dat was all dah style den."

"Yeah," said Frances. "Too bad you gave it to Poland. I woulda wore it. I loved dat gown." The girl's lips trembled and her eyes fogged with tears. She then threw her arms around her mother's neck. "I'm sorry, mama. I'm sorry."

The mother cried as the two held each other in their arms. A cloud of jealousy passed in front of Nelly at that moment. Frances was the oldest, the first child. She was closer to her mother and father as well. Nelly realized that nothing could alter that biological order of things. Anything she ever did, or would do, was second best.

Upstairs the two sisters sat on the edge of the bed. It was the first time Nelly was invited into the room. She stared at the mirror and looked at her sister out of the corner of her eye. Frances seemed the same person, yet a baby was growing inside of her. In nine months or less Frances would be a mother.

"Hey, I'm gonna be a auntie," Nelly suddenly shouted. "I never thought a that. You want a boy or girl?"

"A boy. Vince wants one too. Dey're easier to raise, and dey pass on dah family name. Dat's important to Vince."

"What's it like?" asked Nelly with a quick glance at her sister. Frances avoided the question. "Tell me, sis. I wanna know. What's it like?"

"What are you talking about? You an yer stupid questions."

"It's like ma said. She never told us nothing. I don't know nothing. What do you do? How do…"

"Leave me alone," Frances interrupted. "You'll find out when yer married."

When Nelly tried on her Maid of Honor dress, it was as though she had been touched by the wand of some fairy godmother. Pani Novak stood transfixed at the sight of her niece. Frances was stricken with jealousy because she never had the good looks or coloring of her younger sister: the blond hair and blue eyes. Frances was quite mousey really with her bath water complexion and dull brown hair. And now on the eve of her wedding she had to watch as Nelly unintentionally stole the show.

"You better keep a eye on her for sure," said Frances. "She's growin up fast. Maybe daddy was right about not dating until she's twenty."

Despite the Ostarski family's poor financial status, as well as the short notice, over three hundred people were invited to the wedding reception at the Pulaski Post. A good Polish band, the Kaisertown Rythmaires, had been hired, and the extended family worked together to prepare a meal of breaded pork chops, roasted chicken, kielbasa, mashed potatoes, corn, red cabbage, fresh green salad and oven baked rolls and butter. A full bar was set up with Nelly's various uncles and older cousins alternating as bartenders.

All of Nelly's relatives were at the hall, some of whom the girl had not seen for years. As the family members grew older, they also drifted apart. And the occasional wedding and funeral now replaced the more frequent birthday celebrations, communions and confirmations of the past as the social fabric which held them all together.

The one person Nelly really wanted to talk to was her cousin Jason whom she had not been close to since the ride home from Corpus Christi over a year ago. There had always been something special in their relationship, something just under the surface that each of them felt but did not dare to uncover.

Now, bedecked in her new dress and filled with confidence about her looks and maturity, Nelly felt bold. Seated at the head table with the wedding party, Nelly kept a steady eye on Jason. She lost no opportunity to stand up, bend over, and move around giving him a good view of her assets. She did all this in the most casual manner, of course, as though unaware of her cousin's hot stare in front of her.

Immediately after the meal Nelly was busy posing for photos, chatting with her aunts and uncles, and being generally pleasant and polite to Vince's family and friends as well. During this time she was constantly shadowed by one of the ushers on the groom's side, a boy named Henry, Hank.

The band had been playing loud, raucous polkas for some time before they toned down to a slow dance, the first of the evening. Nelly was standing beside her mother still panting from the last dance when she felt a soft touch on her bare shoulder. When she turned she found herself face to face with Jason, his warm romantic eyes smiling straight at her.

"Such a handsome couple," the relatives commented as the two stepped onto the dance floor.

"Bedder den dah bride an groom."

"Too bad dey're cousins, nie?"

"Kissin cousins."

The old Pulaski Hall was enormous, and it needed all its room to accommodate the crush of dancers that thronged the floor. Everyone, including the youngest children, danced. Some of the teenage boys tried to abstain, but their efforts proved futile as their aunts and female cousins constantly pulled them onto the dance floor.

"So what have you been doin lately?" asked Nelly as she swayed within her cousin's arms. "I haven't seen you for a long time."

"Busy with high school and the basketball team. Got to keep my marks up if I want to get into a decent college. Why? Did you miss me?"

"Yes, I mean after all you are the only boy I'm allowed to see. I can't date until I'm eighteen thanks to Frances. I been thinkin of becoming a nun."

"Now that would be a waste," said Jason while surveying Nelly from head to toe. "You look great in that dress."

Suddenly the music stopped. In the middle of the dance floor a crowd gathered in a circle around Frances and her father. All the recriminations and anger of the past were gone. Nelly could see her father's eyes sparkling with tears. Of course, he was also as drunk as a pickled egg by this time too. The band started up with the accordionist leading the way. Everyone joined in the singing.

"Nie smuc sie dzis tatusiu. Nie smuc sie dzis o mnie. Bo dzis jest me wesele. Usmiechil sie do mnie."

Nelly's father took his now married daughter in his arms and waltzed slowly around the room. He was indeed a great dancer. Frances dropped her head on her father's shoulder. He patted her on the head and whispered something in her ear. A pang of jealousy pierced Nelly's heart barbed by the plaintive strains of the music.

"Nie zapomne tatusia. Bo on tez kocha mnie. Zawase on robil dla mnie. Dal mi wszystko co mam."

The couple continued to waltz in a wide circle while the assemblage sang. Nelly's mother was in tears. Aunt Vickie was also sobbing: an infectious emotion that soon spread to all the aunts. For their part Nelly and Jason avoided the family celebration. They took a seat at a far table.

"The thing is," said Nelly who had consumed a couple of high balls and grown loquacious. "I don't know nothin about boys. I don't know what to say; what to do. I feel like a idiot."

"Girls are bold nowadays," Jason put in. "You know, they put the make on guys. You, you're different. You've got a certain wholesome look…"

"The look of a dumb virgin, you mean?" Nelly blurted out.

"Whoa," laughed Jason. "That's not what I meant."

"What did you mean?"

"I mean that you… ah. How can I put it?"

"I'm listening," replied Nelly with a mischievous batting of her eyebrows and a tapping of her fingers on the table. She was enjoying her cousin's discomfort. Then she suddenly remembered the mirror in Frances' bedroom and the image of her sister's bare foot drumming rhythmically against the naked body of her then boyfriend and now husband, Vince.

"Well, what I mean is that you look, you look like you're better than you look," stammered Jason. "Does that make sense to you?"

"No."

He's got the most beautiful eyes, the most beautiful smile, the most beautiful everything thought Nelly. But why should he pay any attention to me? I'm just his cousin. He's probably just being nice, giving me a shoulder to cry on, poor little cousin Nelly.

At that moment Henry arrived at the table. He gave a contemptuous glance at Jason and then asked Nelly to dance. "You don't mind my cutting in on yah? Do yah?" Henry intoned in a voice that indicated he didn't much care what Jason thought.

"No, he don't mind. He's only my cousin," replied Nelly before Jason could say anything.

Jason grabbed a cold beer as he watched the two vanish into the throng of dancers. He was lost in thought when someone called out his name.

"Oh, hi Uncle Florian," said Jason. "Great wedding. You must be proud of your daughter today. She looks beautiful."

"Who dah hell is dat dancin wit Nelly?" replied the man ignoring the compliment. "I seen him makin dah goo-goo eyes at her all day long. Some dida from dat's Vince's side?"

"He's one of the ushers. I don't know him."

"Well, I doan trust him," continued the uncle. "Nelly doan know nuttin about boys. Dat's dah trouble. Some guy ged in her pants in a minute, she's so stupid. I'm gonna break dat up right now."

"Uncle Florian, I really don't think that would go over very well. They're just dancing. You're going to hurt some feelings for sure and maybe even spoil the wedding celebration. Look, I'll tell you what. I'll cut in and dance with Nelly myself. Keep an eye on her for you. How's that?"

"Jason, dat's a good idea. No wonder yer so smart an goin to college an everyting. And I'll get you another beer. You wanna beer? I'll put it on the table here. Dat's good and Nelly won't tink it was me buttin in."

Nelly saw Jason approach from across the floor which was just what she wanted.

"Hope you don't mind?" Jason said tapping Henry on the shoulder.

Before the boy could react Nelly was already in her cousin's arms. She snuggled up to him and put her head on his shoulder. She felt him draw her closer until his knees rubbed softly against her thighs. Nelly's face flushed.

"What was that all about?" inquired Jason

"All what?"

"Well, you left me sitting there looking pretty stupid while you went off with that cretan. What happened?"

"Nothin. It's just dat yer my cousin and he isn't. Dat's all. And the poor guy just joined the Marines. He's leaving town and he doesn't even have a girlfriend or anybody to write back home to."

"Are you sure? I thought you had to pass an I.Q. test to get into the Marine Corps?"

"Very funny, Jason, but he isn't that bad. Let's go outside," Nelly suggested. "It's hot in here and they're havin the "Czepina" anyways and I don't wanna be around for that."

"Good I can do without that old Polack stuff too."

They exited through a side door onto a narrow alley. Up ahead they saw their Uncle John bobbing from heel to toe with a pool of liquid gathering around his shoes and spreading slowly across the sidewalk.

"He'd be farther ahead if he unzipped his fly," Jason whispered as they shuffled past the man.

"I'm sorry about the way I behaved in there," Nelly explained. "I just feel so stupid when I'm around boys. I blush, my hands sweat, I don't know what to say. And den there's my father spyin on me all the time."

Jason turned Nelly around facing him.

"Jason, I don't know about this," said Nelly closing her eyes at the same time.

His lips were warm and moist. She felt her mouth open slightly and the boy's tongue run softly along the edge of her lower lip. Nelly moaned as she felt Jason's hand slip down the small of her back and pull her forward until her belly rubbed against his and their thighs met. Before she could say anything he kissed her again, harder this time with his tongue plunging into her mouth until it met hers. The second kiss took her breath away. She felt disoriented and even struggled for balance.

"Yes," she whispered to an unasked question. "Yes, yes, yes."

Nelly's parents were invited to spend the weekend at their friends' cottage at Rushford. The couple had no children so Nelly was not obliged to go along. Nevertheless, her father promised to call her twice a day to make sure everything was alright.

"Don't worry dad. I'll stay home and keep the doors locked. If I got a problem, I'll call Jason. He can be here in a few minutes."

"Yes, dat's good, real good. Jason's the one. Dat way I don't have to worry so much."

When the car pulled out of the driveway she immediately called Jason and invited him to her house. All those final weeks of school after Frances' wedding, Nelly had been unable to concentrate on anything other than Jason. She watched the clock stand still up on the classroom wall as Sister Honorata droned on about the wonders of god in science class.

'Dey call it science,' the nun had scoffed. 'Science is only the miracles of Our Lord revealed to man.'

Nelly dreamed of the miracles she wanted revealed, and who she wanted to reveal them to her. Yes, Jason was perfect. He knew what he was doing. She had heard all the stories about him from her Kaisertown friends. How he hung around with an older crowd, how the girls there called him "Lover Boy", and how he had had lots of girlfriends. And, of course, he was the only boy who could come and go at her house without creating the slightest bit of suspicion. He was her cousin, after all.

And if the ideas she had were so bad, so sinful, why did god put them in her head in the first place? She was only reacting to what was stirring inside of her. If this was a test then god certainly knew she'd flunk it with flying colors. But, if things did get bad, she could always go to confession and god would forgive her. He had to, that was the rule.

And then there was Jason sitting at her kitchen table. Nelly had on a pair of bright red shorts, very tight red shorts, and a white blouse. Her blond hair was done up in a ponytail and tied with a red ribbon. She had on just the slightest bit of lipstick. She didn't need much makeup because she was, in fact, very pretty.

"Frances was always picking on me," Nelly said to Jason. "I don't miss her. Hey, do you want a drink, maybe? I put some of my father's beer in the fridge. You wanna beer?"

"You're not trying to get me drunk so you can take advantage of me?" Jason laughed.

Nelly gave him a smile over her shoulder as she opened the fridge door and bent over to get the chilled bottles of Simon Pure. Her father kept several cases of beer in the cellar. He'd never miss the few bottles she had brought upstairs.

"You have the most beautiful eyes…" Nelly began as she handed the beer to her cousin. Goosebumps ran up her legs and arms like a high school marching band parading on a football field.

"You always were one for eyes. Remember Aunt Stella's bedroom?"

"Oh God, don't remind me. That picture of St. Veronica's veil. Strange that Jesus could be so scary."

There wasn't anything scary about Jason's eyes, however. They were warm and welcoming and flecked with patient passion as he led her upstairs to the attic bedroom that had recently been relinquished to Nelly. This was it. There was no going back now, the girl realized.

Jason kissed her repeatedly, then his lips moved down her neck as his hands rubbed her ass cheeks and the backs of her thighs.

"Oh God," sighed Nelly. "What's happenin to me?"

Jason grabbed Nelly's hand and placed it between his legs. Nelly felt the hard bulge and rubbed it with the encouragement of Jason's hand on top of hers.

"What's that?" she stuttered; confused, excited and curious at the same time.

"What do you think it is?" Jason laughed.

Nelly's eyes clouded and her chin crinkled ever so slightly. "I'm so stupid, I could just cry," the girl said. "I don't know nothing. I never been wit a boy before. One time, Bobby Gomulak was showin his, his "thing" to the girls in the school yard at St. Casimir's, but before me and Marsha got there Sister Superior had already dragged him to the office."

"That's precious," chuckled Jason. "You're something else."

"It's no fun bein stupid," Nelly protested looking at her cousin with frightened expectation. Before she could voice a protest of any kind, Jason removed her sneakers and socks and her blouse and shorts. He undid her bra with enough ease to tell Nelly that he had obviously done this before. Then he unceremoniously yanked her panties down and stepped back to admire her.

Nelly stood open mouthed with embarrassed excitement. She instinctively cowered. Jason stepped forward,

"God, you're beautiful," Jason gushed.

Nelly could see that the boy's erection had not subsided. My God, what was gonna happen next, she wondered.

Jason led Nelly to the edge of the bed where he sat her down.

"Keep your legs open," he said. "You ever play with yourself?" he asked. "You ever get an orgasm doing it?"

"What's a orgasm?"

Nelly watched in awe as Jason rubbed her; slowly, gently, but steadily.

"Jason, Jason, I think maybe we should stop? I never felt like this before. I..." Nelly stammered.

"Forget it," Jason said. "Alia jacta est."

He then planted the heels of her feet on the bed and spread her legs wide open. Nelly watched as her cousin's finger disappeared inside of her with an accompanying rush of blood to her head that made her dizzy. She looked puzzled. Her face was as red as her discarded shorts on the floor.

"Take a deep breath," Jason commanded as he stood beside her and moved his finger around and around while massaging the tip of her pussy with his thumb.

Nelly gasped. Faster and faster went Jason's finger. The girl's thighs began to twitch. She couldn't speak. She couldn't breathe. She looked around for help. Her hands knotted the bedspread in a death grip.

"Stop, Jason. Stop, please, matka bosca," she finally managed to whisper. "Something's happening. I'm afraid."

Her cousin merely laughed and continued his assault.

"Jaason! Jason! Oh, my God."

The mounting tension followed by the sudden release exploded over Nelly. She didn't know where she was. She involuntarily clamped her legs shut and fell backwards onto the bed. Her head was spinning. When she opened her eyes again Jason was kneeling next to her. His clothes were off and he was fitting something around his penis. He snapped it into place and smiled at her.

"Ready?" he asked.

She didn't know what he meant. There was more?

"I'll be as gentle as I can, but it's going to hurt a bit. You OK?"

Nelly nodded and unquestioningly spread her legs. Later as they lay tangled in the bedspread and each other's arms Nelly and Jason casually talked and confided in each other like a familiar married couple.

"No wonder the nuns don't want us to have sex. If the girls ever found out how good it was dere'd be nobody left in Catholic school," said Nelly. She kissed Jason on the forehead.

"You're not in pain?" he asked.

"A little bit, but when you hold me, it goes away."

"I don't know how you can tolerate those nuns," Jason added.

"We can't wear no make-up, or fix our hair. It's a sin. Everything's a sin. I remember one time Sylvia Burkowski came to school wit her hair all done up in a French twist. It looked real nice. She just stood up for her cousin's wedding. Sister Superior grabbed her by the hair, dragged her into the bathroom and stuck her head under the cold water. I seen Sylvia leavin school. Her hair was all straight and wet and she was cryin."

"Jesus, it sounds like the Inquisition. Why do you put up with it?"

"My parents, whadda you think. Remember, there are boys in the public high schools. And after Frances getting pregnant I can hardly leave the house. My father called before you got here just to check up on me."

"Well, Catholic school didn't do your sister much good."

"Me neither I guess, but it just feels so good being with you," Nelly said. "And I'm glad it's over and you were the one. When do you gotta go home?"

"I don't," said Jason, his eyes with a sparkle that drew Nelly like a magnet. "I told my parents I was sleeping over at a friend's house in Kaisertown."

Nelly realized that she had told Jason her mother and father were gone for the entire weekend and this was only Friday. She looked at him inquisitively.

"Because I was hoping," Jason continued, "that if everything worked out, I'd spend the night with you."

"Here? With me?"

"Sure, if you want me to?"

"Ha," stammered Nelly in happiness. "And I could fix us something to eat. It would be like playing house, but more real this time. And we'd sleep together too? All night?"

Jason grabbed Nelly and swung her on top of him. "Yes, but only if you ask me real nice. Ask me to stay here and sleep with you and fuck you all night long."

"Jason, I'm shy to say that word."

"Come on. I want to hear you say it. Say it for me and the nuns too."

Nelly sat up straddling Jason's body. She made the sign of the cross, then laid her face on his shoulder and whispered in his ear.

"Please," she said. "Stay with me tonight. Stay and fuck me. Fuck me. I want you to."

Barney's Tavern: Casimir Street:

Pije Kuba do jakub

Jakub do michala

Pije ja pije t

Kompania cala

Polish Drinking Song

The pink neon sign outside the tavern blinked sporadically in the night: "Barne", "Barn", "Barne". The passage of years had exacted a steady erosion of its letters. The "s" was the first to grow pale and wink out of existence. The "y" vanished next. Currently it was the "e" which struggled for survival trying desperately to prevent itself from following its alphabetical brethren into the dark Kaisertown night.

The tavern's owner, Barney Andrzejewski, however, wasn't about to replace or repair the sign. After all, the saloon's clientele was a fixed commodity, a known number of neighborhood men, and a few women, whose presence was dictated more by weather and the arrival of the weekly paycheck than to any advertising. If there was no sign at all, Barney reasoned, the exact same number of customers would show up.

"Barney's" was set in the middle of the block on Casimir Street between Weimer and Weiss and it drew its customers from a five to six block area which extended along Casimir and down several side streets to Clinton Street. It was an average sized Kaisertown drinking establishment, not as spacious or fancy as Ray's Supper Club at the edge of town, nor as run down as Onkoniewski's just down the street. It nevertheless provided Barney and his wife with an income that made them the envy of all their patrons and neighbors as well as few of their competitors as well.

A long, high wooden bar with a dozen stools ran the length of the front tavern. On the wall beyond the bar stood a large mirror which served to reflect and exaggerate the number of liquor bottles lining the staggered shelves in front of it. A counter top door that lifted on hinges allowed access to the area behind the bar and to the kitchen beyond. A large, noisy, old fashioned styled cash register monopolized one end of the bar. Bare, round topped, wire legged tables and matching chairs filled out the room proper. The floor under them was gray with age and speckled with bits of mop that clung like lost hair to the rough sections of the narrow hardwoods strips. The windows were opaque with dust and settled cigarette smoke.

There were no pool tables or juke boxes inside Barney's place. Little in the way of adornment graced the rooms. A lone plastic Corbie's parrot swung on a perch over the kitchen door, a Simon Pure clock kept incorrect time above the back room entrance, and on one wall sat a large framed photograph of a group of dancing krakowiankas. Several of the peasant women had their skirts blown high in the festive air revealing plump, bare Polish buttocks underneath.

The back room, which had been used primarily for Friday and Saturday night dinners and dances, contained a dozen tables as well as a small dance floor and an elevated stage at one end of the room. An upright piano, three music stands and chairs occupied the stage which was abandoned now.

It was Saturday morning and Barney was setting up the bar at his usual hour of 7:00 AM. Large jars of sliced pickles, blind robins and pickled eggs were set out on the counter accompanied by baskets of salty soda crackers, fat pretzel sticks thick with salt and trays of salted peanuts.

Barney checked the beer spigots above the sink after making sure the big kegs in the basement were tapped and ready. All liquor bottles were examined. Those containing only one or two shots were replaced with new bottles.

Jeanette would be down at ten o'clock to get the kitchen ready for serving later in the day. However, Barney and his wife no longer bothered with elaborate meals. At one time they had a good fish fry, but it proved to be too much work.

'By the time you pay for yer help, it ain't wort it,' reasoned Barney. So now they served just sandwiches: good roast beef on weck, fried baloney on an egg roll, and kielbasa on rye bread. Barney and Jeanette did almost all the work themselves hiring one extra girl only on Saturday nights.

Barney instinctively distrusted all hired help anyway, convinced they were either lazy or deceitful, or both. In this regard he often told the story of Joe Chipua from Orange Front and how Joe once hired a bartender to help out after the old man had a minor stroke. Help out for sure! The guy robbed old Chipua blind, screwed his wife, and took off with the cash receipts and half the liquor stock. Old Chipua, unable to cope with the financial loss and embarrassment, "took the pipe" as they said.

Barney was a big man, fully six feet tall and over two hundred pounds. He was good looking and at age forty-five had a full head of black hair. He was good natured as a rule because it was good for business. He didn't have much formal education, but he knew how to make a buck, and that, after all, was what life was all about, wasn't it?

A bartender was a good catch in Kaisertown to say the least, and

Barney had his pick of women, but he chose plain Jeanette Sobczyk as his bride. No pretty, delicate baby dolls with their fancy hairdos, polished nails and expensive clothes for Barney. He needed a worker, plain and simple, and he got one in Jeanette. She was loyal, thankful, and deferred all decisions without question to her husband.

At eight o'clock Barney's first customer of the day walked through the door. It was Jimmy Pajak, owner of Pajak's Plumbing across the street. Jimmy always stopped in for a shot or two before beginning his own work day.

"Ale zimno, nie?" Jimmy began as he took a seat at the bar. "Snow priddy soon."

"Good for the business. Gets the customers inside," replied Barney. "But den you got yer heatin bills too. Always somtin when you work for yerself. An how's the plumbin business?"

"Shitty, I gotta go by Formek's and fix the sewer pipe. I tink the old lady flushed down one of her rags again. Taki pipa jaki fox hole," Jimmy chuckled. "When the old man's screwin her he's gotta strap a two by four to his dupa so he don't fall in."

Barney passed a shot of Wilson's over to Jimmy, and poured one for himself.

"Ten co rychlo staja, temi pan Bog daje," he said with lifted glass. "And as long as people drink, dere's gonna be saloons."

"And as long as people shit, dere's gonna be plumbers," added Jimmy with a smile that flashed two golden teeth in the front of his mouth.

By ten o'clock there were a dozen men in Barney's place. Two of them, Eddie Gowron from Weiss St. and Vince Ziemba from Cable were seated at a table near the front windows. Vince smoked a corn cob pipe and sent blue circles of smoke into the air at regular intervals while his companion constantly shuffled a pinochle deck. They were waiting for two more pals to arrive to round out a game: twenty-five cents for four hands around and an extra dime for a bid hole.

"Hey Barney," shouted Vince across the room. "Pamietasz dat time Thadeus got dah thousand aces? Dat Thadeus, he doan know how to play for gowno, but he's got dah luck, nie?"

"I radder have dah luck," added Eddie. "You can be dah bess player, but witout dah luck an dah cards, you can't do nuttin."

"Hey, when's Tony comin?" someone else chimed in. "I taught he'd be here by now."

"Pretty soon," replied Barney. "What you got a winner dis week?"

"I dunno."

And the man dug into his pockets and pulled out several pieces of thick green folded paper. He unraveled them and put them on the bar pressing the thick tickets down with his thumb.

"Jim Rogowski won fifty dollars lass week," someone volunteered.

"Yeah, but how much he spend over dah weeks and weeks he play? He never tells you dat."

Two men in the middle of the barroom were listening to a third tell a story about two sisters. Each man had an empty shot glass and a partially filled beer glass in front of him. Like all the men in the establishment, they were between fifty and sixty years of age.

"Dah young sister," the man recounted, "who was real good lookin and had lots a boyfriends, was always pickin on her older sister who was taki plain, you know, a real old maid who never had no dates.

"After a while dah young one got married. Her husband was a foreman by Moog Valve, makin good money. Dey moved by Orchard Park, a beautiful house. But still she was always pickin on her old sister, makin fun out of her. 'Poor Alica, too bad you can't find a man. Yer not getting any younger. Runnin out a time.'

"Den sure enough," the man continued. "Dah old, ugly one, she gets a man, a guy at her work by Trico. Dah old maid she's like a new person now. Wearin makeup and new clothes. Goin out wit her man. Happy. So what happens next?

"Dah husband of dah good lookin sister dies, heart attack. He leaves her wit everything all paid for: house, two cars, cottage by Silver Creek, from the insurance, you know. Den what do yous tink?"

The man paused for effect. "Dah young one turns around and steals dah boyfriend away from her own sister, dah ugly one, and marries him. Weddin was jus dis spring by Precious Blood and she sent a invitation to her sister on top of it. Whadda yous tink about dat?"

Just then the bar room door swung open and several men burst into the establishment amid an explosion of shouting and laughter. Big Tony Kasinski was the central figure in the maelstrom. An imposing figure at six feet tall and well over three hundred pounds, he was hard to overlook.

"Czekaj! Czekaj!" he hollered as he made his way to the bar and heaved his bulk onto a stool which seemed to cry out from its burden.

"One day dah coppers follow me in and it's all over," he good humoredly complained. "OK, dah winnin numbers now."

Barney pulled out the dozen tickets he had in the cash register drawer. He bought them more in order to keep Tony coming around and drawing in the crowds than in any expectation of actually winning. Also, if one of the customers won, they would more than likely spend a good deal of the prize money right there in the saloon. Last year Mickey Gomulak won thirty dollars and had half of it spent before that bastard Black Vic persuaded him to go home and share the money with his family. Tony shouted out the winning numbers amid grumblings from the crowd. No winning numbers.

"Number 764! What about 764?" someone shouted from the rear of the room.

"Zeby babka miala jajka to by byla dziadkiem," came a voice in reply amid a hail of laughter.

When the number calling was over Tony bought a round of drinks for the house. Five kids and not a pot to piss in, thought Barney. He was glad he and Jeanette did not have children. Couldn't afford them.

Thadeus Nowicki strolled into the bar dressed in his weekend best topped off by a wide hat with a small red feather stuck in the band.

"Chodz tutaj, Thadeus. We're waitin. I'm dealin dah aces for partners."

The card players and other patrons of Barney's place were in the best of moods. This was Saturday, their first day off after a long week of work, and this was their place, their sanctuary. No women. Just friends, laughing, drinking, smoking, and telling stories and lies.

"Saturday is dah best day a dah week," proclaimed Lefty Gardon as he lifted his glass in an informal toast. "Friday yer still tired from work, and you only got half a day. Sunday it's church and get ready worrying about dah job on Monday. But Saturday dere's nothin but Saturday all around and you got no worries."

"Twenny-one," said Eddie Gowron peering at his cards through a cloud of cigarette smoke which wafted up from the butt tightly clenched in his teeth.

"Pamietasz, extra ten cents a bid hole," cautioned Thadeus.

"Hey, no cross boardin yous two," said Vince Ziemba. "Pass."

At ten o'clock Jeanette came down from the upstairs apartment. She was a small, puddle plain woman, flat chested with a slight pot belly. Her graying brown hair was pinned behind her head with two large plastic clips. A cigarette dangled from her lips which were insincerely pasted with red lipstick.

Barney eyed his wife suspiciously checking to see if she had been drinking again. That's all he needed on his busiest day: a loud mouthed wife and her stupid irritating laugh, forgetting orders, and giving away drinks. Then Barney would have to take her into the kitchen for a few quick sobering slaps across the face. Jeanette waved to everyone.

"Hiyah guys. Who's winnin? Thadeus again? You owe me a drink from lass time. Remember when I said you were gonna win wit dat hand? Ha, ha, ha."

Jeanette tilted her head back and laughed showing her nicotine stained teeth.

"Hiyah honey," she said to Barney and pecked him on the cheek.

Barney compressed his lips, but did not kiss his wife. No odor of alcohol though so Barney smiled contentedly. Back at the bar he watched Jeanette through the open kitchen door: a good cook, a good worker, good.

Once the smell of cooking kielbasa filled the air, the patrons' thoughts turned to food. Of course, there were a few holdouts who preferred the glow of unadulterated booze sloshing in their stomachs, but the majority grew ravenous.

All sales were rung up by Barney who loved nothing more in life than the sound of the cash register: the "chick", "chick", "chick" of the numbers popping up on the top of the machine, the tally button with its "jing, jing" sound, and then the loud "ka-ching" when the door opened. The sweet sounds of success.

By three o'clock the tavern was in high gear. Twelve men squabbled and played pinochle at the three tables nearest the windows. Opposite them another six were engaged in a poker game. The stools at the bar were all occupied. The air was blue with smoke and cooking odors. And all around this whirled Barney, serving drinks and collecting money with both hands while Jeanette fed order after order of food onto the bar.

The only female patron to enter the saloon during that busy afternoon was Florence Wilczak who was naturally escorted by her husband, Hank. Although many women used to show up on Saturday nights when Poncho and his band were playing hardly any ventured in now. This was the man's time, and women were not welcome.

"What's he bringin his wife in here for?"

"He takes her everywhere. Piorun! When he goes to dah corner store for a quart a milk, it's like he's goin overseas. 'Oh honey, doan be gone too long. I miss you. Kiss. Kiss.'"

"Psia krew, dey still hold hands when dey walk down dah street. He can't wipe his ass witout her checkin dah paper for rough spots."

Pan and Pani Wilczak made their way into the back room where Jeanette set up a table by putting on a clean white tablecloth. When she came back into the bar area she accosted the gossiping men.

"Jesu Kochany, yous oughta be ashamed of yerselfs. Just jealous a man spends time wit his wife."

"I spend enough time wit my wife," responded one of the men. "She ken give me one day a week outa dah house."

"Dah only woman I wanna see on Saturday is you, Jeanette."

"What yous got married for if yer always tryin to get away from yer wifes?" Jeanette continued. "Maybe dey like to go out sometimes too, have some fun insteada workin around dah house all day."

"How come I never hear you squakin and I don't see Barney takin you no place," someone added. "Yer workin all dah time."

"What do you tink Barney married her for," called out another.

The men at the bar fell silent and glanced at Barney who paused ever so slightly in his drying of the bar glasses. Jeanette didn't say anything. She just put down her tray and repositioned a few loose strands of hair.

She then cleared her throat.

"For your information, Mr. Smarty Pants, Barney already promised me a vacation in Florida. We're gonna get somebody to run dah bar for a while an he's takin me to Miami Beach. I already got dah folders and everyting. Right Barney?" she added for emphasis.

The barkeep smiled and nodded to his wife before turning an icy stare at the customer who had broached the topic in the first place.

"Dere. What I tell yah," Jeanette said proudly as she walked into the kitchen.

Several men swirled the beer in their glasses, or shuffled their feet along the foot rail of the bar until one broke the silence.

"Florida, hey Barney? Suppose to be real nice down dere. Wit dah Buffalo winters Florida's dah place to be, nie? You wouldn catch me complainin."

"Yeah Florida," Barney smirked. "I go to Florida, I gotta pay somebody to look after dah place for me. Need tree, four people an den dey rob you blind. So bedz cicho on dat Florida stuff. I can't afford it right now."

Naturally the first thing Jeanette mentioned to Barney when they had a moment alone was the Florida trip.

"Maybe dis winter, nie, Barney? You know, we gotta make plans early. Dat place, dah Seaside Castle, dat looks real good, nie?"

Jeanette's voice was filled with timid optimism and restrained excitement which needed only the slightest hint of acceptance in order to burst free. She didn't get it from her husband.

"Tak, tak, we'll talk later. Now get dem sandwiches out. Dah table's waitin."

Jeanette was only temporarily crestfallen. "I'm fixin. I'm fixin. But we ken talk later, nie? You said."

Barney looked resignedly at his wife. She had put on a babushka while cooking and looked homelier than ever with her ears sticking out from behind the multi-colored fabric. Taki duzy ears, he thought. She should cover them.

At four o'clock the doors of the tavern swung open and in walked a tall, wiry man about seventy years of age. He took long strides into the room. His hair, which was only partially hidden by a brown fisherman's cap, was as white as his cotton colored handlebar mustache. The latter, however, was darkly yellowed along the upper lip from years of cigarette smoking. The man wore a sheepskin vest, a checkered flannel shirt, and well-worn overalls held up by thick red suspenders. It was Eddie, the Red, Kaisertown's most notorious citizen.

Eddie stood in the corner of the bar. He never sat down in a saloon and never presented his back to anyone. He was a bit "spooked" he claimed from the constant assaults in the Western mining towns where the cops, bosses' men, and scabs regularly tangled with the Wobbly miners.

Eddie was proud to call himself a Wobbly back then in what he called the most dramatic era in American history. That was when the working class almost won its battle with the capitalists before the social-ists split apart and the workers settled for Gompers' sellout unionism.

"The IWW was the only real class conscious union America ever had," he proclaimed. "We were together in everything. We never wa-vered. Nobody crossed our line. We felt for each other, fought for each other, and died for each other and our union. Your unions today are sell outs. They bargain away the rights of workers. They say that the unions and capitalists are brothers. Yeah, Cain and Abel were brothers too."

"Hey Eddie," one of the card players shouted. "We ain't got it so bad. We got a good union at Worthington. I got a nice house. Pieniadze. I'm here in dah saloon spending it. What more do I want?"

"Freedom, economic freedom, control of production, call it what you want, comrade," replied Eddie. "The capitalist bosses ain't so stupid like you think. They know you better then you know yerselves."

"Aw, go on," the man insisted. "If you ask me our union is doin good."

"Give the slaves a union, does it mean they're free?" replied Eddie.

Barney stood on the far side of the bar listening only casually to Eddie, the Red's harangue. Barney had heard it all before, and frankly, if Eddie had not been good for business he would have told him to get out long ago.

He probably never worked a day in his life anyway, mused Barney. What does he call me all dah time, "a pretty capitalist"? Yeah, if workin around dah clock, an worryin, an savin to fix up yer business is bein "pretty" den maybe he's right. But dere ain't nuttin pretty about it. It's hard work.

Eddie, the Red, drained his glass of beer, and walked to the door.

"Remember, stick together as working class brothers," he cried. "You have nothing to lose but yer chains."

"Solidernosc? Who's he tryin to kid?" someone at the bar muttered. "It'll never happen."

Barney looked up at the clock: almost five o'clock. Time for his nap. "Chodz tutaj," he called to Jeanette who came promptly and happily to the bar.

"Id's OK, honey," she said. "I take over. You go an have a nice nap."

Barney made a mental note of his wife's excessive cheerfulness. She wasn't fooling him. She still had that Florida business on her mind. He'd deal with it later. Right now he needed a break. Forty-five minutes would do. Then he'd be ready to go once again. As he climbed the stairs to their apartment he could hear the jingling of the cash register. Good. She's a good woman. If I could afford dat Florida trip, I take her, he thought.

Upstairs Barney shut the windows and began to close the blinds. Just in time too because he could see and hear the cars filled with wild teenagers racing down Casimir Street. Their radios were blaring, bodies hanging out of the windows, screaming and shaking their fists at one another.

"Young punks," Barney said lout loud. "Taki idiots wit dere stupid cars. What's dis world comin to? Everybody's godda have a car."

Jason: Stonewallski to the Rescue

Jason sat in the parlor waiting for his mother to get dressed for
church. Why the hell does it always take her so long, he wondered. Opposite him his father sat reading U.S.A. a novel by John Dos
Passos, while the strains of Beethoven's "Kreutzer Sonata" played in
the background. His father was well dressed also, but he wasn't going to
church.

"I sympathize. Believe me," Jason's father said without looking up.
"But I promised your mother you'd attend church until you were sixteen
at least. I spared you Catholic school, can't you hang on a little longer?
You're almost sixteen now."

"This summer, but I'll be a raving lunatic by then," Jason answered.
"I'm so bored I could chew my arm off."

"Look, I've got an idea," said his father. "Let's find something good
for you to read in church. It will keep your mind occupied."

"If the Polish panis or the priest see me reading something other than
the Bible or a prayer book, I'll be excommunicated on the spot. As it is I
get dirty looks from Pani Dombrowski whenever I move a muscle out of
turn. 'Whad you got it ents in yer pents?'

His father smiled. "Life is full of sacrifices," he said. "But here, I've
got just the thing for you, and it's pretty ironic for church too."

He handed Jason a three volume set of books with soft purple leather
covers and golden edged pages and similarly colored ribbon markers.

They looked exactly like three small prayer books. Jason knew them immediately from his father's library, The Complete Works of Edgar Allan Poe. He had already read, "The Tell Tale Heart", "The Cask of Amontillado", and "The Raven" at school. He thumbed through the other titles: "Masque of the Red Death", "The Black Cat", and "The Murders in the Rue Morgue". Perfect!

If Father Kolinski ever saw these he'd choke on his communion wafers, Jason thought as he tucked one volume under his arm. "Thanks."

It was obvious that Holy Mother, the Church, no longer held Jason in its spell. Now he merely went through the motions to appease his mother. And as far as he could tell the church's teachings hadn't done her, nor her church going relatives and neighbors, much good either. Pani Dombrowski, who sat behind Jason every Sunday at mass, still poisoned dogs and drowned kittens. Mr. Durlak swore and chased after anyone who so much as stepped on his grass, yet he never missed church. Every Halloween old man Mynka tarred his driveway to keep the kids away. Pan Grabski drank up his paycheck every Friday night at Stan's Bar while his family went hungry. And he and Hank Adamchek, who beat his wife and kids regularly, were up standing members of the Holy Name Society.

The entire ceremony of the mass seemed absurd and barbaric to Jason. People kneeling at an altar with their mouths open waiting for the "flesh and blood of Christ". Bells, candles, holy water, and censors belching smoke. This was the 1960s for Christ's sake, the age of science. The church was stuck in the Dark Ages, and that's where it belonged. Now at least Jason had his Poe books. No one detected the switch and although his mother may have had her suspicions, she never said anything.

Many things changed for Jason that year. A few weeks into the winter season, for instance, found him on a bus with his father traveling to see, "the Professor", his father's secret friend. Jason did not know much about the man except that he loved literature and classical music and was totally detested by Jason's mother. In the past, the mere mention of his name was enough to initiate a terrible argument in the Novak household.

The NFT bus moved along Clinton St. The Novak family had no car. The familiar sights of Kaisertown passed by as Jason looked out the window: St. Bernard's Church, Kent's Drug Store, Dr. Kalinowski's office, Buszka's Funeral Home, Orange Front, Mr. Frost's Shop, the Garden of Sweets, and the Strand Show. Periodically the big bus was pelted by a cascade of snowballs as the Kaisertown children indulged in one of the favorite winter pastimes. There was certainly no shortage of ammunition. When the bus passed Kelburn Street Jason's father nudged him.

"Your other grandmother lives there," he said. "Third house from the corner."

"How come I've never met her?" Jason inquired.

"Your mother doesn't like her very much."

"Oh boy, another one. I know she also hates the Professor so how come all of a sudden she's letting me meet him?"

"I convinced her that he would be an invaluable aid in your schooling especially once you're in college, which is true, of course."

"What does she have against him anyway?"

"It's a long story. Let's just say they don't share common interests and aren't willing to compromise."

"Why do they call him the Professor? Is he a teacher?"

Jason's father laughed. "No, it actually began as a derogatory term, from your mother naturally, which somehow humorously stuck. Allen Clark, which is his actual name, ironically works for the City of Buffalo as an operator at the South Ogden incinerator plant. He's a garbage man in other words.

"You're kidding?"

"No, you see he doesn't want the time consuming worries of a career cluttering up his mind. He wants it free to pursue the classics of music and literature. Nothing else matters. You won't find him discussing sports, or the movies, or the weather."

"Thanks for the warning."

From downtown Buffalo, Jason and his father transferred to a Niagara Street bus which took them to DeWitt Street It was a short walk to Number 1865.

"He rents an upper flat," Jason's father explained. "Spends all his money on books and records. He doesn't much care where he lives as long as it's inexpensive. He's taught me a lot over the years, and I hope he does the same for you."

The more Jason knew about the Professor, the more worried he got. How would he measure up? What would he say?

The house at 1865 DeWitt was, in Jason's mind, a total dump. Alongside a rickety front porch, a long narrow enclosed stairway led to the second floor. This was the entrance to the Professor's lair. It could have been a scene from a Dickens' novel. The stairs were narrow and slanted and lined with debris. Grocery bags filled with dozens of empty cans of tuna fish and tomato juice along with wooden cases of Vernor's Ginger Ale crowded the top landing.

The apartment door was partially open and a puff of hot, humid, and musty air hit Jason square in the face as he stared wide-eyed at the entrance. Never, even on her death bed, would his mother have allowed her kitchen to look like this. The sink and countertop were buried under an avalanche of unwashed cups, plates, glasses and utensils. The Professor must have exhausted his entire supply, figured Jason. The faucet dripped a steady staccato of water into a grease slicked sink while pots and pans obscured every element on the stove. Atop the kitchen table stood piles of magazines and newspapers: "Life", "Look", "The New York Times", and "The Weekly People" among them. Standing in an interior hallway that led into the rest of the flat stood a tall, barrel-chested man with a decidedly ugly twist to one side of his mouth. He wore a loose fitting, wrinkled maroon colored bathrobe. On his feet he had on a pair of un-laced salt-stained black shoes with no socks.

"Hi there. You must be Jason. Come in," said the man and he disap-peared into the darkness behind him.

Entering the living room, the boy saw books everywhere: books on shelves, books on the furniture and spilling off the coffee and end tables, books piled on the floor. Jason's father had a library too, but this was an Alexandria, though a totally messy one. The Professor motioned Jason to a chair nearly inaccessible save for a narrow pathway through piles of literary debris. Jason's father sat on the one exposed cushion of the couch. The Professor preferred to stand. There wasn't another clear spot available in the room anyway.

The man immediately offered Jason several books to peruse while the bulk of the conversation took place between the adults. Jason felt like a child bought off with a bag of candy. Nevertheless, he soon found himself engrossed in one of the books entitled, Our Living Planet. It dealt with the Earth's origin and the evolution of life on the planet and was filled with fascinating illustrations and photographs. Every now and then snippets of the adults' conversation would intrude on his reading and Jason would stop to listen.

"There's another point I want to mention about this here Kennedy," the Professor said. "He's not going to be any hero of the working class. Daddy's millions got him elected and he's not about to forget whose side he's on. Let me just read you this from one of his campaign speeches and you tell me who he sounds like." 'The enemy is the Communist system itself – implacable, insatiable, unceasing in its drive for world domination. For this is not a struggle for the supremacy of arms alone – it is also a struggle for supremacy between two conflicting ideologies: Freedom under God versus ruthless, godless tyranny.'"

"Sounds like our friend, Joe McCarthy, for sure," replied Jason's father. "But who was it that said the Communists are so invaluable for propaganda purposes and the suspension of civil rights here in America that if they weren't around the U.S. government would have to invent them?"

The Professor let out a squeal of laughter. Rather irritating, Jason thought. "That was none other than Dwight Eisenhower. He understood that all this government repression with the CIA and Hoover's FBI, wouldn't be half so easy if you didn't have the bogeyman of Communism around to scare the American people into actually giving up their own hard won rights and freedoms. It's an age old trick, but it always seems to work."

"So much for learning from the lessons of history," Jason's father added.

"And another thing," continued the Professor. "This here Kennedy's got so much goin for him right now: boyish good looks, Harvard education, ex-Navy man, high society wife, but do you remember the story of Croesus?"

It took Jason a minute to realize that the Professor was actually talking to him on this last point. He tried to gather his wits, then finally blurted out.

"Wasn't he some ancient king; very wealthy, obsessed with wealth like Midas?"

"True. He's got it, Ed. But Croesus was historical, of course, and Midas just a character in Greek legend. Anyway the thing about Croesus was this. He was very rich, you're right, sort of the J. Paul Getty of his time. One day he was bragging while displaying his wealth to the wise man, Solon.

'Wouldn't you call such a man who possess the riches I have, happy?' he said. To which Solon replied: 'Call no man happy until you see how he dies.'

"Many years later in a war with Cyrus of Persia, Croesus was captured and as he was tied to a stake and about to have molten gold poured down his throat he shouted out those fateful words of Solon: 'Call no man happy until you see how he dies.'

"I always remember that story, Ed. Here's another thing. I wanna give you this here copy of Dos Passos', "Three Soldiers". I know you're reading, U.S.A. his great opus, but I'll tell you this "Three Soldiers" is worth a place on your bookshelf. I was in the army stationed in Hawaii after the war and I know all about this bullshit military discipline. I can relate to the book. This god damn oppressive regimentation, it kills your spirit. You're a nobody in the army; no rights, no freedoms, no individuality. Even the toilets in the bathrooms were lined up in a long row with no partitions in between."

Jason cringed at the thought and looked with sympathy at the Professor for the first time. But the Professor did not dwell on himself for long.

"You know, Ed, it's shameful to recount that Dos Passos, after the Depression and the Thirties, became a turncoat to his own artistic personality. I often question what really happened to cause him to become so reactionary. Did you know that after the genesis of his great novel, he turned around and became a F.D.R. man?"

Jason's father nodded. "Yes, I know, but there was some great social criticism in that book. I love the quote he's got in there from Debs."

The Professor immediately turned, took a book from one of his shelves, and thumbed through it. "Here it is," the Professor proclaimed with a wave of his hand. 'I am not a labor leader. I don't want you to follow me or anyone else. If you are looking for a Moses to lead you out of the capitalist wilderness, you will stay right where you are. I would not lead you into the Promised Land if I could because if I could lead you in, someone else could lead you out.'"

The Professor shut the book with a thump; then held it up. "You got this on the one hand," he said. "And then you got that Hemingway. I mean, yes, Hemingway has this literary style: clipped, blunt, journalistic, but his stuff is a constant reiteration of the same old themes: men without women, war stories, the aimless superficialities of the Thirties. His reputation is way over done. You watch, Ed, all his best stuff is behind him and that can be limited to <u>For Whom the Bell Tolls,</u> and his short story, "The Snows of Kilimanjaro". The former is a truly great story, an epic poem virtually, and the latter, I would rank that as one of the best short stories ever written. You can't touch him when he writes like that, but he doesn't write like that very often.

"You know, Ed, there were a lot of writers of the era who showed great promise, and then lost it, or abandoned it like Dos Passos. I'm thinking now of a poetess. I would consider her one of the three greatest female poets in the English language."

Jason's father furrowed his brow as the Professor pointed at him for an answer.

"She's America's greatest sonneteer. Been dead a decade now."

"Millay," replied Jason's father.

"Correct," the Professor shouted. "Edna St. Vincent Millay. I love the melodious ring of her full name. It's like Wolfgang Amadeus Mozart. It's the Amadeus that gives the name its magic. You know Gotlieb in German has the same meaning, 'Beloved of God' as Amadeus. Thank goodness

Papa Mozart also had a musical ear when it came to selecting a name for his son."

Jason recognized the name of Millay from his high school English class. He almost raised his hand.

"Is, isn't she the poetess who wrote, "My Candle Burns at Both Ends" he stammered.

The Professor turned a sardonic smile on the boy. "Yes, but I'm not talking about that twaddle pushed for mass consumption."

He returned his gaze to Jason's father.

"It's her sonnets that are works of art and for these she's been almost totally forgotten. You know she wrote that propaganda shit during the war, and she always regretted it. The pressure on these artists to compromise their work is enormous. Difficult to say, no, to the money that is thrown at you."

In the meantime, Jason felt like a bird shot out of the sky on its fledgling flight, but then he caught the eye of his father. Jason saw his dad wink, then smile. Don't let it bother you he seemed to say. Jason returned the smile and picked up the next book. It was a pictorial history of the Civil War filled with Mathew Brady's photographs. The Professor obviously knew of Jason's interest in that conflict.

"Do you know in which war the U.S. suffered the most casualties in its history, Jason?" the Professor asked.

"The Civil War."

"That's right. Most people would have answered, World War II, but you see in the Civil War every dead and wounded soldier on both sides was a U.S. casualty. Now here's another one for you. Which army in the year 1865 was the largest single fighting force on the globe?"

"The Army of the Potomac."

"Right again," said the Professor with absolute glee.

"I know the commanders of the Army of the Potomac," added Jason trying to press home his redemption in the Professor's eyes.

"In order?" the man asked.

"OK," Jason checked the names off his fingers as he went along. "First there was George McClellan, but he spent too much time organizing and stalling and not fighting so Lincoln replaced him with General Burnside. But Burnside was just no good and he lost to the Confederates at Fredericksburg. Then Hooker was given command, but he lost at Chancellorsville. Just before Gettysburg General George Meade was put in charge and he fought Robert E. Lee. Then it was Grant who stepped in and finished the war."

"Good, very good, said the Professor. "For a while there John Pope worked with McClellan, but McClellan was the actual commander so Pope don't count. He did a terrible job anyway."

The Professor turned to Jason's father.

"You notice how he's got them memorized? He relates the commander to some battle or some little quirk in their nature. 'McClellan stalled.' 'Hooker lost at Chancellorsville.' These extra details help you remember better. They give the memory more bulk so that it's easier to recall. I do the same thing myself."

Jason breathed a sigh of relief. Now sit back and keep your mouth shut for the rest of the meeting, he told himself. During the next two hours the meeting covered the topics of Stonewall Jackson's Valley Campaign, Cortez and the Aztecs, Shakespeare's heroines, and dueling scars in Germany. For most of the time the strains of Mozart's, "Marriage of Figaro" floated in the air. Whenever a particularly beloved passage was played, the Professor immediately waved his arms like a school teacher demanding silence. Then he'd stand with his eyes closed as though in a trance. Afterwards his eyes would flash open and he'd continue the discourse as though nothing had happened.

When Jason's father finally rose to terminate the session, the Professor got upset. "I got more stuff here to cover, Ed. I didn't get to Emily and her sister, Vinnie, and this here Mabel Loomis Todd."

"Allen, look at it this way," Jason's father explained. "If this meeting works out, and Jason's mother approves, we will all be able to see each other more frequently."

"Vale! Vale! The Professor called as Jason and his father descended the stairs.

After his inaugural debut Jason nevertheless missed the next session with the Professor. Turned out he had a meeting already set up with his cousin Larry Bingkowski.

"I didn't know you and Larry got along so well," commented Jason's father. "He's a fair bit older than you isn't he and not exactly the studious type?"

"He's nineteen. He's a working class kind of guy."

"OK, fair enough."

Jason wasn't that familiar with the Houghton Park end of Kaisertown where Larry lived. It was a rough neighborhood filled with young toughs eager to bully and fight any strangers who ventured inside their turf. And Jason, with his slim build, and "bedroom eyes" certainly would have attracted the bullying element except for one factor. He just happened to be the first cousin and close friend of perhaps the toughest guy in Kaisertown, Larry Bingkowski. With the acknowledgement of such kinship any hostility was immediately brushed aside like the waters of the Red Sea with Moses standing on the shore.

Just what drew Jason and his cousin, Larry, together was a mystery to both boys. Maybe it was the absolute disparity of their backgrounds that attracted them like the opposite poles of a magnet. Each was fascinated by the world represented by the other, a world shut off from them by background, personality, and opportunity.

Jason met his cousin in front of Babe's Ice Cream Parlor where several cars were parked with windows rolled down and radios blaring. The drivers and male occupants talked to friends along the sidewalk and tried whenever possible to coax young ladies in for a ride. Everyone was enjoying the refreshing exuberance of a new springtime in the city.

As usually happened Jason found himself regaling the guys with stories from history and literature. He had a multitude to choose from since the boys were generally unfamiliar with anything that happened beyond the borders of Kaisertown itself.

"Hey man, tell us dat story about dah mummy. You know, dah real one dere dat dey found in Egypt dat time," asked Deano, one of the regular gang.

"That was when and why all those Boris Karloff movies came out," Jason said. "Wee, Ohh, Wee, Ohh," he continued, mimicking the sounds of eerie movie music. "The mummy walks the night searching for the sacred… tanna fly leaves, and the reincarnated body of his ancient love, Clit-o-patra."

"Yeah man," said Corny Cornichewski, "I love dat fuckin mummy. Everybody's tearin ass away from him an he's barely fuckin movin, draggin dat leg a his, you know. And what happens later on when everybody's tired out? Who's dat comin around dah corner? You guessed it, man. It's dah fuckin mummy. Dat cock sucker never stops."

"Just like the tortoise and the hare," Jason said.

"What's a tortoise?"

"What dah fuck is a hare?"

"Never mind," replied Jason. "Actually, it was a guy named Howard Carter who discovered the tomb of Tutankamen. It was buried under the debris from other temples and tombs that had been looted in the past. Grave robbers were always bustin in and stealing all the gold and jewels that were buried with the pharaohs."

"I like dem big words he uses," cut in Pruny, a bulky, strong fellow.

"Anyway, when Carter opened the tomb it contained the richest find ever discovered: priceless artifacts, gold, ivory, gems. And remember Tut was just a minor pharaoh, a kid, but his tomb was the only one that had not been robbed. But after a while several members of Howard Carter's expedition died, some unexpectedly. It was from that that the idea of the mummy's curse got started. Just a myth really."

"I don't give a shit," said Deano. "You wouldn't catch me digging around in dem old pyramids with all dem curses and dead bodies."

"Hey," interrupted Corny. "How about dat time we went to St. Stan's Cemetery?"

"Don't remind me a dat one. Fuckin Pruny busts into one a dem above ground graves, yah know. He figgers dere's bodies in dere wit rings and jewelry on dat we can steal."

"A mausoleum," Jason said.

"Fuck man, I don't know what dah name is," replied Corny, "but dere was a whole family buried in dere from way back, years ago."

"We crawled thru dis little window," Pruny continued. "You shoulda heard Deano cryin he doan wanna go in. He's afraid a ghosts."

"Fuck you, man. I was on probation."

"Was dere anyting inside?" someone asked.

"Jus names on dah walls, and you could see where dey were closed up like drawers in a dresser. But dere was nothin you could pull on to get em open. Den asshole here says he can hear somethin movin inside dah walls where dah bodies was."

"Hey, man, I did hear somethin."

"Jerk off."

"If you weren't so tough, I'd beat dah shit outa you right now," laughed Corny.

All the older and tougher guys in Kaisertown were by now either friends or so evenly matched in strength that fighting was a waste of time and energy. Their serious battles were waged with boys from outside the neighborhood. Most of the in-house fighting was done by the younger boys working their way up the pecking order.

Jason was sitting in the front seat of Larry's car and Tommy Grow-chowalski was in the backseat with his girlfriend, Linda, when Pruny stuck his head in the window to talk to Larry.

"Hey man," he said. "You know dem wops we beat dah shit outa at dah last Ryan dance? Well, dey're comin back. Joey Lombard, he goes around wit a dego broad and she told him dey were getting a gang together for dah next dance."

"How many," asked Larry?

"Maybe thirty. One bunch is comin from dah West Side, and anudder from Lovejoy, plus some is already gonna be at dah dance waitin. Once dey all get together, look out!"

"Mother fucker, we can't get half dat many even wit Chevy and Mack an some of the younger guys."

"Yous an yer stupid fights," said Linda.

"Don't kid me, baby," said Tommy flexing his arm. "You love dese muscles."

"Only one muscle dat broad loves," joked Pruny.

"Hey, watch yer mouth," shouted the girl.

"Watch yers too," laughed Pruny. "I still got yer teeth marks on my cock from last time."

"Wait a minute, man," Tommy interjected. "Doan go talkin to my broad like dat."

"Forget it, Tom," said Larry saving the boy from a fight he could never hope to win. "Pruny's only kiddin."

The group split up planning to meet again in an hour at Babe's to plot strategy for the coming fight, the rumble.

"Why not just forget about this stupid rumble?" Jason said. "Don't show up at the dance. It takes two to fight."

"Hey, dis is Kaisertown. We can't have no wops taken over."

Jason shook his head in dismay, then changed his expression. "Maybe you're right," he said with exaggerated seriousness. "We've got to stop these invading Italian hordes. They started in Italy, but was that enough for them? No, they had to move overseas to New York City, then to Buffalo crowding out the good old Polacks on the West Side. And did they stop there? Oh no! They marched on to Black Rock and Lovejoy. Now they've got their greedy eyes set on Kaisetown. Will they never be satisfied?"

Jason pounded the dashboard for mock emphasis. Larry stared at him.

"Next they'll want our businesses, good solid Polish enterprises. Goinski's Bakery's will become Guido's Pizza Parlor. No, no say it isn't so. The Orange Front will turn into Verdi's Tavern. Oh, god, why have you forsaken us? Tedlinski's into Luigi's. Nooo!"

"Yer fuckin nuts, man. You know dat don't you?" Larry smiled lighting a cigarette.

"Laugh! Scoff! I tell you the Olive Oil Menace is at our doorstep. Next they will want our women. And you know those perverted guinzoes, they, they … go down on their women. Alack, the Polack male is doomed. Arm! Arm and out. Polacks of Kaisertown unite. You have nothing to lose but your kielbasa."

Larry's cigarette bobbed off the end of his lower lip.

"I swear man, you've gone off the fuckin deep end," he said. "But, hey, what else do we got here but our turf and reputations?"

Babe's was overflowing as the Kaisertown boys gathered to discuss the upcoming "rumble". Larry and Pruny presided over a chaotic session of shouting, threatening, and boasting. Jason was going to suggest the adoption of some rules of order, but decided to withdraw to a convenient corner instead. He had no intention of engaging in the fight so why interfere in its planning.

At the next table with their backs to him sat two girls. Each had a half filled glass of Coke in front of her. Jason ordered a strawberry soda for himself, then gallantly told Babe that he'd be glad to pay for anything the two ladies wanted. With a long meeting ahead, Jason figured it might be a good time to make out with a couple of Kaisertown originals.

"Oh goodie," said one girl without the slightest hesitation. "I'll have a hot fudge sundae."

Jason smiled. OK, Diamond Jim, he said to himself. That was a fast seventy-five cents. Any more bright ideas. Let's see what damage her friend does.

"Nothing for me, thanks," said the second girl as she turned around and looked Jason in the eye.

"Ohh, hi Dorothy," gulped Jason. "Wow, how have you been? I haven't seen you since…"

"Since when, Jason?" asked the girl.

"Hey, I'm real sorry about that, but I want you to know that I had nothing to do with telling your parents."

"I know. It was my sweet little brother. Thank god he's out of my life now along with the rest of them bastards."

Jason thought back to that moment in the cellar with Dorothy standing naked in front of him. When the girl's eyes met Jason's again, he looked away.

"On second thought," said Dorothy. "I'll have a Banana Split. Janie, you can finish it for me if it's too much."

"Oh goodie," repeated Dorothy's friend.

Babe arrived with the ice cream a while later.

"Here you are. That'll be two-fifty, Jason. I even put a little extra whipped cream on top. No charge."

"Thanks, Babe," said Jason. "I don't care what all the other customers say about you, I think you're a real prince."

"Thank you, Jason," said Dorothy's companion. "By the way my name is Janie and I'm Dorothy's best friend."

"Nice to meet you, Janie. My pleasure. Enjoy yourself."

Jason watched as the girl dug into the sundae like Stachu Klemp attacking a hunk of roadkill. When he glanced over at Dorothy, she was smiling.

"Thanks, that was nice of you," she said.

In the meantime despair had settled over the meeting of the Kaisertown boys.

"We're screwed," Larry concluded. "Can't get more den twenty guys. Maybe at the dance other guys will help out if something starts up."

Pruny spotted Jason and called him over. "Hey, Jason, yer always reading dem history books. What would one a dem famous generals do? Guys like dat Alex dah Great, or Neopolitan?"

Jason stepped forward. Larry looked up hopefully.

"Actually, you might be able to do what Stonewall Jackson did during the Valley Campaign. The circumstances are similar."

Everyone started shouting. "What did he do? Who dah hell is Jackson?"

"You know, dah Battle a New Orleans, you dumb fuck."

"Yeah, he was president a long time ago. Ain't you never seen a twenty dollar bill?"

"That was Andrew Jackson," Jason explained. "I'm talking about Stonewall Jackson, the Confederate Civil War general."

"Why dey call him Stonewall?"

Jason took a deep breath. "It's a long story, and not really important. The point about Jackson was his Valley Campaign. At that time the Northern forces were planning to attack the Southern capital of Richmond. This would crush the Confederacy and make them surrender. So the Yankees decided to link up several armies that were in the area into one big army and with overwhelming manpower bash the Confederate troops who were protecting the city.

"But Stonewall Jackson messed up their plans. He took his small army and marched quickly over to confront one of the advancing Yankee armies. Since this Northern army had not yet joined forces with the other Northern troops, it was about the same size as Jackson's and Jackson defeated it. Then even as those Yankees were retreating, Jackson turned his men around and marched all the way down to another part of the Shenandoah Valley and attacked a second Northern army. Again he won the battle. The result was that the Yankee armies never did join up and the Confederate capital was saved."

Everyone in the room hunched their shoulders and looked puzzled until Larry shouted. "Perfect."

"What is?" asked Pruny.

"The Stonewall plan. We'll get our guys in cars and go by Lovejoy. Knock off dem wops over dere, den drive to Black Rock. At the end we wind up at the Ryan dance. The wops dere are waitin for dere friends, but dey ain't comin so we finish dem off. Perfect."

It turned out that the Stonewall Plan worked to perfection. Jason was at Black Rock and Lovejoy to watch the action. He almost got himself caught up in the fighting, but Larry rescued him and saved him a certain beating.

"I guess I'm more of a lover than a fighter," said Jason during the ride back to Kaisertown.

After the Ryan dance itself, when all the fighting was over, the gang of friends assembled at the back of Houghton Park to celebrate. Car doors were opened and music blared into the spotlighted darkness. Trunks held cases of beer on ice. Most of the guys were neck deep in lies and exaggerations about their part in the rumbles. More than a few were sporting noticeable injuries. Corny and two others were spending the night in the hospital.

"You know, I almost felt sorry for dem wops at dah dance," said Deano. "Dey're lookin around for dere buddies, den Bang! Man, did dey get dah shit beat outa dem."

Larry was more pensive. "Dat one wop, I seen him. He had a knife. He didn't use it, but it came close. Tings are getting scary. Fists and feet used to be enough. Next it will be knives, you wait. And who knows, one day we'll probably all be shooting at each other wit guns like in a fuckin war."

"Who are the girls over there?" asked Jason pointing to the only two females in the entourage.

"Couple a whores from the dance. Dey're not from here," said Larry. "Tommy invited em. Better hope Linda doesn't find out."

Both girls were incredibly drunk. "Hey, is this the Four H Club?" one of them asked.

"Yeah," added the other amid a squeal of laughter. "The find em, feel em, fuck em, and forget em club?"

"Bingo," said Larry to Jason as they watched from afar.

Pruny immediately strolled off into the night with one of the girls. The other was quickly surrounded by the remaining boys. She was thin and blond, not at all bad looking either, noted Jason.

"Yous really think I got nice hair?" said the girl. 'My mother says my hair was my best feature. I brush it a hundred times a day."

"I don't think she's no real blond," called a voice from the crowd.

"Maybe a bleach job?" said another.

"Only one way to tell for sure."

Several boys made a grab for the girl. "Hey, yous cut that out. And where's Mary? Where did Mary go?"

"She's out walkin wit one of the guys. Don't worry. We ain't gonna hurt you. We just wanna have some fun. Don't you?"

"Jesus, yous guys are all alike."

The boys took that for a yes, and inside a minute they had the girl stripped naked and laid across the hood of one of the cars. Several cigarette lighters winked around her body. "Yeah, she's a blond alright," was the consensus. "Who's first?"

"Hey, wait a minute," said Deano. "Where's Stonewallski? Our hero should be the first. Stonewallski, front and center. Dis is yer commandeer, General Deano E. Lee. Get up here an fuck dis broad on the double."

"Say one word, and I'll turn mercenary and work for the Italians," said Jason to Larry.

Deano looked around and waited. "OK men," continued Deano. "Looks like our hero ain't here. We godda make him proud of us. Follow me."

There were at least a dozen boys in attendance. Those who finished or were waiting a turn stood around laughing, drinking, smoking, and kibitzing on the action. Throughout all this the girl lay quietly unconcerned about the assault on her body. Except for her eyes blinking occasionally she could have been dead. Soon a rivulet of semen collected under her crotch and slowly trickled down the front of the car. Some of the boys, growing impatient, moved alongside the girl and tried to insert their penises into her mouth. The girl then came suddenly to life.

"Hey, get the hell outa here! I don't do that shit!"

The boys didn't argue. They simply circled back and resumed their places in line. Jason had seen enough and resolved to split the scene. Larry stuck around.

"See you later."

It was a beautiful spring night, warm and fragrant. A chorus of frogs sang from the quiet eddies and swampy margins of Buffalo Creek below the park. Jason headed for the gates at the Clinton Street entrance. He was a hero. He was also more than a little drunk. As he approached the exit Jason noticed someone, a girl, sitting atop the park's stone wall near the tall iron gate. The girl pounded her fist against the ledge and muttered something unintelligible. Smashing a bug, maybe a spider, he thought. A damsel in distress. Stonewallski to the rescue. Hope she's good-looking.

Where did it bite you? On the upper thigh? Remove your pants at once. I must suck out the poison. It's the only way to save your life, Jason mused as he approached, then noticed the girl was Dorothy. She was sobbing and talking to herself. Jason coughed and shuffled his feet before looking up at her.

"Oh, it's you Dorothy, thank God," he said. "I thought for a minute there I was having one of those religious visions. You know, Our Lady of Houghton Park descending from heaven to bring a message to the world, or Kaisertown anyway."

"Oh, I could give a message to Kaisertown alright," the girl said. "Go fuck yourself. How's that for a message?"

"Not exactly what I was expecting from the mouth of the Virgin Mary."

"If you're looking for a virgin, you came to the wrong wall," answered Dorothy.

"OK," said Jason. "Fair enough. What are you doing up there?"

"Contemplating suicide if it's any of your business."

"Good vocabulary."

"I guess you're not the only one capable of stringing two syllables together. Why are you bothering to talk to me anyway, now that you're such a big fuckin hero? I heard about the fight, "dah rumble". You assholes are always fighting. Am I supposed to be impressed and pull my pants down for you?"

The girl sniffled and ran the sleeve of her jacket across her nose. Jason stepped closer.

"Mind if I join you?" he asked.

When Dorothy gave no immediate response, the boy hoisted himself up onto the chest high stone wall, trying to hide the strain on his muscles.

"I'm sure your friends told you all about me by now, what a whore I am. You sure you're not looking for a piece of ass, or do you just want to find out if Kraut broads fuck differently?"

"Holy shit," said Jason. "What did I do to deserve this? I told you before, I was sorry…"

"You guys think you can do anything to a girl just because she's got a reputation," the girl broke into sobs. "God damn it, I hate when I'm like this, a little, crying sissy, but I'm sick of it."

She pounded the ledge again in anger. Jason moved closer to Dorothy. He was concerned about her hysteria and wanted to comfort her.

"Dorothy, I'm sorry. Really I am. Look, can I…"

He tried to put his arm around her, but when she felt his touch Dorothy pivoted and slapped at him. Jason lurched backward to avoid the blow and, in doing so, lost his balance. "Whoa," and he fell head first off the wall and into the dark shrubbery below.

"Jason! Jason! Are you alright?" Dorothy called down in panic.

Jason was OK, just slightly disoriented. How the hell do I get myself into these situations, he thought? Next time I see a girl crying I'm going to walk right by. 'What, you just got raped by the 7th Artillery Brigade and need a hand to get off the ground? Sorry, my wrist is sore. Doctor told me not to lift heavy objects. Bye.'

"Jason, say something. I'm sorry. I didn't mean it. Are you OK?"

"Well," replied Jason as he stood up. "If you can call having a rose bush stuck up your ass OK, then, yes, I'll survive."

Dorothy laughed as she slipped off the wall and landed beside Jason. He saw the momentary flash of her tight belly and slim hips when her jacket and blouse rode up as she descended.

"Oh good," said Dorothy. "I didn't mean to push you."

She brushed the dirt out of his hair. The glow from the street light flooded over the top of the stone wall and shined directly on Jason's face.

"Fuck, you're handsome, and those eyes," Dorothy said as she moved closer and put her hands on his shoulders. "You remember that time in our cellar when you made me take my clothes off. The time you're always apologizing for?"

"Yes, and as I said before.."

"Shhh, don't explain. You see. I liked it. It was exciting. It was just too bad my little bastard brother was there, that's all."

Dorothy pulled Jason tightly against her body. "Oh God," she sighed. "How come you're so nice? I'm not used to it."

By this time they had wandered out onto the sidewalk. A passing car suddenly stopped, then backed up.

"Oh, shit, it's him," said Dorothy. She hurriedly straightened up her hair and clothes.

"Where the fuck you been," called a voice from the car? "And who's dat asshole wit you?"

"Hey, what's the matter, Chevy?" cried another voice. "Don't you recognize him? Dat's Jason Novak, fuckin Stonewallski, man."

"He's Bingkowski's cousin," commented another.

"Good for him. Now Dorothy, how about you get yer ass in the car?" said the boy named Chevy.

Dorothy put her head down and walked to the vehicle. The door opened, she got in, and the car sped off leaving Jason alone in the night.

Jason spent more and more time at that end of Kaisertown. In the summer he joined a basketball league at Houghton Park. His asthma was a thing of the past. He had outgrown it at puberty just as Dr. Kalinowski had predicted although Jason's mother preferred to credit St. Jude to whom she had prayed religiously for twelve years.

Jason had been a starter for the South Park basketball team, but after skipping school a few times to play poker at Corny's house, the principal kicked him off the squad. That behavior had created a concern for Jason's father, a minor one anyways.

"As long as you stay focused and your marks don't drop, and more importantly, you don't get yourself into any serious trouble, I have no complaints," his father said. "You can do what you want in your spare time. Just try not to waste it."

Pruny was the captain of their basketball team which dubbed itself the "Kaisertown Confederates". It was a motley crew known for its rough and tumble style of play. They often finished games with less than the prescribed five players because of chronic fouling.

Half way through the season with the team in a surprising second place, the players decided to chip in and buy themselves jackets. They enlisted Casey Switkowski's mother, who was an expert seamstress, to stitch the name of the team on the back of the jackets. Unfortunately Pani Switkowski's spelling prowess did not match her sewing skills. When her handiwork was completed the "o" in Confederates had turned into an "u" and the "f" morphed into a "t". Finally she completely omitted the final two "e"s in the last word. The end product read: Kaisertown Cuntedrats".

"Jesus Christ, Casey, is yer mother retarded or what?"

"We paid ten bucks each for dese, "Rat Cunt" jackets. Ain't we gonna look cool?"

"And what dah fuck was you doin, Casey? Couldn't you see after she done one, dat it was all fucked up?"

"It looked OK to me. How was I supposed to know?"

The players pulled off all the lettering except for "Kaisertown" and left it at that. Anyway it wasn't long afterwards that the team was disqualified for fighting and abusing the referees.

"Dey shouldn given us no technical. Joey was the one dat got hurt," explained Tommy referring to the team's final game.

"Joey jumped on the guy's back," explained Jason. "Bad luck he got thrown off and slammed into the pole, but he started it."

Several of the players began to laugh. "Fuck, man, to see him laying dere on dah court wit his nuts hangin outa his shorts like dat, I nearly pissed myself."

"And the little cock sucker's got a set of balls on him like a fuckin bull. I seen Gloria Kaminski strainin her eyes dere to get a look."

"Hey, Stonewallski," shouted Pruny. "We're goin for a swim. You comin?"

Jason was planning to meet his father and the Professor this afternoon in the park, but he figured he had enough time for a quick dip nonetheless. He ran to the Shelter House. In its cool dark corners couples stood in bathing suits or street clothes and whispered and stole kisses while young children raced shouting from wall to wall trying to catch their echoes which reverberated down from the vaulted ceiling. Stout Polish matrons strolled by pushing baby buggies, their legs and arms red like bright apples. Old men played checkers in the alcoves of the doorways.

Jason dashed past them all, threw his gym bag into a bent doored locker, put on his basketball shorts and jumped into the mandatory shower. He then quick stepped into the long greenish-yellow tray of disinfectant and exited into the bright, colorful moving mosaic of people splashing, wading, and swimming all around him.

The three public pools were packed: the baby pool with its young mothers bouncing their laughing children up and down in the shallow depths as a fountain splashed water high in the air; the five foot pool with its water barely visible for the mass of people congregated in this most popular of the pools; and finally the deep twelve foot section with its three tiers of diving boards monopolized by the older boys of Kaisertown like a jungle tree swarmed by a troop of monkeys.

Jason waded and swam across the five foot pool on his way to the diving boards. When he got out on the opposite end with a strong sting of chlorine in his eyes, someone, a girl, was standing directly in front of him with her back to the sun.

"They say the eyes are the windows of the soul. Do you believe that?" she said.

The figure moved aside letting the full rays of the sun shine directly into the boy's eyes blinding him temporarily. When he could focus again the girl was gone, nowhere to be seen. It didn't matter. He knew it was Dorothy. Then someone distracted him. It was Pruny cannonballing off the ten foot board with his swimming trunks pulled down.

"Hey Pruny," someone shouted amid peals of laughter. "Wipe dat smile off yer face."

Walking through the park afterwards Jason kept an eye out for Dorothy. Somehow he thought she would be there, but instead he came upon his father and the Professor along with another man sitting at a picnic table. The third person proved to be a local character known as, Eddie, the Red. Jason had seen him occasionally coming and going from the neighborhood barrooms. As was to be expected the table was covered with bags and books. The conversation was in full heat when Jason sat down.

"Lenin was forced into a policy of repression, don't you see," exclaimed Eddie, the Red. "If he opened up to so-called Western democratic ideals, he would in fact open up the country to reactionaries and revisionists. He would expose the Bolsheviks to counter-revolution. They had to hold on ruthlessly to what they had won, or else risk losing it all."

"True enough," echoed the Professor. He was not a patient listener as Jason had often observed. "And the U.S. was only too happy to exploit this image of a bloody jowly Lenin feeding on his own people.

"Another interesting facet here is Lenin's initial misconception of Stalin's character," continued the Professor. "You know, Ed, Trotsky saw it first, but even he did not realize the depth of Stalin's corruption. You see most of these old Bolsheviks were such idealists, so dedicated to their cause, that they could not imagine one of their own subverting the revolution.

"But you can't create this tight, closed party system and then not, at least, suspect someone of trying to usurp power and use it for his own brand of tyranny. Stalin was there to take advantage."

"The central problem, of course," added Jason's father, "was the fact that the Russian working class was in no position to take and hold industry. There was very little industry in Russia to begin with. Marx and Engels fully believed the workers' revolution would take place in Germany."

"The will of the worker is gone, today," said Eddie, the Red. "In the old IWW days workers knew who they were, where they stood, and who the class enemy was. Not today."

Jason could detect a growing tension building between Eddie, the Red, and the Professor. It flared into open conflict when the conversation turned to the realm of music and Eddie made an unintended disparaging remark about the Professor's beloved Wolfgang Amadeus Mozart.

"Mozart was like a juvenile delinquent, a bon vivant, who couldn't manage his own affairs, and drove his father to an early grave. He had no friends. That's why no one came to his funeral."

The Professor stood up, his face reddened with rage. "There is no historical accuracy to any of these allegations," he thundered turning beseechingly to Jason's father. "If anyone does not believe that this child musician, this tiny prodigy, was not the most marvelous little boy ever born on Earth, then that person I have no use for. By the age of five, I told you this, Ed, he composed his first concerto. The little Mozart sitting at a chair in his father's study, a large feather pen in his small hand.

'What are you doing, Wolfgang?" the father, Leopold asked.

'I'm writing a concerto, papa,' was the boy's reply.

"The old man smiled kindly not wanting to dampen his son's enthusiasm. 'You want to see it, papa?' The old man held out his hand and read the paper and then a tear glistened in his eyes. Before him was a perfectly adept musical score, from his five year old son. Five years old!" thun-

197

dered the Professor. With that he threw his books and articles into two shopping bags and stomped out across the grass.

Eddie, the Red, looked at Jason's father, shrugged his shoulders, and walked off in the opposite direction. Jason and his father exchanged wan smiles.

"I better go after the Professor," he said. "Should have known it would happen. Do me a favor. Don't go home right away. Give me a couple more hours.'

"OK, don't worry."

Jason grabbed a hot dog and soda at Babe's before slowly strolling home. The house was dark except for the eternal kitchen light. Pillows and blankets were thrown across the parlor couch.

"Dat you, sonny boy?" came his mother's feeble voice from the bedroom.

"Yes. Dad's not back yet?"

"Dat bastard wit his Professor again. No time for dah famly. I'm layin here wit such a bad headache, my head explode."

"I've got a headache too," Jason answered. "I'm going to bed. Good night."

Timmy Klein: *"Zeby cie Diabli Wzili. May the Demons Take You."*

Timmy held out the deck of cards for Wladek to see in the dusky light of the evening.

"Oh, yeah, you like these babies don't yah, you fuckin moron. Ohh, ohh, nice titties. Yeah, look at this one, Ace of Spades. Jesus Christ, don't touch em with yer dirty monkey paws. I'll hold em. You just look. Yeah, that's it. Drool, you fuckin ape. I'd have you give me a blow job, but I wouldn't put a baboon's cock in that rotten snagged mouth a yers."

Timmy put the cards back in his pocket. Wladek yowled and cried in protest and reached out for them like a religious supplicant grasping for one last touch of a holy icon. His big hands clenched and unclenched while his clumsy feet did an awkward jig.

"Holy fuck," said Timmy. "Yer some sight, you are. I don't know why the doctor didn't strangle you at birth. If I was yer poor mother, I'd put you in a fuckin home, home for retards. Yer good for a laugh anyways, and I'm sorry to say but yer the only friend I got here in Kaisertown which don't say too much for me either."

Wladek grunted and continued to dance around as he unslung the canteen from his shoulder and opened the flap of his little school bag. It was the same Mickey Mouse bag he had carried when he first met Timmy at Okie Diamond where Stachu Klemp had Timmy trapped in the pond. The boys had met periodically after that, mainly by chance, for Timmy would never be caught dead in public with Wladek. And Timmy was always careful to refer to himself as "Jason" just in case Wladek's garbled speech became suddenly intelligible to someone else. Besides, Timmy figured, old lady Khula probably knew what that retard son of hers was saying so better Timmy's name be kept out of the conversation altogether.

Wladek rummaged through his knapsack and finally pulled something out. He held it up for Timmy to admire.

"Well, well," said Timmy with surprise. "I never would a figured it. Guess the old hard-on is stronger than the heart strings. Does that fuckin thing still work?"

Wladek smiled his rotten toothed smile and held the watch up to his ear. "Tig, tog, tig, tog," he grunted and shook his head in the affirmative.

"If you don't mind, please take that watch away from yer ear. Take me a week to disinfect the fuckin thing," said Timmy.

Nevertheless, Timmy smiled with satisfaction. He had stolen the cards from his father's tool box in the cellar months back with no repercussions. And that old watch Wladek had was made of sterling silver. Stamped right on the back along with the initials N.Y.C. and W.K. Timmy had admired it for months, but every time he tried to bargain for it Wladek had thrown a fit.

"You can stay and jerk off," said Timmy as he handed over the cards. He pocketed his new prize and broke from the copse of sumac and crab apple trees. He then strolled onto the broken, weed lined sidewalk that ran parallel to the width of Okie Diamond. Very little traffic ventured that barren way with its vacant lots, open fields and distant railway yards.

On the opposite side of the street Timmy saw a figure coming towards him, familiar, a girl. She carried a small transistor radio in her hand. A thin wire led to an earplug which was stuck into her left ear. She was lost in the music and her own thoughts and did not notice Timmy.

"It's that conceited bitch, Tina Kasprczyk," said Timmy after a moment's squinting into the setting sun. "Stupid bitch, just because she met Jason here one night a couple of years ago she thinks it's gonna happen again. Like he's out here just waitin for her. And then they got married and walked off hand and hand into the sunset to raise another bunch of sniveling Polack brats to fill up the slums of Kaisertown. What a idiot. She should marry Crazy Wladek. More her type."

Timmy was then seized with indignation and envy. Fuckin Lover Boy Jason, he thought. Broads followed him everywhere and Tina was the worst. She's eat a mile of his shit just to kiss his ass. And Jason experimented with her, tried out all sorts of sex stuff on her. She gave him blow jobs too. Jason bragged about it to Timmy and inadvertently filled his neighbor with seething jealousy and rage.

But Timmy got nothing. Girls never even waved back at him. They just gave him that familiar look of contempt as though he was worse than Glupi Wladek or Stachu Klemp. He hated them for it, and he hated Tina Kasprczyk most of all.

Afterwards it was difficult for Timmy to recall if it was a conscious plan he hatched that evening there on the edge of Okie Diamond or a bit of inspiration that just came to him. Somehow it seemed to fall into place like the procurement of the watch. Things had a way of working out sometimes.

"Tina, Tina," Timmy called and waved the girl over to him.

She pulled the earphone from its resting place and stepped tentatively into the street unsure who was calling to her. Timmy could hear the far away strains of music singing like a buzzing insect from the dangling earphone. It excited him.

"Hiyah Tina, funny thing yer here because me and Jason was just talking about you."

The girl's apprehension faded. "Jason? Jason? What did you say about Jason? He was talkin about me? Where?"

"Well, yeah, that was the whole thing. We were in the trees there. You know the old fort, and he was talkin about meetin the love of his life, the girl that got away, and he was getting all choked up and romantic. Said that girl was you. Anyhow, I'm not much for that romantic shit and he wanted to be alone."

"Is he still there?" asked the girl.

"Hell, yeah, I just walked out myself. You remember where it is, the old fort by the apple trees where we used to play when we was kids?"

"Kind of."

"Then here, I'll show you. Careful, it's getting a little dark in the trees."

"Just a minute," the girl said and she opened her purse and put the radio inside. She then quickly removed a tube of lipstick and gave her lips a quick swipe. Pink.

That would look good wrapped around my cock thought Timmy as they entered Okie Diamond. They walked through the high grass until they came to the red topped sumac bushes and the umbrella like entanglement of the wild crab apple trees. The girl grew hesitant.

"Jason's here? Yer sure?"

"Yeah, right over there. You can see him just a few more steps."

The girl's reluctance vanished when she saw a boy sitting cross legged under the drooping branches of the apple trees in a hollowed out area like the entrance to a cave.

"Jesus, Mary, and Joseph, it is Jason. Oh god, I was afraid, you know. I didn't believe at first that he was here. Really here. Jason! Jason!" she called and ran ahead.

When she got up close and recognized Glupi Wladek with his cock in his hand she stopped dead in her tracks. She turned to Timmy.

"What the hell?" was all she managed to say before Timmy socked her square in the jaw.

Uppercut. Drops em like a ton of bricks just like Jersey Joe Walcott, mused Timmy with a broad grin on his face. He dragged the girl the few remaining feet under the low canopy of trees. With Glupi Wladek staring down with his mouth open and drooling Timmy stripped the girl naked and proceeded to rape her. He slapped her constantly across the face, cursed and laughed at her even though she was unconscious and oblivious to the violation forced on her.

"Is that you Jason, my darling? Fuck me, Jason. Fuck me. I want to have yer kids. I love you," Timmy shouted out loud.

Wladek was jumping up and down with excitement and bewilderment. The cards lay spilled across the ground as he now stared at the real live naked girl in front of him. As Timmy withdrew Tina moaned and blinked her eyes into semi-consciousness.

"She's groanin. She likes it," said Timmy to Wladek. "She wants more. She's a whore. You give it to her now. Go ahead. Put yer cock in her. Do it."

Timmy grabbed Wladek's canteen, then moved behind Tina. He splashed water into her face and pinned her arms above her head. The girl sputtered and stared wide eyed at the pimply face and rotten teeth of Glupi Wladek as he laid heavily on top of her and pushed himself between her already spread-eagle legs.

"Jason couldn't make it so we got you a stand in husband. Meet yer new husband. Look at him. Yer makin babies together. How sweet, baby Wallys. He likes you too. What a nice couple. Everybody in Kaisertown is saying what a nice couple yous make."

Timmy laughed and laughed drowning out the girl's hysterical sobs.

He cupped his hands across her mouth. She bit him.

"You bitch," he hissed. "Here I set you up with the love of yer life and that's the thanks I get? Why there's a hundred girls in Kaisertown right now who'd love to be in yer place, you ungrateful bitch."

He grabbed the strap of the nearby canteen and slung it around the girl's head and neck. As Wladek bucked and howled, spitting in ecstasy and delirium, Timmy tightened and twisted the strap. Tina's eyes bulged.

"What, you can't believe it's true?" said Timmy as he watched her. "It is true, all true. True! True! True!"

Glupi Wladek stopped thrashing and rolled off the girl, grunting and sputtering in the process. The sudden odor of the boy's unwashed body exposed during the rape swept over Timmy. He gagged and turned away. When he looked down again, Tina's face was a deep raspberry blue. Red foam bubbled from the corners of her mouth. Her wide open eyes were protruding and veined with red. The canteen strap had all but disappeared beneath the swollen flesh of her neck. The other end was tightly twisted around Timmy's now cold white hand.

"Holy fuck," cried Timmy. He loosened his grip and shook the girl's shoulders. "Tina! Tina! Come on, Tina!"

Timmy turned to Wladek. "You fucking asshole! She's fuckin dead. You made me do it. It's all yer fault."

At that moment, the street lights across Griswold Street blinked, then sputtered into life. Glupi Wladek stood up in panic. He pulled up his pants and crudely brushed the dirt from his clothing. He sobbed as he tried to gather up his scattered belongings.

Timmy was in a panic of his own. What the fuck! What the fuck am I gonna do? His breath came heavily and labored. Just like that asshole Jason with one of his asthma attacks he thought. Yeah, Jason, just like that asshole Jason. Timmy turned to Wladek again. His tone changed to one of concern and conciliation.

"Wally, let me help you. Let Jason help you. Here, I'll get yer stuff. Look, here's yer cards. Good ones, nice. Jason's yer friend."

Timmy was careful to slide the packsack across Tina's body smearing the runnel of blood that had seeped from the girl's vagina and run down her thigh.

"And here, I'll help you put it on. Yeah, good. Jason's yer friend, you know. Good friend, Jason."

In the process Timmy grabbed Tina's bra and panties and stuck them deep into Wladek's pack. He handed the canteen back to the boy as well being careful to hold it by its straps.

"There you go, Wally, you poor stupid moron. What difference will it make to you? Everywhere is Moronville to you. Maybe they'll let you keep yer cards in jail. Now you better get home to yer mother. Yeah, and Jason will see you later, maybe tomorrow, maybe in hell. Yeah, good, Jason's yer friend. Don't forget. He helped you. Now go."

Glupi Wladek stumbled out across the fields and down Griswold Street to the corner of South Ogden where he turned and disappeared. A passing car blared its horn as the boy cut in front of it. Good thought Timmy watching from the edge of the field. Maybe they will remember that gorilla. He glanced down again at the dead girl.

"Thought you were so smart. Too good for me. Yeah, look at you now. Just a dead slut ready for the cold ground. They'll bury you in a few days and you'll be gone and forgotten and the worms will eat yer skinny ass to bones. All yer big dreams are over. Hot stuff, you got nothing now. Just what you deserve."

Timmy knelt down and masturbated in front of the girl's body. Then he ground the wetness into the dirt with his heel and reluctantly pulled the silver watch from his pocket, wiped it carefully and threw it on the ground next to the Ace of Spades that lay half hidden under Tina's body. He grabbed her purse and looked through it finally stealing the transistor radio and some change. He left for home with the faint clanging of distant box cars coupling together. It sounded like the tolling of bells.

Pani Khula: "Ja Niewiem. I Don't Know."

Pani Khula knew there was trouble when she heard the knock on her front door. It was years since anyone came to her house and never, but never, did anyone come to the front door. The front door entrance meant a stranger, an unknown entity, and therefore trouble. And when she saw the two police officers standing there with Father Kolinski from St. Bernard's Church, her knees buckled.

"No, no, no" she pleaded. "He's a good boy. A good boy."

The men looked at one another. "How do you know we're here about yer son, Walter? Has he done anyting wrong dat you know about?"

Pani Khula stammered, afraid she had unwittingly condemned her boy. But she knew it could only be one thing. She had done her best, tried to turn his attention away from bad thoughts and deeds. Although she had lighted candle after candle on her little bedroom altar to the Virgin Mary and baby Jesus, she knew it was a losing battle. She had no idea of the breath of his trouble, but she knew it was inevitable that this day would come.

After the first visit by the police regarding the Bartkowski girl years ago she had beaten her boy, whipped him mercilessly with the pyda. But she couldn't sustain the punishment. She couldn't be cruel to him, her only link to life and love. So she gave up over the intervening years, tried to distract him, save him from himself.

"Lulajze, Jesuniu, lulajze, lulaj... easy Wladek, doan be so rough wit yer matka. Easy. Let mommy help you. Dere, dere's my boy. Good boy. You come to mommy. Leave dah liddle girl by demselfs. Big trouble if you touch it dah liddle girls. Dah police will come and dey will put you in dah jail and you ken never see yer poor matka again."

Now despite all her sacrifices here were the police again. They wanted to talk to Wladek and check his room and personal possessions, and, oh yes, did she recognize this?

"Yes, dat was my husband watch. Wladek had id. Id was his favorite ting. He carried it wid him all dah time. He never led it go. How did yous ged id? He musta lost id or somebody stole id on him."

Again the exchange of glances and again Pani Khula's feelings of panic and betrayal. The cuckoo clock in the kitchen sounded. Wladek who was peering around the corner, smiled and clapped as the little bird popped out three times and sang.

"Looks like something here," said one to the policemen pointing to the edge of a knapsack where a dark stain had discolored a faded red and yellow Mickey Mouse face.

"Dis is Walter's packsack, nie?"

"Yes," replied Pani Khula with a panic stricken look towards her son.

Inside they found a bra and panties and a deck of girlie cards with the Ace of Spades missing. The priest made the sign of the cross and shook his head sadly. The two policemen approached Wladek. One of them took out a pair of handcuffs. Pani Khula screamed.

Detective Sojka and Officer Abramowski: "Bedz Cicho! Be Quiet!"

Officer Abramowski and detective Sojka discussed the case over a cup of coffee at the Deco restaurant around the corner from Precinct #5. At one time the station had been a bastion of Irish and German police power on the city's East Side and its officers rose through the ranks of Buffalo's city hegemony in step with their ethnic and political counterparts. In more recent years, as Polish immigrants moved into the Eastside, the ethnicity of the local police force changed with them. Many of the beat officers were now Polish, a few of them made it to detective rank, but only a smattering had risen higher.

"Look it. The fuckin retard done it," emphasized detective Sojka. "We found the evidence right in his knapsack and dat driver seen him leavin dah scene of dah crime. What more do we need?"

"Yeah, yeah, yer right. I know yer right," replied officer Abramowski. "Still, it don't add up. I mean I don't see him draggin dis girl all the way into dem bushes like dat wit her kickin and screamin. She never would a been caught dead anywhere near the likes a him. You seen what he looks like. And what about his mother's talk about another boy, some kid named Jason?"

"Look it. Dis is a big case, a murder right here on the Eastside," explained detective Sojka. "A case like dis don't come around too often, yah know. And we got it solved overnight. It fuckin fell right into our laps. What we gonna do now? Start actin like we ain't sure we got the right guy? No tanks. You know how many captains, or lieutenants of police dere are in Buffalo dat's Polacks?"

"Jesus, I can't think of any right now."

"Exactly, and right now city hall is just beggin for promotable Polacks, and dat's us partner, you an me. We're the fuckin heroes of the day. Let's not screw it up. And dat other suspect, dat Jason Novak kid, I checked him out. His old man is a supervisor over by Worthington. The kid is a bright student and a basketball player over by South Park. He ain't gonna get involved in sometin like dis. Dat retard Khula's got it all mixed up. Anyway, nobody is gonna figure out no Jason name from all dat mumbo jumbo talk dat retard was sayin."

"No, but the mother knew and what about dem other footprints, and the radio, dat transistor radio, the girl's mother said she had it wit her. We never found dat on the retard."

"Dere's tons of fuckin kids playin around in dat field. Footprints could a come from anybody, at any time and we found the watch, don't forget dat. The radio, I dunno. Maybe the retard tossed it away. Afraid it might incriminate him."

"Incriminate him!" said officer Abramowski. "He had her panties and bra in his knapsack. He can't tink dat straight. He would a kept the radio too. And another ting. The victim's clothes. Her blouse was unbuttoned and her bra unsnapped, her shoes and pants were pulled off. Nothin ripped. You seen dat Khula kid. He could hardly tie his sneakers. He woulda torn her clothes all to rat shit getting em off. Somebody else was dere. I'd bet on it."

"OK, fine, I'll tell you what. For our own peace of mind we'll check the fingerprints on dem cards, and the watch. Maybe dere's somebody else's dere. And we'll talk to dat Jason kid, Novak. If he ain't got a alibi den we'll worry about it, OK? But if he's clean on dat, den dat's pretty much the end of the story. Deal?"

"Deal, but what about a blood test on the rape victim. Could show something."

"Deal?" the detective repeated with emphasis, ignoring his partner's suggestion.

"Yeah, deal."

Jason: *"Pomodz mi. Help Me."*

Jason was standing in front of Babe's with his cousin, Larry Bingkowski, and a bunch of the Kaisertown guys. It was a year after his "Stonewallski" fame and he was solidly entrenched as one of the gang although by his own admission he was a loner and did not make the street corner a familiar hang out. Everyone was smoking except Jason. He never took up the habit and his asthma had precluded any earlier attempts.

The topic of conversation was the recent murder of Tina Kasprczyk. Nobody knew much about it outside of the general circumstances, but nothing like that had ever happened in Kaisertown before so gossip and speculation ran rampant.

"I betcha it was dah wops from over by Lovejoy. Dey coulda come down dah tracks at South Ogden, crossed by Dingens, and got in dah field from dah back way. Dey seen her walking down dah street and jumped her."

Everyone nodded and muttered in agreement. It must have been them because no one from Kaisertown would have done such a thing.

"Wops, dat's what they want most of all, you know, is a Polish girl. Ginzoes, they're all greasy and dere skin is dark and oily. Dat's why dey love a white broad so much."

"Fuckin A, he's right," someone else chimed in.

"Dis is revenge for dat beatin we laid on em back at dat Ryan dance.

Dey're getting even."

Pruny, looking uncharacteristically serious, spoke up while unrolling the sleeve of his tee shirt to extract a pack of Lucky Strikes.

"Alright, yous guys, everyone here dat wants to head down to wop town right now and beat dah shit outa dem ginzoes on dere own turf, take one step forward."

All the boys looked quizzically at Pruny at which point he himself took one decided step backward.

"Son of a bitch, yous Kaisertown Polacks ain't afraid a nuttin. Dat's what I admire about yous. Me, I'm helpin Babe serve up some banana splits today. Udderwise, I'd be right dere wit dat rest a yous guys."

He bobbed his head knowingly, popped a cigarette into his smiling mouth, lit it with his Zippo lighter, snapped the top closed with a click, then took a comb and straightened a few loose strands of his Vaseline slicked hair that had managed to disturb his perfect DA haircut.

"Somebody said the cops arrested Crazy Wally, that retard used to run around dressed like a fuckin cowboy."

"I can't see him doin nuttin like dat. He's harmless."

"Fuckin big and strong though."

Then another voice spoke up from the back row, and shouted, "It was niggers."

Jason winced as the word snapped the boys into silence like a conductor holding a baton above the heads of an expectant orchestra. Everyone waited, not saying a word. Jason felt like he was having an asthma attack with its long deathlike pauses between shallow breaths of air. The boys moved instinctively closer together as if in a football huddle. Then their voices erupted in cacophonous unison.

"Holy fuck! God damn! Jesus! Dey wouldn't dare. Not right here in Kaiserstown. Man, we got real trouble, fuckin A."

"I heard down by Shea's Buffalo a little white kid, he went to the bathroom dere and niggers fuckin cut his cock off," volunteered one of the boys. "Kid bled to death. My cousin goes to McKinley, and was tellin me. You know, dere's nuttin but niggers downtown now. Dey're takin over."

"Hell, she's better off dead."

No one noticed the police car pull up. It wasn't until both doors slammed shut that the boys looked up. Everyone froze, then stared at each other in puzzlement. A few tossed their cigarettes on the ground. Larry Bingkowski was the only one who appeared calm. He had met the police many times before.

"Which one a yous is Jason Novak?" one of the cops asked.

The boys all looked at Jason, relieved but puzzled by the unlikely target of the police inquiry. Larry's cigarette bobbed off his lip and fell to the sidewalk in a spray of sparks.

"Well, I guess dat's you den," said the cop with a quick step towards Jason whose face had taken on a decidedly ashen tone since the initial mention of his name. Jason turned to his cousin.

"What seems to be the problem, officer?" asked Larry.

"None a yer business, Mr. Bingkowski," came the reply.

"He's my cousin."

"Yeah, we noticed the family resemblance right away. We just wanna talk to Jason here for a few minutes, in private. If that's all right wit you, of course."

"Actually…"

But before Larry could complete the sentence Jason was inside the police car. The frightened boy immediately noticed that there were no handles on the back seat doors. His knees knocked together involuntarily and his hands shook. The driver looked at Jason through the rear view mirror.

"Look it, kid, don't get yerself all pissed up. Yer not under arrest or nuttin. We just got a few questions and den you ken go. We'll even drive you home."

Jesus Christ, thought Jason, my mother will have a heart attack if she sees a cop car dropping me off. What the hell did I do?

"You know a girl named Tina Kasprczyk?"

"Yes, she lives, lived on Wheelock Street, one block over from South Ogden."

"How good did you know her?"

Jason hesitated.

"I said how good did you know her?" repeated the officer

"We went around for a while, a little while, couple of years ago."

"Were you wit her in the days or hours before she got… before she died dere out in dat field behind Wheelock Street?"

"Okie Diamond, no I wasn't with her. I hadn't seen her. Maybe walking around or something like that, but that was all."

"You ever have sex wit her?"

"Ahhm gee, maybe, I guess when we were going out together."

Jason's head began to pound. Why ask him about Tina? And this sex stuff, what was that all about?

"And you weren't tempted to see her again? Have more sex? It ain't easy, is it, getting a girl to have sex wit you?"

"Well, I don't know…"

"Oh yeah dat's right. Don't dey call you Lover Boy or something like dat around here? A real Casanova?"

"Casanova," Jason said recovering himself somewhat.

"What was dat?"

"Nothing."

"How about a kid named Walter, Walter Khula?"

The name sounded familiar, but Jason couldn't quite place it. The driver handed him a picture over his shoulder, then turned to his companion in the front seat. "What do dey call him around here?" he inquired.

"Glupi Wladak," came the reply.

"Oh, Crazy Wally," said Jason grabbing the photograph. "Yeah, I know him. Did he do it? Kill Tina?"

"How good do you know him?" added the detective.

"Well, I know who he is. He's retarded. You know, mentally deficient. He's no friend of mine or even an acquaintance. I just know him from the neighborhood. He lives at the end of South Ogden Street."

"We know where he lives. You sure you ain't been hanging around wit him lately? Seems his mother, she tinks the two a yous are good friends," the detective continued.

"Jesus, I don't know where she got that idea from?"

"You think yer pretty smart, don't you, Jason, Mr. Lover Boy? Big shot wit the broads. Lots of big words. You know, maybe you just figured you had sex wit Tina comin to you. Get it any time you wanted even if she said no."

Then the other policeman spoke up. "Take it easy, detective," he said to his companion. "The kid is alright. He's answerin our questions."

He turned around and faced Jason.

"Jason, my name is officer Abramowski. I know yer a good kid. Look, we just gotta get some facts straight. It really ain't got nothing to do wit you like we tink yer guilty of a crime. Now one more ting. Where were you on Friday, the 10th of July? Dat was two weeks ago."

"Was that when Tina got killed?" Jason asked.

"Just for the record. Help us clear dis up. Where were you between say 6:00 PM and 11:00 PM on dat day?" the officer repeated while ignoring Jason's question.

"God, I don't know. I can't remember."

"Come on, kid, tink. It was only two weeks ago," interjected detective Sojka.

Jason didn't like him. He preferred officer Abramowski.

"Give it some time. We ain't in no hurry," added officer Abramowski. "Two Fridays ago between 6:00 and 11:00 at night. And did you see Glupi Wladek dat day? Anytime at all dat day?"

"No, no I never saw Crazy Wally that day or any day for a long time. I'm usually down at the other end of Kaisertown, this end here, with my cousin and the guys. Hangin out at Babe's or Houghton Park, you know."

"Who were you wit dat night? You got someone who can vouch for you?"

"I'm trying to think."

"Well for god's sake, you must a been somewhere dat night? Where the hell were you?"

"I, I don't remember just now. I'm too nervous to think straight."

The two police officers looked at each other. Detective Sojka shook his head slowly in dismay.

Of course, it had only taken a moment's reflection for Jason to recall exactly where he was that night. That was the night his aunt and uncle went to their friends' cottage in Rushford and he spent the night fucking the brains out of his cousin, Nelly. Then he lied to his parents and friends about where he had been. Son of a bitch, what was he supposed to do now?

Jason's father was in the yard at South Ogden when the police car pulled up. His calm demeanor and politeness impressed the two officers.

"I'm sure Jason was with his cousin, Larry Bingkowski, that night officers. They slept over at a party in Kaisertown. I remember being concerned that there might have been some drinking involved and I didn't want Larry driving my son home at that late hour. Isn't that right, Jason?"

"Yes, yes, I think that was it, now that you mention it," replied Jason remembering now the excuse he had given his parents.

The father saw there was something wrong with this explanation. He didn't know what, but he knew beyond any doubt that there was no way his son, Jason, was involved in something as horrible as Tina Kasprczyk's death. He listened to the policemen's dilemma about Jason's name coming up during the investigation. Then he offered a quick solution.

"Why not just introduce Jason to this Walter Khula and see if Walter recognizes my son as his good friend? We will be glad to accompany you right now if you like."

That saved the day because at the holding cell in Precinct #5 it was obvious that Glupi Wladek had no idea who Jason was. If Glupi Wladek had a companion on that dark evening at Okie Diamond, it wasn't Jason Novak.

"Look it," said detective Sojka turning to Jason's father. "Wit yer word dat Jason here was wit his cousin dat night and wit Walter not recognizing him, I tink we can all agree dat yer son had nuttin to do wit dis unfortunate incident in any way. Wouldn't you say dat's true, officer Abramowski?"

"Yeah, I guess maybe we should a stayed and had a word wit Mr. Bingkowski after all. He could a vouched for you right den and dere."

When they were alone, Jason told his father part of the truth about that night saying he was with a "girlfriend" the whole time, and not with his cousin Larry. His father was not as upset as Jason had imagined.

"I knew there was no way you were involved. God damn, I'd kill myself if I thought I had raised such a child. Poor girl, I can just imagine what agony her parents are living through right now. And on another topic, since you brought it up, I hope to hell you are wearing protection like we discussed before?"

"Yes, I got rubbers from one of the guys in Kaisertown. I used to get them from Larry, but he ran out that time. Don't worry."

"Good, because that's one thing that would cut your future off short. No college, no education, You'd wind up like the rest of these poor working stiffs in Kaisertown, trapped in a miserable, unrewarding job with a young wife and family to support."

Dorothy: "Love Me or Leave Me."

Dorothy wasn't sure what love was although she had played the game of love for some time now. She just had never won the grand prize, settling always for the consolation of sex and acceptance even with the attendant violence they often brought her. She knew, of course, that she had been looking in all the wrong places. The boys of Kaisertown were not for her, not for her with the exception of Jason Novak, the one that got away. Dorothy's instinct, however, told her that there was still a chance. The two former neighbors were both odd ducks, misfits, uncomfortable in their surroundings. Perhaps they could find each other and a way out of Kaisertown.

Dorothy knew that Jason spent a lot of time around Houghton Park and Babe's Ice Cream Parlor. His cousin, Larry Bingkowski lived on Gorski Street nearby. The two boys were often together although Dorothy could never understand the relationship between them. Jason was seventeen and in his last year at South Park. He was an honors student, a bookworm and athlete. Larry was twenty-one, never finished high school, worked in an auto repair shop, and was a petty criminal. Just what Jason saw in his cousin or the rest of those moronic Kaisertown hoodlums Dorothy could never understand.

The girl was living with her babcia Hanka for a couple of years now. With dziada Andy dead some seven years, babcia welcomed the presence of her granddaughter. She also detested Dorothy's father with a passion so she was glad to help the girl. The fact that Dorothy's father mercilessly beat his wife and kids was a minor concern for the old woman. Babcia Hanka had received enough poundings from her own husband in her day to take such behavior as normal. It was the man's German heritage that damned him in the old lady's eyes.

"Drogi Boze, jak swiat swiatem Polak z niemcyn nie be dzie bratem," she often proclaimed.

Furthermore, Dorothy came in handy when babcia Hanka needed someone to interpret the ever changing world around her. The old woman barely spoke English and was steeped in the culture and traditions of the old country and she was reluctant to embrace anything new or unfamiliar. She was considered a healer and soothsayer amongst the elder members of the Kaisertown neighborhood who flocked to her for spiritual advice and medical healing.

Babcia's garden was overflowing with herbs, weeds, and flowers, all with medicinal and/or magical properties: piolun for menstral pain and upset stomach, lupszczyk for the kidneys, rumianck for croup. There was also rhubarb and cabbage and lily of the valley, milkweed and chicory. The back kitchen was filled with jars and vials of salves and potions made from their roots, leaves, and flowers.

Dorothy's babcia was also in frequent conference with Mr. Frost, the apothecary on Clinton Street who likewise fashioned his own remedies and cures. Prominently displayed in his old fashioned shop was a large jar of twisting and writhing leeches that the neighborhood children loved to watch as their parents and grandparents discussed symptoms and remedies with the white haired, green visored owner.

Dorothy infrequently helped her grandmother minister to neighbor patients who crowded her door step. More often she just watched as she did one day when Pani Jardinski arrived. The girl stood transfixed as her babcia burned several spikey clove buds on her old wood stove, then ground them to powder between two spoons, added some granulated sugar and finally, taking a hollow duck's feather, blew the powder into the woman's right eye.

The girl winced in sympathetic pain as the woman squirmed in her chair, her eyes running with tears and black streaks flowing down her cheeks. The procedure was repeated three times along with some prayers and numerous spitting on her babcia's part.

"Glowka, for to take away dah cloud in her eye," the old lady later explained to her bewildered granddaughter.

The 1963 assassination of John F. Kennedy, as well as the unexpected death of Pope John XXIII, had a devastating effect on Dorothy's babcia.

"Rany bozka, dah worl's gone crazy," babcia Hanka lamented as she made the sign of the cross and recited rosary after rosary on her knees before the portraits of the president and pope that hung on her parlor wall.

The old woman was not alone in her grief. All of Kaisertown was devastated by the tragic news of the year especially that relating to the young President. Kennedy's good looks, his Catholicism, and boyish charm had trumped, in the eyes of Kaisertown's devote Polacks anyway, his otherwise fatal flaw of being, after all, an Irishman.

Dorothy and Janie stopped in Babe's for an ice cream cone. It was a warm afternoon. Jason, the object of the visit, was nowhere to be seen. However, Dorothy did spot Larry's car parked along the curb. The two girls walked past.

"Hi," Dorothy said addressing the lone occupant of the vehicle. "Where's your sidekick, Boswell? Home writing his memoirs?"

"Yer one crazy broad, yah know," answered Larry. "But if you mean Jason, he's in the back of the park lookin at some fuckin birds and keeping a low profile. Hey, yous girls wanna go for a ride?"

"Sure," said Janie. "Can I sit in front? What station you got on?" And she bounded in the car not waiting for a reply. Larry grimaced, but was too polite to protest.

"What about you?" he added looking Dorothy up and down.

Dorothy licked her ice cream cone slowly, purposely leaving a smear of vanilla on her upper lip before licking it off.

"No thanks," she replied.

"Dorothy jus wants to meet Jason. Dat's why we came down here in dah first place," added Janie.

Dorothy rolled her eyes. "Thanks for sharing that with the world."

"The two a yous would make a good couple," said Larry. "Nobody else can figger out what the hell either one a yous are sayin half the time. Maybe yous can talk together."

"Dorothy don't wanna do no talkin," added Janie quickly.

"Next time I want a secret kept, I'll just hire a skywriter," said Dorothy as she moved off.

Jason was at the very end of Houghton Park where the manicured lawns gave way to high fields of weeds and shrubs, and the tall willows and sycamores that lined the shores of Buffalo Creek. He must have seen her approaching because without saying a word he motioned her towards him indicating that she be quiet. He was holding a pair of binoculars. A small book was wedged under his belt.

"Look, he's on that branch on the left of the sumac bush, a little above the fence post."

Jason handed the binoculars to Dorothy while pulling her close to his body with his freehand. His demeanor and actions were so natural that it seemed as though Dorothy had been there the whole time sharing a familiar past time.

Dorothy put the glasses to her eyes, but couldn't see anything except a blur of greenery. Jason stared distractedly at the binoculars in the girl's hands. He seemed momentarily lost in thought.

"What's the matter?" asked Dorothy. "Am I doing something wrong?"

"Focus them on top," Jason instructed, "and watch closely. He's back in the sumac now. He's a warbler, fast moving, a yellow warbler."

Dorothy finally got the binoculars into focus and moved them back and forth not sure what she was supposed to see.

"What the fuck is a warbler?"

"A bird, a beautiful yellow colored bird. You'll see. Keep watching."

Dorothy swept the glasses back and forth. "There! Oh no, he's gone. The little cock sucker won't stay put," she hissed in frustration and stamped her foot.

"I do love when you talk dirty to me," Jason replied.

"Sorry."

"Be patient. They also serve who only stand and wait. He's still back there. He'll come out."

And then, there he was, an image of bright yellow with red streaks on his breast, his beak open and singing. Dorothy had never seen anything like it. He was beautiful beyond words.

"Wow," was all she could muster. "They must be rare, these, what did you call them, warblers?"

"It's a yellow, or summer warble. There are lots of different warbles. This one is actually one of the most common."

"Wow," Dorothy repeated. "I never would have known."

"I got interested through my Uncle Teddy," Jason explained as the two of them walked back up towards the civilized part of the park where the scattered picnic tables, horseshoe pits, and water fountains stood.

"Uncle Ted works at Bishop's Food Terminal at the Bailey Market. He loves bird watching and is a bit of a bingo fanatic too, but that's another story. He can identify a bird just by its song. What do you think of bird watching anyway? Like to give it a try? This park is a great place. I've counted about twenty species here just this past month including an oriole and a scarlet tanager."

"Fuck, I didn't know there were so many damn birds," replied Dorothy. "Figured a bird was a bird. Funny though because I was just listening to a song by Carmen McCrea called, "Baltimore Oriole."

"Do you always swear this much? Not that I mind. It's a bit of a turn on if you want to know the truth."

"Not that you guys need any encouragement," Dorothy replied. She figured she was a bit of an expert when it came to boys and what turned them on and off.

They walked up the hill suddenly holding hands. It seemed so casual, so natural that Dorothy didn't know if Jason did it on purpose or merely forgot himself. She felt self-conscious somehow. She wasn't used to boys holding her hand. Oh, they liked to feel her up, and fuck her whenever they could, but things like holding hands, such an open acknowledgement of affection, that was uncommon for her. The two finally sat down at a park bench.

"Mind if I have a cigarette?" Dorothy asked.

"Go ahead."

Dorothy noticed the sunshine gleaming in Jason's eyes. She smiled and held up her hand with his still clutching it.

"Kind of difficult," she replied.

"Oh, sorry."

"Want one?" she asked. "Oops, it's my last."

"No thanks, but help yourself. I think it looks sexy actually although you're not doing your health any good."

"So, you'd rather have me look sexy for you, sucking on a butt," said Dorothy as she blew a smoke ring into the air, "even though I'm ruining my health doing it."

"That's not what I meant."

"What did you mean?" Dorothy asked trying to provoke him.

"You're right," Jason replied. "Give me that," and he pulled the cigarette out of her lips.

"Hey, you bastard, give that back to me," Dorothy snapped.

"No, your health is more important."

"Fuck off, and give me back that cigarette."

"No, I can't let you do that to yourself."

"I'm starting to get angry."

"And you know what?" Jason added. "You look damn pretty when you're angry."

"Hey, and you know what? I'm not your girlfriend that you can boss around. Hand it over."

"Oh, how quickly they forget," Jason said shaking his head.

"What are you talking about? Forget what?"

"Up in old man Pankow's garage. The vows we exchanged. You pledged to love, honor, and obey and be the mother of my children. Now it's suddenly over."

"Why you little bastard," Dorothy replied unable to suppress a smile from slowly spreading across her lips.

Jason jumped off the bench and ran up the hill. Dorothy was right behind him. She tackled him at the top noting as she did that he had purposely slowed down. They rolled over in the grass and came to a halt with her body on top of his. They were both breathing heavily. The cigarette was nowhere to be seen, but neither seemed to care.

"I love when you pant like this," Jason smiled.

"I thought you had trouble with asthma. Anyway right now you are the biggest prick in all of Kaisertown."

"Flattery will get you everywhere."

Just then Jason rolled Dorothy over, and reversed positions. He looked down into her eyes and lowered his face to hers. She instinctively turned away. She never like kissing boys. She couldn't help herself now although she regretted her actions immediately. Jason looked puzzled. Not used to rejection Dorothy figured. Well, then maybe it was a good thing she resisted, but resistance wasn't one of her strong suits and she knew if she looked into those eyes of his again, she'd be doomed.

At that moment both were startled by the honking of a horn and the sudden appearance of Larry's car in front of them. It had driven across the grass of the park, a point they both noted since no vehicles except those belonging to the park maintenance men were allowed inside the gates.

"What the hell are you doing?" called Jason. "They're going to fine your ass off for driving in here."

Dorothy stood up and shook the grass from her clothes. She noted Janie still in the car with Jason's cousin.

"It's yer old man," Larry said. "He's been in a accident comin from Worthington. Hit by a car crossin dah street. Dey took him to dah hospital, but it ain't too serious. He was conscious and everything."

Jason jumped into Larry's car and the two boys were gone leaving Dorothy and Janie standing on the grass.

"What were yous doin?" asked Janie.

"Listening to the "Lullaby of Birdland" until you two showed up. I guess I got screwed without a kiss again," said Dorothy. "Got a cigarette?"

Jason: Ciotka Rose and the Blue Monday Club

Jason's father's cracked ribs and fractured arm landed him in the hospital for a couple of days and off work for several weeks. Jason's mother's often repeated boast that Edda's got dat good job rang true because Worthington provided excellent insurance coverage. The family's psyche, however, became permanently damaged by the accident. As his parents were thrust together more often now their complete incompatibility showed through like a sunshine behind a broken venetian blind.

"Psia krew, wastin yer time wit dem books and dah records not to mention dat Professor too. I don't wan you seein him no more not even by his house. Funny, nie, dat you got time for him, but yer own family nuttin. It's a good ting I make it a good home for you udderwise you wouldn have a pot to piss in."

Jason's father sat there like a whipped dog. Even Stachu Klemp had more backbone than his father, Jason thought. Why don't you just get up and belt her one? Adding to his depression was the fact that Jason had no regular girlfriend at the time, no outlet for love or release from frustration. He often thought about his cousin, Nelly. She was pretty and had a great body, and was pliable as putty, but her dependence of Jason unnerved him. And if he ever got caught with her, god, a jail cell with Crazy Wally would be a longed for sanctuary. His Uncle Florian had trusted him, and loved him like the son he never had. The thought sent shivers down Jason's spine so he just avoided Nelly and since she could not venture out of her house alone, there was no chance their paths would cross for a long time to come.

Most recently, there was Dorothy. She was one of the few girls Jason actually admired and respected although he would never admit that to her. A love affair with Dorothy would be serious, complicated, and passionate. He almost didn't want to get involved with her right now. It was too soon. As it turned out he didn't have to make a decision. It was made for him.

"Jason, I hope you can help me out," his father pulled him aside one day. "Don't mention anything to your mother. She's on a bit of a tirade right now. But I promised my sister, Rose, and her husband Elliot, that I or I should say, we, would help them paint their house this summer. You met them once at a Novak family picnic in Hamburg when we had that lamb roast. I told your mother we were going to the Museum of Science."

Jason remembered and he remembered his Aunt Rose most of all. She had been breast feeding her youngest child at the time. At first Jason did not know what was going on as the baby lay cuddled high on the woman's lap.

"So you're Jason. We finally meet. Welcome to the family," the woman said with a sweet smile. When she held out her hand to greet him, a bib fell from her shoulder and exposed her beautiful full breast for his startled eyes to see.

"Oops," his aunt said nonchalantly. "Let me tuck these suckers back in," and she slipped her breasts casually under her loosened blouse.

It all happened so quickly and naturally that Jason wasn't sure he had seen correctly although he did recall being overcome with a sudden urge to pluck his suckling cousin from his aunt's tit, and take over himself.

Jason's aunt and uncle lived in Clarence, a suburb of Buffalo. Elliot, of course was no Polish name so Jason wondered how in the hell his aunt managed to meet, let alone marry, a non Polack. It wasn't a common occurrence, certainly not in his mother's family.

The house in Clarence was a huge two story wooden structure with a large front and back porch. It sat on a very large lot with the next house on the block nowhere in sight. It was a strange set up for Jason who was used to the Kaisertown neighborhood with its closely set houses, narrow sidewalks, and tiny yards. Even the old Irish neighborhood around South Park High School looked for all intents and purposes the same as his own Kaisertown haunts.

Jason had helped his father with other painting jobs during the summer months. They did Aunt Stella's house on Glenn Street and Aunt Mary's on Olsen Street after Uncle John died. All of Jason's relatives on his mother's side lived in Kaisertown. It was only his father's clan that was scattered outside the area with one aunt actually living out of state entirely.

Most of the money the father and son painting team earned was given to Jason for his education. He was a bright student and destined for college. The current job plan was for Jason to stay out in Clarence and work on the house all week long with Uncle Elliot helping out on week-ends and Jason's father stopping by occasionally to supervise. It was August and Jason slept in the back screened porch. His aunt and uncle had two other children beside baby Anders, a boy named Steven and a girl Erika. Turned out that baby Anders had been a surprise addition to the family.

"After that last one, I might add," said Aunt Rose. "I had the doctor tie my tubes. One more kid and I'd kill myself."

Aunt Rose played the piano and she liked jazz music: Duke Ellington, Count Basie, Errol Garner, Teddy Wilson. Jason was unfamiliar with all of them having been brought up on the usual rock and roll music that pervaded the rebellious Kaisertown scene of his peers. His father's and the Professor's love of classical music never rubbed off on him.

"The essential ingredient in jazz," explained Aunt Rose, "is improvisation. You take the basic melody and then give it your own spin. You improvise."

She played a bit on the piano, "Satin Doll."

"The trick is to retain or return to that essential melody or rhythm or signature of the song so that, although you are creating something new, you are honoring its origin. You incorporate your version in with the original. And since you are basically making it up as you go along you never play the song exactly the same way twice. Creation at its most fundamental. It's sexy.

"That's why I love Erroll Garner, though some people, like your Uncle Elliot, find him too self- absorbed. Too much Erroll Garner not enough "Satin Doll." Wait a minute I'll get a record and we can listen together. I've got a bunch of stuff. You'll like it. So here's Billie Holiday, great interpreter, and, oh gees, I haven't played this one in a while, my favorite, Chet Baker. I love his trumpet playing, of course, but his singing. I just want to drop my pants when I hear his voice."

"Put him on for sure," Jason quipped.

"Later," Aunt Rose replied.

Jason and Uncle Elliot worked together for the first weekend, although Uncle Elliot was not used to physical labor and preferred to leave the bulk of the painting to Jason.

"I'd rather pay than stay," he'd say as he'd pack it in early.

The Magnuson children were asleep every night at eight o'clock. At that point Jason would fix himself a late snack: a ham sandwich with lettuce, tomato, and cheese. Then he's sit in the kitchen on the edge of the living room and listen to his aunt play the piano.

"You've got quite the appetite," she commented one night. Aunt Rose wore a bathrobe thrown over a thin, see through slip. When she played the piano the bathrobe often fell open. She didn't have any bra or panties on underneath. Jason had a great view which may have been at least partially responsible for his nightly hunger.

He also noticed Uncle Elliot perpetually asleep in his chair, a folded copy of the "Weekly People" across his lap. Every night was the same. Uncle Elliot would settle down with a drink and his paper and before long he'd be fast asleep. The piano playing, the conversation, nothing disturbed his slumber.

"Narcolepsy," his aunt said.

"Narcolepsy? I thought that was making love to the dead or something like that," commented Jason.

His aunt smiled. "No, but I might have suffered from that myself these last few years. May I get you anything else? Anything?" inquired his aunt.

"Ah, well, no, I think, Aunt Rose…"

"Please, don't call me Aunt Rose. I makes me feel so old."

"Alright, I just…"

She came right up to Jason forcing him to shuffle his feet out of the way and bend backwards in his chair. "You know, Jason, you have the most beautiful eyes I've ever seen. How old are you?"

"Seventeen."

"Seventeen. My god, half my age. How sinful." She stared at him a moment longer, then seemed to refocus her thoughts. "I imagine you're sexually active by now. In this day and age it's nothing unusual. Don't be embarrassed. We can talk this over as adults. As they say, 'Ah youth, too bad it's wasted on the young.' Anyway I think you're a bit precocious in a lot of aspects of life in talking to your father and what I've seen myself. So let me give you some advice when it comes to women, or girls in your case.

"If you want to be a lover, not a sex crazed screwing machine, show some tenderness. A woman wants to be loved not fucked. Do you know what I'm saying?"

"Yes, I think so."

"And you might even want to masturbate beforehand. It takes the pressure off and you can satisfy a woman better instead of hopping on and off like a rabbit. No woman wants a Minute Man in her bed. The Revolutionary War is over."

Wow, Jason thought, maybe if she just showed me in person.

"And oral sex. Let me tell you it's a two way street. As much as you guys are delirious over the proverbial "blow job" women are just as happy with the return favor. That's something you guys completely overlook. And when you're done, don't just turn over and go to sleep. Hold the woman, squeeze her gently and give her a sweet kiss on the forehead. If you do all this, believe me, of all the men in her life, she will remember you.

"Right now, if I was even ten years younger and not married, or if you were ten years older we might get something going. Hell, if I was single and free again that might do it. Who cares about old fashioned morals? I gave up on the church long ago."

"So, I guess I'll have to check in from time to time," Jason smiled. "Just in case."

Throughout the heated conversation Uncle Elliot didn't move. He snored on contentedly.

"How does he manage at work?" Jason asked.

"As long as he doesn't sit down, he's fine. Your uncle actually works standing up. He's a draftsman so it comes naturally."

Jason's father arrived the next Sunday to check up on his son's progress on the paint job. "Doesn't look like you got that much done in the last few days," he commented. "Bad weather out here?"

"Jason wasn't feeling well," volunteered Aunt Rose. "I told him to take it easy. If he pushes too hard, he'll exhaust himself prematurely. He's taken on a big job."

In their nightly intimate talk sessions, Jason and Aunt Rose spent a lot of time playing records and listening to jazz and the blues on the radio. They especially enjoyed, "The Blue Monday Club" broadcast late at night and live on WBEN from Johnny's Ellicott Bar and Grille in Buffalo. They'd also often just sit together on the living room couch talking about everything from politics and bird watching to sex and literature.

"I see you're reading Dickens," his aunt commented after noticing a copy of Hard Times in Jason's suitcase. "I read all his stuff in college. Dickens had a great social conscience although he could never translate that into an outright condemnation of the capitalist system. He was a reformer not a revolutionary. Of course, you can't really blame him. He was a writer not a politician. Then again, Dickens had to throw in all that moral crap about fallen women and lost family values, poor Nelly. That much was bullshit. Matter of fact, now that I think of it, fuck Dickens. He didn't mind screwing around himself. Male superiority. I got a real problem with that.'

Jason noted his aunt's wet lips on the filter, the sucking and resultant glowing red tip of the cigarette, the tilted head and spirals of smoke issuing from her open mouth.

"There's just too much I want to do for myself. Hell, I've got enough trouble with a marriage and family eating up all my time. To tell you the truth, I don't know if I can take this shit anymore, spending my time cleaning, cooking, washing. It's ridiculous. I should have been born with a cock. You bastards have it made. You can even fuck without repercussions. It's the woman who has to worry about getting pregnant and raising children. What the hell did I get an education for?"

"Uncle Elliot seems like a good man though," Jason interrupted.

"Yes, Elliot's a good man, a good man. You're all good men."

During his quiet moments painting the house Jason often contemplated the extreme difference between his two parental families. His father's side was populated by strange characters, book enthusiasts, bird watchers, jazz and classical music fans, and political radicals. His mother's family on the other hand was petty, backbiting, fervent Catholics and adherents to the old country morals and customs. The odd thing was, they were all Polish. It made the boy wonder.

After his stay in Clarence Jason decided to visit Johnny's Ellicott and experience "The Blue Monday Club" first hand. He was intrigued by the pounding blues music and the background crowd noises and the bustling sounds of the bar room scene. He got his cousin Larry to lend him his ID and drop him off.

"I ain't goin in dere, sorry," said Larry, "too many niggers. I'd get in a fight for sure and I'm already on probation. Be careful you don't get knifed."

Jason had never seen so many colored people in one place before without a white face in the crowd other than the bartender whose voice Jason recognized as John Weiss, the owner himself. A waitress came up to him. She was a colored girl, pretty with a slim shape, short skirt and a beautiful round ass.

"What can I get you?" she asked.

Jason hesitated. He had noticed several cocktail glasses along the bar and on the tables. Somehow he figured a mere beer would be too plebeian and he remembered his Uncle Elliott back in Clarence.

"I'll have a bourbon Manhattan, neat, please." The waitress raised her eyebrows and seemed impressed. Jason could see her at the bar nodding in his direction as she spoke to the bartender.

"Here you go," she said upon her return. "Hope you likes it. My name is Pearl. I'm Johnny's woman. What bring you in here?"

"The music. I like jazz, and the blues too, of course."

"Good, enjoy, and be sure to tell all yer friends about Johnny's Ellicott Grille. We like to see white people in here. Everyone's welcome at Johnny's."

Jason felt self-conscious at first, but after a few initial glances in his direction, he quickly blended into the crowd. Everyone simply melded together, drinking, talking and introducing themselves. The music made them one. They were colorblind.

The band was set up in the back corner of the room: three men; a drummer, bass player, and Mr. Monty Hall, singer and organ player extraordinaire. They were playing "Hey Bartender" with Monty Hall modifying the lyrics. "Hey bartender, buy the organ player a drink. Hey bartender, have everybody buy the organ player a drink."

Before Jason left the bar that night he sent up a drink to all three band members. He was flush with money from his paint job. They raised their glasses to him as he exited. Pearl smiled. Jason met Larry outside in the car.

"Yer in one piece anyways," said Larry. "I don't know how you can listen to dat jungle bunny music. Give me Elvis any day."

"To each his own," Jason replied.

"You oughta hook up wit Dorothy dere," continued Larry. "Dorothy Klein. She likes dat same shit music."

"That's a thought," replied Jason.

Pani Khula: "Nic Niema. There is Nothing"

Pani Khula pulled the empty coaster wagon down South Ogden Street to the corner of Clinton, then down the block until she entered Tedlinski's Butcher Shop. She walked slowly, pained by the flood of memories that burdened her. She glanced back at the lonely wagon and imagined little Wladek there, smiling proudly and holding on to the sides of the wagon with white knuckles. She saw him with a bunch of long stemmed gray headed dandelions, waving and frantically blowing on them to let loose the flight of the fuzzy little parachutes. Invariably he'd bounce a fat fist against his nose or eye and the tears would flow. Pani Khula would then cuddle and comfort him, her most precious of cargoes.

The neighbors knew them well, Pani Khula and her son. Yes, the boy was different, and at first, the women would make the sign of the cross when they saw them approach. But later they accepted the mother and child. He was, after all, such a happy boy, and who can question the ways of god.

When he was older, Wladek pulled the wagon himself. He was careful and proud. He'd grin, clap and point at the shiny wagon as he moved it along the streets. In Tedlinski's store he'd arrange the packages on the wagon, carefully in his mind's eye, but haphazardly to any onlooker. Invariably the parcels would fall off along the way back, but he'd patiently stop, retrieve them, and then once again heap them amid the others to continue the trundling trip down the streets. Pani Khula never interfered. It was his journey.

Now the shopping trip was a chore filled with sadness. Even the jovial, fat nosed face of Mr. Tedlinski could not cheer Pani Khula. It only reminded her of the big round suckers the store owner had habitually given to Wladek. How the boy looked forward to his reward, smiling at the long glass counter, his little fingers working an unseen instrument and his feet tapping out a rhythm that only he could hear.

Mr. Tedlinski filled Pani Khula's order himself, prompting her occasionally to make sure she got all she needed and also take advantage of the specials on offer that day. The aroma of fresh sausage that pervaded the market reminded Pani Khula of Wladek's favorite time of year, Easter. That was when all his seasonal goodies were on display: fragrant kielbasa, fresh baked sweet rolls, and the butter baraneks, and colored eggs. Oh how he loved the Easter eggs. When he was very young he'd bite right through the shells and Pani Khula would have to brush the smashed egg shells off his tongue with a spoon. Then there was the candy. That was when his teeth started going bad. It was all the chocolate he ate at Easter. He wouldn't stop until it made him sick.

Her house, near the end of South Ogden Street across from the open fields and swamps that the children called Okie Diamond, was a small, brown insul-brick affair. It was neglected now having been without the services of a man for many years. Pani Khula had tried with Wladek's clumsy assistance to cut the grass, maintain the yard, and do minor repairs required of the property, but now she stopped. The place looked deserted, almost spooky in its dilapidation. The windows were shut tight and the curtains forever closed. The house ceased to breathe, echoing the suffocation in Pani Khula's own soul. The children on the block called her, "the South Ogden Witch" and crossed the street and ran away rather than pass directly in front of the old house. Even Father Kolinski abandoned her, frustrated by her unbreakable sadness and inability to let go of her feeling and trust once again in god.

Pani Khula took to drinking in the year of Wladek's arrest and incarceration at the Wendy Home. The criminal mental hospital was too far away for her to visit and she was crushed by her separation from her helpless son. Her first and only visit there had been a nightmare. The place was filthy and filled with restrained and celled prisoners and patients. The stench was unbearable and the screaming, pleading and swearing more than she could stand. Wladek was in a ward with seven other men half of whom were tied to their beds or wheelchairs. Wladek did not recognize her. He just rocked in his chair hugging himself and sobbing. She had to leave when medication time came around. She stopped at the chapel on her way out, but the priest was too busy to see her.

The occasional swallow of Krupnik had become a half a bottle a day habit, a tranquilizer for Pani Khula. She saw Wladek's face everywhere. Many, many a time in her drunken delirium or grief stricken hallucinations she saw her son enter the back door, or stroll out of his bedroom, his bright Mickey Mouse pack on his back and the little toy gun on his hip. She did not fight the images. She clung to them as the only reality that mattered. She rarely retired to her bed, choosing instead to sleep on the faded horsehair sofa where she regularly passed out after drinking all night. She kept the candles burning in front of the bambinko on the buffet as the only illumination in the room. Although she kept all the religious icons in the house, she ignored them completely. Even the basin of holy water at the doorway was dry and she no longer bothered to cross herself when passing the holy pictures. Her life was at an end. She wept for what used to be.

Barney: *"Pamietasz. Remember?"*

It was a Saturday afternoon and Barney surveyed the barroom from his favorite perch behind the cash register. There were three men in the establishment: one at the bar nursing a draft, and two at a nearby table hoping a couple of friends would show up to round out a pinochle game. "Play cards, cy co?"

Another quiet day, one of many in recent years, lamented Barney. Where had all his customers gone? It didn't seem that long ago when his bar was a veritable circus, teeming with life and laughter, and Barney was the ringmaster; jovial, confident, and commanding. He occupied center stage, the social spotlight shining directly down on him. He loved it then. People confided in him. They borrowed money from him, asked his advice, valued his opinion and envied every dollar that dropped into the constantly jingling cash register.

Well, for one thing, a lot of the old timers were gone. Eddie, the Red, was dead, and Tony, the numbers man passed on along with the game itself. Nobody played the numbers anymore. Poncho, his weekend piano player, Ed Przepyszny, and Larry Stanikowski, all who had regularly dropped their paychecks in the bar on a Friday night had retired and moved away from Kaisertown, gone with hundreds of their neighbors and thousands throughout Buffalo to the suburbs of West Seneca, Amherst, Cheektowaga, Clarence, and Orchard Park.

And the young piss pots nowadays, they didn't come into the

Kaisertown bars like their fathers and grandfathers had done. Barney remembered clearly just a couple of years ago, when five young men stepped into his bar. They were Kaisertown boys. He had seen them in the neighborhood. The men took a quick look around as though they had accidently stepped into some foreign land.

"Holy shit, how long this place been here? Looks ancient," blurted out one of the guys.

"You got a jukebox in this dump, old man?" inquired another. "Pool table?"

They exited laughing and shaking their heads. "Guy's a fuckin dinosaur," he heard one of them say.

Punks, he thought. Dem and dere God damn cars. Dat was dah problem. Drivin around everywhere. Don't spend no time or money in dah old neighborhood. If you don't have to drive to a place, it can't be no good. Nobody ate in the bars no more either. Instead they drove out to the hamburger joints, the drive-ins, and the plazas with their Your Host and pancake houses. How was a local business man supposed to make any money?

Barney's world was disappearing. Already a lot of the bars in Kaisertown were shut down, or converted into private homes with awkward entrances and overly large windows. His was the only mid street bar remaining. All the other and several on Clinton Street itself were gone: Pump Inn, the Orange Front, Bill's and El's, Frank's, the Clinton Lounge, all vanished.

It was a bitter pill to swallow, a fall from a high place. But in a way he was lucky too. He and Jeanette owned the house and the business outright and they owed no money to nobody. Their bank book was large, especially when you took into account the seven thousand dollar nest egg Jeanette had saved over the years for that trip to Florida. What was more, they never had any children. Who could afford kids anyway with all of them wanting allowances and cars, and dreaming of collage. It was ridiculous and furthermore, it would have pulled Jeanette away from the bar. What would he have done without his wife back when business was booming?

And Jesus, speaking of Jeanette, he really should pick her up a little gift or some token of his appreciation. All these years. He barely remembered her birthday or their anniversary. Maybe a nice new apron for her upcoming birthday, one with her name stitched on it, or a new cigarette case. He had given her an initialed lighter, a good Zippo, a number of years back. She was thrilled and it hadn't cost him anything except for the engraving because he got it complimentary from the Wilson's distributor. He was going to have her full name put on it, but the "J.A." in big letters looked good enough.

Poor Jeanette, she was not looking good lately. Lost weight, and she coughed a lot. Her smoking habit, two packs a day, didn't help. Then there was all that second hand smoke from the barroom. Barney cleared his throat repeatedly just thinking about it. Luckily Barney never picked up the habit himself. Too expensive first of all. What was the sense of spending money on something that you lit up and then watched burn to ashes. Stupid.

"Maybe I should see a doctor, Barney? What do you tink" Jeanette asked one day when she was too sick to come down into the bar.

"Just relax in dah bed today," he replied. "Take id easy. Dah bar isn't too busy no more. I can handle it. We close now at nine on weekdays, eleven on Sadurday. No sense boat of us overdoin it. You stay here."

"I hope it ain't nuttin serious, you know Barney. We got dat trip to Florida comin up soon, nie? Been savin for so long. We godda go dis winter, nie, Barney? It'll be nice too. And you know dat's probably just what I need, some nice fresh air, dah ocean air. It's supposed to be real good for you. And dah sunshine and dah nice warm water. Wouldn't dat be nice, Barney? We're gonna go dis year fer sure, right honey, right Barney?"

Barney just nodded his head.

"I gotta go get dah bar ready. We'll talk later. Watch yer shows dere in dah afternoon and take it easy. I'll put a couple a hankies next to dah couch for you. I hate dose Kleenex boxes you buy. Such a waste. You blow in dem and den throw dem out."

Downstairs Barney set up the bar. He had his routine, but it was not as involved as it used to be since there was little point with business down as it was. Jimmy Pajak came in.

"Budweiser," intoned Jimmy. "Stomach can't take it dah whiskey no more. Doctor said I shouldn't drink at all with dah medicine, but what dah hell, you gotta die a sometin, nie? Look at President Kennedy," he said raising his glass. "Piorun, we finally ged one of our own in dere, good Catlick, an dey kill him. Jews guarantee."

"Yer right dere. Wasn't it a Jew shot Oswald? Ruby, he was a Jew. How come a Jew was in dere an got right up to dah guy? Kennedy was breakin up dah Jewish control a dah banks and dah big money. Dey didn't like dat, nie. Had to get rid a him so dah Jews got a commie dere to kill him. Den dey knock off dah killer. Dat's how dey do it. Mafia too. Kill dah killers so dey can't talk."

"Too bad we didn't give Hitler more time. Would a got rid a dah Jews and finish off dah Russians on top of it. Now we gotta fight em all over again. And how's Jeanette doing?" Jimmy added changing the topic.

Barney shook his head. "Not good."

"What dah doctor say?"

"Piorun, you know Jeanetta. She won't see no doctor. I couldn't drag her."

The two men reminisced, recounting the lost lives of former customers and decrying the general deterioration of the Kaisertown neighborhood.

"Over by Weichek's he put in a whole new bar," said Jimmy. "My boy Stan, he did all dah plumbin, and one a dem new Formica tops, looks like marble, you know, dark green and white. And he's got new tables too and all new chairs and stools wit green and white plastic seats. Real nice. Dobze. Got a juke box too. Some women are going over by there now. Busy."

"Maybe dat's what I need around here," mused Barney. "Change tings around. But what would dah old timers tink? You know dey like tings to stay dah same, nie?"

"What old timers?" Jimmy said.

"Yeah, you got a point dere," Barney admitted, "but where would I get dah money for all dat? Must cost a fortune."

"Five thousand, it cost Weichek. Dah juke box, he just rents dat. Gets a percent a dah songs it plays."

"Five thousand," Barney mused out loud. "Five thousand."

"Yeah, dat's a lot of pienwenze, but wort it. Business is good by Weichek's. Gimme another Budweiser."

Nelly: "Trzynajsie Wiatru. Cling to the Wind."

Nelly made the sign of the cross as she stood in her bedroom beneath the small but resplendent bambinko and the flickering red candle in front of it. She kissed the rosary and hung it around the infant Jesus' neck.

"Oh god, please," she whispered.

She was late with her period, almost a month, and she was in a panic. How could this happen? She had only done it that one time with Jason, and he knew what to do. He had worn one of those things. It was perfectly safe. He said so. He promised.

"A month, are you sure? Did you keep track of this before?" Jason stammered at the news.

"I think so. I mean I never thought about it. I trusted you. I never figured. My father's gonna kill us."

"Jesus Christ, what a stupid thing to do. I don't have enough girls to screw around with I've got to fuck my own cousin but, never mind," lamented Jason trying to contain his concerns to the current problem.

"I'm gonna tell my mother. I can't stand it no more," Nelly cried.

"Holy shit, don't do that. Let's make sure first. I mean, maybe you're not pregnant. It's possible you could be mistaken. Once you open your mouth, it's all over any way you look at it."

Nelly felt a pang of sympathy for her cousin. After all the whole affair was her idea. She sought out Jason and encouraged him. Maybe, this was the Lord's way of punishing me also, Nelly thought, for not believing in him and turning my back on the ways of the church. Sure, the sisters had been miserable and cruel, but that didn't mean they were wrong. Now it looked like everything they said was true. She had looked into her cousin's burning eyes and seen his naked body and lusted after it. She wanted and then enjoyed the sex and never thought about the consequences. Now they were upon her. She was caught in her own sinful trap. And what could she do now? Jason was her first cousin. They couldn't get married and cover up the pregnancy like her sister Frances did. And oh my god, the baby. What about the baby?

Nelly pictured herself in a home for unwed mothers just as Sister Superior had warned her and her classmates. Nelly was walking the halls amongst other sinful girls with their bellies stuck out in shame and the nuns laughing and pointing. She'd live in a cell of a room and spend hours on her knees saying the rosary over and over again. And once the baby was born he'd be immediately taken away and put up for adoption.

"I swear I will never, ever have nothing to do with boys again," Nelly shouted at Jason. "I wish you weren't my cousin no more."

Nelly was alert and sensitive to everything around her now. She checked her body in the mirror every day to see if her stomach was expanding. The more she looked, the fatter she seemed to be getting. And she kept a close eye on her father wondering if somehow he sensed her predicament. He did seem to be particularly quiet of late as though he was worried about something.

"Oh god," Nelly prayed, "if you'll just do this one thing for me, I will learn my lesson. Don't let this happen. Don't let my father find out. It will break his heart. I'll do anything, anything."

It was Saturday morning and Nelly still lay in bed. She could hear her mother fixing breakfast in the kitchen just outside her bedroom door.

The smell of eggs frying in butter and the crisp crackling of kiska in the frying pan did nothing for her appetite. She was apprehensive and nauseous.

Suddenly a crashing sound jolted Nelly out of her melancholy reverie. Something had fallen to the floor in the other room. The bambinko on her dresser shook from the impact, and the votive candle flickered. What? Then she heard her mother's voice.

"Florian, Florian, you OK in dere? Florian?" Then the scream. "Oh rany bozka, Florian!"

Nelly ran into the kitchen. The bathroom door was open and she saw her mother kneeling across the prostrate form of her father. His large chest and protruding stomach, long the object of family jokes, did not rise and fall. He wasn't breathing.

"Rany bozka, run an get Pani Flisakowski next door," shouted Nelly's mother. "Call dah police, or dah firemens to come. Go."

The firemen huddled around Nelly's fallen father. His face was already blue. Nelly's mother was held by Pani Flisakowski while a clutch of other neighbors looked on. Nelly stared at her father's body. Then she remembered her prayers. No, her body trembled and tears rolled down her cheeks.

"No, daddy, no. I'm sorry. I didn't mean it that way," she cried out. The crowd looked upon her pityingly. Her mother gestured and one of the neighbor ladies walked over to Nelly and put her arm around her. The girl began to shake uncontrollably. Her knees got weak. Her stomach tightened and she felt sick. Then a collective gasp was heard in the room.

"Oh bozka, help her," Nelly's mother shouted. "Get her out. Here, I get dah towels."

There was a blurred, confused movement of people. Everyone's attention focused away from the bathroom and clearly on Nelly. Their eyes moved across her body from head to toe. Nelly followed their stares. A bright stream of blood flowed down the inside of her thigh, behind her knee and onto her left heel. Nelly's mouth opened, but no sound came out. She fell to her knees. Through her bedroom door she espied the bambinko. A strong breeze rushed past the girl's body from the open kitchen door. The red candle on the dresser top flickered and went out. Nelly collapsed.

Jason: "Life is Like a Faucet. It Turns off and On."

Jason sat at a booth in Babe's Ice Cream Parlor, an untouched chocolate milkshake in front of him along with a worn paperback copy of <u>Bleak House</u>. Everyone in the establishment knew Jason by name. Ever since the cops had pulled away from the curb with Jason firmly ensconced in the back seat of the squad car his reputation had grown to celebrity status. Everyone figured it was because of the "big rumble" and other gang activity that he was questioned about back then. No one knew the truth. In fact, since the arrest and incarceration of Crazy Wally, the rape and murder of Tina Kasprczyk was almost a forgotten event in Kaisertown.

Jason had not forgotten Tina, however. After all, she had been his first sexual partner, his live experiment, his Kinsey Report so to speak. But trouble developed with Tina fast enough. She became more and more dependent and clinging until Jason was so socially stifled that he couldn't breathe anymore.

"I don't care what happens," Tina had said. "You can do anyting you want to me. I don't care. I just wanna be wit you. I wanna get married and have yer babies."

That was it for Jason. Of course, he was reminded of that predicament again when at the funeral home he was accosted by Tina's mother.

"Jason, Jason, oh jenna! If onny you woulda marry my Tina, none a dis woulda happen. She was such a good girl. Woulda made a good wife and mudder too. Now she's gone, my baby, my Tina. Boze wanned her. He took her to heaven with dah angel. My Tina."

If they were so eager to be with god, Jason reasoned, why all the grief when someone actually died? Weren't they then in heaven? Wasn't that the longed for destination all along?

Of course, after the experience with Tina, what did I do, Jason reminded himself. I moved right along into the same dead end relationship with Nelly. She was beautiful and pliable sure, but that affair would have gone nowhere too. Thank god she wasn't pregnant either and had the good sense to keep her mouth shut. That would have been a disaster.

'Oh yeah, dad, everything is fine except for the fact that I just knocked up cousin, Nelly. Thought I might throw that in while we discuss what university I'm enrolling in. And would you mind telling ma the good news, and maybe Uncle Florian and Aunt Bertha too?'

That was the beauty of older woman, Jason reasoned turning his thoughts to his Aunt Rose. They could take care of themselves. He wondered too just when and how he would see his aunt again and if they'd ever have the sex together that both of them had been imagining during those long conversations over the past summer. In the meantime he was through with virgins. It wasn't a moment later, however, that the image of Pearl, the colored waitress at Johnny's Ellicott, flitted through his mind.

"Jesus, get a hold of yourself," he mumbled. "You just got out of a tight corner with your cousin and now you're thinking of fucking some black girl down in the ghetto."

Jason mechanically turned the page of his book. He did not notice his cousin Larry and their buddy Corny, enter the building.

"How yah doin asshole?" Larry said trying to get Jason's attention, but the boy did not reply. "Hello inside," Larry repeated.

"Hey, Stonewallski, dere's four girls outside from Villa Maria. Dey wanna take turns suckin yer dick," Corny added.

Jason blinked a couple of times and looked up. "Oh, what? Hi, how you doing?"

"What dah fuck is wit you?" asked Larry. Then he changed his tone. "Upset about Uncle Florian? Yeah, me too. He was a good guy. I heard Nelly's pretty fucked up about it too."

"Hey man, what you readin dere?" asked Corny. "Dat a book? I read a book one time an it wasn't even for school. Was about des guys, you know, was in a gang and…"

"You mind?" said Larry before continuing with Jason. "I liked Uncle Florian too. He never had no steady job, but dah guy was smart. Anyting mechanical, electrical, or plumbin, he could do it all. Remember when we took dat car radio over to him. Helped us put it in my Chevy."

"Yes, because you lost the instructions."

"Found em later."

"That was after Uncle Florian already installed the radio and he put it in exactly as the instructions indicated. That was cool."

"Yeah, I remember dem barbecues dey used to have in dere backyard over by Glenn Street. Whole family show up and play cards. And dem pigeons he raised up in the old garage. Used to eat em."

"What does a pigeon taste like?" asked Corny.

"Fuck if I know," replied Larry. "You wouldn't catch me eatin one a dem little cock suckers, but Uncle Florian and his family was poor."

"Dat cousin, Nelly, of yers though," said Corny. "I seen her a couple of times. Dat is some broad. I wouldn't mind…"

He looked at the other two boys.

"I mean if she wasn't yer cousin and everyting."

"Fuck, I almost forgot," said Larry to Jason. "You ain't seen dat prick

Chevy around nowhere, have yah?"

"No, I've been in a kind of trance here. He could have come in. I wouldn't have noticed. Why?"

"Cause we're gonna kick dah shit outa him, dat's why," said Corny.

"Yeah, wait till you hear dis one," continued Larry. "Bunch of us was down at Diamond #2 watchin the softball game. Barney's Ballers was playin Stan's Tavern and stupid Tommy Novacewski, he takes out dis safe and fills it wit water from dah fountain. Gonna make a water balloon, you know."

Jason nodded.

"So he fills the safe up and brings it over to dah bleachers and we're all lookin at it because the fuckin ting is pissin water like one a dem tings the priest uses to sprinkle holy water all over the place."

"Yeah," said Jason.

"Was full of holes," said Corny. "Turns out it was one a dem safes dat Chevy's been sellin around Kaisertown. Fuck, I bought some myself. Buck each, you know, dat's a good price."

"Where is this going?" asked Jason. "I bought a few myself."

"We all bought safes from Chevy," said Corny. "But dat fucker all along was prickin holes in dem. You know, dey was wrapped in dat gold foil. So he took a pin and jabbed it along dah edges. Fuckin sabotaged dem safes."

Jason turned pale and swallowed hard. 'Ohh my fucking lord," he stammered.

"What's dah matter? You use one a dem lately?"

"Oh man," Jason continued, the image of his cousin Nelly standing in tears in front of him flashed through his mind.

"Well, you ain't dah only one sweatin it out," said Larry.

"Yeah, how about Frankie, Donny, and Pruny?" interjected Corny.

"Dem poor fuckers was gang bangin dat scrag Lois Stachowski over by Donny's house one night when his parents were over by Weichek's for a fish fry. Dey were all usin safes from Chevy. Fuck, I'd cut my dick off I had to marry dat ting."

"Hey stupid," said Larry. "Who's she gonna prove was dah father? Every hard up dick in Kaisertown's been fuckin her for years."

The two boys left on their quest for revenge while Jason dropped his head in his hands, If I had known about this a couple of weeks ago when Nelly thought she was pregnant I would have been swinging from Black Bridge by now, Jesus Christ. Of course, I can't say I was much comfort to Nelly either, Jason recalled. Maybe I can talk to her at the funeral, smooth things over, and we can at least be friends or cousins again.

At the funeral, however, Nelly ignored Jason completely. He tried to catch her glance by staring at her until she felt the pierce of his eyes just like in the old days, but his tactics failed. Nelly was too absorbed in her grief and shut Jason out.

At St. Stanislaus Cemetery the assembled relatives broke into mournful song as Uncle Florian's casket was lowered into the grave. It reminded Jason of his babcia's burial many years before. He had not attended Tina's service. The visit to the funeral parlor was enough for him.

"Witaj Krolowo nieba I Matko litosci, Witaj Nadziejo nasza w smutku I zalosci, K'Tobie wygnancy Ewy wolamy synowie, K'Tobie wzdychamy placzac z padolu wieznioie."

Nelly turned to Jason for the first time. The look on her face told him more certainly than words could express that he would no longer be part, any part, of Nelly's life. The bond that had held them together for all those years was broken. Jason hung his head, but did not pray.

"O Jezu, niech po smierci ciebie ogladamy, O Maryo, upros nam czego pozadamy."

Nelly grabbed her mother's hand and together with Frances the grieving women gathered the loosened dirt from the edge of the grave and sprinkled it down on the coffin. It sounded like a hard rain upon the heavy metal lid below.

"O Jezu, Jezu, Jezu, Jezu kochany! Jezu wielkiej dobroci nigdy nit Przebrany."

At the Pulaski Post where the funeral supper was held Jason sat with his cousin Larry. The hall was filled with the din of people as they arrived in bunches from the cemetery. Two long buffet tables were laden with the usual food fare: smoked and fresh kielbasa, noodle and potato salads, rye bread, pickled beets, horseradish, sliced tomatoes, and cucumbers. Coffee, cheesecake, and poppy seed kuhas rounded out the desserts. Relatives and friends stood around or took seats as they pleased. A free bar had been set up. There was much talking and reminiscing.

"Dey're gonna have to sell dah house, nie. Not a pot to piss in."

"Poor Nelly, she talkin it hard, nie? I heard Berta's gonna get her in by Drescher."

"She was close to Jason, Vickie's kid. If dey weren related I bet you dey get married."

"Best ting for her to find someone, a man to take care of her."

"What's wit Nelly?" asked Larry noticing the difference in attitude. "I thought yous two were close. Kissin cousins wasn't it? Somethin happen?"

"I'm the lowest of the low," Jason said in reply.

Larry tapped Jason on the shoulder. "Dat's Ok, cousin. Don't worry. Wit all yer faults I love you still."

"Where the hell did you hear that?" said Jason. "I thought you were an Elvis man?"

"Dat crazy broad Dorothy Klein. I run into her once in a while 'cause she hangs around wit Janie, dat new broad I'm seein. Janie's kinda chubby, but she's cute and sweet and has a great pair of tits. I like her."

"Yes, Dorothy. I've come close with her a few times, but we never quite clicked."

"It wouldn't take much, believe me," added Larry. "And you don't have to worry about Chevy no more. Dey broke up. Matter of fact he just got out of the hospital. Lucky I didn't kill him which is what I wanna talk to you about. I got into trouble over dat beatin I laid on him. Got charged wit assault. I already seen dah judge. Dat and some other shit I been in was gonna mean jail time."

"What? No way, man. Did you get a lawyer?"

"Oh yeah, I got dat F. Lee Bailey guy lined up."

"Seriously, what are you going to do?"

"Already been done. I signed up for the army. Only way I could get outa jail. 'The army could use a good man like you,' the judge said to me. 'Learn to control dat anger you got in you. Might turn yer life around. Done good for udders. One thing for sure, you ain't gonna improve in jail. It's up to you, Uncle Sam or Uncle Slam.' Funny guy dat judge. I'm gone in a mont. Basic trainin."

"Holy shit, I hope you don't get sent to Vietnam. It's starting to get serious over there."

"Maybe I could get a job in dah motor pool. I'm good wit engines and shit like dat. Who knows? Anyway, I also wanted to tell you dat one time, a while back, the cops had me in the precinct, and dey started askin about you."

"Me?"

"Yeah you and Tina Kaspryzck. Dey wanted to know if I seen you dat day when she was killed out dere in Okie Diamond."

"What did you say?"

"I told em you were wit me the whole night. We was drinkin and hangin around the park. You know, like we do all dah time anyways," Larry smiled.

"But, you know, I wasn't with you that night," Jason said.

"I been questioned by the cops lots a times," continued Larry. "I knew dey were fishin for information and dey weren't gonna get nuttin from me."

"Thanks," said Jason. "You know I never would have had anything to do with hurting Tina."

"I know dat, but sometimes you don't have to try too hard to get into trouble. It finds you. You know, Jason, yer smart and you got everyting goin for you. Get outa here while you can. Dere ain't nuttin but trouble hangin around Kaisertown, and I won't be here no more to protect you. And one more ting. I want to know if you'd take care of my car for me while I'm gone. Insurance is paid up for the year. After dat you just gotta pay it yerself."

"I don't even have a driver's license."

"You can get one inna month before I leave. Up to you. Want it or not?"

"Yes, sure, I'll just have to talk to my dad."

Jason looked around the hall for his father. He found him sitting alone near the cloak room, his jacket thrown over a chair, a bottle of beer on the table in front of him. He looked tired. Of course, Jason's father and Uncle Florian had been close all their lives despite the wide differences in the lifestyles and interests. The discrepancy reminded Jason of his own relationship with his cousin Larry. Jason explained the situation regarding the car. His father seemed lost in thought and uninterested.

"Well, what do you think?" Jason finally asked.

"I'm leaving your mother," came his father's response.

"What? Jesus, you Novaks are certainly blunt if nothing else," Jason said thinking back to his Aunt Rose and her sexual advances towards him. "Can't you break the ice a bit first? Some kind of prelude maybe?"

"Why, it wouldn't change anything. I just can't put up with it anymore. I'm stifled. I'm getting older, for god's sake, and what have I done with my life? What can I point to as a lifetime achievement?"

"You godda nice house," Jason offered with a smile.

"You know, son, you've been lucky. You've had lots of girlfriends, and I know you've slept with some of them. You've had experiences. I've actually envied you these past few years. When I was a young man, hell, we didn't know a thing about sex, and had no way of finding out. To get a copy of the god damn Kinsey Report you had to prove you were a medical student. This sex thing, it preoccupied a man's thoughts.

"Now your mother was a beautiful woman, beautiful. She still is for that matter, but I got carried away with that idea. I wanted her, had to have her, and in those days, don't kid yourself, that meant marriage. And I was egotistical. I thought I could have it all: pursue my own interests in music and literature and have her at home taking care of my other needs."

"Sounds a bit like the Professor," replied Jason.

"I'm afraid you're right. Exactly. And it wasn't realistic, or fair to her. It was a losing game and it has finally come to an end and I'm sorry."

"I can't say I blame you," Jason commented. "So where would I go?"

"Well, it would be nice if your mother did not contest the separation. We could just settle the whole thing amicably. She can have the house and then there will be support money. Now if you stay with your mother that means I'd have to pay out more for you also. It's up to you. I don't know how your mother is going to take it."

"Not well."

Not well indeed. The first thing Jason's mother did, on the advice of her sisters, was to get a good lawyer, a good Jewish lawyer. Of course, this was to be expected, not only because it was vindictive and would cost the old man plenty of money, but also because there was a genuine element of ignorance about divorce within the Kaisertown community. Of Jason's seven aunts on his mother's side, and even those on his father's and taking into account any neighbor he ever knew, no one, but no one, had ever been divorced before.

Like a medical patient discussing her ailments, Jason's mother toured the neighborhood recounting her matrimonial woes and soliciting sympathetic advice and comforting words from her bewildered friends and relatives. Pani Novak was the talk of Kaisertown, and as the wronged and pitiful center of attention she somehow managed to put a brave face on her fate.

Deep down, of course, even Jason knew the wound was deep and maybe even fatal and the social stigma was huge. And for all the expressed sympathy and indignation, the undercurrent of shame was palpable. The neighborhood was abuzz with gossip. Obviously that damned Edda wanted too much. After all the years she had given him, how could he betray her like this? But still, some of the fault must also lie with Pani Novak. And all those who envied her good looks and suffered her noticeable condescension, those whose husbands did not have as good a job as her Edda, whose house was not nearly as nice as hers, whose furniture was more worn and outdated, and whose child was not as handsome and popular, to all those people, she got just what she deserved. Jason remained with his mother.

The family house was sold, a crushing blow to his mother's pride and reputation. He and his mother moved into a flat above Pani Lusychin's house on Meadowbrook Street. Jason had Larry's car, and less than a year left in high school. He saw his father frequently, and often drove him to meeting, appointments, and assignations. Jason wasn't bitter. He enjoyed the freedom and notoriety his parents' divorce had given him although he found living with his mother difficult and frustrating and pretty soon impossible.

Timmy Klein: Juden Rat

Timmy didn't have any friends in Kaisertown. There had been one or two younger boys that he had played with for the past couple of years, but the children's parents ended the relationships. They didn't trust, nor like, Timmy and for good reason. One time Timmy forced the young Langosinski kid to steal cigarettes and candy off the shelves of Charlotte's store. He then taught the boy how to smoke and every now and then he'd take the lad up to the garage loft, get him drunk, and make him suck Timmy's cock.

"Here, wash it down with a beer and stop cryin. If you squeal I'll tell all yer friends that yer a cock suckin queer."

Timmy was stuck with his little boy friends because absolutely no girl in Kaisertown would look at him, not even that slut of sluts, Lois Stachowski. That was particularly galling to Timmy because it was said that at a drunken party at the back of Houghton Park, Lois had even let Stachu Klemp fuck her on a five dollar bet from some of the guys.

One night Timmy resolved to get his revenge on Lois. No slut was gonna tell him to go fuck himself, he vowed, so he secretly followed her home. She had been drinking and sucking guys off in the parking lot at Babe's. Timmy figured she must have been fed at least a dozen beers. Why anyone would waste so much beer on such a scrag he couldn't understand, but he thought he might as well take advantage of the situation.

Lois was wobbly walking home that night. None of the Kaisertown gallants offered to escort her. Timmy waited until she got into her yard before grabbing the girl from behind. Trouble was that her neck was so big and fat that he couldn't hook his arm around it for proper leverage. Lois promptly slammed her elbow into his ear, then pivoted around, surprisingly quickly too for a fat broad, Timmy noted, and kicked him in the nuts. It took the wind out of him and gave Lois enough time to clock him several times in the face with her fists. As he turned to flee in terror he heard Lois yell after him.

"You little cock sucker, you ripped my blouse. I ged my hands on you I'll sit on yer face till you stop breedin."

Just the thought of Lois Stachowski's big sweaty ass in such close proximity to his breathing passages made Timmy forget his pain and begin running like Stach Klemp after a garbage truck. He also had a new found appreciation of Lois' strength and her capacity for alcohol.

"That bitch could drink the Doyle II Volunteer Fire House under the table. Hope she chokes on a cock and dies."

From that time onward Timmy figured unless something virtually fell into his lap, he'd best stop looking for trouble. After all it was only two years ago that he sweated out that whole affair with Tina and Glupi Wladek. He had seen the cop car pull up next door with Jason inside. It was nice to pin the blame on that bastard neighbor of his, but if the cops figured out Jason wasn't with Wladek that evening, which they did, then they'd just might start looking for someone else. Best just keep to himself.

Timmy infrequently attended school. His mother never pushed him and his father was rarely at home since he had gotten a new job driving trucks for the Bailey-Ogden stockyards. Whenever the old man was in town, Timmy stayed away. He slept up in Pankow's garage although he'd often creep down to eavesdrop at his parent's bedroom window at night.

He liked to hear his father beating and fucking his mother.

"I'd like to go in there and finish her off some night when he's done."

Up in the garage Timmy had a bed roll, pillow, a stash of cigarettes, a few beers, a hunting knife, his rat club and extra clothes. He kept souvenir items hidden behind some loose wall boards. That was the resting place of Tina's transistor radio which he'd often take out and listen to through the earplug. Timmy liked the Wolfman Jack Show, "Ahh-ooo. Ahh-oo."

Timmy's arch enemy remained Stachu Klemp. The old dog still survived and maintained its abiding hatred for Timmy. Once in a while when perched in his loft, Timmy could see the mangy mongrel lope through the yard below. He'd sniff, sniff, and then follow the trail to the garage itself. Timmy could hear the growling and scratching on the double sliding doors.

"Why doesn't that old cock licker just die?" said Timmy to himself. "He must be a hundred years old. What the fuck is keeping him goin?"

Timmy's favorite activity, when he wasn't engaged in petty crime, was rat hunting at the North Ogden dump. It was also something he had become quite adept at over the years. Late at night with his nail studded baseball bat in hand Timmy would head for the railroad tracks beyond Rosseler Street where the Kaisertown houses ended amid the wide open, unorganized fields of Okie Diamond. He loved the silent, stealthy night walk amongst the desolate fields. There was something primeval about it.

He'd follow the New York Central tracks across Clinton Street Bridge all the way to Black Bridge which ran over Buffalo Creek far from its flow near Houghton Park. From atop the bridge Timmy could see the smoky glow and occasional flash of flame that marked the fires of the municipal dump. Along the tracks and bordering the creek restraining fences had never been erected so the boy could walk right in from the unguarded back way.

The dump was deserted at night, the front gates locked and a row of trucks parked near the entrance. There was a maintenance shed near the gate where the caretakers spent their days drinking coffee and having lunch. Nearby were piles of salvageables: various types of wire, hubcaps, mounds of aluminum, returnable bottles, heaps of rags, newspapers and clothing. Timmy raided the piles and broke into the shed infrequently and only on those occasions when he would not be returning to the hunt for a while. Otherwise he stayed at the far end amid the smoldering and burning piles of garbage.

Once he had come down to the dump with Tommy Langosinski and Bobby Durlak, his little pals before their parents forbade them from associating with Timmy. He had fashioned a nice club studded with old nails he found in the garage for each of the boys.

As the three of them approached the fetid, glowing mounds of burning refuse, they could already sense an unseen presence long before their eyes could focus on anything specific. Blackness was everywhere except adjacent to the smoldering piles of garbage where an eerie glow hazily illuminated a small circumference of ground. Occasionally flashes of flame and sparks would ignite the night sky when something particularly combustible fell into the cauldron of hot coals that made up the heart of each mound. The sudden burst of light provided a fleeting glimpse of detail before the darkness descended again.

Hugging the garbage strewn ground amid this smoky inferno moved irregular, pulsating, waves of scurrying shadows like dark clouds sweeping across a moonlit landscape. As the boys got closer audible scratching and high pitched squeals filled the air. It was then that they finally could discern the object of their hunt; the rats, thousands and thousands of long tailed, humped backed, sharp toothed rats feeding on the garbage mounds.

The sight of the creatures instilled an instant and instinctive loathing in the boys, a loathing that demanded the unconditional and immediate extermination of the vermin. Rats were hideous, a menace, full of disease and there were thousands, maybe even millions of them. They had to be destroyed. In fact the boys were actually doing the broader community a service in ridding them of such a menace. Rats beware. On to the kill.

Spacing themselves so as to avoid accidently hitting one another, the threesome ran screaming and flailing their clubs at the pack. The boys kicked and stomped on the rats with their heavy engineer boots. They beat them to bloody wet spots on the ground, or tossed them stunned and crippled into the smoldering fires. A frenzy overtook the youngsters. The squeals of the rats, the sight and smell of blood, the brimstone blackness and the breathless exertion fed their fever. The more grotesquely an animal was killed, the more it elicited braggadocio and humor from its human assassins.

"Lookit dat bastard. His guts is draggin on dah ground. I got him good."

"Mine's on fire. He's runnin in circles."

"Hit him again. He's screamin."

"No, don't waste your time. Let him die on his own."

Killing was easy. The boys enjoyed it. The rats deserved it. On the long way home that night no one spoke. The younger boys had been through enough. They stumbled mindlessly along the tracks, then parted company at the Clinton Street Bridge. Timmy continued alone. He descended the track bed, crossed Rosseler Street and walked along the margin of Okie Diamond. In the distance he could see lights from a house at the far end of South Ogden. How solitary it was, separated from the others by dark vacant lots. Then he realized it was Glupi Wladek's old house. His mother lived there now, alone.

"Fuckin retard," said Timmy. "Wonder if they got you suckin cock at the prison. Or are you tied up with a straight jacket blubbering for yer mommy and pissing yer pants. I wonder how yer old lady is doin all alone in that house."

It was then that Timmy noticed movement in the tall bushes ahead of him that bordered the broken sidewalk. Timmy clutched his bloodied club and walked out into the street and listened carefully. Then the hair on his neck and arms stood up.

"You mother fucker! Come on. I know yer in dere. I got something saved up for you."

The movement in the bushes became more pronounced, followed by deep, demonic growling which turned into sharp barks punctuated by horrible gnashing of teeth as if the hidden animal was tearing at the shrubbery in misplaced rage.

Timmy widened his stance and raised the club as he backed away. Stachu Klemp then emerged from the undergrowth and approached the frightened boy. The animal's fur was mangy and matted, and one side of his head was shorn almost to the scalp by the shovel blow delivered by Timmy years ago.

"Stay away, you one-eared, nut lickin bastard if you know what's good for you," screamed Timmy. But he knew that dogs could sense fear in people, and there was no doubt that right now Timmy's pores were broadcasting absolute panic. Timmy backed up. Stachu Klemp stalked forward. All along the edge of Okie Diamond they continued the deadly Mephisto waltz each waiting for the other to make the first wrong move.

"Come on. Let's get this over with once and for all. What I need is a shotgun to blast yer mangy ass. I'll blow yer legs off and watch you bleed to death."

The death march continued to Timmy's house where Stachu Klemp stopped, huffed and turned away first pissing on the basement blocks to mark his accomplishment. Timmy breathed a sigh of relief. How long does a fuckin dog live anyways, he wondered. He's like a fuckin elephant. One day he'll slip up and I'll get him.

Dorothy: "I'm so Black and Blue"

Dorothy's babcia's izba had become the girl's sanctuary, free from apprehension, humiliation and pain. Within the private and protected walls of her own bedroom Dorothy's joy was sublime. There she could relax and enjoy her beloved music without criticism or interruption. Miles Davis, Jakcie MacLean, Donald Byrd, Coltrane, Parker, Billie Holiday, Clifford Brown, and her all-time favorite, Lester Young, all kept her company. They gladdened or delightfully saddened her world, a favorite song tipping the scales of sentiment with just a few bars of its melody.

Dorothy was gainfully employed now, but after giving her babcia money for room and board she spent virtually all her money on clothes and jazz records. Her babcia thought she was crazy.

"Matka bozka, dah pienenza on dat music an you gonna go deef too."

On those infrequent occasions when Dorothy's mother visited babcia's house, Dorothy made it a point to leave, or not be there in the first place. The mere sight of her mother's hunched posture, her scarred and beaten face filled the girl with an odd mixture of sorrow and loathing. She couldn't abide the presence of her mother, the abused dog that she was, walking the streets of Kaisertown for all to see.

And only the lord knew what Dorothy would have done had she ever run into her father again. As for Timmy being left behind, Dorothy didn't care. Timmy was just an evil embryo, an Otto Klein in the making. When her brother was a youngster he stole, lied, and tormented Dorothy and every friend he ever had. She couldn't do anything about his behavior. He did not respond to either fear or persuasion. He was incorrigible, beyond redemption. She merely endured his presence until she could finally leave the house.

In the passage of years Dorothy couldn't say that her luck with boys had ever changed very much. They all took advantage of her, had their fun: Danny, Chevy, Mack and all the others. Most wanted sex. After that was over, which wasn't very long or enjoyable, she noted, there was precious little left to say or do. And although she had actually liked a couple of the boys along the way, she was always disappointed in the end. The only one who was different and still continued to fascinate her was Jason Novak, but he frightened her at the same time. He made her feel vulnerable because she cared. What would happen if she actually fell in love with him? What then?

Dorothy dropped the loose tea in a steaming pot of water for her babcia's morning cup. "Please, no readings today," she smiled. "I don't have time." On her way out Dorothy picked up her babcia's copy of the Polish newspaper, "Dziennik Dia Wszystkich" and tossed it on the table. She was off to work at the Sol Steinberg Corporation, makers of Queen-O beverages, sweet syrups that were mixed with water in the household and drunk like soda pop. They came in various flavors.

The office and factory were located on Fillmore and Genesee Streets. It was a transitional neighborhood where the old Polack homeowners mingled uneasily with recently arrived colored tenants. Rosaline was Dorothy's sole office coworker. Together they kept the company books and operated the switch board. Dorothy had taken a three month bookkeeping program out of high school to learn the fundamentals of office work.

The Queen-O operation was as dysfunctional as most of its employees, who ranged from the Jewish owners and salesmen to the all immigrant and colored labor force that made the product in the factory below the offices. Sol Steinberg and his brother owned the business. Both were men of exceeding girth and appetite providing the witty Rosaline with lots of verbal ammunition to fire away at their expense much to Dorothy's surprise and amusement.

One day the phone rang and the switchboard lit up. Rosaline flipped the key. "Hello, Sol Steinberg Corporation. How may I help you?"

Dorothy sorted some files nearby and raised her eyebrows. Rosaline was in a good mood. Polite, friendly.

"I'll ring his office," Rosaline continued on the line and waited while the phone rang in Mr. Steinberg's office. She waited some more, then looked at Dorothy and hunched her shoulders. The phone continued to ring in the inner office.

"I know that fat fucker's in there somewhere. What the hell is he doin, jerkin off?"

Dorothy's mouth opened in a silent but spreading grin. She pointed to the open switchboard key. The customer had heard the conversation.

"Fuck," cried Rosaline in alarm, then clamped her hand over her mouth. "Ah, ahh, I'm sorry about that," she apologized to the customer. "He should pick up in a minute."

The person on the other end of the line evidently knew both Rosaline and Mr. Steinberg well enough. He laughed it off, but Rosaline later said to Dorothy that she'd probably have to suck the guy's dick next time he came around just to keep him quiet.

Rosaline's outspoken approach often caught Dorothy off guard. One day after work as they stood at the bus stop having a cigarette and waiting for their ride a colored boy on a bicycle pedaled by, then stopped.

"Hey, yous little white girls want some good black meat to play with?" and he grabbed his crotch and laughed.

"I got a black dildo at home twice as big as yer little dick," said Rosaline looking the boy straight in the eyes. "Now fuck off before I kick you in those marble sized nuts a yers and cripple you for life."

The boy left in a hurry.

"Wow, that took nerve," said Dorothy staring at Rosaline in amazement.

"Not really. You stand up to these assholes, no matter what color, and they almost always back down."

"And if they don't?"

"Lay back, spread yer legs, and enjoy it."

"I gotta stay away from you," Dorothy said. "You're bad for me, but at least I don't have to worry about swearing. For fuck sake, you swear more than I do."

"You know," said Rosaline. "Let's miss the next bus and stop in on the corner for a drink. I could use one."

"Is it safe? I mean in this neighborhood?" inquired Dorothy.

"Safe enough. Half the guys at Queen-O hang out here after work. We'll get them to buy."

The Moon Glow Bar was filled with after work patrons, most of them colored. The girls made an impressive unescorted entrance.

"Hey baby, what cha doin tonight? Want some company? What's some fine lookin womans like yous doin here all on yous own?"

A familiar face stood up and waved the girls over to the back of the bar while another man approached them smiling broadly.

"Charlie White and his cousin Donald," said Rosaline. "They work in the bottling section. Nice guys. I went out with Charlie a couple of times. They'll buy us a few, guaranteed."

It turned out that Rosaline was doing more than just casually dating Charlie. She was his steady girlfriend. Dorothy was surprised, yet curious. What was it like, she wondered, to sleep with a colored guy?

"That's not all of it either," said Rosaline back at the office a few days later. "He's married too and has five kids. Said he was gonna leave his wife for me, but I don't trust that black two timing prick. He cheats on her, he'll cheat on me too. But I love him so what the hell."

Dorothy felt suddenly sorry for Rosaline. Such a confident, aggressive girl and she was just as insecure and fucked up as Dorothy. The two became fast friends. Dorothy also struck up an acquaintance with Donald. It turned out he was a musician working at Queen-O to earn enough tuition money for college. And they liked the same kind of music, jazz. Donald played the trumpet and he flamed Dorothy's enthusiasm for jazz, be-bop jazz in particular, into a passion. She wasn't sure if it was Donald with his clean cut good looks and dark brown skin, or the music which drew her into his world. Maybe it was just sexual curiosity or the illicitness of an affair with a colored man that compelled her to pursue the relationship. Whatever it was, she didn't care. It was beyond anything she could ever experience in the closed world of Kaisertown and she embraced it eagerly.

The foursome took in sets at Nietzsche's, The Green Door, The Moon Glow, Dan Montgomery's, and the Royal Arms which was their favorite because it featured top of the line entertainment. Furthermore, Charlie was good friends with the owner, Lew Gallanter who personally introduced them to a lot of musicians. Dorothy met Miles Davis and Ahmad Jamal and watched Thelonious Monk fall asleep at the piano while playing to a crowd of half a dozen people. She sat for dinner with Mel Torme, the Velvet Fog, who was in town for a gig at the Arms. Dorothy found him quite the self- centered, petulant bore.

"I had to come on the goddamn scene a little too late, you know," Mel protested as he let Lew Gallanter buy him several rounds of drinks before dinner. "I got the voice, everyone knows that. Better than most even, but the timing, damn! You know Sinatra, Martin, Williams, they all got in when crooning was at its peak. Then I start up and it's ebb tide. Gotta play the two bit clubs. Not fair. God damn, not fair."

Dorothy felt sorry for Lew. She noticed him wince at the reference to "two bit clubs". She slept with Lew that night. It was too late to go home. She was drunk and wanted the warmth of someone's arms. Lew wasn't much of a romantic. They just laid in bed and talked, but he was kind and caring and Dorothy liked him for that.

Dorothy also began to visit Donald at his apartment which he shared with a couple of college students and musicians in the Fruit Belt area of Buffalo. She'd grab a bunch of her record albums and take the Clinton bus to Jefferson where Donald would meet her and they'd walk to the apartment together. He lived upstairs and had the place to himself whenever Dorothy showed up; his friends being the understanding type.

"Oh my god," Dorothy gasped that night when Donald removed her clothes and first placed his black hands on her white body. He laid her down on the rug and kissed her neck and breasts. His breath was sweet. She moaned and squirmed restlessly and her legs twitched when Donald spread them apart and positioned himself in between. She ran her hands over his glistening black shoulders and dropped her head back. She virtually jumped in place when he entered her although she could feel that his erection was not strong. It didn't matter. Dorothy sensed something was decidedly different this time around, something building inside of her. She began to gyrate and push up to meet him. Donald got harder.

"Keep, keep going," she urged him. "A little more, more. Oh fuck."

Then suddenly Donald stopped and slipped heavily off her as though exhausted by the brief effort. Dorothy was dumbfounded but recovered herself quickly as Donald asked her if she had come.

"Yeah, yeah, of course," she lied not wanting to wound his pride. As for "coming" she was certain that had not happened, not now or ever before. "Fuck yeah," she continued taking his hand and rubbing it gently. "You were great. Exciting as hell. Wow!"

Donald smiled and at least pretended to believe her. Their subsequent sex life did not amount to much. Donald was often uninterested, moody, and maudlin. Dorothy tried everything, but even giving him blow jobs did not always work and afterwards Dorothy would have to drink nearly a half bottle of wine to restore the flow of saliva into her mouth. Her jaw was sore for the rest of the day too.

The lovers spent most of their nights together listening to their beloved music, drinking wine, and sucking lollipops. They both loved Billie Holiday, and, of course, Donald was partial to the great trumpet players: Miles Davis, Clark Terry, Donald Byrd, Clifford Brown, and Louis Armstrong.

"You know, Louis Armstrong, some people think he was just a old time Dixieland player. Big, smiley faced, raspy voiced Uncle Tom, stupidly happy all the time. But, man, you know he was the greatest trumpet player ever. I mean ever," ranted Donald one night when he seemed particularly blue. He then started crying.

"That bastard, nobody should be able to play like that. How does he do it? He hits these notes, high fuckin notes, and sustains them. It's unnatural."

Dorothy had listened to Donald play a few times at the apartment and then at a couple of the local clubs. She thought he was good. Evidently Donald's musical peers thought otherwise. His opportunities to play dropped off. Other trumpet players took his place at the gigs.

"They say I got no wind, man. I'm blowin as hard as I can. That's all I got."

Dorothy tried to console him. "Is that so important," she asked? "You're good, isn't that enough? How about Miles Davis? You can't say he blows hard. His music is soft, muted. He purposely did it that way, turning a weakness into a strength."

"I'm not good," Donald replied. "And even good ain't enough. This isn't like playing bugle in a high school marching band. You know how many really good trumpet players there are out there? A handful. That's it. You don't make the grade, you out. You understand, you little white bitch?"

Donald slapped Dorothy a couple of times across the face. He then pulled down her pants, put her on all fours and tried to fuck her from behind. He was limp. He slapped her ass hard, then harder and harder. When he stood up to kick her, he slipped and fell down.

"Fuckin white bitch," he cursed. Then he started to cry. Dorothy pulled up her pants and walked slowly to the door. When she turned around and tried to say something, Donald just waved her off.

"Sorry," he whispered. "I just want to be alone for now. See you next week. Feel better then. Next week, yeah man."

The next time she visited, Donald was not at the bus stop to meet her. His friend Clarence showed up instead.

"Dorothy, Donald, he ain't feelin so good. Maybe you shouldn't come tonight?"

"He doesn't want to see me anymore?" asked Dorothy, hurt by the apparent rejection that Donald's friend was trying to cover up.

"No, it's just maybe it would be better to stay away."

"That's sweet of you, Clarence. Does he have another girl up there? Is that it?"

"No, not really, but…"

"But then, I'd just as soon see him if you don't mind."

Dorothy walked purposely through the hallway to Donald's apartment. "Strange Fruit" by Billie Holiday was playing somewhere in the downstairs apartment. Upstairs Donald was sitting on the floor in his jockey shorts when Dorothy opened the door. He was swaying and blowing discordantly into his trumpet. Feeble honks, hisses, and sour notes issued forth. Donald put the horn down. He was drooling. A shoelace was tied tightly around one arm. On the floor in front of him lay a syringe, a lighter and a spoon. He looked right at Dorothy and smiled, but made no movement. Then he took up the horn again and continued his feeble efforts at producing something that might even vaguely resemble a musical note. He had no success. Dorothy shut the door. Clarence was down at the stairs waiting for her.

"What the fuck happened?" Dorothy asked. "When did this start?"

"Dorothy, Donald's been an addict for years. Long before he met you. Just getting worse now. He can't play no more. Can't get no gigs. You know he ain't even been to work the last couple of days."

"That's another reason I wanted to see him," Dorothy answered. "I thought he might be sick."

"He is, that's for sure. Maybe I should drive you home? I ain't safe to walk back this time of night by yerself. And here, I got these albums of yours out of his room. I see you like Billie Holiday."

Dorothy nodded. "I like Ella Fitzgerald quite a bit," she added trying to be pleasant and conversational.

"Yeah, but Billie's got the soul," Clarence continued. "I figure that Billie, she like a shot of whiskey, you know, dark, strong, even bitter, but, man, she packs a punch. Ella, on the other hand, she's like a cool glass of water, clear, refreshing, but really kind of tasteless. Give me Billie any day."

Dorothy had Clarence drop her off at the corner of Kelborne and Clinton Streets. She didn't want him taking any chances in Kaisertown. Jesus, she couldn't ever remember seeing a colored man in her neighborhood. The local Polack hoodlums would go crazy and kill him.

"Maybe sometime, if you ain't seein Donald no more, you an me could go out? Take in a few gigs around town," said Clarence as he opened the door for Dorothy.

"Yeah, maybe," Dorothy replied.

Donald did not show up for work the next few days so Mr. Steinberg fired him. Dorothy wasn't surprised, but she was worried about his addiction and his dashed musical dreams. She, on the other hand, would get over her own rejection. She always did. Dorothy and Rosaline in the meantime were engaged in an immediate struggle to balance the month's invoices.

"Fucking thing, we're still out thirty-nine dollars," said Dorothy.

"We've been wastin enough time on this shit," replied Rosaline. "Give me that last invoice. Here." And she promptly tore the pink paper into dozens of little bits, then, she walked to the open window and threw them out.

"Presto, magico. Look, we balanced."

"Somehow that's not the way they taught us at Bryant and Stratton," Dorothy replied. "You know, one day you're going to get us both into a lot of trouble."

A few minutes later and Mr. Steinberg came in from his lunch hour. There were bits of pink paper stuck to the top of his hat brim.

"Son of a bitch," hissed Rosaline. "Luckily the cocksucker is as blind as a gefilte fish. I'm goin outside to pick up them paper scraps. Next time we'll flush em down the toilet like I used to do. That's what I get for showin off. I'll be back in half a hour. I wanna check out Ruby's Shop for something while I'm out."

Rosaline came back in short order carrying a bag with, "Ruby Dooby Doo's Ladies Wigs and Hair Pieces" written on it.

"You didn't," said Dorothy. "What color?"

"Red, kind of. Wait till you see it. I always wanted one ever since I been passin her shop. What do you think?"

Rosaline held up a large, flowing orange wig and tossed it on her head like a cowboy throwing a saddle across a horse's back. She endeavored to straighten it out with not a lot of luck. Her dark Italian strands stuck out underneath the wig in all directions. "How's it look?"

"Like a rabid fox jumped on your head and died there."

"Very funny. Charlie always wanted to fuck a redhead so now's his chance. Ruby said first thing to do is wash it, comb it out good, and dry it. Then it's ready to wear. I'm goin in the bathroom right now and get started."

She emerged fifteen minutes later. "I got it drying on the window still. Be careful when you go in."

Just then Charlie and one of the foremen from the plant come into the office. They had to see Mr. Steinberg right away.

"What did you assholes fuck up now?" asked Rosaline.

"Found a couple of rats drowned in one of the syrup vats, root beer, our best seller. If we dump it we're gonna be short this week's shipment."

"Going to dump it?" questioned Dorothy. "What the hell else would you do?"

"Don't fuckin dump it," said Rosaline. "And don't even tell the old man. Everybody knows you guys are pissin and jerkin off in them vats all the time. What's a rat or two?"

Charlie smiled. 'Hey, dat syrup, it's all boiled first. Boilin kills everything."

"And I used to drink that fuckin stuff," said Dorothy.

"Fuck, are you crazy?" added Rosaline. "You think it's just coincidence that nobody, and I mean nobody, here at the plant actually drinks that shit. Not even Steinberg himself."

There was a hurried knock on the outer door. Everyone looked around as a young colored girl ran into the room.

"Hey you," she shouted. "You cat just done fell outa dah window dere. Right down dah ground in dah alley. We didn wanna touch him 'case he hurt and bite us."

Everyone looked at one another, puzzled. "Cat? We ain't got no cat here, girl. Maybe downstairs in the warehouse, but not up here. You sure it was this building?"

"Sure nuff, big orange cat fell right outa dah window. I seen it wit my own eyes."

"Oh my god," screamed Rosaline and she ran out of the room.

"What was that all about?" asked Charlie.

"Hopefully you'll find out in a little while," smiled Dorothy.

"Dat lady, she sure love her cat, don't she?" said the little girl.

Donald came in for his last paycheck. He looked dejected and sullen, may be a little angry as well. Dorothy tried to soothe him with kind words, but it was obviously over between them. All the better, she thought. I had to put up with a drunk most of my life, a heroin addict can't be much of an improvement.

"I guess you ain't heard then what happened to Clarence, that night you made him take you home?" said Donald on his way out.

"What do you mean?"

"Yer white friends, they stopped his car at a traffic light. Pulled him out and beat the shit outa him. He's still in the hospital. Beat his head and broke his arm. Might not be able to play no more."

"Oh my god, I didn't know. I never heard anything. I …"

"Oh yeah, news flash, "Nigger beat up by white boys."

"What hospital is he in?"

"What do you care?" and Donald left.

Dorothy wound up at Mercy Hospital that evening. She brought along a new Ahmad Jamal album for Clarence and one red rose. When she got to his room there were several young men there already. Donald was not one of them. They stared at her when she entered. None moved.

"Clarence?" Dorothy inquired.

One man stepped away from the bedside. Dorothy walked forward. Clarence's face was swollen and discolored. He had a cast on one arm and his protruding fingers looked as if they had been dipped in ink. He also had a tight, wide bandage wrapped around his ribs.

"Clarence, oh my god, I'm so sorry. I didn't know," Dorothy gasped.

Clarence looked at the girl, then turned away. One of the colored men bumped into Dorothy knocking the record album to the floor. When she bent to get it, a foot kicked it under the bed.

"Hey, boys, I'm sorry. What's the matter? Don't I know some of you from the apartment?"

"We ain't no boys to you," said one of the young men and he stepped toward Dorothy menacingly.

At that moment two colored women entered the room carrying a package and flowers. One looked considerably older than the other. They were in fact Clarence's mother and sister.

"Who you?" said the older lady. "You dat little white bitch got my Clarence all beat up. Huh, dat you?"

She didn't give Dorothy time to reply. "Don't think I don't know what you up to. Shakin you little white ass around these black boys.

Havin a little fun and then go back to yer nice white neighborhood where dere's no niggers allowed. Some black boy put you white ass against the wall, cops be down here in a minute, roustin everybody outa bed to find out who done it. Nearly kill a black boy and who cares? His fault for bein down in "Whitey Town" in the first place."

Dorothy stood with her mouth open, unable to speak. The younger girl stepped between them. "Momma, let her be. Let her get out here. Dat's all. You go over to Clarence. Take him the flowers."

The girl took Dorothy by the arm and led her to the door.

"Thank you," said Dorothy. "I...

"Don't thank me. I don't want my momma get upset, that's all. You just sashay yer white ass on outa here and leave us alone. You ain't got enough white boys you ken fool with in yer own neighborhood, you gotta come down here and mess with our black men?"

"I'm sorry," said Dorothy with tears in her eyes. "You wanna give this to Clarence?" She held out the rose.

"Shove it up you white ass," was the reply and the woman walked back into the hospital room.

Dorothy staggered out of the building. Poor Clarence, she thought. He was doing me a favor. Now look at him. Nice reward for all his trouble. What a loser I am, what a fucking loser. I can't do anything right."

The next day Rosaline tried to cheer Dorothy up. "Don't worry about one stupid guy. There's a lot of fish in the sea."

"This said by a white girl whose first and only boyfriend is a black man who's married and has five kids."

"Hey, I'm only human," smiled Rosaline. "Come out with me and Charlie this weekend. We'll hit a couple of clubs and you'll feel better."

"What's this place called," asked Dorothy the next day as they parked the car and walked towards a blinking neon sign. "I don't think

I've ever been here before."

"Some joint Charlie knows. He's been to every dive in Buffalo."

"Hey, this is a good bar. They got the "Blue Monday Club" here. Good entertainment and the drinks are half price today," Charlie replied in protest.

"Oh great, the blues, just what I need to cheer me up," said Dorothy.

There was a small crowd at the door. The threesome weaved their way through. There was some incidental bumping and shoving.

"Sorry," said Dorothy. "Pardon me."

She tried to move around an imposing body so she could follow Rosaline and Charlie, but the person in front of her didn't move. In fact, he seemed to purposely block her way. "For fuck sake," she finally hissed and looked up, up into the smiling face, and sparkling, bright eyes of her old Kaisertown neighbor, Jason Novak.

"Sounds as though your vocabulary hasn't changed very much over the years," he laughed. "How have you been? You look great."

"Thanks, you too, but what's a nice guy like you doing in a place like this?"

"Just slumming until university starts," Jason explained. "Going to UB as it turns out. My parents separated and that killed any chance of getting out of town. Money is pretty tight right now. By the way, this is my buddy Carl," and Jason introduced Dorothy to a tall, good looking black man. "Hey, we're just on our way out, but maybe some time we can get together for a drink? Rehash old times."

"Who was that?" asked Rosaline when Dorothy caught up with her and Charlie.

"The man of my dreams," replied Dorothy. "He just doesn't know it."

Sergeant Sojka and Detective Abramowski: "Zeby Babka Miala
Jajka to by Byla Dziadkiem. If grandma had a beard (balls) she would
be grandpa."

"Well dere, detective Abramowski, how does it feel to be a detective on dah Buffalo police force?"

"Dobrze, dobrze, police sergeant Sojka."

"See, I told you that Kaspreczyk case would make us. Smood and efficient, dat was you an me partner. We cracked dat case in record time. Now dah public is safe, the chief is happy, and city hall gets to promote a couple of hero Polack cops. Dah krauts got dere turn, den dah micks, and dah degos so now it's our turn, nie?"

"Yer right, but you know, back den I really did tink dere was someone else involved besides dat retard Khula," added detective Abramowski. "Dat's all I'm sayin."

"Oh, yer probly right about dat, but it wasn't dah Novak kid. He didn't fit dah profile and anyway his fingerprints didn't match."

"What fingerprints?"

"Dah ones on dah watch and dem girlie cards. Dah prints I told you to follow up on."

"I took dem to dah lab, but forgot about em after dah meetin wit the retard and the Novak kid and his dad. What was the point after dat? Dah kid was cleared. Dah retard didn't know him."

"No point like it turned out," added sergeant Sojka, "just good to know all dah facts. Dah facts come in handy especially when you gotta move dem around a little bit later on to cover yer ass. Dat watch was wiped clean. The deck and dah Ace of Spades had lots a different prints, mainly dah retard's 'cause he pawed em up pretty good and blotted out most of dah udders. But dere were a few sets of recurrin prints, pretty clear ones, on dah canteen too and dey didn't belong to Wladek or Jason Novak."

"How do you know? I don't remember ever fingerprinting the Novak kid. Madder a fact I know we never did."

"I know 'cause when I had him take dat photo ID of dah retard in the squad car, I took dat picture with his prints on it back to the lab myself. No match. He wasn't dere."

"But dat meant you were suspicious too, like me. You musta figgered dere coulda been someone else dere. Dah retard, he wouldn't a wiped dat watch clean, and why didn't he take it wit him? His mudder said he never let it out of his sight. Maybe we shoulda pursued all dah leads? See where dey took us."

"You doan listen too good, detective. Nobody wants to hear about no leads if dat means someone is still out dere planning to rape and kill liddle girls. Dat scares dem. Dey want a suspect. Dey want him arrested, put on trial, convicted and locked up for good. All as quick as possible. An dat's just what we gave dem."

"But what if dere is a accomplish still out dere?"

"Start talkin like dat and we ain't gonna look so good, nie? Anyway, wouldn't be dah first time someone got off scot free. But we know dah retard was involved for sure, so justice has been served. Don't worry."

"Just like dat nigger dah udder day?" Detective Abramowski said.

"Exactly. He gets dah shit beat outa him, but whose fault is dat? If he hadna been where he shoulda been, nuttin woulda happened to him.

He shares a good burden a dah guilt. You gotta know yer place. If it ain't yer place, don't go dere. If you go dere anyways, be prepared to pay dah consequences."

"Yeah, he sure did dat, but maybe we shoulda gotten outa dah car sooner when we seen dey were layin a good beatin on him."

Sergeant Sojka smiled and shook his head, "I had to finish my cigarette. Anyway, if we got dere too soon a couple a problems come up. Number one, dah nigger doesn get dah beatin he deserves, an what kind a lesson is dat? Number two, we jump in and den we see dah guys dat's doin it, and den we gotta arrest somebody. And for what? Dey was just protectin dere home turf. Good Polish boys. You know, we live in dat neighborhood too. You let one nigger in, more will follow. Stop dah first one dead in his tracks, dat's dah end a it."

"You got a point dere, sergeant."

"Lookit. It's tree o'clock. We got a appointment wit Monsignor Majewski by St. Casimir's. Let's go."

"Monsignor will be wit yous in a minute," said a comely woman, the housekeeper, who answered the door. She ushered them into a sitting room the walls of which were lined with dark wooden bookcases with glass doors. Heavy leather furniture circled the room. A large marble topped desk sat near an adjoining entry way. Several leaded glass lamps provided a dim illumination. The blinds were drawn to keep out the afternoon sun.

"You know," whispered detective Abramowski, "if it wasn't for dat no screwin law dey got, dis wouldn be such a bad life."

"What no screwin law?" winked Sergeant Sojka as he nodded towards the retreating housekeeper. "An don't say no to nuttin he offers us."

The Monsignor came in. He was a ponderous man who walked slowly and sat down behind the desk with an audible puff.

"Well officers, id's good to see yous. Maybe I ken offer yous something to drink, nie? Pani Durlak, come in here please," he shouted. "Pani Durlak. Scotch, officers, or maybe a good sherry? I use it myself for dah communion. Good for dah blood, nie?" the old priest laughed.

Pani Durlak poured out the libations from a set of crystal decanters and glasses. The three men exchanged pleasantries and consumed a couple of drinks before Sergeant Sojka broke the silence.

"Fadder, I know dis is a uncomfortable subject, but it's been tree times now dat Fadder Thomas from yer parish has been stopped for drunk driving, and each time he, ah, had a woman wit him dat was, how can I say it, a woman maybe wit a bad reputation. We haven't reported nuttin officially, but…"

"Officers, officers, Fadder Thomas is very involved wit dah underprivileged, dah poor people, of not only our parish here at St. Casimir's, but dah whole city of Buffalo. He is a volunteer all over."

"Fadder Thomas during his last stop was very belligerent. He didn't have his collar on. The arrestin officers didn know who he was till my partner, detective Abramowski and me came on dah scene. We saved him from a very uncomfortable situation to say dah least."

"Dobrze, dobrze, I'm sure," said the Monsignor smiling knowingly.

"Fadder Thomas was caught in dah nigger section of town," continued the sergeant. "The women, dey were all niggers, and dey were all prostitutes, every time he got stopped. You know, it's getting harder and harder for us to cover dis stuff up."

"Tank yous again, officers," the Monsignor interjected. "I appreciate yer concern, but I have already spoken to Fadder Thomas. He has agreed to stop dah drinkin. You see, officers, I have left no stone unturned here. Now, Pani Durlak will see yous out."

"One more ting," added sergeant Sojka upon leaving. "Dah parking tickets dat Fadder Thomas got, we took dah liberty of tearin dem up."

"Dziekuje," Monsignor Majewski replied automatically, but then he hesitated. "Czekaj, officers. Fadder Thomas doesn't got no car. Whose car was he driving all dem times?"

"Why, yours of course.

Monsignor Majewski staggered back as though hit in the head with a ball peen hammer. His face flushed.

"My, my car," stammered the priest. "My, my Cadillac?"

"For sure. We got the description and yer license plate number. You know Monsignor, in dat neighborhood, it's not safe parkin a expensive car like dat."

"Piorun, if dere's a scratch on dat car," spat the good monsignor.

"Same wit dah speedin an dah reckless drivin tickets, monsignor. We tore dem all up," added Sergeant Sojka.

"Ahhh, ahh," the priest babbled. "Pani Durlak, Pani Durlak, get dat, dat Fadder Thomas in here right away. Now,"

The police officers left the room. "I don't remember no speeding or reckless drivin tickets," said detective Abramowski.

"Maybe I exaggerated a bit," replied his superior. "Anyways, dah old s.o.b. had it coming. He coulda offered us a few of dem cigars, maybe a bottle of booze. The captain scarfed two tickets to the Boni game against St. John's last year. Cheap bastard. Screw him."

Jason: The Senior Prom and Aunt Catherine's Note

"Inever tink I wind up like dis," said Jason's mother as she looked around her apartment. After the large, well-furnished house the family had owned on South Ogden Street, this was a decided step down, living in a flat on rent. "At least dah bastard's gonna pay."

Jason's aunts visited frequently to commiserate with his mother. "Piorun, a divorce. Taki terrible, terrible. Everybody's talkin."

"What did he god damn it want from me? What?" cried Jason's mother in despair and anger. "I give him dah best years a my life and dat's dah tanks I get."

"Good ting you got Jason here to help you out, nie? An he's got Larry's car too. I jus hope he doesn't take after dah old man."

"No, he's a good son. He would never leave his mother like dat. He knows I need him more den ever now."

Jason listened from the kitchen. He was in his last year at South Park and was expecting to go to Geneseo College in the fall, his father agreeing to pay his tuition and room and board. His other option was the University of Buffalo where he had a Regent scholarship. It would cost him next to nothing to go there and Jason already had a tidy sum saved up from summer and part time jobs. The rub with that option was that he'd have to live at home with his mother.

Jason also had to admit he had no real affinity towards his Kaisertown cohorts especially now that his cousin Larry had gone into the army. Although he continued to enjoy the prestige and freedom within that rough neighborhood, he never felt completely at home there.

At South Park High Jason had been dating one of the varsity cheerleaders, but when he got kicked off the basketball team, she dumped him. He always thought that Paula was an idiot, but, boy, could she suck cock and that, in Jason's mind, more than compensated for her intellectual deficiencies.

Paula was Jason's date for the senior prom so when they broke up Jason was stuck looking for a replacement. He wasn't sure he even wanted to bother, but he also didn't want to give Paula the satisfaction of seeing him without a date. And his former teammate, Frankie Woijehowski was encouraging him to attend.

"You can find somebody else. Might be a challenge for you. Some other broad's pants to get into."

"Yes Frank, you're such an incurable romantic."

Jason entered the study hall after his math class nodding and saying hello to the students he knew. Sitting in the first seat of his aisle was Mary Anne Bartchiewicz. She was a tall, awkward girl who self-consciously walked in a slumped over manner to minimize her height, a technique which actually had exactly the opposite effect. Mary Anne was pretty in an old fashion manner. She never put on makeup and wore unusually long dresses with white socks and black buckle shoes. For some reason, unbeknownst to even Jason himself, he always greeted her especially warmly.

"Good afternoon, Mary Anne. You look lovely today. I like your dress."

For her part Mary Anne would turn beet red, lower her head and mumble, "Tank you." And when Jason passed she would turn and stare at him until he got to his desk. When he'd wave back at her, she would quickly spin around.

Frankie Woijehowski sat opposite Mary Anne. He and Jason were still fast friends despite Jason's departure from the basketball team. Jason always gave Frankie a ride home from school and they occasionally went out cruising and drinking on weekends now that Jason had his cousin's car at his disposal.

"Hey Mary Anne," Frankie whispered to the girl. "You know dat Jason broke up wit Paula and he's lookin for a date to the prom. You goin wit anyone?"

Mary Anne turned her customary shade of raspberry red and shook her head.

"Good 'cause I'm gonna tell Jason. I think he might ask you. He likes you."

Mary Anne immediately raised her hand and asked the teacher for permission to go to the bathroom.

"Hey, Mr. Asshole," Jason chided Frankie, "you're getting her hopes up and then I'll look like some insensitive, heartless bastard when I don't ask her out."

"Don't worry. She's gotta know I'm just kiddin."

A quick look the next day told Jason that Mary Anne was obviously not in on the joke. To make matters worse, Frankie was back at it.

"I think Jason is really goin to ask you to the prom, Mary Anne. He's sweet on you. You know he likes tall girls."

"Once a prick, always a prick," said Jason to Frankie.

The date of the prom fast approached and the atmosphere in the study hall grew tense. Frankie, as usual, didn't help matters. Finally to clear things up once and for all, Jason stopped in front of Mary Anne's desk and stood there until the girl looked up at him.

"Mary Anne, I just wanted to…" Jason began. Then he saw such a look of expectation and joy on the girl's face that it brought him up short. He took a deep breath and started again.

"Mary Anne, about the prom. I know that…"

The girl's eyes were wide and fluid and there was a timid smile on her lips. Her face was beyond red and Jason could see, if not hear, her heart pounding in her chest. And she didn't have all that bad a chest he noted at the moment. Fuck it, he thought.

"As I was so awkwardly saying, Mary Anne. Would you like to go to the prom with me. I'd love to take you."

Behind him he heard Frankie Woijehowski fall off his seat and onto the floor.

Jason picked up Mary Anne at five o'clock. The prom started at seven. After that Jason and Frankie and a bunch of the guys were taking their dates to the Carriage House Restaurant for a late dinner. Then a few couples were going on to Frankie's parent's cottage for the rest of the night or all night if the guys were lucky. Jason wasn't sure just how much of the itinerary he'd be able to complete or wanted to complete for that matter.

"Jason, dese are my parents. Daddy, mommy, dis is Jason Novak, the boy I been telling you about. He's my date for the prom."

Mary Anne's parents acted as though the Pope had just walked into the room. The mother hugged Jason. The father took his hand and pumped it several times, reluctant to let go.

"Novak, a good Polish name, nie. Dobrze, dobrze."

Mary Anne looked as though she was wearing a cut own version of her mother's bridal gown which turned out to be exactly what it was minus the veil and train. Jason gave Mary Anne a corsage. He was a bit overwhelmed by it all. "You look lovely," he said.

"Sid down it, you. Sid down," the parents urged. "We god it dah eats for yous. Such a big day, you need it dah energy, nie?" The house was extremely hot and reeked of cabbage, onions, and garlic. The dad smiled and nodded furiously. Jason didn't know what to do.

"I believe we have dinner reservations for later this evening," he finally spoke up. The parents looked at each other, and hunched their shoulders.

"What? No eats?"

"Mommy, I tried to tell yous. Dey doan do it like dat. We're goin to a big fancy restaurant to eat after the dance."

"Yous gotta pay for dat. We got it all dah eats here for free."

Jason smiled. "Maybe we could have a little taste before we go," he suggested by way of compromise. That seemed to work.

Just a few minutes into the meal and the doorbell rang. The mother jumped up expectantly. "He's here. He's here. Everybody to dah parlor."

Jason looked around. "Who's here?"

"Dah picture man," the father shouted.

A man walked in the door carrying a large chest and a tripod. The father assisted him. Lights and the tripods were set up in the next room and for half an hour bulbs flashed as Jason and Mary Anne sat for a dozen pictures: Jason and Mary Anne holding hands, three poses; Jason putting on Mary Anne's corsage, two poses; Jason and Mary Anne and her mother, two poses, same with her father, then Mary Anne with each, then with both of her parents.

"Ale ladna," Mary Anne's mother cried. "My baby, ale ladna."

"And what time would you like me to bring your daughter back home tonight, Mr. Bartchiewicz?" Jason inquired politely.

"Around it ten," the man replied.

"Ten," Jason repeated incredulously.

Mary Anne's mother interceded. "Zaplomnial wol jak cielenciem byk.

Maybe eleven is good, nie? Mary Anne never been out past ten before."

"Mommy," whined the girl. "This is the senior prom."

"OK, OK, at dah midnight. Dat's all dere is, at dah midnight."

The prom itself did not turn out badly. Mary Anne knew a few of the girls there and everyone was happy and excited enough to get along and content themselves with general smiles and compliments.

"Expecting to get laid tonight?" asked Frankie to Jason. "Hot date you got dere. Where the fuck did she get dat dress?"

"Don't press your luck, you cock sucker," replied Jason good-naturedly. "It was you who got me into this mess in the first place. At least she shaved her legs for the occasion. I was getting worried there at first. Who is Paula with?"

"Al Zizzi."

"Well, he will have fun tonight, no doubt."

Jason had several dances with Mary Anne. She was a poor dancer and her breath smelled strongly of garlic from the Polish sausage she had for supper. After the dance they attended the restaurant with about ten other couples. Mary Anne was radiant with joy. She talked and laughed more than Jason had ever known her to do. It was almost a little irritating.

Before the two of them got out of the car at Mary Anne's house, the girl turned to Jason. Her face was again cherry red even in the subdued lighting of the car.

"Jason, I, I just want you to know that this has been the most wonderful day of my whole life. And I know my parents are a little crazy and old fashioned, and that stupid photographer they hired, but you know, I've got those pictures of us and when I look at them I will always feel happy and remember how good you were to me." And she started to cry.

Jason leaned over and kissed her. Her lips were wet and salty. Her chest rose and fell with halting sobs. He would have loved to slip her out of that dress and into the back seat of the car, but that was not meant to be.

"I better kiss you again here," he added. "I'd do it at your door, but I'm afraid your father might shoot me."

Mary Anne laughed. They walked into the yard together. Her parents were both staring out the window. They moved to the dining room window, and then the kitchen keeping pace with Jason and their daughter on the sidewalk outside.

"Good night, Mary Anne."

"Goodbye, Jason."

Jason did not attend his high school graduation ceremony. Too corny he figured and he didn't like the cap and gowns. Furthermore, he didn't want a confrontation between his parents if both of them decided to attend. Nevertheless, his mother held a party for him at the apartment. She figured the aunts owed Jason some cash for his academic accomplishment.

His relatives gave generously, but Jason did notice a decided reticence on their part to discuss or even listen to any plans he had to attend college. He found out why later in the evening as he helped his mother clean up. His aunt Catherine was present also.

"Yer mother needs to talk to you, Jason," his aunt began.

Jason knew this was trouble since his mother was fully capable of talking for herself under most circumstances.

"She doesn't think it's a good idea for you to go to college right now like you want to. She needs you around here. Yer the man of the house. I talked to yer uncle, Dan and he said he could get you into Trico with him.

Good money dere."

Jason looked over at this mother who was washing dishes and listening, but not participating in the conversation. He had seen this technique many times before. His parents used to communicate through him as though he was some sort of spiritual medium during their past arguments.

'Tell yer old man dat I'm not washin his clothes no more,' his mother declared to him. Jason would then turn to his father, sitting a few feet away, and repeat the sentence.

'Tell your mother, thanks a lot. I'll take them to the dry cleaners myself.'

"I can't stay in Kaisertown," Jason explained. "I don't want to work at Trico. I don't want to work at Worthington, or Bethlehem Steel either."

"You gotta work," his aunt implored. "Everybody's gotta work. If you ken get a good job now right outa high school, why bother wit college?"

"Look ma," Jason said turning to his mother. "I am not sticking around here to work in some factory in Buffalo. I already got accepted at Geneseo and dad said he'd help me with tuition and my room and board."

His mother turned to face him, angrily tossing a dish cloth into the sink.

"Doan you mention dat bastard's name in dis house after what he done to me. You always stick up for him. You wanna be like him, big smart man. Everyting is not good enough for him. Whad about me? Who's gonna take care a me? You know I got it dah bad headaches and nerves."

His aunt Catherine jumped in. "I didn't wanna say nothing to you, Jason, with everybody here, but yer mother went to the doctor and she's gotta take pills now all dah time. She's sick. Who knows even how long she can work. She needs somebody to take care a her. Yer the only one. It's yer responsibility."

"Is Paulie going to work at Trico and miss college? Is uncle Dan getting him a job there? I don't think so. I've got to talk to dad. He will help me. He understands."

"You go to him. You always like him more den me. You go and you don't come back," his mother cried.

Jason walked out the door and down the steps. He could hear his mother yelling after him. "Jason, come back. My son, come back. Don't leave me."

Her voice grated through is body like fingernails across a chalkboard. He cringed. His skin crawled. He felt like screaming.

Jason's father was the epitome of understanding.

"Your mother hates me and she's taking it out on you. It will go away, but there is no chance that you will miss college. That's definite. In the meantime, let's get you a small apartment somewhere, something cheap, but nice that you can stay in until school starts in September. I won't have to pay her as much with you gone. I feel guilty as hell for putting you through all this and even your mother for that matter. I must be hard on her."

"She's enjoying every minute of it," Jason replied. "Wallowing in self-pity and being the center of attention."

Jason returned to his mother's apartment the next Monday while she was at work at the Drescher Box factory where aunt Bertha had gotten her a job. As Jason gathered up his belongings, he looked around the apartment and an overpowering feeling off remorse washed over him. He saw his mother's apron thrown across a kitchen chair. A few knickknacks salvaged from the South Ogden house were displayed in the tiny living room. Copies of the Enquirer lay on an end table.

"This is it," Jason said. "This is all she's got left."

On the kitchen table was a handwritten note. It wasn't his mother's writing. Her penmanship was poor and her writing lacked any measure of grammar, syntax, or sentence structure, not to mention spelling. Aunt Catherine had undoubtedly written it.

'You are no longer any son of mine. You always loved your father more than me. Now that I need you the most you leave me. Thanks. I don't expect nothing from you no more. Don't come back and don't look around for the money you had here. I took it. It was mine anyway because I gave it to you. Go to your father. You deserve each other. I am not your mother no more.'

Jason and his father picked out an apartment on Cherokee Drive in West Seneca for Jason. The flat had a kitchen, a small bedroom and a bathroom which was shared with the landlady, a reclusive woman in her forties who lived alone in the adjoining apartment. Jason rarely saw her and merely slipped the rent money under the bathroom door and the next day a receipt was dutifully slipped back onto his side.

In the meantime, Jason's father got him a summer job at the foundry and machine shop at Worthington. Jason needed the money. He had insurance coming up on Larry's car and living expenses as well. In fact, the combination of Jason's need for money, and his new found sense of freedom, as well as his father's diminished financial resources reversed Jason's decision to attend Geneseo College. He enrolled in the University of Buffalo instead.

Nelly: Rany boskie and the Jew

Each day Nelly lit a candle at St. Casimir's for the soul of her father until virtually the entire votive offering at the Virgin Mary's altar was dedicated to him. She prayed to the Holy Mother for mercy both for her soul and that of her father's. Was he taken too soon, before he was prepared? Was it all because of her sins and selfishness? Nelly also attended her father's grave at St. Stan's Cemetery once a week with flowers and pulled weeds from the grass and kept the monument stone polished and shiny until the snowy blasts of the Buffalo winter interrupted her sojourns of sorrow.

That Easter was filled with sadness for Nelly. There was no redemption nor resurrection in her life. All was misery. She attended mass every day starting with Passion Sunday when the images of Jesus throughout the church were covered in satiny velvet cloth. On Fridays she dutifully followed the priest, Father Benkowski, through the Stations of the Cross kneeling at every niche which depicted the Lord's torture and crucifixion. Jesus suffered for her and all people in the world. She should be eternally grateful for his sacrifice and beg for the forgiveness of her sins. "Bless me father, for I have sinned."

On Good Friday Nelly prostrated herself before the life size statue of the crucified Jesus as it lay across the steps of the altar. The velvet cloth had now been removed and Nelly followed the others as they kissed the wounds of the Lord, hands, feet, crown of the head, and side, where the spear of the pagan Roman soldier had pierced the lily white flesh of Jesus.

She remembered happier times of her youth when she and Frances and her mother brought their Easter basket to be blessed for swieconka. And all the Polish ladies showed off their finest embroidered basket coverings and eyed those of their neighbors with contempt or envy as the case warranted. She and her sister could hardly wait to get back home and pile into the fresh sausage, ham and boiled bacon along with the caraway rye and the cross stitched egg bread smeared liberally with the butter lamb. And, of course, there were the colored Easter eggs and the candy bunnies and marshmallow chicks. Easter was a joyous time back then, back when she was young, and her father was alive, and the family was happy.

Finally Nelly's mother stepped in out of worry for her younger daughter.

"Nelly, you can't go on it like dis. It's not right and yer fadder he wouldn wann it to see you like dis too. Yer a young girl and priddy. You god yer whole life to lead. You godda ged over it."

"It's all my fault," Nelly cried. "My fault."

"Doan be so foolish. Boze wanned yer fadder, dat's all. Our time comes, an we can't do nuttin aboud it."

"It's just, you know, I didn't get to spend enough time with him at dah end. We used to do so much togedder. He built those doll houses for me, and all the little furniture. And we went for rides in the car, just him an me and he'd buy me ice cream cones. Den we drifted away somehow and now it's too late and I can't bring him back or tell him that I miss him and that I'm sorry, so sorry."

Nelly cried as her mother held her.

"Cicho, cicho, don't blame yerself. You got older an got udder tings on yer mind; school and friends. Dat's dah way it is. And I was wonderin too how come you don't see yer cousin Jason no more? You know dah two a yous was close, kissin cousins, nie?" she added with a smile. "Be good to talk to him. Maybe even go out. Get yer mind off tings."

"I don't wanna see him ever again," Nelly replied catching her mother off guard.

"What's dah madder? He do something to you?" The woman's curiosity, even her suspicion was up.

"No, no, I just don't want anything to do wit boys right now, not even relatives. Daddy was right. I shouldn't date till I'm older. What do I know about boys?"

"You need it someting to get yer mind off dah troubles. I got just dah ting. It always work for me."

Admission to the bingo hall was fifty cents apiece which got the three women the standard issue of two cards each. Extra cards could be purchased for ten cents. Eddie Gordon and two other members of the Holy Name Society at St. Casimir's passed out the cards and greeted everyone at the door. Inside the foyer a picture of a bespectacled and unsmiling Pope Pious XII hung on the wall.

Eddie Gordon handed Bertha, her friend, Celia Lewandowski, and Nelly their cards. "Good luck," he said with a smile.

"Piorun," Bertha hissed. "He's trying to jink us."

"I must be jinxed myself to let you talk me into coming here," commented Nelly.

Nearly two thirds of the tables were already occupied by women jealously guarding their places against all interlopers.

"Move it yer purse dere. It's in my way," protested Bertha.

"Dese seats are saved."

"You got it more room down dere. Move over by her," added Celia.

Celia was Bertha's bingo playing partner. She was also the only woman Bertha knew who had a car. Her husband let Celia use it strictly for bingo trips which often amounted to three times a week venturing into various parts of Kaisertown.

"My god, what's come over you two?" asked Nelly. "Talk about yer split personalities. This hall is attached to the church you know."

In addition to their seating obsessions every player had her own special way of arranging their cards. Some had the cards spread out in a large square with all the letters lined up in columns. Others preferred one long train like set up. Some just glanced from one bingo card to the other in no apparent order.

"Look it dat woman over there," nodded Nelly. "She must have twenty cards. How can she keep track of all of dem?"

"I use to take dat many too," added Celia. "But if you don't win, gets expensive."

Many women used plastic discs to cover the bingo numbers on their cards. Others preferred pennies or dried corn kernels. The tables were also filled with innumerable good luck charms from plastic four leaf clovers, and miniature horseshoes, to rosaries, icons of the saints, vials of holy water and pictures of movie stars.

In the large crowd there were only a handful of men. These undesirables usually attended with their wives much to the horror and disdain of the other women. Only rarely did a man venture into the bingo hall alone. Chief amongst these gate crashers was the infamous Teddy Swiatek whose reputation as a lucky player was well known and thoroughly detested throughout the Kaisertown bingo circuit.

Whenever Pan Swiatek approached a table the women would pile every conceivable item of clothing atop every empty chair. When the man did finally sit down, a long sorrowful groan welled up from the nearby unfortunates. It was the death moan of a collective spirit getting its bingo luck drained for the evening. Counterbalancing this sound, however, was the audible sigh of relief emitted by the occupants of the other tables whose luck had just been preserved.

Bertha's steady bingo playing friend, Celia Nockowicz, was an exceedingly homely woman in her early fifties whose face was marred by numerous bulbous warts and moles. A dime sized purple scar in the shape of a small crater rested on her left temple. Many years ago, following an arcane Polish home remedy, Celia had taken a stout sewing thread and looped it around the base of her largest and most irritating mole. After several ties and tugs to tighten the string around its fleshy target Celia yanked the string with all her might. The growth was torn from her temple followed by a geyser of blood which spurted high with every beat of the woman's frightened heart.

Luckily Stan, her husband, heard the sound of Celia's body hitting the floor. He managed to staunch the bleeding with another tried and true remedy of a compress of spider webs and stale bread. Needless to say, the rest of Celia's warts stayed exactly where they were.

Three men ran the bingo from atop a small stage. One man rotated the large mesh drum where a mass of ping pong balls poured back and forth with each revolution. Each ball was marked with a prominent letter-number combination. After a series of turns, it was the job of the second man to reach into the cage through a small trap door and remove one ball. In doing so it was of utmost importance that the man never, never, so much as glanced at any of the balls. To do so was to invite rioting on the part of the highly suspicious Polish ladies in attendance.

Once extricated the ball was handed over to the third member of the Holy Name triumvirate who promptly read out the letter and number imprinted on it. The man then inserted the ball into a pigeonhole board set at an angle for the audience to see and check.

Throughout the night these poor men were bombarded with critical remarks from the crowd.

"Hurry up. We ain't got all night."

"Too many Bs. Where are dah Ns?"

"Shake dem balls."

Nelly had to be constantly reminded by her two companions to check her cards. Her nonchalance irritated them.

"You pay good money for dem cards."

"Dat Diane Cheiwoska, she win again," said Bertha. "Lucky dat one. She won id dah big jackpot last week."

"Dey got it lots of money at home," added Celia. "She doan need no bingo."

"Maybe she just likes getting out with her friends?" suggested Nelly whose comment was met with silence.

Bertha grew tense as she needed only one more number for the ten dollar bingo, N-43. How many times just one number, she thought, only to have someone else beat her to it. "B-3," the caller shouted. "I-19, 0-68, N-43."

N-43, the number echoed in Bertha's mind. N-43, psia krew, that was her number. "Bang-o, bang-o," Bertha shouted as she stood up and waved her hands in the air like a shipwrecked sailor hailing down a passing boat. Celia almost choked on her Verner's ginger ale.

"Drogi boze," she cried. "You scare me to death. It's Ok. Dah man is coming."

Eddie Gordon checked Bertha's card. Everything matched so he gave her a crisp ten dollar bill. She was the sole winner and didn't have to share her reward with anybody.

"Such a nice man, dat Eddie Gordon, nie?" added Bertha. "I always like him."

Nelly shook her head good naturedly.

"An for dah luck I'm takin all of us to dah Deco for some eats," concluded Bertha.

When the twenty-five dollar cover the board grand prize came up, the hall dropped into silence. All eating, drinking and talking ceased. Anyone who dared violate this unspoken law was summarily stared down into submission. Even Nelly suddenly took an interest in her cards.

The call of the numbers trumpeted from the stage and echoed off the walls. The rasp and bang of the tumbler sounded like distant thunder while the cascade of ping-pong balls rolled like a rumbling avalanche. But before the three women got excited and with fewer than half their numbers covered, a voice rang out in the hall. It was a male voice. It was Teddy Swiatek's voice. Pan Swiatek had won the grand prize, again, and by so doing confirmed his status as the most hated man in all of Kaisertown.

Shortly afterwards Nelly joined her mother and Aunt Vickie working at the Drescher Box Company. The factory was located off Fillmore Street in a rundown industrial part of the city. The company made cardboard and specialty paper boxes. Its nearly all female work force of machine operators and packers totaled fifty. The foremen and supervisors and sales staff were all men.

The work was good for Nelly. Though it was repetitious and tedious it was enough to keep her mind occupied. She soon worked herself up to the position of operator's helper, and then to machine operator itself. This was the most prestigious and highly paid position on the factory floor. It involved a great deal of piece work. Nelly was fast and nimble and she and her helper made a lot of money. Her mother was proud of her because Nelly's work ethic attracted attention from the bosses.

"Dey like my Nelly, nie. She's fast. Even dah big boss himself, Mr. Drescher, he come down an talk to her about how good she's doin."

"Long as she don't kill dah job on us," someone mentioned.

"Nelly's not no job killer. Just does her work, dat's all. Piece work's for herself anyways. It doan bodder dah rest of us."

The Drescher workforce was equally divided among Polish and Italian women with a small minority of Jews and a couple of colored women thrown in. Most conflicts, petty as they were, were generally confined to the Polish-Italian segment with each group seeing in the other its chief rival. The Jews and colored were so far removed from the everyday experiences of the other women that they hardly counted for competition. Although circumstances sometimes required the women to work together, they sat for lunch and gossiped amongst themselves strictly along ethnic and racial lines. Since the supervisors were men and they assigned the various jobs, there came about a fair bit of flirting and occasional exchanges of favors offered by some women in order to get the better jobs.

Bertha Ostraski was a veteran of the factory and well understood the sexual politics of the plant. She was a wiry and strong woman with a personality hardened but not broken by adversity. The strength of character showed in her face. She was respected by her fellow workers and by the supervisors as well. The latter never challenged her and gave her daughter a wide berth when it came to soliciting sexual favors.

"How come dat Helen Vincente gets all the Whitman orders?" Nelly asked one time at lunch. "She's not that good of a operator. Aunt Vickie is better than her."

"Yer Aunt Vickie doan lift her skirt for dah supervisors like Helcha does," replied Bertha.

"What do you mean?"

"You see when Helcha goes out for dah lunch, she comes back and nobody says nuttin about how long she been gone? Where you tink she goes all dat time?" Aunt Vickie added.

"I heard too dat dah old man Drescher, he had something to do wit her."

"She was a handsome woman when she was younger, doan kid yer-selfs," added Bertha.

"An she's single now anyways so what does she care?"

"Maybe you should try dating too," said Nelly to her Aunt Vickie. "Yer divorced now so yer free to do what you want to."

The expression on Aunt Vickie's face changed immediately. She threw her food wrappers and the rest of an unfinished sandwich into her lunch bag.

"I'm not divorce for yer information, young girl. I'm separate. Dat's a difference." She left the table.

Nelly's jaw dropped. "What did I say? I didn't mean nothing."

"Doan worry," said her mother. "Yer auntie's just sensitive right now wit Jason gone too an everyting. She get over it. I talk to her later. Now, go back to work."

One day at the box factory while Nelly worked alongside Helen Vin-cente filling a special order of gift jewelry boxes for Kleinhan's Depart-ment Store, she noticed Mr. Lewis, the foreman, walking the floor with a young man in tow. Mr. Lewis was pointing things out to his companion and stopping at various machine stations to talk to the operators. As he approached Nelly's machine she noticed Helen fluffing up her hair and smoothing down her skirt. There was also a slight tug at the woman's blouse which exposed more cleavage to public view.

"This is my nephew, David," said Mr. Lewis to both Nelly and Hel-en. "I'm trying to interest him in a job here at the Drescher Folding Box Company. So far with no success."

"I don't know, uncle. Things are looking up on this side of the plant. Maybe I'll change my mind," the young man replied while looking straight at Nelly.

All the while Helen was making googly eyes at Mr. Lewis, Nelly couldn't help admiring David. He was probably Nelly's age. Not good looking, but not unattractive either. He seemed friendly and full of good humor and he was very well dressed. The next time Nelly saw David was at lunch that same day when he asked her out to the local deli for a sandwich and coffee.

"Go on it you," said Nelly's mother, happy that a man, and a seemingly important one at that had paid attention to her daughter.

"I packed my lunch though," protested Nelly.

"I eat it for you," replied her mother. "Now go you."

David had recently finished a two year course at Eric County Tech and was looking for work. His father was a businessman who owned a couple of hardware stores and a discount retail store that just appeared in the area, called, "Three Gals". David had his own car, a new Buick. He explained what model it was and some of its unique features, but it all went over Nelly's head. She was more conscious of the fact that at age nineteen this was her first actual date, lunch at Mel's Deli with a virtual stranger.

"Hey, you ever been to Niagara Falls in the winter time?" asked David. "What do you say we drive over there this Sunday. We can have dinner afterwards, and maybe take in a show?"

"That's quite a lot for one day," replied Nelly.

"Just the Falls then, and dinner. What do you say?"

"OK, but make it after two o'clock. I can't miss mass."

The first date was followed by many others. Nelly was happy. Bertha was thrilled for her daughter.

"You see it. Good to get outa dah house and be wit people you own age. He seems like a nice boy. Takes you to nice places, nie? Dat Klein-han's Music, taki beaudiful I hear it. Who was dere you see?"

"Johnny Mathis."

"Ohh, he's nice. I wanted to see Liberace. He was dere last year. Maybe next time me and Vickie and some of dah girls from work, we go. I love dem outfits he got. Ale ladne, nie?"

David dabbled in photography and wanted desperately to take pictures of Nelly, nude pictures. She refused out of hand, but later compromised as their relationship grew closer. David had his own apartment on Jewett Parkway. They were there one evening after dinner.

"OK, how about you wear this mink jacket," explained David. "I take a picture. Underneath you've got nothing on. You hold the coat open. I take another picture."

"No."

"OK, you wear this mink jacket. I take a picture. Underneath all you've got on is your bra and panties?" David hesitated. Nelly didn't say anything. David tentatively continued.

"OK, you hold the coat open. I take another picture or two. You've got a beautiful body, you know. You've got a beautiful face too. You really are just simply beautiful all around," he concluded.

Nelly was nervous as she disrobed for the shots. When she held the coat open she could feel the rush of blood crimson her face. David snapped away. He came closer and slipped his arm around her and kissed her. Nelly took a deep breath as images of Jason rushed through her mind. She remembered that hot night in her sister's bedroom, but hesitated.

"No David," she whispered. "I'm not ready. I don't know."

"That's OK," David replied. "I understand. Just let me look at you for a while longer and dream a bit more."

Nelly smiled, opened her jacket widely and stuck out her tongue playfully.

The Polish women gathered at the lunch table at Drescher's Box Factory.

"He gave you a mink coat?" one of the women said to Nelly.

"It isn't a coat, just a jacket," she replied.

"Just a jacket, a mink jacket. Psia krew, I take it a mink hanky and be glad."

"He's rich I heard. Got a big car, nie? Nelly, you lucky."

"An he takes her to taki nice places where dey got dah good eats. Lots a times," added Nelly's mother trying to get her two cents worth in to praise her daughter's prospects. "His fadder's a big shot who owns a lotta property in Buffalo. Got a big house, like a mansion dere in Orchard Park."

"Maybe he's gonna ask you to marry him? What you gonna say, Nelly?"

At that moment Helen Vincente passed by. She glanced back at the Polish ladies and said distinctly and loudly. "He's a Jew."

The women's mouths dropped open. Some crossed themselves hurriedly. Others finished their lunches and left the table to Nelly, her mother, and Aunt Vickie. When they got home Nelly's mother put her face in her hands.

"Oh jenna, jenna, I shoulda known it was too good to be true, a Jew. And he seemed like such a nice boy, so polite, and den he was rich. You know, Nelly, you never had it much in dis world. Now when you maybe got a good chance, turns out for nuttin. A Jew."

"Mom, listen to yerself. David is nice to me. He buys me expensive presents. He takes me out to places I never been, never would have went.

He's always nice to you too. So now everything is finished just because he's Jewish? The world comes to a end because he's a Jew. Think about what yer sayin."

"I know it. I know he's been good to you, but why does he gotta be a Jew? Piorun, just our luck. Did you know? Did you know he was a Jew?"

"Mom, I don't even know what a Jew is supposed to be like. I never met one before. I never thought nothing about it. What was I supposed to say? 'Hey, by the way are you a Jew?'"

"Nelly, my Nelly I doan know eider, but what you gonna do for getting married? You gotta get married in church. An what about dah kids. What's gonna happen to dah kids, oh jenna, jenna kohane."

Nelly didn't say anything to David about her mother's outburst. She was too ashamed. Jason was right, Polacks are the most prejudiced people in the world. They even hated each other because David may be a Jew, but Nelly also knew that he was Polish. His family was from a village outside of Krakow.

One day David picked Nelly up from work and asked if she wanted to come with him to his parents' house for dinner. His mother was preparing a special meal.

"Great," said Nelly. "It will be nice to meet your parents. Have you mentioned me to them, by the way?"

"Oh yes," David smiled. "They certainly know how I feel about you."

David's house was indeed very large, maybe even a mansion worthy of servants and grounds keepers. Nevertheless, it was David's mother herself who prepared the meal. The family sat in a separate dining room decorated with elaborate French provincial furniture. The dinnerware was fine china, the wine glasses crystal, and a beautiful monogrammed silver service flanked each plate.

Nelly would never have known what fork to use at the table were it not for the many meals David had taken her out to at various restaurants throughout the city. The conversation was eager and friendly although David's father was a bit on the quiet side. If this was how Jews behaved Nelly mused, great. Everyone bowed their heads before the meal. Nelly did the same and made the sign of the cross. When she looked up everyone, with the exception of David, was still praying. Old fashioned she thought, just like her mother, aunts and uncles.

Nelly did not recognize any of the food being served. Even the water in her glass seemed unusual. It tasted bubbly. Out of politeness she did not say anything. People have their own ways. That was fine and even interesting.

David's mother seemed to sense Nelly confusion. "Is something wrong with the soup, my dear?"

"No, no it's delicious," Nelly replied. "What are these little dumplings or whatever?"

"Why those are matzo balls, dear. Surely you've had matzo balls before?" said the woman with a shallow smile. David pleasantly changed the subject, asking his father how business was doing at the newest store.

The main dish was served: a large roast of beef surrounded by small rounded mounds of baked dough, carrots, and sweet potatoes.

"Boy," said Nelly. "These are just like little pierogies, filled with potatoes too. They're very delicious. We have these mainly at Christmas time, wigilia."

David's parents exchanged glances. Their brows seemed to furrow somewhat. They simultaneously looked at their son who merely smiled back and continued eating.

"And what temple do you go to, dear?" continued David's mother.

"Temple?"

"Yes, of course, dear, what temple? What temple do you worship at, belong to?"

Out of simple ignorance Nelly presumed that the words temple and church were interchangeable. "Oh, I go to St. Casimir's. That's on the corner of Gorski and Casimir Street in Kaisertown. I don't imagine you know where dat is. Pretty far from here and not as nice a neighborhood either."

The jaws of the two older people dropped open in unison. David's father abruptly excused himself from the table. His wife stared hard at David and was about to leave, but got the best of her manners.

"I see. Well, David has told us so much about you, but it seems that he has left out certain facts, important facts his father would say. You'll excuse me. I'll get the dessert and be right back."

Nelly looked helplessly at David. Her eyes were wide and wondering.

"God, you're beautiful," David said. "I'm sorry, but my parents…"

His mother reentered the room carrying a tray of pastries.

"As I was saying," continued David. "I'm sorry, but my parents are a bit prejudiced, you see. They aren't used to gentiles being invited for dinner."

"David, really. That isn't fair. You should have said something. Prepared us. You said you were dating the girl steadily, and she was special to you. We naturally assumed she was Jewish. You know how sensitive your father is after what happened to his family during the war."

"Please, if I hear about the war one more time, I think I'll puke," replied David.

His mother took a deep breath. "These are called blintzes by the way, dear," she said and left the room.

On the way back to Nelly's house David tried to explain. "I never said anything because it's really none of their business who I date, or how we feel about each other. I'm tired of all their Jewish bullshit. Jewish this, Jewish that. Screw it."

"What did you mother mean when she said that about your father's family during the war?"

"Nothing."

"No, tell me. I want to know."

"When the Germans came to my grandparents' village they rounded up all the Jews and sent them away in box cars. My grandfather and grandmother and their kids, one of them was my father, escaped and were hidden by my grandfather's best friend, a Polish farmer. He put them in a root cellar underneath his barn. My grandfather gave his friend all the family's money, silverware, and jewelry to hold until the war was over and the Germans left Poland. A few days after the trains pulled out the friend called in the German soldiers and gave up my grandfather and his family.

"The Germans had the neighbor dig a hole with his tracker and they buried my grandfather's entire family alive. They laughed that the Jews had lived in a hole, so now they could die in one. My father somehow stayed breathing under the dirt and escaped. He fought in the French underground until the end of the war. He never went back to Poland."

"Oh, my god," sobbed Nelly. "The poor man. That's horrible."

"Mel Lewis at Drescher, he's my mother's brother. Their family was already in America before the war started. None of my father's family escaped the Holocaust. They were all killed."

"Who could ever forget or forgive that?" Nelly said. "But weren't your grandparents Polish too?"

"They were Jews who just happened to live in Poland. And the farmer friend who betrayed them all, he was a Catholic."

Back in David's apartment Nelly let David seduce her for the first time. It was more of a charity offering, a kind of apology for all the wrongs done to David's family in the past. Nelly continued to date David, but the frequency of their meetings dropped off until they eventually melted into nothingness like the late snows of a Buffalo winter.

"You find it someone else," said Nelly's mother. "Doan worry. A nice Polish boy next time dough, nie? You stay wit yer own. Dat's dah best."

In the spring time Nelly resumed her visits to her father's grave at St. Stan's Cemetery. She brought bright tulips and yellow daffodils. "Daddy, daddy," she whispered. "I'm so sorry. Things were better back then when I was your little girl."

Barney: "Sczesliwa bestija! Lucky Bastard!"

The sign shone brightly in pink and green outside the old tavern, "Barney's Bar and Grille." Several smaller signs in bright neon colors lit up the windows: Budweiser Beer, Utica Club, and Genny Cream Ale. The street was lined with cars on both sides. A few patrons stood outside waiting for a line of men in baseball uniforms to file in ahead of them.

"Barney"s Ballers," they shouted. "Kings a dah diamond. Houghton Park softball champions."

Inside the barroom Barney stood at his customary spot of pride and privilege behind the cash register and beamed proudly at the large crowd of young people in front of him. There was a fair proportion of women thrown into the mix, most of them drinking out of cocktail glasses. Barney now featured several beers on tap and also had a menu of cocktails for the ladies. Whiskey sour with cream was his featured drink for the weekend and they were selling like hot dogs at a firemen's picnic. Barney could barely wipe the smile off his face. The steady ring of the cash register was like an aphrodisiac to him. He had to regularly look down at his pants to make sure he didn't have a hard on.

Another reason for the inspection of his drawers was the pretty cook and waitress Barney had working for him this past year. Susie Tishka was a long time Kaisertown beauty who retained her good looks and coupled them with a pert petite figure. She favored short skirts which did justice to two of the finest legs that ever polkaed across a Kaisertown dance floor. Susie had bright strawberry blond hair done up in a stylish French twist which was regularly highlighted and maintained at Wanda's Beauty Salon just down the block on Clinton Street. Susie and Barney had actually dated before he met Jeanette. It was only the latter's exceptional work ethic and dedication to business that had swayed Barney to select Jeanette over Susie in the first place. Susie was now a widow having been married to John Bramokowicz. They had two children, both grown.

Of course, Susie Tishka would never have been at Barney's in the first place had it not been for Jeanette's failing health and subsequent death only a year ago. The warning signs of the lung cancer that killed Jeanette had been there for a long time. It was after one dark coughing fit, however, during which Jeanette coughed up blood that Barney finally called in Dr. Kalinowski. Jeanette was frantic for medical attention by that time.

Barny pulled the good doctor aside before they entered the room. "Doctor, please don't say nuttin to Jeanette if it's serious, you know, cancer. She's afraid and it would kill her right away if she knew what she had dere. We talk after. Just give her some hope, you know, and den some pain killer to make her comfortable."

The doctor confirmed Barney's suspicions. Jeanette had terminal lung cancer and it was obvious that she was terrified of the diagnosis.

"Your wife was insistent on knowing how long she has to live if she does in fact have cancer. Seems to be important to her," said Doctor Kalinowski to Barney downstairs in the bar. "Some things she wants to do before she dies, I guess."

"You didn't tell her, did you?" Barney said in a bit of a panic which the doctor attributed to the man's concern for his wife's mental state.

"No, I didn't even confirm it was cancer although the signs are obvious. I told her she could recover yet with some bed rest and lots of liquids and some pills I will prescribe for her. I'm afraid they're only painkillers. She has about six months."

Barney shook his head sadly. "I will tell her when dah time is right. Leave it to me doctor. I don't wanna upset her especially if it don't do her no good."

"That's probably best," confirmed the doctor.

Barney fixed Jeanette's bedroom to make it self-sufficient when he was busy downstairs in the bar.

"I want you to be comfortable so you don't need nuttin. I even gonna put a little potty seat so you don't gotta go all dah way to dah batroom. An dah TV too. I'll put it on yer dresser. I will sleep on dah couch. It's OK."

He saw the panicked look on his wife's wizened face. "It's only temporary anyways, till yer feelin bedder. Doctor says you take yer medicine an everyting be alright. Take time dat's all."

"Barney, what about our trip to Florida? Maybe we should go right now while I can still manage at least a liddle bit. I could sit inna chair dere on dah beach wit my feet in dah water like in dah picture we seen, nie? Nie, Barney? Dat would make me feel bedder too I tink. Nice warm sun beatin down, and dah blue sky. Dah sky, it looks so blue in all dem pictures, doan you tink, Barney, Barney?"

"Dere's plenty a time when yer feelin bedder. Just stay in yer room an get lots a rest. Doan worry about dah bar 'cause I take care a dat."

"Maybe it's too much fer you, Barney, honey. Maybe we should hire someone come in once in a while to look after me. Would be nice to have someone to talk to when yer busy all day."

"Psia krew, I'm workin my fingers to dah bone an tryin to save money an right away yer spendin it on a nurse. Nurse cost money."

"I doan mean a regular nurse, no. Just a neighbor lady maybe, like Pani Heina, come in an keep me company for a hour or two, and clean up around here so you doan gotta do it all yerself."

"I taught you wannid to save money for Florida. How we gonna save?"

"Don't we got enough by now," Jeanette's voice faltered. "I, I'm afraid Barney. I'm afraid I ain't never gonna get dere, never see dah Florida beach or nuttin." She began to cry.

"Doan cry. Doan worry. Dah doctor said you just gotta touch of pneumonia or something in yer lungs. Gonna clear up with dah medicine an some rest. Dah most important ting is dah rest."

"An we're goin to Florida when I ged bedder? We're goin for sure?"

"Yes, yes."

"Promise."

"Promise."

"Dat's my Barney. We gonna have lots a good times yet, nie, Barney? Me and you."

Jeanette slipped off to sleep dreaming of ocean breezes and warm sunny skies and blue waves lapping at her feet. She died two months later. She was fifty-two years old.

Barney was setting up the bar late one morning when Jimmy Pajak came in leaning heavily on a cane.

"Jimmy, long time no see. Where you been hidin?"

"Psia krew, I hardly go out no more. Artridis, an den I got dah shingles too, nie. Matko boska, nearly kill me. I stop by a couple a times, but you weren't open. I just see yer new hours now, noon?"

"No sense wastin dah electricity an heat when dere ain't nobody comin in. Late night crowd now."

"I seen dah youngsters."

"Dey got dah pieniadze."

"An piorun, lookit what you done to dah bar. I wouldn recognize dah old place. What dat in dah back?"

"Come in. I show you," said Barney.

The two men walked towards the darkened rear of the barroom past two pool tables, a shuffle board game, and two bowling machines.

"Jesu, you got all new stuff in here. Where's all dah card tables gone?"

"Doan need em no more. Nobody plays cards, an wit dese machines everytime somebody plays, dat's money in my pocket."

The back room lit up when Barney threw a switch. There were couches and comfortable chairs and coffee tables placed around the former dance floor. A brightly lit juke box stood under a sign on the rear wall that blinked into life as Jimmy Pajak's mouth dropped open.

"Barney's Lounge" it displayed in soft blue and pink letters.

"Dah young kids, dey sit here togedder wit dah lights down low and lisen to dah music and drink. I even catch em playin wit dah girls sometimes, feelin dem up."

"Piorun, yer kiddin."

"No, right in dah open. Dey doan care. Good for dah business an I'm makin taki fancy drinks now too. You should see."

"Where'd you ged dah money for all dis fancy stuff? Must a cost a fortune, nie? I taught you were goin outa business almost dere for a while."

"Me and Jeanette saved over dah years. Had some good business an we owned dah building an stuff."

"Poor Jeanette, she never seen none a dis, how good it turned out," said Jimmy. "You got my flowers, nie? I couldn't go to dah cemetery wit my artridis."

"Yeah, dziekuje, dobrze. Jeanette, no but she would a wanted it to turn out good. She was a good business woman, and work. Dat woman could work, night an day, didn't matter. Work like a dog. Dey doan made em no more like Jeanette. Dat's for sure."

"Yous two ever go on dat Florida trip she was always talkin about? Psia krew, every time I seen her she was showin dah picture an dah pamphlet about dah Florida. Florida, Florida, dat's all she talk about."

"No, we never made it. I waned to go, but she was too weak dere at dah end. She couldn't even ged down dah stairs."

"Ahh, dat's too bad, nie?"

The two men heard the front door of the bar open and a woman's voice call out. "Barney, Barney, honey, you back dere?"

"Who's dat?" asked Jimmy.

"You doan know? Dat's Susie Tishka. Me an her, we're seein each udder now. She got her own house, paid for, you know, but she helps me wit dah bar. Dis lounge, it was part her idea what she seen in downtown Buffalo where all dah big shots go. She been around places. For me she looks after everyting. Does dah books. Everyting. I doan godda worry about nuttin."

"She still good lookin like before?"

"Here she comes."

Introductions were made, then Susie excused herself to get the kitchen ready and fill out the beer and liquor orders.

"Ale ladne, she's still a beauty," said Jimmy.

"She's got dah hot pants too," Barney said with a wink. He pulled Jimmy's collar and whispered in his ear. "One time after we close we did it right on dat couch over dere." Barney's voice sank even lower. "She puts it in her mouth too. Taki blow job."

"Zebys struchla," Jimmy made the sign of the cross. "You lucky bastard."

"Yeah, yer right, Jimmy. I been lucky. I had Jeanette an we build up dah business good togedder but wit lots a years a struggle, an doin witout too. But, you know, dem days is over. Now, I enjoy myself. What's dah use a savin, savin all dah time? You jus gonna die and dat's dah end. No, me and Susie, we travel now. Close dah bar right after New Year's dere an we go to Florida for dah whole mont an part a February too. Come back for dah Valentine's Day.

"You ken rent a place down in Florida dere real cheap. An you got yer sun and sand. And yer eats are cheap too. Cheap and good. Me an Susie, we got it a good time dere. We doan grudge us nuttin because you onny live once, nie? You onny live once."

"Sczesliwa bestija, sczesliwa bestija," Jimmy repeated.

Jason: "Love's Labour's Lost"

Since he moved out of his mother's flat and onto Cherokee Drive, Jason rarely ventured into Kaisertown. The long string of friends and family he had there faded into the background of his life. He never had much in common with them anyways and his attendance at UB now severed the tie completely. In pace requiescat.

The only Kaisertown relative he kept in touch with was his cousin Larry who was involuntarily entrenched in an army career; a circumstance that worried Jason more and more as U.S. involvement in Vietnam deepened. Jason himself was exempt from the draft until the end of his four year university term. That gave him a couple more years of freedom. Larry, however, was on his way overseas after his next leave.

The two cousins exchanged letters on a regular basis. Jason was impressed with his cousin's writing skills. Larry wrote as he spoke, directly and thoughtfully, although a bit ungrammatically. Jason's letters in turn entertained Larry with accounts of life back home in Buffalo. Family news was limited since Jason's access to the mother's clan was cut off. He could only inform Larry second handedly through Larry's sister, Diane, who worked at the Ben Franklin Store on Clinton Street. Larry was particularly concerned about his mother and siblings who suffered under the harsh hand of the head of the household, Larry's drunken dad.

The old man was a "chipper" at Worthington where he had worked for over thirty years. His occupation made him virtually deaf and he refused to wear a hearing aid. As a result he was constantly crabby and suspicious of any conversation around him.

"Whadda yous sayin dere? Huh, Huh? Yous talkin about me? Watch her mout."

It was apparent that there was no love lost between Larry and his dad and the boy had endured many a beating in his day. However, Larry had blossomed into a strong young man. When he stood up he was six feet tall and had biceps on him like Malecki hams. When he left for the army he issued a stern warning to his father.

"You lay a hand on ma, or Allison, or Diane, when I'm gone, you bedder not be here when I get back."

Jason picked up his cousin at the train station. "You lost weight," Jason said. "And that hair."

"Army food. Stachu Klemp wouldn't eat it. And what? You don't like my baldy sour? 'Course, it's even worse now dat everybody's got long hair tanks to dah Beatles. Not my kind of music either. Hey, you still into dat jazz shit?"

"Yes."

"You and Dorothy. No, give me dah King any day."

Larry was silent for much of the ride until he finally spoke up after lighting a cigarette. "I been training for a gunner on a chopper. Heading for Vietnam right after I get back."

"Jesus fuck," replied Jason. "I thought you were getting into the motor pool? Hell, it would be a lot better to repair jeeps and tanks and stuff behind the lines than be up in a fucking helicopter."

"Dat's all bullshit promises to sucker you into joinin up. Dey promise you stuff, great career moves and den when yer in, it's dah grunts for you, infantry. I figgered dah chopper shit was better. I hate the army. It don't make no sense.

"Like when we had dis jerk off sergeant, Sergeant Steward, in boot camp. He told us to take a pile a bricks and load em onto some skids and put them on the other side a dah exercise yard. Den along comes a lieutenant when we're done.

'What dah fuck are yous doin wit dem bricks?'

'Sergeant Steward told us to move em here.'

'Oh yeah, well I'm tellin yous to move dem fuckers back to the other side where dey belong. Now move yer asses. I want it done before mess call.'

"So what did you do?" asked Jason.

"Fuck, we moved em back. You can't reason wit dem assholes. Anyways we found out later on dat it was all a set up. Dem two pulled dat shit on every new batch a recruits just to prove a point."

"Some point. And what if they told you to charge a machine gun nest?"

"Fuck, I don't know. Pretend I didn't hear maybe."

"What if they ordered you to shoot a bunch of women and children?"

"I don't know and I don't wanna tink about it. Anyway, why don't you just shut up? You and yer fuckin questions. Dis ain't no college classroom. Guys are fuckin dying over dere, you know."

Jason jumped in his seat. "Hey, I'm sorry. I didn't mean it like that."

"I remember what you said about all us poor working stiffs being stuck in the front ranks," Larry continued. "Cannon fodder. Sure enough, all around I seen a bunch of slobs like me, niggers too, and you know what? We were all trainin togedder and workin togedder and we were all scared shitless togedder and pretty soon we'll all be dying togedder."

"Janie's been asking about you," Jason volunteered in an attempt to change the subject to something more pleasant.

"Yeah, I wrote her a few letters. She wrote back. Good handwriting, but fuck, she ain't dat bright. I shouldn't say dat. But she's sweet and does have a great set of tits, sucks a mean cock too. I could use some tender lovin after all the hookers and tramps around the base. Pay yer money and get your cock sucked or fuck some broad up against a wall in some alley."

"Sounds romantic."

"Speakin of romantic, you been seen Dorothy lately?"

"Funny you should mention her. I actually ran into her the other day at that blues club you used to drop me off at when I borrowed your ID. She looked damned good too. All these years in Kaisertown, you know, I've been tempted to look her up, but something always got in the way."

"Like some other piece of ass?" quipped Larry.

Jason smiled and shrugged his shoulders.

"She's a good broad." Larry continued. "You know she wrote me a few letters, nothing romantic, just friendly stuff. And she can write, I'll tell you. Got some big words and good ideas. She wrote about you too."

"Me, what did she say?"

"I'm not tellin."

"Prick."

"Asshole."

The two cousins laughed and it was old times again. They bought a six pack of Genesee beer at Wesmart and pulled into the NFT turnaround just behind the store.

"You want to take the car, you can drop me off in West Seneca?" volunteered Jason.

"No, you keep it. I'm stickin close to home. Make sure everybody is doin OK. But maybe we can go out later and hit some of the old bars."

Before Larry left for overseas, he signed the car over to Jason. "Give me a few hundred for it later. I'm getting something brand new when I get back, probly Impala, top of dah line. But let me tell you about dis Vietnam shit. I'm fuckin scared as hell. I don't care so much if I get killed right off, clean, you know. But I doan wanna wind up no cripple. Guys steppin on landmines and getting dere legs and nuts blown off or getting captured by the VC. Dat's dah worst. Man, best to kill yerself first. And just another word of advice. I'd look up dat Dorothy if I was you. I really would and take off to Mexico or somewhere wit her. Leave all dis shit behind."

Jason's father had recently moved out of the Professor's flat on De Witt Street and got an apartment of his own of Holly Street.

"The Professor is a brilliant man," Jason's father explained. "but he's a total slob. That flat of his is right out of Dante's Inferno. It merits a separate circle of hell."

"I still think he should have become a teacher or university professor," Jason said. "He'd be great at it with all the knowledge he has and his insight into literature."

"I told you his priorities. Also, he doesn't have the formal education. Plus, he doesn't have the patience for teaching. He couldn't tolerate anyone who didn't love the classics as he does. It would drive him crazy."

"Was he ever married?"

"Twice, believe it or not. His first wife, Edith, was an English lady, very pleasant, sweet, maybe even a bit simple, or naïve might be a better word and quite attractive actually. Other than for sex, of course, Allen ignored her completely. He'd more or less lock himself inside his study and read and listen to music for hours by himself. She was forbidden to disturb him."

"Sounds pathetic, but vaguely familiar."

"It was tragic really. After a while he even encouraged her to go out on her own; visit friends, take in a movie, anything that would leave him free to pursue his own interests. Naturally she wound up finding another man, one who paid attention to her. The Professor was crushed, but, it was his own fault although he never saw it that way.

"The second time he married a high school English teacher. Seemed like a perfect match, but she had two young children, a boy and a girl, by a prior marriage. Naturally the kids were not allowed to disturb the Professor while he was reading or listening to his music. He sneered at any childhood activities or interests they had like reading comic books or playing with toys. He said it was all a waste of time and he forced them to read the classics: Dickens, Shakespeare long before they were ready.

"So after years of this kind of emotional abuse the boy had a nervous breakdown, and talk about irony. In his schizophrenia the kid would scream out lines from Shakespeare taunting the Professor. 'It is a tale told by an idiot, full of sound and fury, signifying nothing.' I'm telling you, Jason, it was a classical tragedy in its own right."

"Yes, complete with the Professor's own tragic flaw."

"Oh sure, he still blames Edith for the breakup of the first marriage and the kids for the second. You know, he would sob when reading a son-net by Edna St. Vincent Millay, but his own wives' misery and solitude did not move him in the least. He had a detachment for the real world. Everything was funneled or filtered through the lens of literature. He could be moved to rapture by a poem about the moon, but he wouldn't bother to walk outside on a dark night and look at it for himself."

Jason and his father arrived at the Professor's apartment to remove a few personal belongings, but also to have another literary session. The clutter and debris Jason had seem on other visits was minimal now, but starting to regenerate.

"I have certain books which I treasure," explained the Professor. "They are the classics that have stood the test of time. By that I mean, they have endured generations of readers and have maintained their relevance, their grip on the human psyche.

"Here's my unabridged Shakespeare. Six volumes with everything: tragedies, comedies, histories, and, of course, the sonnets. Next my King James version of the Bible. It is poetry second to none. The clear, unadorned crispness of the text, 'Jesus wept,' says it all. And then there's my Keats, the best of the Romantic poets and far superior to any of the others like Lamb, Shelley, Byron, and even Coleridge."

"I liked, "Ode on a Grecian Urn" Jason volunteered, but the Professor instead turned directly to Jason's father.

"You notice in Keats' poetry, Ed, the emphasis on aspiration, breathing. His poetry is filled with it. You can feel the labor in his poetic voice, a reflection of his own mortal struggle with consumption. And then!"

The Professor raised his hand in the air like a cop halting traffic at a busy interception. "And then that bastard, Wordsworth, a mere versifier at best, when asked to comment on Keats' "Endymion" says it's "a pretty piece of paganism". The talentless son of a bitch. I will never forgive him for that slight, you know, Ed.

"Calm down," Jason's father implored. "I know how you feel."

The Professor took a deep breath and proceeded. "Ok, to speed things up here. I've got the classical poems of Homer naturally, The Iliad and The Odyssey, the Professor continued. "The other of my literary gems are: James Joyce's, "Ulysses" and Finnegans Wake."

The Professor laughed talking again to Jason's father. "This Joyce, you know, Ed, he seemed to think that he was the only author around, and that people would spend all their time reading just his stuff. And Mark Twain, of course. Huckleberry Finn is without a doubt the greatest American novel ever written. Now another classic is Crime and Punishment, with a very good translated by Constance Garnett. That reminds me of the tremendous importance of having a good translator. As a reader, I am dependent on the translator for not just the story line, but for the feel of the narrative, the nuances of the language, the poetry of the words. I couldn't enjoy Homer's Iliad without the Lattimore translation. And then you have Edward Fitzgerald with the Rubaiyat and Burton's The Book of a Thousand and a Night. I always use the translation of the title of Proust's classic as an example of the interpretive power of a good translation.

"Think of it. Here you have the French. A La Recherche du Temps Perdu which you can render any number of ways. Literally, "In Search of Time Lost, or Lost Time". But the translator, taking liberties in the cause of poetic license comes up with, Remembrance of Things Past. It's beautiful. Simply beautiful and that is what good translation is all about."

When Jason and his father finally departed, they were burdened with books and articles. The Professor had a habit of giving away books he had finished reading and analyzing. Jason picked up a copy of Rebels and Redcoats and Lincoln Finds a General.

"Lincoln was the last U.S. president worth his salt," proclaimed the Professor. "All the rest since then have been capitalist toddies."

"I wonder if you could drop me off somewhere?" Jason's father asked as they drove away from DeWitt Street. "I'm meeting a lady friend at her house. She has her own car. We're going out dancing tonight. This is our third date."

"I'm happy for you dad. You deserve some fun in life, and by the way, how is Aunt Rose doing lately? After Uncle Florian's funeral and Larry's signing up I've lost touch."

"Uncle Elliot has had enough of her. They separated. He's settled with the kids. My sister can be difficult. She was dissatisfied with marriage and took it out on her husband and the children. Felt like she was missing out on life."

"I should stop by and see her. It's been a while."

"Good idea, I think she's been lonely and depressed lately. Probably could use some cheering up. You two seem to hit it off intellectually."

At his aunt's apartment they drank manhattans and listened to Billie Holiday. 'My man don't love me. He treats me oh so mean.' The time was right and having sex with his aunt didn't bother Jason in the least. Frankly the illicit sex excited him. He loved the intrigue and taboo and he enjoyed the experienced hands of his aunt. What a difference.

"Jesus, you're so beautiful, and your eyes, such depth of blue," purred his aunt at the door as Jason took his leave. "Your father was right, you are a good student only in more ways than he figured. And remember, don't go to strangers. Come to me."

Jason bent down and kissed his aunt on the forehead. "Goodnight."

Another reason why Jason had lost track of his aunt of late was that he was seeing a girl from one of his UB English classes. She was a Jewish girl from New York City. Her name was Amy Levine and she was intelligent, well built, and pretty with a boyish cut to her jet black hair.

Jason took Amy to several Buffalo restaurants: the Anchor Bar, Leonardo's, Victor Hugo's, as well as the Studio Arena Theater where they viewed controversial foreign films before they wound up one night at his Cherokee Street apartment. They undressed in the dark and lay down on the bed teasing and testing each other.

"Jewish boys don't kiss like that," Amy admonished Jason as he attempted to heighten the level of their intimacy.

OK, strike one he thought.

"Jewish girls don't do that," Amy informed him in reference to his attempt at oral sex. When a particular position proved equally forbidden as in "Jewish boys don't do it that way," Jason was long out of strikes.

However, the strength of his hard on and the feel of Amy's naked body next to his drove him on. She was going to get it one way or another, he resolved.

The legs of the bed beat a steady staccato on the floor as the girl's words of protest finally turned into whimpers and groans of passion. At least she enjoyed the basics, but with that many restrictions, it's a miracle there are any Jews left in the world, Jason reasoned. The next day Jason received a note from his landlady which was slipped under the bathroom door. It demanded a rental increase of $20 a month.

Nevertheless, after their class on 18th Century English Literature ended, Jason never saw Amy again. They did exchange a few letters over the summer. Amy was particularly taken up with the Jewish struggle of the Six Days War. She dreamed of finishing school and then moving to Israel to live on a kibbutz. Jason dreamed of Amy on her knees sucking his cock. Such a dichotomy of interests, coupled with a few lines of sympathy for the Palestinian cause in some of Jason's letters cemented a termination of their brief affair. Amy summed it up in her last letter.

"You're too busy concentrating on " screwing girls" to devote any real passion to world affairs. And your bullshit ideals are just an excuse to remain on the sidelines of political struggle. Give me instead the cause of the brave people of Israel, struggling for their very existence against the entire world. This is a real battle with real people and real consequences. I'm leaving in a week. I don't care if I ever see you again. P.S. You were the worst lay I ever had."

At least I was circumcised, Jason mused. That should have counted for something. After his rebuff from Amy, Jason decided to revisit the Blue Monday Club at Johnny's Ellicott Grille. He remembered the first time he was there and the beautiful colored waitress. What would it be like he wondered? That night while sitting at the bar, he met a new friend, a black guy named Carl Gerard.

"I likes the Blue Monday Club," said Carl, "because drinks are half price and I like Monty Hall. You hear him before?"

"On the radio a few times, and once in person," replied Jason.

"I likes the Blues; B.B. King, Arthur Prysock, Lou Rawls. How 'bout you?"

"I prefer jazz. Count Basie, sometimes Duke Ellington, although he's a bit too orchestral for my taste. Then there's Erroll Garner, Teddy Wilson. He played with Billie Holiday, and I like Chet Baker, both his singing and trumpet playing."

"Cool. Hey man, why don't go come down the neighborhood for a visit? Have a drink with me. Hit a couple of bars afterwards."

"Where do you live?" inquired Jason.

"On Peckam Street, 85 Peckam. I lives with my woman, Julia. Why don't you come on over, man?"

One Saturday afternoon Jason did just that. Peckam Street had long ago been part of the vast Polish neighborhood on Buffalo's East Side, but the people Jason saw walking around now we're certainly not Polish. Jason looked around for 85 Peckam Street. The fact that half the houses did not have any numbers on them did not facilitate the search. With number 79 a few houses away Jason narrowed down the options. He parked the car and walked up to the building. A long stairway ascended from an open interior hallway to the second floor. There was no exterior door on the house itself.

Jason climbed the stairs and knocked on the door. A voice called out to enter. He wasn't sure it was Carl's voice, but, what the hell, he had come this far. When he looked inside the apartment he was on the edge of a large living room with one couch, a coffee table, a single chair and a TV set. The floor was devoid of any rugs or carpeting. Three large windows overlooking the street were thrown wide open. The thin, worn curtains were tied in knots and hung out the windows. Two men sat on the couch drinking from mayonnaise jars.

"Hey man, look who here," one of the men stood up and shouted. It was Carl although Jason did not immediately recognize him. He wore only a tee shirt and a pair of tan colored pants. No shoes or socks. Jason noted how lightly colored the soles of his feet appeared.

"Dis is the guy I was telling you about, man. My good friend, Jason, from down the Blue Monday Club. Hey, you wanna drink? We got us some good gin here?"

"Sure," Jason replied. He knew that accepting a drink was good manners, although he did have a few reservations about the condition of the glasses.

After Carl's neighbor left, Jason was startled to hear a baby cry. The sound came from an adjacent room where a small black baby lay in a crib. His head was rubbed bald on the back. His diaper was dirty.

"His mama be home in a while," Carl said ignoring the distressed infant.

"Your wife?" Jason inquired.

"Hell no, man. I ain't married."

"And the baby?"

"Yeah, he mine. I'm livin here with Julia. She treat me good. She got two other kids. They out with her now and her cousin from down South here too till she get her own apartment. Want another drink?"

"No, this one's got me half blasted already. The glass is kind of big," Jason smiled.

The outer door opened and a group of women walked into the room talking loudly and carrying several parcels. When they saw Jason the conversation stopped abruptly. The little girls scampered behind the back of one well-built and very pretty colored woman. The other, younger woman, was smaller than her companion. She had a thin figure, with a beautiful round ass, Jason was quick to observe. She also had the typical colored features of a flared nose and large lips which the older woman did not possess. Carl broke out laughing.

"What, ain't none of you peoples ever seen a white man before? This is my friend I was telling you all about, Jason."

It was obvious that the two little girls hadn't actually seen a white man before, at least not close up in their living room. They continued to hide behind their mother who smiled and nodded.

"Why sure, we done seen plenty of white people. Don't be no fool."

That very night Jason found himself sleeping on a mattress on the floor with the younger woman. Her name was Illa May. She was Julia's cousin. Jason couldn't believe the sexual opportunity coming so fast. Hell, he thought, if this was a white woman I'd have spent a fortune on dinners and dates before I even got to grab her tits.

After everyone else was settled in their bedrooms, Jason pulled the covers off Illa May and stared at her naked body in the light of the lone lamp in the room. The girl immediately hid her face in her hands. "I'm shy," she meekly protested, but it wasn't long before she peered between her fingers at Jason's nude body.

"You handsome," she said. "But you got devil eyes."

"You're very pretty yourself," Jason replied.

The sight of the girl's naked body gave Jason an erection that he could have driven through the stone walls of St. Casimir's basilica. The girl's lips were full and soft as Jason kissed them. He ran his hands across her body. Her pubic hairs were wiry, and her nipples hard. Her entire body mesmerized him. He didn't know what to do first.

"Put my cock in your mouth," he finally said. "Put those big, beautiful lips around it."

Illa May shook her head. "I don't do none a dat stuff. No, but you can put me in any different positions you want. I ken do it a lot of different ways, but I don't do none of dat other stuff."

"That's OK," Jason replied. He didn't want to do anything that spoiled the mood. "How about protection? Should I put something on?"

"No, dat don't matter. It's not my time. You can do it to me. Go ahead, do it to me."

When the sun was beginning to flood into the room, Jason heard the hall door open. A colored man reached in and deposited several bottles of milk on the floor. He saw Illa May's half exposed naked body asleep next to Jason. He smiled. Jason smiled back and then the man was gone.

Carl and Jason frequented a lot of the black neighborhood bars. The women never accompanied them. Carl didn't want them along probably because he was often flirting with other women and didn't want to admit that he couldn't afford the extra outlay of cash.

"I gotta get myself outa there, man," Carl confided in Jason. "Woman's always askin me for money. Money, money. Hell, I ain't got no money. Been laid off for a three months now. Where I'm gonna get no money?"

"Well, she does have your little boy, Carl Junior there," Jason said. "You want to make sure he's taken care of."

"Hell man, I ain't even so sure he is my son. I was just goin with her and all of a sudden she's pregnant. Too soon you asks me. Hey man, you borrow me ten bucks? I'm broke right now."

"No problem."

That summer Jason had a steady job at Worthington in the machine shop. He made and saved a lot of money. During the school year he organized his classes so that he had the mornings off and could work four nights a week unloading trucks at the new Twin Fair store in town. He had lots of money, but little sleep.

Julia's older girl, Brenda, finally overcame her fear of Jason and would often sit on the couch holding his hand and staring at it. Then she'd look up at him examining his features and skin and eyes.

"You got funny eyes," she said. "You color them?"

"No, they came that way.'

"How can I get me some eyes like that?"

"You can't. You have to live with the eyes you've got. Some things you can't change." Jason looked at her small fingers intertwined with his.

"You be my friend?" she asked.

"Sure."

"I never had no white friend before. You be the first."

"Hopefully I won't be the last and you can call me Jason. It's OK."

When Julia came into the room she corrected her daughter. "You can call him Mr. Jason. You shows some respect for yer elders."

"That's OK," Jason intervened. "By the way, where are Illa May and Carl?"

"Illa May ain't here no more. I kicked her sorry black ass out 'cause she been here long enough without no money. No money, no job. All she got was money you give her."

"Where did she go?"

"Back home down South, Mississippi. Dat's where her folks are at. And here, she left this for you." Julia handed Jason a folded paper. It was a note from Illa May.

"Dear Jaysen,

My cosin Julia kiked me out an I gotta leave cus dere is people goin an I ken get a rid wit dem. I luv you an if you wan me to come back sen some money for the address I give you an I ken come. We ken hab budiful babys you an me. My address is 2256 Myrtle St. Laurel, Mississippi. Luv, Illa May."

"Her writin ain't too good," said Julia.

"I get the message."

"Illa May more a little girl herself, not a real woman," continued Julia. She subtly held her head higher and pulled her shoulders back and gave Jason a profile of herself.

"How old was she by the way?" Jason inquired. She did have a great shape, he thought.

"Fourteen."

Jason almost swallowed his tongue, but Julia did not seem the least bit concerned. "Well, she sure did look older," he finally replied.

"There's a difference between a real woman an just a girl," Julia added.

"I'll say amen to that," added Jason.

When Carl showed up an argument and an actual fight broke out between him and Julia. Jason stepped in quickly.

"Hey, please, let's calm down. The kids are getting upset. Look, I've got an idea. What do you say we get dressed up and go out to dinner, just the three of us. Today was payday so it's my treat. I know a place called The Cloister. You'll love it. What do you say?"

"Hell, she ain't never been to no nice place. Wouldn't know what to do," Carl said.

"I sure been to fancy restaurants before just not with yer cheap nigger ass."

Carl laughed, but took no offence at the word. "The Chicken Shack, that ain't no fancy place."

"It was the Swiss Chalet and that was a real nice restaurant what Bernie took me to. You too cheap take me out no place."

Jason could see that this wasn't moving any too quickly in the right direction. "Please, forget the past. Let's go out together now. I'll go home and come back and pick you up. Carl and I will have to wear a tie and sport coat. You've got a sport coat, right Carl?"

"Yeah, I got me one, good one."

"What am I gonna wear?" asked Julia. "I ain't got nothing good."

"I thought you been goin to big restaurants all the time. Now you ain't got nothing to wear?"

"How can I have something to wear when you ain't brought no money in this house since you been here?"

"Mommy, how about dat dress you wears to church?" said Brenda who was peeking around the corner of her room.

"That old thing?"

"Looks pretty."

"I guess I could get it out and all ironed up in time."

Jason was determined to show his friends a good time. He sensed that they were both nervous and ill at ease. He ordered a couple rounds of drinks and then selected a bottle of wine with the meal. They ended with great desserts and after dinner liquors. Everyone seemed to have a good time and Jason was happy to pay the bill. Carl even bought a cigar and lighted it up with satisfaction. He enjoyed the good life. He only lacked the means to obtain it. Julia on the other hand was noticeably quiet. On the way home in the car, Julia, who was alone in the back seat, started to sob. Carl turned around.

"What you doin back there, woman? You cryin? What wrong wit you?"

Jason slowed down and adjusted the mirror so he could see Julia. Sure enough, her dark eyes were twinkling with tears.

"Are you OK, Julia? What's the matter, dear?" Jason asked. "Somebody say something that hurt your feelings?"

"No," Julia replied. "It's just that, that when I seen all that money you done paid."

"Oh, don't worry about it," Jason insisted. "It was my pleasure. You two are my friends. I can afford it. I'm working."

Julia shook her head and continued to cry. "That, that was more money than what I spend on groceries for all of us for two whole weeks. You spend that on one meal like it was nothing, a whole weeks of groceries."

"You a fool," Carl added. "No sense takin yer sorry ass out no place."

They drove the rest of the way in silence with Jason glancing occasionally at Julia. She stared straight back at him. There was a strange look in her eyes, defiance almost.

By the end of the week Carl had left Julia. He moved in with a skinny, but pretty woman named Althea who lived a dozen blocks away. Jason helped Carl move his few belongings to Althea's flat. Julia did not seem to mind in the least.

"I shoulda kicked his worthless black ass out of here long time ago," Julia said as Jason carried bags and boxes down the stairs. "He ain't never bringed no money in this house since he lost his job at the NFT. Stealin my money most the time and sellin my food stamps for liquor money. I ain't cryin over him. And he's only yer friend 'cause you got money and yer white," she added with her arms folded. "Make sure you tell him to stay away from here. He want something then you can get it. I don't mind you."

Julia wore a loose fitting house dress with thin straps across her brown shoulders, Her skin glistened and a thin runnel of perspiration collected at the nape of her neck and ran slowly down the cleavage of her breasts. She was beautiful. Julia caught his fixation. She looked hard at him.

"Why don't you come by later tonight, get the rest of his junk. I'll look around see if anything's left. Come by after the kids are asleep."

The apartment was almost dark inside when Jason returned.

"Got the lights off 'cause of the heat," Julia explained. "I'm here on the couch. Sit down. I'll get you a cold drink. I got some orange Queen-O with gin. Dat OK?"

"That's fine," said Jason.

He sat down giving his eyes time to adjust to the darkness. There wasn't much to the room. Same old furniture. There was a new throw rug on the floor though, and a clock in the shape of a rayed sun disk on the wall. It didn't have the correct time. Julia sat close to Jason. He had never been this close to her before out of deference to Carl. Julia handed Jason his drink. Her body smelled faintly of Fels Naptha soap.

"How are the kids doing?" asked Jason stricken by the quiet in the apartment.

"They at their auntie's."

Jason could see Julia's chest rising and falling in the shadowy light. She was breathing heavily. He could smell the pine scent of juniper berries on her breath. He leaned over and kissed her. Her lips were thinner than Illa May's, but she pressed back with an open mouthed passion that caught Jason off guard.

In a moment they were lying naked and hot on Julia's bed. Julia was strong and rough. She ran her hands all over Jason's body. She grabbed his cock with her full hand and jerked him into a rock hard erection. She breathed heavily in a combination of anger, passion, and resentment. Jason wasn't sure if they were making love or having a serious wrestling match.

Jason conducted his own hands on an exploration of Julia's body. He didn't seem to have enough hands for the job. Everything was moving fast. He would have loved to switch on the light and get a good look at the woman's naked body, but he couldn't leave the arousal of the moment.

He finally disengaged her hands and pushed her down on her back and spread her legs widely. She didn't resist. Afterwards, they lay together panting in silence. Finally Julia rolled onto her side and looked at Jason. "How come you pick Illa May?"

"You were Carl's woman," Jason explained. "I couldn't cut in on him like that."

"You didn't like me enough? You liked Illa May better?"

"No, I didn't like her better. And I didn't think you were interested in me. You had Carl."

"You could tell when I looked at you. You musta known."

"You're right. The minute I saw you, I liked you, a lot. I should have said something and not gotten involved with Illa May. Of course, she did have a beautiful ass, I must say."

"Why you," Julia slapped Jason hard on the chest.

"Hey, I was only kidding. You've got a much better figure."

"I do?"

"Yes, your ass is much nicer, rounder, harder, and you've got full, firm breasts. And you're beautiful. You're the most beautiful woman I ever met."

"I am?"

"Yes, and you know what else? I like your slender neck right here where it meets your collarbone." Jason leaned over and kissed Julia's neck and shoulder.

"You just sayin that 'cause you wanna do it to me again."

"No, I don't want to do it anymore. Once was enough."

"Why not? You done it with Illa May lots of times more than once."

"How do you know that? Why you little sneak, you were watching us. Weren't you? Well, maybe you picked up some pointers from that girl. She might have been young, but, man, she knew how to make love."

"That skinny thing! She hardly move her behind. Just layin there like a dead fish on a table."

"And naturally once you saw my big cock, then you just had to have me, right? That's what got to you in the first place. One look at my big manly cock and you was gone. Gone woman, gone."

"Dat tiny little thing. Little baby boy, he got a bigger one then that."

"Why you no good..." Jason tickled Julia who laughed and curled into the fetal position. As Jason continued she rolled over on her stomach. Their bodies rubbed. Julia stuck her ass in the air and wriggled it around. Jason was hard in a minute and easily slipped into her from behind. From there Julia took over the action and gyrated and humped and bumped and wrung Jason's member dry.

"How that?" she said after she too had satisfied herself.

"That was the best. You're wonderful. The best lover I ever had." He kissed her glistening shoulder and patted her ass. They fell asleep side by side until morning.

When Jason got back to his apartment the next afternoon, he removed his shoes while sitting on the edge of the bed distracted by the memory of the night before. Then something on the floor next to his overturned shoe attracted his attention.

"What in hell?"

There on the floor was a large, bronze colored insect struggling to its feet and trying to get its bearing amid new surroundings. Is, is that a, a cockroach, Jason gasped never having seen one before in his life? He recoiled in horror and his toes curled in panic before he grabbed his other shoe and beat the insect into a wet paste on the floor. He took a shower immediately.

Jason and Julia remained lovers for most of the fall, a fact that Jason hid from Carl. This made double dating with Carl and Althea impossible which Jason remedied by inviting his Aunt Rose out instead. Since the couples stayed exclusively in the black neighborhood they wouldn't ever run into anyone they knew,

One evening Carl and Althea were late and Jason and his aunt got pretty looped on manhattans while waiting for them. They were at Dan Montgomery's, a quaint and recently renovated old hotel that served dinners and had entertainment on weekends. It was located in the dilapidated warehouse section of Buffalo between the rail lines and the New York State Thruway near the downtown core.

"This is also a boarding house, right?" said Aunt Rose. "I'm horny. Got any ideas?"

Just then Carl walked in, but without Althea. "We had a argument," he explained. "'bout spendin too much money goin out to dinner and stuff. Woman just wanna sit around the house doin nothing."

"Don't worry about it," said Aunt Rose and she reached over and patted Carl's hand. Jason saw a strange glance flit between them.

Late that night after numerous more manhattans and much laughter and storytelling Jason felt a wave of depression sweep over him. The merriment of the other two people grated on his nerves. He suddenly wanted to leave.

"I don't want to spoil the evening," Jason said, "but I think we should take off. I'm tired and have to work tomorrow night. Let's go." He held out his hand to Aunt Rose who looked at him inquisitively, then turned to Carl.

"I don't want to leave right now," she insisted. "You go by yourself.

I'm staying here with Carl."

"How are you getting home then?"

"We'll take a cab. Don't worry about it. I've got money. I'll get home alright."

After settling up the bill Jason paused at the doorway and noticed Carl and his aunt holding hands and ascending the stairway to the upstairs rooms. The sky was faintly light in the east as Jason drove back to his apartment. The sun was about to rise.

Nelly: "Idz z Bogiem. Go with God."

After the break up with David, Nelly withdrew into a protective shell. She refused to go out even for the traditional Friday night fish fries with her mother and she avoided her sister whenever Frances came to visit. The arrival of her new nephew did nothing to alleviate her misery. If anything it made her feel worse. Nelly rode the bus to and from work even though one of her co-workers offered her a free ride each day. On the bus she sat alone while mechanically fingering the rosary in her pocket.

One day someone sat down beside her. She was annoyed even though the after work busses were always crowded. Furthermore, the person next to her kept clearing his throat and incidentally nudging her. She finally looked up. The young man looked familiar. It was in fact Bobby Gomulak, her old elementary school classmate and the first boy to ever plant a kiss on her lips. The goofy cowlick still stood up on the back of his head despite a glistening glob of Vaseline that tried to keep it in place.

"Hiyah," Bobby said. "Remember me? St. Casimir's?"

"Yes I do," Nelly replied, cheered by the young man's blushing face and good natured manner. "Some of the stuff you pulled was hard to forget." For the next week they traveled home together on the bus and talked and laughed over the school day memories they shared.

"I felt sorry for you," said Nelly. "The sisters were always picking on you. It wasn't fair.

"I didn mind," replied Bobby. "Classes were so boring, yah know, but Sister Felicia, that one, she really drove me crazy. I tink I had a detention from her almost every day. But I got back at her too just like Sister Paulicarpa.

"I was a altar boy wit Fadder Majewski. Man, he was one miserable s.o.b. for sure. Even Sister Felicia, tough as she was wit everybody else, she jumped when he talked to her. 'Oh yes, Fadder. No Fadder. Whatever you say Fadder.'

"So the altar boys, you know, we used to change in the cloakroom at the vestry before mass. One day Sister Felicia came in with dah communion wafers. The nuns used to bake em just before mass. She didn't see me. When she left, I came out and ate the whole two bags of wafers. Gobbled em all up, musta been two hundred. Ha, ha, ha. Den Fadder Majewski came in and I helped him get dressed like usual. When he didn't see no communion wafers he called out into the church for Sister Felicia.

'Where's dah communion wafers?'

'I put em right on the table.'

'Well, I doan see em anywhere.'

"Sister Felica came in and looked all over the room for dose wafers. Nothin. Nowhere. Dey didn't figger on me. Never knew I was even there at the time, so den Father Majewski let her have it.

'Psia krew, cholera. Get back dere and bake dem wafers and fast. What are you doin all day long, playin wit yerselfs. Go on. Ged out.'

"Sister Felicia was almost cryin. 'Yes Fadder. I'm sorry Fadder. Right away, Fadder.'

"Man, I laughed my fanny off over dat one and she deserved every bit of it too. Dey were all mean, dah whole bunch a dem, Father Majewski and Father Benkowski too. When the altar boys worked a wedding or a funeral we sometimes got a tip from the people, you know. Maybe the groom would give us a few bucks, maybe even a five dollar bill, but den the priest would come and make you hand it over to him."

"No," Nelly said incredulously.

"It's true. I'm tellin you dah trut. Dey'd put out dere hand. 'Turn it over.' Sometimes dey'd even search yer pockets. I used to hide my money in my sock. Dey never looked dere."

"What are you doin for a job now, Bobby?" Nelly asked.

"I work at the Chevy plant on Delevan. It's dah engine plant. My uncle got me in. Good money."

Nelly soon found herself looking forward to the bus ride home with Bobby. She was buoyed by his good will and unflappable spirit. She found out later that he purposely had a friend from work drop him off at the bus stop so he could ride home with Nelly. He had his own car all along, a Chevy, of course.

One day Bobby asked Nelly out on a date. She still wasn't ready for male companionship, but when he told her it was to the Doyle #2 Fireman's picnic, she relented.

From a distance, the night time sky was lit up by the glow of the carnival lights. The fire hall itself was dedicated to the pursuit of bingo while the parking lot and nearby streets were closed to traffic and filled with people, mechanical rides, food stands and booths offering games of chance. The mingled smells of French fries, and hot dogs, hamburgers too and Polish sausage filled the air. There was also cotton candy, and bright red candied apples and caramel corn, clams on the half shell and steaming clam chowder and corn on the cob with pads of butter. Bobby bought them a large order of French fries which they carried in an upside down paper cup soon soaked through with spots of grease, vinegar, and ketchup. Nelly was radiant.

"These fries are delicious," she exclaimed. "I can't remember when I had em last. Seems like a lifetime ago."

Bobby tried his luck at knocking down the kewpie dolls and spent over five dollars in the effort. When Nelly wasn't looking he handed the vendor another five dollars for the rights to a big teddy bear.

"Oh, you won one. He's beautiful. I'm going to call him Doyle."

"Is he goin to sleep in bed wit you?" Bobby asked.

"Why, yes, of course, I wouldn't have it any other way."

"Lucky bear," and Bobby grabbed Nelly's free hand and held it. She didn't resist. They both tried flipping rings over the necks of Coke bottles at another game of skill. Nelly got frustrated with her futile efforts.

"Them bottles are too close together," she protested. "The ring can't fit over dem."

The man came and took one ring and slipped it perfectly across the neck of one of the bottles. He smiled at Nelly.

"Sure, if you set it right down on top like dat," she said.

To win a gold fish you had to throw a ping pong ball and have it stay on the top of a little fish bowl about the size of a small mason jar. Each of the dozens of bowls contained a live goldfish swimming around in different colored waters. The different hues in the bowls and the fish and the bright lights shining down on them all made for a sparkling magical scene.

On the side of the booth a young man was putting on a performance for his friends and passers-by by swallowing the live fish offered to him by different game winners.

"That's terrible," protested Nelly. "The poor fish. They shouldn't let him do that here. There's little kids around, you know."

Bobby just smiled. "Must tickle going down. Hey, you wanna go on dah Ferris Wheel."

"Only if you promise not to rock the chair, and I hope we don't get stuck on top. I'm afraid of heights."

Naturally their car was immediately stopped at the very top of the Ferris Wheel.

"I knew it. I just knew it," moaned Nelly with her eyes tightly shut. Then she felt the car sway. "It's moving. No, Bobby, you're not swinging it, are you? You promised."

"Maybe I changed my mind."

"No, stop."

"Maybe if you kissed me I would."

"You no good, conniving rat," said Nelly. "You probably planned dis, didn't you. You knew it was going to stop on top."

"It always does, sooner or later," he replied. "Now how about dat kiss?"

"I hate you. OK, but I'm not moving, and if you rock dis seat even a little I'm going to throw up all over you."

Bobby carefully leaned over and kissed Nelly dryly on the lips. He put his arm around her, then the Ferris Wheel started up again. Bobby took Nelly home with the spoils of the night: Doyle, a small stuffed tiger, two green glass plates and a pink cup. Bobby kissed her good night in the car and once again at the back door of her house. Nelly felt a slight tremble in his lips.

"I had a very nice time, Bobby," she confessed. "Except for the Ferris Wheel which I'm never going on again."

Bobby now picked Nelly up from work in his car every day. Nelly filled Bobby in on all the gossip about the girls at Drescher's while Bobby befuddled her with explanations of horsepower, torque, and cubic centimeters. They got married the next year.

It was a gala affair at St. Casimir's followed by a reception at Ray's

Supper Club. Both came from large extended families so the haul in money and shower gifts was prodigious. Nelly was the most beautiful of brides while Bobby could best be described as plain. The contrast in appearance between the bride and groom prompted many a whispered comment.

"Taki szkaradny. What does it she see in him?"

"He damned lucky to get such a bride like dat."

"I heard she's pregnant. Had a Jew boyfriend before. He knock her up, den dump her. Bobby was dah onny one who take her."

Others took the more common and practical approach pointing out that Bobby had a good job.

Of course, there was no tatusiu waltz and she had insisted on walking down the aisle alone. The memory of her father was still there in Nelly's mind, but the pain and guilt had faded. She knew that he was looking down on her and would understand. She did laugh, however, when Bobby removed her garter and they put the carrot topped hat on Bobby's head during the czepina. He looked so adorably silly she could not resist the laughter. And in the midst of the assemblage and the celebration she spotted her mother standing there in tears, her dreams having finally come true. Frances left the wedding early saying she was concerned about her baby staying with Vince's sister.

Nelly got undressed for bed in the bathroom on their wedding night. She only emerged after the lights were off and Bobby was already under the covers. They had never had sex before.

"I love you Nelly. I love you so much from the very first time I saw you getting your knuckles rapped in school by Sister Fidencia in the fourth grade."

There was a slight wheezing to Bobby's words. His breath reeked of beer and cigarettes. As he raked his calloused hands under her nightgown and across her body, he groaned and began to pant heavily. Suddenly he lifted Nelly's nightgown to her neck and jumped on top of her. Out of self- preservation Nelly repositioned herself as she gasped and groaned from the pain. Bobby took this as encouragement and started thrusting feverishly. Before Nelly could articulate a protest Bobby arched his back and let out a muted howl as his body shuddered convulsively.

"Oh man," Bobby exclaimed. "Dat was what I call heaven. An now dat we're married, we ken do it all dah time, anytime we want. Are you OK, Nelly? I didn't hurt you too much, did I? Don't worry. You get used to it. The first time is the worst."

Nelly straightened up her nightie and got out of bed.

"I'm fine, but I tink I might be bleedin a bit, I'm goin to dah bathroom for a minute and check."

"Yeah, I figured as much," Bobby replied. "It's like dat on the first time, I guess."

Nelly was fine as it turned out, but she didn't want to tell the truth to Bobby. No sense hurting him. She crawled back into bed and draped her arm around her new husband's body and snuggled him tightly.

"I love you too, Bobby," she sighed. "Yer a good man, a good man, and you'll make a good husband and father."

Timmy: *"Psia Krew. Dog's Blood."*

Timmy had observed the lonely house for many nights. He knew old lady Khula was in there by herself. He spied on her through the windows. He watched as she drank heavily from the bottle of Krupnik and prayed on her knees in the living room. He laughed as she moaned and cried and rent her hair calling out for her dear lost son. And often while in the throes of her drunkenness Timmy also watched as she lifted up her house dress and spread her legs as though accommodating some unseen lover.

"What the fuck is that old cunt doing?" mused Timmy. "Horny old witch."

Nobody in Kaisertown ever locked their doors at night. Crime was almost non-existent although that had changed momentarily right after Tina Kaszpczyk's murder. But things got back to normal soon afterwards and the unlocked door at Pani Khula's house gave Timmy easy access. He just walked in.

The old lady was passed out on the couch. Red votive candles cast an ominous glow onto the walls and ceiling of the room as Timmy looked around for something to steal. He rummaged through her purse finding seven dollars in bills and some loose change.

"The old bitch must have some money hid around here somewhere," mumbled Timmy. "Polacks don't believe in banks."

He went into a bedroom next, the old lady's. He turned on a small dresser lamp. It was night time so no one would be suspicious. There was some costume jewelry inside a small heart shaped glass container on the dresser. Timmy threw the contents on the floor and stepped on them. He searched the drawers. Nothing but the old woman's underwear.

Timmy moved on to the next bedroom and once again flicked on the light. The room looked as though a child lived in it. The bed was made up with cowboy blankets and matching pillows. Pictures of horses, cowboys and Indians were stuck on the walls with curled yellowing strips of Scotch tape barely holding them in place. A cowboy holster with toy guns was slung across a bedpost.

It was then that Timmy heard a voice from the other room. "Jesu kochany. Jesu kochany."

The old lady was sitting up on the sofa now and staring at the open bedroom door. Her mouth fell agape when Timmy stepped towards her silhouetted against the muted light of the bedroom. Pani Khula tried to get up, but fell back down on the couch. Her chubby white legs flashed in the semi-darkness. She wasn't wearing stockings.

"Wladek, synulek, chodz tutaj."

"What are you babbling about, you old cunt?" said Timmy. "Wladek? You think I'm Wladek? Thanks for the compliment. Must be the lighting."

Timmy turned and shut off the bedroom light as he exited. The old lady was totally disoriented in the near darkness again.

"Mommy take care a you, Wladek. Matka take care."

"Fuck, this is getting creepy," mused Timmy out loud. "What the hell was going on in here? Sick fuckers."

Pani Khula's hand reached out in supplication. As a joke Timmy unzipped his fly and put his cock in her hand. To his shock the old lady squeezed it knowingly, familiarly.

"I don't believe it, you sick old bitch." He slapped Pani Khula in the face knocking her to the floor where he pulled up her dress and removed her panties. The woman groaned. "Dziekuje, dziekuje, boze."

"If that retard was fuckin you, there ain't no way I'm putting my cock in that black hole a yers." Timmy punched her several times knocking her false teeth from her mouth. He then pushed his penis past Pani Khula's bleeding lips.

"Uhh, ughh, mommy, fucky, fucky. Ohh, ahh, fucky fuck," he grunted and laughed as he fucked the old lady's mouth. "You should be in jail along with that crazy retard son a yers."

When he was done, Timmy dragged the disoriented woman into Wladek's room and pulled her onto the bed where he wrapped her in sheets and blankets like a mummy. She couldn't move. Her body was covered to the level of her eyes. He then returned to the living room and came back with two votive candles. The light from their flames danced a macabre waltz on the ceiling. Pani Khula's eyes blinked in horror as Timmy whispered in her ear.

"Yer son, Crazy Walter, he had nothing to do with that girl's murder. It was me who killed her, me, Jason Novak, and me alone. Wladek was just walkin by and I stole his watch and put them things in his knapsack. He didn't even know her. Ha, ha, ha. Where's he now by the way? Ha, ha, ha."

Timmy placed one candle amid the rumpled blankets on each side of the bundled helpless woman and waited a moment to make sure the flames took to the fabric. Then he left.

Outside on a far off hill that had once been part of Okie Diamond, Timmy smoked a cigarette and watched the flames break out of the bedroom window and engulf the house. Then he walked home crossing in part an unopened section of the recently constructed New York State

Thruway which had obliterated the playground fields of his youth and was destined to link the Buffalo suburbs and beyond with the city core itself. As he walked into his driveway he could hear the wail of fire sirens in the night air.

"Is dat you Timmy?" his mother called from her bedroom as he shut the door behind him.

"What's dat noise I hear outside?"

"Sirens, I guess. Something musta happened. Who knows?"

"You OK?"

"What, after nineteen years yer suddenly worried about me? Too late. Go to sleep and be glad I'm not the old man come home to beat the shit outa you."

The next morning Timmy joined the throng of neighbors and pass-ers-by who had gathered at the charred remains of the Khula home. Only one wall was left standing, badly burnt and leaning into a pile of mangled debris. A couple of volunteer firemen from Doyle Number 2 were dous-ing a few smoky spots. The fire hose ran a long distance down the street to a hydrant. It lost half its water along the way leaving a line of wetness across the sidewalks.

"Anybody know what happened?" Timmy asked an elderly man standing beside him. The man was wearing an old coat and had morning slippers on his feet.

"Piana," the old man replied.

"What?" Timmy responded.

"The cops said the old lady was a bad drunk," someone else volun-teered. "She probably knocked over a candle and burnt the place down. You know everybody's got electricity now days but dese old people dey gotta try and save a penny. Lookit what happen."

An old woman with half blind rheumy eyes tottered up to Timmy.

Speaking not directly to him she said in a high pitched voice. "Zeby cie diabli wzili."

"Jesus Christ, don't anybody speak English around here?" replied Timmy.

"Doan pay no attention to her," said the same person next to him. "She's old and crazy."

Timmy noticed a man dressed in a long coat walking through the rubble pointing at things while talking to a fireman. The man had a gold badge on his chest. Timmy and the cop unexpectedly exchanged glances. Timmy walked purposely away immediately. When he looked back over his shoulder, the cop was still watching him. What the fuck is he staring at me for, Timmy wondered. There are lots of other crazy assholes standing around here.

Timmy decided to lay low for a while. Somehow the look on that police officer's face at the fire scene unnerved him. The boy, therefore, rarely ventured out during the day unless his old man happened to be at home which did not occur often. At night he spent much of his time hunting rats at the Ogden dump, or just sitting up in the old garage smoking cigarettes and listening to the transistor radio he had stolen long ago from Tina Kaszpczyk. He was growing progressively restive and anxious and isolated. He longed for a friend, but those days were over long ago when he and Jason had parted ways. On the positive side, however, there had been no sign of Stachu Klemp lately. Hopefully the mongrel was dead, mused Timmy. The old cock sucker can't live forever.

Timmy rarely thought about his sister, Dorothy, although he sometimes fantasized about fucking and abusing her. He regretted that on the day when he and Jason forced Dorothy to strip for them, they weren't smart enough to get her to suck and fuck the both of them. Maybe that would have cemented a more long standing relationship between the two boys.

After too many nights alone, Timmy couldn't stand it any longer and he left the garage with Tina's radio concealed in his pocket. He also had his Lucky Strikes and his wallet with a few bucks left from the robbery at Pani Khula's. He figured he'd follow his familiar route along the railroad tracks beyond old Okie Diamond through the B&O/Lackawanna switching yard and onto Lovejoy Avenue and the Italian section of East Buffalo. He had met a dago girl there a while back who let him fuck her for five dollars.

Once into the remnants of the fields of Okie Diamond Timmy removed the radio from his pocket and put the earpiece in place, and tuned into WKBW his favorite station. He took out his cigarettes, tapped one out of the pack and contentedly lit up. Life was good.

Up on the elevated track bed he turned around and surveyed all of the new Thruway lanes and broken fields below him. As he approached the switching yard he could hear the banging of rail cars although the noise was muted by the music of the radio. He had to be careful here as dozens of tracks lay before him with box cars descending from a small slope hundreds of yards down the line. The cars had been pushed into position by a work locomotive then left to slide down the proper track designated in advance by a train man in a control tower.

It was at this point that Timmy got the feeling of being watched. Maybe it was that railroad cop who had chased him from the property in the past. Or maybe it was that detective from the fire scene tailing him. Or maybe? The boy stared back at the shrubbery bordering the fence and track. Could it be? Timmy removed the ear piece and listened carefully, but the shunting cars made all other sounds impossible to hear.

"Son of a bitch," he hissed. "I thought somebody said that nut sniffer was run over on Dingens Street?"

Timmy began to sprint across the tracks, keeping an eye on the brush line but also on the box cars that glided around him front and back. Perhaps he had taken that route through the rail yard too many times before and the old dog finally caught his scent.

"Ball biting bastard. There he is," shouted Timmy and the race was on.

Timmy thought of stopping and smashing Stachu Klemp with a rock, but the rail yard was uniformly covered with only small cinders. Flight was the boy's only salvation, and what was he worried about? After all he should be able to out distance an aged, lame, half blind old mutt. And he would have too had he not tripped, fallen, and lay spread eagle across the last set of tracks. In panic Timmy watched Stachu Klemp lope closer and closer. The boy never noticed the freight car till it was just a shadow above him.

Detective Abramowski and Sergeant Sojka: A Coffee at Deco's

"I heard you had some action in Kaisertown," said sergeant Sojka as he entered the precinct office.

"Yeah, busy. First dat house fire on Sout Ogden wit poor old lady Khula. Probably better off dead anyway except for the way she went, burning up like dat. She had no life after we took dat retard son a hers away," replied detective Abramowski.

"I felt bad for her too. I was by dere dah next day wit dah fire inspector."

"Was a accident, nie? Candles in dah house? I guess she was drinkin real bad at dah end. Figured she knocked over a candle and was too drunk to get out."

Detective Abramowski studied his onetime partner carefully before continuing. "Dat dah way you saw it too, or is sometin boddering you?"

"I seen a kid dere at dah scene when I was walkin around. He caught my eye. Turned out he was killed up by dah switch yards a few days ago. Name was Timmy Klein, kind of a bad apple in dah neighborhood I hear. You know anyting about him?"

"Yeah, we stopped him a few times for fightin and shop liftin. Had some complaints too from parents didn't like him hangin around wit dere kids. Nuttin specific. He was a juvenile back den so we just gave him a warning."

"Have any close friends, relatives in the neighborhood?"

"Old man was a wife beater and drunk, out of town a lot. Mother was pretty mousey. She didn't have much to say. Took dah kid's death hard dough. No friends dat I could find."

"He ever know the Novak kid, Jason Novak?"

"Dat kid from dah Kaszpczyk case we was lookin at for being a accomplice with dah retard? Not dat I know of."

"Dey was neighbors, next door neighbors," added Sergeant Soyka.

Detective Abramowski swallowed hard and took a deep breath as the sergeant continued.

"You got dah belongings found on dah Klein kid when he was killed? What happened up dere best you ken figger?"

"Tripped over dah tracks. Must a been runnin away from dat old Kaisertown mutt we found up dere too. We taught it was his till we talked to the kid's mudder. Was a pretty sick scene. The boy's legs were cut off. Dog was chewin on dem when anudder train car hit it too. I got dah stuff here in dah evidence locker. Was gonna take it to his old lady. Come on, I'll show you."

The two men leaned over the large box from which detective Abramowski pulled various items.

"Wallet wit no money, a Zippo lighter, transistor radio…"

"What's dose initials on dat radio?"

"T.K. Timmy Klein," answered Abramowski.

Sergeant Sojka smiled wryly. "T.K. Tina Kaszpczyk. Ever see a boy wit a pink colored radio?"

"Piorun, yer kiddin me?"

"Take dat radio over by dah Kaszpczyk house and ask dah mudder if it belonged to her daughter. Tell her it was just found in dah evidence room or something. Leave dah Klein kid out of it. Dat's just between you and me. And for yer own satisfaction, you ken double check dah kid's prints wit dah ones on file from dose girlie cards and dah retard's can-teen. Dat should clinch it."

"Holy shit, I never woulda taught."

"I know," replied sergeant Sojka. "Come on. Let's get a coffee over by Deco's. You ken buy."

Dorothy: Body and Soul

Dorothy, her mother and grandmother were the only ones at Timmy's funeral. It was held in a small private chapel in a former grocery store front in the Ghost Town neighborhood. The Kleins did not belong to any of the Kaisertown churches. Dorothy's babcia paid for the priest who came in for a few minutes of prayer. He referred to everyone as "my dear ones" since he didn't know any of their names.

Except for the horror of Timmy's death, Dorothy was unmoved by the loss of her brother, her only sibling. They had never been close, never shared in any good times, no childhood bonding, no common dreams. It was perhaps best that he died early, she reasoned, before he could mature into a hateful, sadistic woman abuser like his father. God only knew what he would be capable of in later life.

Dorothy's mother cried throughout the brief service. In short order the woman's grief irritated Dorothy. Her mother had done her best over the years to ignore her children and never interceded on their behalf against her raging husband. When they desperately needed help none was forthcoming. Now that it was too late to do any good, the old lady's emotions overflowed. Well, fuck her, Dorothy thought.

The three women shared a meal at a nearby Deco restaurant. Dorothy paid. Other than the sound of cutlery scraping on plates, they ate in silence. It was only when they were about to leave that Dorothy's mother spoke up.

"I was tinkin," she hesitantly began. "If yous two doan mind, maybe I could come and live wit yous by babcia's. Otto, he's never home, and I can hardly afford dah rent money. If I leave he probly wouldn't even bodder to look for me."

"He'd come here and beat the shit out of all of us, babcia included," replied Dorothy.

"What do you tink, mom?" asked Dorothy's mother turning to her own mother for support.

"Ja niewiem," said the old lady.

"It would give me a chance, ma, Dorothy, at least a chance."

"Jesus, we hardly see you for years and suddenly you want to move in with us," said Dorothy. 'It's not my house anyway. It's up to babcia."

"Ja niewiem," repeated the old woman plaintively. "Ja niewiem."

Dorothy figured if it came to that she could get an apartment with Rosaline. They had talked about it already for some time. And with the two of them splitting the rent she could afford the move.

"Yous two tink about it, nie," said Mrs. Klein. "I don't have to move right away. I waited dis long. I was hoping maybe one day he would just not come back."

Dorothy and her babcia returned home alone that evening. Dorothy was silent and depressed.

"I'm going to my room," she said. "Play some music for a while. Find something suitably suicidal. I got a new Chet Baker album. That should do it."

Just then the telephone rang startling the two women. After several more rings the old lady answered it.

"Dorty? She goin spac."

"That's OK," the girl replied turning back into the kitchen and taking the phone. She recognized the voice immediately.

"Thanks, nice of you to call, but really, I wasn't close to Timmy. We never got along. Truth be told I hated his guts."

"I suspected as much," replied Jason Novak. "I haven't seen him myself in years. Took me a while to find the funeral parlor. It was closed by the time I got there so I thought I'd call. How's your mother?"

"She's a punching bag, same as usual."

"I see. Sorry to hear it. You know, while I've got you on the line," continued Jason. "I was wondering if you're doing anything this Friday night? I've got tickets to the Nina Simone concert at Kleinhan's and thought maybe you'd like to come. I know you like jazz."

"What, no other girl available for old Lover Boy?" Dorothy inquired.

"Ah, no, that's not really it."

"I haven't seen you for quite a while. Why the sudden interest?"

For some inexplicable reason Dorothy found herself giving Jason a hard time, punishing him almost. She knew that was the last thing she really wanted to do, but she couldn't help herself.

"I wouldn't exactly call it "sudden interest," Jason replied after a pause. "We have known each other since we were kids."

"That was a long time ago."

"Yes, you're right about that."

"A lot has changed since then."

"Right again," Jason admitted. Then he cleared his throat and seemed to take a deep breath. "Well, to tell you the truth, Dorothy, I've always found you interesting. You're different and I like that. And you're witty and smart with a good vocabulary when you're not swearing like a lake freighter captain. You're sensitive too even though you won't admit it. You're certainly very pretty and you have an unbelievable body. So I finally said to myself, I just can't go on ignoring the one and only girl in Kaisertown who has intrigued me so much for so many years."

"What time did you say you were picking me up?" Dorothy asked.

When Dorothy hung up the phone her hand was trembling. She started to sob. Her babcia turned to her in alarm.

"Oh Jenna, honey, what's dah madder?"

"Nothing, nothing at all, babcia. In fact everything is great. I just can't believe it. Out of nowhere. Just when you think it's turned off and gone."

The gloom of that bleak afternoon vanished. Dorothy ran to her bedroom and put on a record. Billie Holiday singing, "What a Little Moonlight Can Do" and she started rummaging through her closet looking for something to wear to the concert, something sexy but not too slutty. A Miles Davis record came up next while she dressed and undressed in rapid succession. "My Funny Valentine, Round Midnight" and "Green Dolphin Street" followed. Dorothy had seen Miles at the Royal Arms. She loved his soft muted trumpet sound, but she was cautious about Davis himself. He looked lecherous and mean and he paid particular attention to the prettiest white girls in the audience. Dorothy stayed close to Lew.

Now Dorothy vowed things would be different with Jason. He was not going to slip through her arms again. She remembered those meetings at Houghton Park, at Babe's, and the numerous chance encounters on the streets of Kaisertown and even most recently at Johnny's Ellicott of all places. Not that she was exactly expecting permanence in the relationship. She'd settle for temporary from someone intelligent to talk to, someone to appreciate her music and share it with her, someone to hold and love, someone who wasn't a complete fucking idiot obsessed with cars and fighting and drugs and booze. And if it didn't last forever, so be it. She'd cherish the memories and get on with her life. Right now it was time for a change. "Things ain't the way they used to be," she said out loud. "Finally."

At the concert Dorothy and Jason sat close enough to clearly see Nina Simone seated at the piano. Dorothy had not realized that the jazz singer was also an accomplished pianist and it turned out that Dorothy enjoyed the piano playing more than the singing which she found a bit strained and off beat.

Half way through the performance, with Nina Simone lost in a hot rendition of "Love Me or Leave Me" Jason reached over and took Dorothy's hand. When she looked at him, he simply smiled back and squeezed tighter. Those eyes of his, thought Dorothy. I'd fuck him right here and now or slip between his legs and suck his cock. But god damn, I better control myself and show some depth. Hell, he's going to university. Probably has a bunch of intellectual, hippy co-eds at his feet and they do say the brain is the largest sex organ in the body.

"I'm the Keeper of the Flame" was Dorothy's favorite song of the evening. At the same time the girl noted a strong racial edge to many of Nina Simone's offerings. Numbers like "Young Gifted and Black" and "I Wish I Knew How It Would Feel to be Free" reflected themes of racism and black pride, themes which came to a fever pitch when a guest performer named Miriam Makeba made an appearance.

Later that night when they were having a bite to eat at a place called, Cedars of Lebanon, Jason and Dorothy discussed the concert.

"Man, there was a lot of tension in the room," noted Jason. "Some of those songs of hers were pretty provocative and that Miriam Makeba! Holy Christ, she got the crowd in a frenzy."

"Fuck, they just roared at everything she said. It startled me," said Dorothy. "I thought we were going to get lynched as ironic as that sounds."

"I didn't realize until then that there were so many black people in the audience," continued Jason. "Gives you a taste of what it must be like to be in the minority. I've noticed recently too that whites are not as welcome as we once were in the black neighborhoods. At one time you could go through there anytime, no problem. Now you're taking a chance."

"Funny, how it never worked the other way around," said Dorothy. "I had a black friend who was almost killed for just driving into Kaisertown."

"Sorry, but good for you. I mean for even having a black friend. For someone from Kaisertown that's a major achievement, if not a risky one as well. At one time I really thought there was a common bond, a mutual understanding developing between the races. You could feel it in the black neighborhoods and hear it in the speeches of Martin Luther King.

"A lot of my Jewish friends at UB said the same thing and some of them became pretty active in the civil rights movement. But when the Black Panthers and that element came on the scene everything changed. I remember going to a bar in the colored section of Buffalo with my black buddy Carl. The Moon Glow Club. Never had a problem there before, saw Joe Williams and Arthur Prysock live. When we walked through the parking lot I noticed a crescent moon and star emblem on some of the license plates. Turned out to be the Black Muslim insignia.

"Inside Carl and I got separated and I was given some sage advice by a guy I had met there before. He had always been friendly to me, but this time was different. 'I like you, white boy,' he said. 'So I'm going to give you some advice. Don't come around here anymore. This is our world now, and we don't want you in it.'"

At that juncture of their conversation the entertainment began at Cedars of Lebanon and Dorothy was distracted by a group of men who gathered on stage and began to play rousing songs on strange looking instruments. Soon a belly dancer appeared. She was middle aged, tall, and veiled with long black hair, slightly chubby, but extremely sexy. Dorothy was fascinated by her. Exotic fragrances of perfume and enticing foods mingled with the unusual music filled the air with a mysterious romanticism. The relative darkness of the room and the multicolored rugs, curtains and drapes which hung everywhere gave the place a sensuous, tent-like appearance.

Dorothy turned smilingly to Jason, but he was not there. A momentary panic seized her before she realized that her errant date was ascending the stage where he soon began dancing in a circle with other male patrons and members of the band. Someone handed him a knotted handkerchief which he waved at Dorothy while kicking his feet and twirling around in a comical, uncoordinated jig. He looked so lovingly awkward that Dorothy wanted to run up to him and hug him on the spot. She was happy and most probably in love.

They ate lamb shish kabob and stuffed grape leaves and hummus and flat pita bread. They drank lemon flavored water and then sweet tea and had something called baklava for dessert.

"You had some pretty slick moves up there on the dance floor, Lover Boy," Dorothy commented.

"Natural rhythm," Jason joked. "I cut it short, held back my best moves, because I didn't want the locals to get envious. Nothing worse than a Polack kid from Kaisertown showing them up.

"Very considerate of you."

"Speaking of Kaisertown, how is your good friend, Janie, doing?"

"She's happy. Just finished up some beautician's school and is working at Wanda's on Clinton Street. She writes to your cousin Larry in Vietnam. Did you know that?"

"Yes, he told me he was sweet on her. I just hope he gets out of that hell hole in one piece. God damn nightmare. Half the gang is there now.

They drafted Joey Radominski the minute he graduated from Erie County Tech. Jimmy Paton, who went to South Park with me was killed just last month. At the cemetery they gave his mother the flag that was draped over his coffin. I saw her stare at that flag for the longest time. I'll never forget it. This is it, a flag for my son?

"What are you going to do?" Dorothy inquired.

"I don't know yet. I heard that teachers were getting exemptions. If you're married, you'd better have a kid real fast. No child, no exemption. Then there's always Canada."

"That sounds good to me," said Dorothy. "It's beautiful there. You just have to cross the Peace Bridge to notice."

"I'm going to have to look into it soon enough. If you get in before your draft status changes to 1A you can get exempted and avoid being a draft dodger. Then you can come and go across the border any time you want. Otherwise you're trapped in Canada. By the way, I haven't seen you reach for a cigarette, yet."

"I gave them up, but put on a few pounds as a result.'

"Well, you certainly put them on in all the right places. You look beautiful in that black dress. You know, many times, in Kaisertown, when I saw you with different guys I was jealous. Yeah, I couldn't understand what you saw in some of those dumb Polacks, guys like Chevy. All that time you could have had me."

"Maybe a touch of masochism," replied Dorothy. "As for you, I was always trying to run into you, but you were so fucking stupid you never figured it out. But let's not dwell on our past affairs. I've seen you date a few airheads in your day too."

"Your point is well taken. We'll call it even."

They ended the night at "The One Eyed Cat", a new quiet and romantic cocktail lounge in town. They found a couch in a corner and sat down for a drink as "Blue Train" played over the sound system.

"I love the music here," said Jason. "None of that shit rock and roll. You like jazz too. Where did you develop that taste coming from the polka capital of the U.S.?"

"Out of nowhere, I guess. Probably as a reaction to everyone else's rock and roll infatuation. I purposely went in the other direction. I bought a couple of albums at Sattler's and then found myself spending almost my entire fucking paycheck on jazz records."

"Always the odd ball," said Jason. "I wouldn't mind listening to those albums of yours. Want to invite me over to your place and play some music for me?"

"I'm still at my babcia's actually, and, as a matter of fact, I've got to get up with her tomorrow at eight o'clock for church, Polish mass," Dorothy explained.

"I didn't think you were the religious type?"

"Why, because I was a whore from an early age?" Dorothy snapped back. She felt that antagonistic mood creep over her again.

"No, it's not that," Jason tried to explain. "And I don't think that religion stops anybody from screwing around. Look at the Catholics. They break all kinds of sexual taboos because they know they can go to confession and get all their sins forgiven"

"You smart college boys, always analyzing everything and everybody.'

"Just what's wrong now?" Jason asked. "We were having a great time."

"What, not used to being argued with?" Dorothy persisted. "Don't like broads with brains especially if they don't have a university degree to go along with them?"

"You certainly can be an argumentative bitch at times."

"What are you going to do about it, Lover Boy?"

Jason grabbed Dorothy roughly by the shoulders. "Kiss me," he said.

"What?"

"Kiss me. Don't be angry. I don't have time for it."

Dorothy was taken aback by the simple request. She never thought much about a mere kiss. Most guys hardly bothered. They just wanted to fuck or get their cocks sucked. She leaned forward into Jason's body and fell into the abyss of her first true kiss. Their lips met softly, then their mouths melted together. Dorothy had trouble breathing, but was thrilled with the breathlessness.

"There, thank you," Jason said with a smile.

Dorothy didn't know what to do. She felt lightheaded and tingly. Goosebumps ran up her thighs. If and when he actually fucks me, she thought. I'll need cardiopulmonary resuscitation to bring me around.

"Sorry, I don't know what comes over me at times," she explained. "I think sometimes I'm going crazy."

"Such beautiful insanity," Jason said. 'We'd better go now. When can I see you again?"

"Anytime. I'm all for you body and soul."

Sergeant Sojka and Detective Abramowski: "Eenie, Meanie, Minee, Moe. Catch the Nigger by the Toe"

"Did you see dat nigger jump when dah rock salt hit his ass? Whoa, just like in dem old time silent movies," laughed detective Abramowski.

"It don't get no better den dis. Good to be togedder again, partner," replied sergeant Sojka. "An we got 'card blanche' to do whatever it takes to get dah situation under control. No worryin about criminal rights or police abuse. Just do dah job."

"At double time and a half and hazard pay to boot. And all dah booze, cigarettes, jewlry and any other shit we can get our hands on. I got Mary's anniversary and Christmas gifts all set for ten years to come. Our trunk's packed. We gotta start putting stuff in the back seat of the squad car."

"Make sure we take dem things right home. Don't stop at dah station."

"Hey, lookit dat spook over dere," detective Abramowski shouted and poked his fellow officer in the ribs with his elbow.

Across the street a black man was emerging from a ransacked grocery store juggling several packages of food in his arms. A carton of milk slipped from his grasp and broke open on the sidewalk. As he turned a corner to enter an alley, he ran right into another Buffalo cop, nightstick in hand. The officer brought the baton down on the man's shoulder sending him to his knees and spilling the rest of his ill-gotten goods across the ground. Sojka and Abramowski entered the scene.

"Get up and get yer hands in dah air," shouted the sergeant asserting his rank. He looked down on the fallen man.

"Lootin dah same fuckin businesses dat set up shop here in dah first place to help yous niggers out. Tink it's easy for dese people to run a business in dis neighborhood wit all yous jungle bunnies running around? Is dis dah tanks dey get for putting up wit you thiefs all dese years?"

Detective Abramowski grabbed the man's wallet, took all the money out, then threw it into the refuse filled curbside.

"Hey man, dat money is mine. I ain't took nothing out dah store, but some food for my woman and kids. All dah stores is burnt down or looted out like this one. We ain't got nothing to eat. I ain't no thief. I got me a job. I work for the NFT. Man, I got paid on Friday."

"How dah fuck stupid do you tink we are? A nigger wit a good job? Who you trying to kid, boy?" The other officers laughed.

"Hey man," the black man continued to protest. "I don't want no trouble, but I need dat money."

Officer Golas, the third cop at the scene, shook his head in dismay.

"Even if dis is a mistake, it only makes up for dah other hundred times you were breaking dah law and we weren't around to nab you. You break dah law, you take yer chances and yer punishment. Now take yer clothes off so we can determine dat you ain't got other contraband hidden on you."

"Hey, man, come on."

Another blow landed across the man's shoulders as the policemen gathered around the victim.

"Don't even tink about it," said sergeant Sojka unbuckling his holster strap as detective Abramowski slammed another shell into the breach of his shotgun.

"Ha, ha, you call dat a cock? My wife's Chihuahua's got a bigger dick den dat," said officer Golas.

"You wanna live to screw dat black pussy you got back home, you bedder just grin and bear it."

"Please," the man now begged as he sensed the situation was spiraling out of control and might soon reach a point of no return. "Please, I... I know some white people. Yeah, I'm their friend. We go out together and like my friend says, 'We're all the same underneath, you know. We're all workers, brothers. Color don't matter."

"What?" gasped sergeant Sojka. "You tink we're all brothers? Us and you?"

"Not brothers like that, but working class brothers."

"I can't believe dis. Yer friends must be a bunch a dem fuckin commie flower children. Probly you want some a dat white pussy, right? Dat's why yer hangin around wit dem hippies. You ever fuck some white pussy, boy?"

The police immediately noticed the expression on the man's face, and caught the hesitation in his voice. They looked at one another in disbelief.

"You mother fucker," cried officer Golas as he kicked the naked man between the legs. "I can't fuckin believe dis. A lesson is long overdue for dese cock suckers. Who dah fuck do dey tink dey are?"

The three policemen began kicking and beating the fallen man with their night sticks. "All togedder now," shouted detective Abramowski. "Eeeny, meeny, miney moe."

Each word was accompanied by a three-fold blow to the man's body as the police struck in unison. The man twitched and writhed finally rolling onto his stomach to absorb the punishment.

"You remember, sergeant Sojka, dat white girl dat was raped behind dah Clinton-Bailey Market? Gave us dat description of the nigger who done it. Now, I ask you, don't dis boy look a lot like dah one wanted for dat rape?"

Officer Golas lifted the man's head by his hair. "Yeah, now dat you mention it. He's a goddamn dead ringer."

"Who said all niggers look alike?"

"Where were you on dah night a September 10th at exactly nine PM?" asked sergeant Sojka.

"Please, please," the man stammered. "I don't remember. I don't know."

"Can't say dat's a very good alibi. Would you, officer Golas?"

"You know guys, I can take it from here," replied the officer. "No sense tying up all our man power on one half dead nigger. I'll meet up wit my partner and see yous guys back at dah station."

Sergeant Sojka and detective Abramowski nodded in agreement and left.

"What you tink he's gonna do back dere by himself?" inquired detective Abramowski.

"I dunno," added the sergeant, "and I don't care."

Two days later when the rioting on Buffalo's East Side subsided and firefighters were able to return to the neighborhood, the charred body of a black man was discovered in the burnt out shell of Weisenstein's Grocery Store. The body was never identified.

Jason: The Maple Leaf Rag

The morning after Dorothy spent the night at Jason's apartment she went to the bathroom and emerged with a folded note in her hand. "It was under the door," she said.

Jason opened the note. "Son of a bitch, another god damn rental increase from the landlady. What the hell is up with her? Every time I have a girlfriend over she god damn well raises the rent."

"Fuck," said Dorothy. "You must be paying a thousand dollars by now, Lover Boy."

"Very funny."

Jason drove Dorothy to work.

"You heard that your cousin, Larry Bingkowski, and Janie are planning to get married?" Dorothy commented.

"No, you're kidding. I haven't heard anything from Larry lately. His letters sort of dropped off. Last I remember, he was coming home on leave."

"I'm happy for them," Dorothy continued. "She's a sweet girl and will love him forever. And he needs someone like that. To tell you the truth he's been sounding a bit strange in his last letters."

"I hope he gets the hell out of there soon."

The car pulled in front of the Queen-O building. Dorothy swung around to get out.

"Jesus, that skirt doesn't leave much to the imagination, does it?"

Jason said.

"You seemed to enjoy it last evening."

"That's when I had you all to myself." Jason grabbed Dorothy's hand. "Tell me you love me."

Dorothy hesitated.

"Lie if you have to," Jason joked.

"I love you," she said.

"Was that the truth or were you lying?"

"Bye." And Dorothy bounded out of the car with a smile.

"As I said before, you can be one miserable bitch when you want to," Jason shouted back good-naturedly.

Jason swung around to the UB campus to get his schedule for next semester's classes. This was his last term and he had several difficult decisions to make. First what to do about his draft status. He was protected while a student, but he knew he was a goner the minute he graduated. The letters he got from Larry, expurgated as they were still did not paint a comforting picture of life in the Vietnamese jungle. The daily news footage did not help either. There was no way Jason was going into the army. He cared too much about his own skin and knew too much about the capitalist system to tolerate any involvement in one of its wars.

Conscientious objection was one avenue of escape, but proving his status on political grounds was not going to be easy. The thought of prison time if he refused to serve did not sit well with him either. As a felon he was never going to land a teaching job. Jason had argued many of these points with Rick Slater and Dave Garner of the campus SDS chapter. However, he felt their outlook was too narrowly focused and short sighted.

"You're all fired up now," he said, "but if the war ended tomorrow and you didn't have to serve, everything would be fine. God's in his heaven, all's right with the world."

"Hey, man. You can't fight the system if you're dead," said Rick.

"I agree with you," added Dave speaking to Jason. "But the issue is more immediate. We're talking about guys dying over there, getting their nuts blown off. Killing innocent people, simple villagers who never did them any harm. And for what? Hell, who the fuck ever even heard of Vietnam before this shit started?"

"American interests," shouted Rick. "The administration is defending vital American interests in Vietnam and Southeast Asia. What the fuck interests do you or I or anyone else you know, have in all of Asia put together?"

"I'm changing majors. Should buy me a couple of years," added Dave.

Jason figured his best bet was emigration to Canada. His initial inquiries told him that if he got accepted as a landed immigrant before he got called up in the draft he would be ineligible for service in the U.S. army. He would be what they termed, "an alien not subject to the draft." Perfect.

Jason stopped by the Ben Franklin store on Clinton Street to see Larry's sister, Diane.

"What do you mean, you don't have time to talk. The store is empty. There's nobody here, but me. What's wrong?"

"He made me promise not to say nothing to nobody."

"Who made you promise? What are you talking about?"

"Larry, he made me promise not to tell nobody he was back home."

"Home? As here in Buffalo?"

The girl nodded.

"Jesus, and he doesn't want to see me? He said that?"

She nodded again. "But I'm worried about him, Jason," she continued. "He stays in his room all day by himself and when army guys came looking for him he took off and camped out at Houghton Park. He told us to say we hadn't seen him. I don't know what's going on and he's always dressed up in his army clothes. He's got a knife and gun. I'm scared he's gonna kill somebody. The old man is so nervous he can't sleep at night."

"Has he seen Janie?"

"No, I'm tellin you. Nobody knows he's back."

"Oh man, look, tell him you saw me today and I was asking about him, that I hadn't gotten a letter in a long time and was worried. Leave it at that. Then if he wants to get in touch with me, give me a call. You got my number, right?"

"Yes, and I hope you see him and talk some sense into him. Everybody in the house is scared to death. He don't seem himself. Somethin's wrong."

On his way home Jason stopped at his father's apartment on Holly Street to pick up some reference books he needed. He had the key and was just leaving when he heard something behind him. He turned around and there was his father standing in the doorway of his bedroom dressed in pajamas.

"Holy Jesus," cried Jason. "I had no idea you were home. Scared the shit out of me. What's the matter? Shouldn't you be at work? Today is only Wednesday. You feeling OK?"

His dad put his head down and started to sob. "It's my fault. I screwed up," he said. "Ruined her life. God, what the hell was I thinking?"

"What's the matter, dad? Whose life?"

"Your mother's. She's a basket case I hear from some of the family. And you leaving her didn't help matters either." The man turned an accusing eye on his son. Jason blinked in disbelief.

"Mom? I thought you left that part of your life behind? Going for a brand new start, wasn't that it?"

"I'm so sorry, so sorry. I've got to get back with her somehow. Make this right. We were married twenty-five years. Oh god, I still remember that pathetic cake she had made with those stupid quarters decorating it, twenty-five years. What have I done?"

"Jesus," stammered Jason. 'Don't you remember the misery you had with her? You couldn't see your friends, the Professor. You couldn't play your music and reading was a useless past time that only ruined your eyes. I don't believe this."

"Believe it. I tell you I'm going crazy with grief and guilt. I can't work. Missed the whole week so far. I'm seeing a doctor and I'm on tranquilizers. You've got to help me, Jason."

"What can I do?"

"You've got to help me get back with your mother."

"I should have said, what can I do besides that. I haven't spoken to her in over a year now. I can't just go back, 'Oh hi mom, remember me, the son you kicked out. And while I've got you here, dad wants back in on the marriage.' This is probably just some temporary guilt trip. You'll get over it in time."

"Can you help me or not? It's not often I ask you for help."

"Oh man, I don't like this one bit."

"Please."

The word gated on Jason's nerves like fingernails on a chalkboard.

"OK, OK, maybe I can spread the word that you're miserable and want to come back. I talk to Diane, Aunt Alice's daughter once in a while. And there's talk of cousin, Larry getting married. Maybe at his wedding whenever that will be."

"Yes, yes, that's good, I could show up at the wedding. Perfect."

"Don't get all excited. Larry's a little screwed up right now. He's just back on leave from Vietnam."

"That's OK. Begin with what you said. That's good, a good start."

Jason left in a daze.

The next evening Jason was at his apartment with Dorothy. He was studying for an English literature exam and she was reading Jason's letter from the Professor, all thirty-two pages of it.

"It's like a fucking book," Dorothy commented.

"Yes, and if I don't reply with a letter just as long, he gets angry. It's a chore just keeping up with the guy."

"He's got a lot of interesting stuff here though. But, you know, I can't really get into Emily Dickinson. I know he thinks highly of her, but I just find her too cold, and calculating, too detached from sincere emotion."

"She lacks femininity if you ask me," said Jason. "Of course, what do you expect from someone who never got laid in her entire life."

"Typical male response," answered Dorothy. "I do prefer Edna St. Vincent Millay. I remember reading one of her poems about the death of a former lover of hers. Jesus, it was so fucking heartbreaking." Her voice began to quaver "It was like a dagger stabbing through my heart. This great love of hers had died and all his handsomeness, and strength and all the love she had for him counted for nothing in the end. Death took him and there wasn't a goddamn thing she could do about it. Nothing."

And Dorothy cried while Jason held her in his arms. "I hate when I'm like this," Dorothy protested. "I'm like a little baby here."

"You're so sweet," Jason replied and kissed her wet cheeks.

"You know, Jason. I meant to…" she said but just then the telephone rang. It was Jason's cousin, Diane, calling to say that Larry wanted to see Jason and that he'd meet him in the parking lot behind Babe's. Dorothy came along. Jason thought her presence might help.

It was unusually dark behind their old hang out when Jason pulled up. Then he realized why. Babe's was closed. "What the fuck happened?"

"All those new hamburger joints," said Dorothy. "They put Babe's out of business."

"Man, the times we had here. It's a shame. Wonder what Larry thinks? This was his second home."

"There he is now, over in the corner," said Dorothy. "What the fuck is he wearing?" She moved closer to Jason.

"Some kind of goddamn camouflage outfit," Jason replied. "Maybe he thinks he's still in the jungles of Vietnam. Man, I don't like this. I shouldn't have brought you along."

Larry got into the back seat of the car almost crouching as he did so. "Anybody see yous come down here?" he asked.

"Only those who had their eyes open," replied Jason. "Why?"

"Dey're watchin me, that's why. I'm sure of it."

"Who? Who's watching you?"

"I don't know. I just got dat creepy feelin. Can't be the fuckin slopes, right? I'm home now, back in the States. I'm safe here, right? Right?"

"Yes, yes, of course," Jason said. "You're perfectly safe here surrounded by friends and family. This is Kaisertown remember. No stranger in his right mind wants to come in here."

"Yeah, man, dat's cool," responded Larry. "I should know dat. Trouble is I don't know what the fuck I know any more. Jesus, my head's spinning. I got dese headaches, and my muscles ache like hell, and dis fuckin rash. I can't sleep, fuckin nightmares, man!"

"You want a beer, maybe?" Jason inquired. "I can drive out to WesMart and get a six pack like we used to."

"Fuck, you got any weed instead?"

Jason was about to say, no, when Dorothy chirped up. "I got some here in my purse. Wait till I roll one."

Jason looked at her. "I thought you quit smoking."

"Yeah, cigarettes. Don't worry I just have the occasional one."

Jason rolled his eyes. "If there are any more surprises," he said, "I think I'll just shit myself and die."

"I been dere," Larry snickered.

After his cousin calmed down with several puffs on the joint, the three of them decided to drive over and surprise Janie. Dorothy went into the house to get her.

"Are you OK?" Jason asked his cousin. "Do you have to go back to Vietnam, or are you done now?"

"I get dese spells. It's tough, man. You got no idea. Vietnam is a fuckin nightmare. Everyting happens so fast you got no time to tink. If it wasn't for the weed, I woulda blown my brains out long ago. One minute you're watchin your shoes and socks rot off yer feet, and dah next yer lookin at some guy dat got his legs blown away. It's unreal, man. Unreal and spooky.

"Let me tell you, man. When yer over dere nothing matters. Yer just tryin to stay alive, you and your buddies. Just pull dat fuckin trigger and hope you kill dem fuckin bastards before dey kill you. Most dah time you can't even see who dah fuck yer firing at except I remember dis one time. We were flying over a village. Who knows dah name. Dere was always some fuckin village. Jets just bombed dah shit outa it and we were bringing dah GIs in on dah choppers to mop up.

"Dere were dese guys, VC, villagers, who knows? Dey were all dah same to us. Dey was runnin for dah bush, you know, dah jungle. Bodies of dere buddies was layin everywhere. Den I see dis one guy fall. Down he goes, and den his pal, or maybe it was a relative, who knows, he looks back and sees what happened. Stupid bastard, he stops and turns around, heads back just when we're comin up on dem in dah choppers. I seen him right below me, grabbin his friend, helpin him to his feet, you know…"

Jason waited. Larry seemed tongue tied.

"And den I shot em. My finger just squeezed dah trigger, automatic. Dey exploded in a cloud a dust and blood. Den we were gone flyin over dah jungle again, shootin at nuttin. You know, I fuckin taught a me and you when we had dat rumble with dah wops on Lovejoy. I told you to stay in dah car but you didn't and almost got yer head caved in except I seen you and got you out of trouble."

"Yes, and was I ever glad of that."

"And dat's where you got dat Stonewallski name, remember?"

"Seems so long ago."

"I tink of it like it was yesterday. Dat VC, he was doin dah same ting, comin back for his buddy, and I shot him for it. Killed dem both."

"It wasn't your fault."

"Sure, sure, I wish it were true, but dey're gonna get me for it. Ain't no doubt and I seen what dey can do. GIs staked down wit dere guts pulled out and dere empty bellies filled with VC shit. Use you like a latrine. Figure you deserve it for what you did to them and their country. Probably right, but getting killed ain't dah main ting. It's how dey kill you dat madders. Never let dem take you alive. Never! Always save one bullet for yerself. Remember dat. Promise me."

"Fuck. I'll never go over there," answered Jason. "I don't want to be killed and I don't want to kill anybody. But I promise, if it will make you feel any better. If it's a choice between me and the other guy, I'll make sure it's the other guy. OK?"

"Good, dat's good, man."

When Janie got in the car it was all hugs and kisses. Larry seemed to mellow. The four of them talked and reminisced, avoiding the topic of Vietnam altogether. At the end of the evening Jason was almost convinced that Larry was back to normal. Dorothy was the last one to be dropped off that night.

"You sure you don't want me to spend the night?" she asked.

"No, it's OK. I appreciated the thought though."

"Don't go to strangers," Dorothy smiled. "Good night."

Jason watched her walk up the sidewalk to her babcia's. She turned and waved and seemed to say, 'I love you,' but Jason wasn't sure. He was sure, however, that he was going to have to figure out his future with her soon enough. Something had to give.

Larry and Janie got engaged that week. The wedding date was set for two weeks. Jason was to be the best man and Dorothy, the maid of honor.

"You think they'll be alright?" Jason asked as he and Dorothy lay naked on his bed sharing a joint, a new habit they recently started. "You think Larry's stable enough?"

"Who's to say what stable is," Dorothy replied. "I think that's what he needs though, the love of a good woman. It's like chicken soup. It can cure whatever ails you."

"Wow, maybe I'll have to take that remedy myself," Jason added. "If I could only find the right woman, that is."

Dorothy slapped him on the head. "It won't be from want of trying," she said. "And by the way, are you still looking into that move to Canada?"

"Yes, I just got a response from a teaching job in Toronto. They're actually crying for teachers up there. I got an interview in two months. If I land that job it almost guarantees my entry into Canada."

"Seems as though you have it all figured out. Aren't you going to miss the States though, family and friends?"

"I'll be glad to get out of here. The country's gone to hell. War raging with no end in sight, blacks rioting in the streets, and my family itself is all fucked up. I don't have much to keep me here. Anyway, I won't technically be a draft dodger as they say so I can come and go as I please. That's the point of getting this paper work done ahead of time. You gonna miss me?" Jason added suddenly.

"No."

"You could at least lie to me."

"Maybe I am."

Jason rolled over on top of Dorothy. "In a Sentimental Mood" with Benny Carter played on the stereo. He smiled at her. She instinctively opened her legs and bent them at the knee. All those other women, Jason reminisced, he had left them without a thought or regret. He just walked away, but that wasn't going to work with Dorothy and he knew it.

Jason drove Dorothy back to her babcia's house. She would be there only another month before she was scheduled to move in with Rosaline. When he got back to his apartment, there was a note under the bathroom door. Another rental increase.

Before he left Buffalo for good, Jason felt it necessary to at least say good-bye to Carl and Julia

"I ain't seen him," said Althea. "Was livin with some woman and her kids on Cherry Street last I heard. Good for nothing nigger anyway. Left me stuck with a bunch a his bills. Never had no money."

Julia was at the old address. She seemed surprised and not particularly happy to see Jason.

"You better not stay too long. I got a new man livin here. He don't like white mens so much. He be home on leave from the army."

"I just wanted to say goodbye. I'm heading to Canada. I'm kind of sorry that things couldn't have worked out a little better between us. You know…"

"You don't gotta say nothing. What you think, I was expectin you to take care of me with all my kids, that we was gonna go live happy ever after in some rich white neighborhood, and eat at some fancy restaurants all the time? I ain't no dreamer. I ain't so stupid."

"No, I never thought you were stupid. I liked you. I liked the kids," Jason stammered. He moved closer, and tried to put his arm around her. Julia backed off.

"There ain't no time for nothing. You got any money, you can leave for the kids?" she asked.

Jason had a few dollars and some change in his pocket. He put them on the coffee table and left the room. "Say goodbye to Brenda and Shirley for me," he said.

At the bottom of the stairway Jason turned and looked up. Julia was standing there watching him leave. He waved. She turned away and walked back into the apartment.

Dorothy: *"Love Me or Leave Me."*

Poor Dorothy, the love affair of her life was coming to an end. What was she going to do without Jason? She couldn't stand the idea of being with another man and the thought of Jason with another woman, leading a life without her, was intolerable. It wasn't the sex. It was the intimacy: the kissing, the hand holding, the embraces, the exchange of ideas, the warm whisperings of love that she would miss.

"There's no other love, but my love for you," the lyrics of Nina Simone played over and over in her mind. "I'd rather be lonely than happy with somebody else."

Oh sure, Jason would venture back to Buffalo now and then if for no other reason than to get his kinky sexual urges satisfied. She knew how to keep him happy that way. She was an enthusiastic lover, experimental, yet compliant and tender at the same time.

Dorothy tried to clear her mind of thoughts about Jason, but she made the mistake of putting a record on her stereo. It was, "In my Solitude" with Lester Young. She immediately sat on her bed and buried her face in her hands.

"How am I ever going to listen to music again?" she cried.

Jason: "Canadian Sunset"

It had all the markings of a glorious spring. The snows of winter had melted away and the ground was warm. The tulips and daffodils were in bloom. Jason and Dorothy, as well as the rest of the wedding party, were gathered at St. Casimir's for the rehearsal. Only the star attractions, Larry and Janie were missing. Father Matthew, who was the ailing Monsignor Majewski's new assistant, was running the affair. He looked at his watch.

"Maybe we take a break, nie, and come back after lunch? Den in dah meantime yous ken find dah two love bird. Lose track of time when yer in love, nie?"

"Where the fuck is that asshole?" Jason whispered to Dorothy. "He said they were going for a walk in the park, then coming right back here. It's ten minutes away and he called an hour ago from his house."

"I'm afraid" said Dorothy. "He's been acting so strangely. Janie told me she was thinking of breaking it off. He's been slapping her around too. She's scared."

"You're kidding? Why didn't you say something to me? I could have talked to him, stopped him from abusing her. It's that fucking war. Once he gets out of Vietnam, he'll be alright. We just have to hang in there with him. Bull shit calling it off. That would kill him. I thought she loved him?"

"She does. That's the problem."

"I'm going to the park. You wait for me here. Say a prayer."

"If I thought it would do any good, I would. Don't be long if they're not there, OK? Janie's wearing her wedding dress, trying it out. She can't be walking far."

Jason drove through the gates this time and parked on the edge of the back lawns, the old gang's stomping grounds with its barbecue grilles, scattered water fountains, and horseshoe pits. Man, the adventures they had as kids and teenagers here in Houghton Park, he could write a book about them. He thought he heard something in the distance as he slammed the car door behind him, then continued on foot along the familiar cindered pathways. Farther up he finally caught a glimpse of the two lovers. Yes, that was them alright. He saw Janie sitting on the ground with her wedding dress spread around her like a white water lily. Larry was standing a short distance away.

"Whoa," said Jason suddenly as he noticed that Janie's dress had been pulled down to her waist. Then he smiled.

"Breaking up, yeah, right. The horny bastard is just grabbing some action out here. He always said that Janie had a terrific set of tits and gave great blow jobs. That's my boy,"

Jason waved and called as he approached, giving the girl time to gather up her things and cover herself, but no one moved. He slowed his pace. Larry had his camo outfit on. He must live in that fucking thing thought Jason. I hope to hell he doesn't plan to get married in that. The picture before him did not change as Jason walked into the frame. Time somehow stood still. He called to Larry. Larry did not move, nor respond. Janie too was motionless and mute. As Jason walked up to her, he became suddenly afraid. She's not the least bit embarrassed, and how can she sit in that awkward position, he wondered. Her head was slightly slumped down on her breast.

"Janie, Janie, Are you Ok?" he asked and then he noticed the rivulet of blood that had seeped from the girl's right temple to the nape of her neck. From a distance he had thought it was a red rose coquettishly pinned behind the girl's ear. Jason's hands trembled. He looked up at Larry.

"What the fuck is going on, man? What did you do to her? Larry have you gone crazy?"

Larry turned and faced Jason. He smiled wanly. "Dey're everywhere, man. Just like I told you before, but you wouldn't listen to me."

"Who? Where?" Jason responded.

"You can't see em. You never see em. Yer too late anyways," he replied. Larry's arm swung forward from behind his back. He held a service revolver in his hand. "I only got one bullet left."

"What the fuck are you talking about?"

"I only got one left," Larry continued like a teacher lecturing a wayward pupil. "I can't cover for you no more. Please don't ask me. It's not fair, man. I need dah last one for myself."

Jason saw the gun shaking in his cousin's hand, then ominously rise up towards him.

"Holy Jesus," Jason gasped and made the sign of the cross.

"I can't save dah both of us," Larry stammered. "Fuck, why you always putting me on dah spot? You know I love you, man. Don't do dis to me. Don't make me choose."

"No, no, it's alright," Jason pleaded. "I got my gun in the glove compartment up in the car. Over there. You can see it on the hill." Tears fell from Jason's face. "I got my own," Jason continued. "I got my own."

Larry let out a sigh. "Man, I'm proud of you. You always was a good student." Then he raised the gun to his head and pulled the trigger.

Jason did not leave his apartment for days afterwards, the gun shot echoing in his ears, deafening him to life as he knew it. He couldn't remember eating or drinking, He let the telephone ring only once before disconnecting it. Day and night people knocked on his door. He didn't get out of bed even when he heard Dorothy's voice calling to him, pleading.

"Jason, I know you're in there. Please, I'm so sorry. I want to help you. Don't shut me out."

He did not answer.

"The wake is tomorrow," Dorothy announced another day although Jason had lost track of time. "Funeral is on Saturday. Everyone is worried about you, asking about you. Bye, and I do love you, Jason. I've always loved you."

Sittniewski's Funeral Home was packed with people when Jason entered. Many of his aunts and cousins were there. He thought he saw Nelly, maybe not. Pruny and Corny were there. He barely recognized them with their long hair. Pani Durlak, the old Kaisertown crone who attended every funeral in town, if she knew the deceased or not, was perched in a corner like a ghoul in a graveyard. Everyone stepped aside as Jason made his way to the casket. A picture of Larry in his army dress uniform stood atop the closed coffin.

Jason's eyes clouded with tears, but he managed not to cry as he rose from the bench. He gave his condolences to Aunt Alice who was too confused by grief and tranquilizers to know who he was. Much of the rest was a blur, but he recognized his cousin Diane in the crowd. Beside her was his own mother. She had her head turned into the shoulder of a man standing next to her. Jason blinked twice. The man was his father.

Jason walked over. He nodded in sympathy to his cousin who smiled weakly and walked away affording him some privacy with his reunited family. His mother looked at him.

"I'm sorry, ma," he said.

"Moje synus," she cried. Jason stood there cringing at his own words and the spectacle he had created. He looked over his mother's shoulder at his father. The scent of flowers and women's perfume that permeated the room made him sick. He had trouble breathing and the warmth of his mother's embrace sent contrasting chills down his spine.

"Hi, dad, nice to see the two of you together again," he lied. Then he left without speaking to anyone else. He drove to the Sol Steinberg Corporation doors. Dorothy spotted him immediately and came running forward.

"I'm sorry," he said,

"Shh, shh, it's alright. Don't explain. I understand. Poor Larry, and poor Janie. What did they ever do to deserve that?"

"You know in all my own selfish grief I forgot how close you were to Janie too. I'm sorry, sorry for all of it."

"Let's not talk about it," Dorothy said. "It's too depressing. Life is too depressing."

"Yes, after life's fitful fever, they sleep well."

"How's your move to Canada coming?" she finally asked.

"I got the teaching job. They sent me a letter. I only have to take a few summer school courses at the University of Toronto. That's all. The job is mine. As far as immigration is concerned I just have a bit more paperwork to do and it's official. I can't believe how accommodating all the Canadian officials have been. It's as though they were on my side in all this Vietnam fuck up."

"Wow, but it sounds so final."

"Not that I had much choice," Jason explained. "If I stayed here, I'd be in the army for sure and on my way to Vietnam and a living hell."

"I know and I couldn't bear that."

"But I was wondering," Jason continued, "if you'd mind taking a trip up to Toronto with me. I've got to look for an apartment and get familiar with the city. I could use some support. What do you think?"

"Sure, what the hell, I'll go, but on one condition."

"What's that?"

"That, that you promise to come back and see me from time to time so I don't go

insane," Dorothy replied with her eyes filled with tears.

"Don't worry about that."

They stayed at the Royal York Hotel and toured Union Station and walked the busy, vibrant streets of downtown Toronto. They held hands and laughed. They were in love although neither one openly acknowledged what any passerby could spot in a moment.

"Even the air is different here," said Jason. "Fresh and clean. No odor of the smoke of war."

Jason browsed through some book stores. Dorothy did some clothes shopping. She bought a miniskirt and a pair of shoes.

"I have to get a little something for Rosaline," she added. "I promised her."

"Hey, let's try Birks. I was thinking of getting my mother one of those mother rings. You know as sort of a peace offering."

"Good, maybe I can pick up a charm for Rosaline's bracelet. Of course, she's got so many charms already that it sounds like a goddamn wind chime every time she moves her wrist."

The jewelry store was a picture of Victorian England: shiny hardwood floors, dark oak woodwork, Tiffany lamps and stained glass windows throughout. Glistening glass cases held sparkling watches, rings, necklaces and bracelets. Sitting atop a short pedestal on the main counter was a gilded bird cage where two life size crystal doves perched looking at each other, beaks open as if inviting a kiss.

"Looks expensive in here," Dorothy commented. "I don't love Rosaline that much."

"Wow, look at these rings," said Jason distracting Dorothy. "What kind of party would you wear these to?"

"Those are engagement rings, dummy, And god, they're beautiful."

"Try one on," Jason joked. "We look like a couple of wealthy young Americans. They'll never know the difference. And you did promise me long ago that you'd marry me someday."

"Don't be silly," Dorothy quipped but she was obvious curious and willing to try one on.

A clerk strolled over and smiled at them. "May I help you?" he asked.

"That one there. We'd like to see that one close up. Try it on," said Jason pointing to the largest ring in the case.

"I'll never be able to lift my hand," Dorothy laughed as she slipped the ring on her finger.

"What do you think?" asked Jason.

"God, it's gorgeous, but I won't even bother to ask how much it costs."

"This one is more modest," said the clerk, "but it's very stylish, one of our newer

settings."

Dorothy exchanged rings.

"What do you say to that one?" inquired Jason.

"It's pretty, very pretty. I like it," responded Dorothy instinctively extending her arm and admiring the ring.

"So, what do you say?" continued Jason.

"Yes, I said I like it. It's beautiful in a modest, stylish way."

"So then, what do you say?" Jason repeated for the third time.

Dorothy turned to him, irritated at first, but then she noticed the look in his eyes, those beautiful, shining eyes that she had loved from the first moment she had gazed upon them so many years ago.

"Don't," she said. "Don't fuck with me you bastard. I'll never forgive you."

Jason smiled and glanced at the clerk. "Sorry," he said, "but my fiancée is a bit taken with swearing. She used to work on great lakes freighters. Got in the habit."

"I thought you had a job here and were moving," Dorothy continued hastily ignoring Jason's comments to the clerk.

"I am, and I've already made the inquiries. Matter of fact I'm going to look pretty stupid if you say no. Might even jeopardize my chances of getting into the country. You wouldn't want my application denied, would you?"

"No, no."

"No?" Jason repeated.

"No, I mean, yes, yes. Jesus, what are you trying to do to me?"

"We'll take the ring," Jason explained to the clerk. "It seems to fit perfectly."

"You know," Dorothy said with her eyes filled with tears. "My babcia she, she predicted this would happen. She said she put a spell on you. She's into that old Polish folklore shit, you know. But I was afraid…"

Jason kissed her before she could finish.

The clerk looked away momentarily then turned back to the couple.

"I will get the matching band and a box," he said. "I presume madam will be wearing the ring?"

The two did not move from their embrace. Jason nodded while Dorothy lifted her ringed hand and twisted it back and forth in the subdued light of Birk's Jewelry Store, downtown Toronto, Canada.

About the Author

Greg Swiatek was born and raised in Kaisertown and the surrounding suburb of Cheektowaga. His education ran through School 69 on Clinton St. to Sloan and then J.F.K. High School and finally the University of Buffalo where he earned a BA in English studies.

He moved to Canada in 1969 to pursue a career in education, teaching high school English for ten years. Looking for adventure he moved to northern Ontario where he tried his hand at trapping, logging, bartending and ultimately owning and operating a fishing and hunting business with his wife and son in the remote area of Biscotasing, Ontario.

After retiring from tourism in 2005 Greg took up writing and made his way back down south to Toronto and eventually settled in the Niagara region where he now lives with his wife, Susie, of 50 years. He regularly travels back and forth to the States visiting friends and relatives. In addition to *Kaisertown* Greg has two other novels available on Amazon.